SUMMER, FIREWORKS, AND MY CORPSE

OTSUICHI

SUMMER, FIREWORKS, AND MY CORPSE

OTSUICHI

TRANSLATED BY NATHAN COLLINS

HAIKA SORU

SAN FRANCISCO

HAIKASORU
Published by
VIZ Media, LLC
P.O. Box 77010
San Francisco, CA 94107

www.haikasoru.com

Otsuichi, 1978-
[Natsu to hanabi to watashi no shitai. English]
Summer, fireworks, and my corpse / Otsuichi ;
[translated by Nathan Collins].
p. cm.
ISBN 978-1-4215-3644-6
I. Collins, Nathan. II. Title.
PL874.T78N3813 2010
895.6'36--dc22

                                2010029880

Printed in the U.S.A.
First printing, September 2010
Third printing, October 2023

CONTENTS

CONTENTS

SUMMER, FIREWORKS, AND MY CORPSE

Kagome, Kagome,
Bird in a cage,
When will you come out?
Just before dawn
The crane and turtle fell.
Who is behind you now?

—from "Kagome, Kagome,"
a Japanese children's rhyme

DAY ONE

I was nine years old, and it was summer.

Vibrant green trees grew thickly around the shrine and shaded its gravel grounds. The cries of cicadas drifted down from branches reaching upward as if to grasp the summer sun.

"I wonder if my brother and the rest of the boys are done talking yet," Yayoi said to me. "You think they are, Satsuki?"

She was twirling her hair with her fingers, and her eyebrows were scrunched down, making wrinkles above her nose. She sounded annoyed.

"I don't know…"

Yayoi Tachibana and I were in the same grade. We were best friends, and we—along with her brother Ken—played together every day.

We were sitting alone on the shaded wooden steps of the shrine, waiting for Ken, who was helping with the preparations for the town's small fireworks show only a few days away.

"He's taking forever," said Yayoi as she looked over at the old stone foundation across the shrine's spacious grounds. "Why can't they just let us girls climb up there too? This is so boring."

The old foundation, a flat, rectangular mound of rocks piled about as large as a warehouse, looked like a small castle built of nothing but dry stone. It stood about as tall as the roof of a house, and I heard that recently, a kid from one of the neighboring villages had fallen while climbing it and gotten hurt.

I was sure some important building had once stood upon that foundation, but that day all that was on top of it were the seated figures of several of the older boys from the village, who were meeting up there to discuss plans for the fireworks show.

I looked jealously over at the dry-stone foundation and muttered, "Boys are lucky, getting to climb up there."

Tall trees grew all around it, providing cool shade from the summer heat. It must have felt nice up there. I bet you could see far away. But girls weren't allowed to climb up. If we tried to, the boys would get mad. Even if we asked first, they wouldn't let us.

But Ken had told me all kinds of things about it. That from up there he could see my house. That the stone felt nice and cool. That there was a hole among the rocks the boys threw candy wrappers into. That the hole was so big they had to warn the younger kids away from it. I knew all this because Ken had told me so.

"Yeah, real lucky," Yayoi said. "I wish I was born a boy. If I were a boy, I'd be able to climb the foundation, and I could play with my brother."

The boys around here didn't let girls join their games.

As we waited, watching for the meeting to end, we grew more and more bored. The shrine had a small playground—a horizontal bar, a swing set, and a slide—but I didn't feel like playing on them. They'd be too hot under the summer sun, and besides, they were all rusted anyway. So I preferred sitting in the cool shade.

But Yayoi apparently felt differently, and she jumped to her feet, stretched in an attempt to shake loose the tedium, and said,

"Come on, let's go do something. I'm so bored I could die!"

"But it's hot out of the shade. I like being cool."

"Okay, fine. What do you want to do then?"

I thought about it a moment and replied, "I want to play 'Kagome, Kagome.'"

"But you can't play that with only two people…" Yayoi slumped back down onto the wooden steps of the shrine.

The staircase was old, about five or six steps tall. During the summer fireworks show or the New Year's bonfire, a box for offerings was placed on the steps. The shrine, also old, was built from dried timber. Although located in the center of the village, it only took on significance when it was decorated for the seasonal holidays.

The buzzing song of an Arabian cicada perched on a nearby tree made the heat feel that much hotter. Even sitting there, idly tracing pictures in the gravel with my finger, I was sweating. A mountainous thunderhead formed animal shapes as it floated in the blue sky.

"Hey, that's pretty good!" Yayoi said, impressed. She looked back and forth between the gravel and the sky. "It's a dog, right? Just like the shape of that cloud."

"Yep. Too bad Six-Six isn't this cute, right?"

We both laughed. Six-Six was a dog that lived in the village. He was a mutt, white and aggressive, with a habit of stealing shoes. And just then, as if he'd heard our laughter and was not at all happy about it, he growled.

We screamed in unison. "Aaaah! Six-Six!"

The white dog stood right in front of us. Up close, he looked terribly large. His extended claws and hateful gaze sent chills down my spine.

"Yayoi," I said, keeping my eyes on the beast, "we'd better run."

That was what the kids around here usually did when faced with Six-Six's stare. But Yayoi didn't move. She couldn't. I too, despite the advice I'd given only moments before, was frozen like a frog caught under a snake's gaze. I had the feeling that he'd leap for us the instant we made the slightest move.

Six-Six advanced toward us step by step. I half expected him to order us to move out of his way.

The story of an older kid being bitten on the face by Six-Six flashed through my mind, and the vividness of it filled me with dread.

But just then, Six-Six yelped as he was struck by a rock right on the butt.

"Brother!" Yayoi cried out.

Ken was standing farther down the concrete path. With a look of sympathy for the creature, he threw another rock at the mutt. The dog howled at Ken in a voice that could have been heard from beyond the grave and then left, repeatedly looking back over his shoulder in frustration as he went. Six-Six didn't usually give up so easily.

"Are the two of you all right?" Ken asked, smiling to console us two younger girls. Behind his kind demeanor lay the courage to stand up to—and subdue—Six-Six. He was two years older than us and deserved every bit of the pride his sister had in him.

"Yeah, we're fine!" Yayoi said as she flung herself at her brother. "Is the fireworks meeting over? Let's go home. Maybe Midori brought us ice cream today!"

Having been rescued from the terror of Six-Six, I felt my energy drain away. I slumped down upon the wooden staircase and watched Yayoi with envy.

"Yeah, I sure hope so," Ken said. He looked over at me. "But first—are you all right, Satsuki?"

I looked up at his smiling face and nodded.

✳

Under the hot sunlight, we walked the winding gravel roads along paddy fields carpeted green with growing rice all the way to their house, which was quite far from the shrine. The fields lay dry, drained of their water. The process was called "field drying." The rice plants were deprived of water, and in their thirst they reached their roots deeper into the soil in desperate search of nourishment. The fields were only dried for a few days each summer, but still, I always felt sorry for the rice whenever I saw the cracked, dry earth. But it was necessary to strengthen their roots.

Just as we'd hoped, Midori was waiting for us at Ken and Yayoi's home.

"Awesome!" Yayoi cheered. "Ice cream! Thanks, Midori!"

"You're welcome," she replied with a grin. "Well, go ahead, you'd better eat up before it melts."

Everyone had finished their work for the day, and Ken, Yayoi, their mother, Midori, and I all sat on the floor around the living room *kotatsu*. (Well, since it was summer, the blanket was no longer draped over it, and the heater beneath it was switched off, so it was less of a kotatsu and more of a low table.) A mountain of vanilla ice cream cups were piled on top of the kotatsu.

"Thanks again, Midori," said Mrs. Tachibana. "Look at all this ice cream!"

"It's nothing. After all, it hardly costs me anything. But when you do buy ice cream, I hope you'll pick ours."

Midori was the daughter of Mrs. Tachibana's sister, or something like that. Even in the somewhat dim light inside the house, her snow-white clothes and pale skin shone as if she'd brought the brightness of the outside in with her. She had an air of elegance rare for village women. Midori had graduated from high school that spring and found a job working in an ice cream factory. She lived in the same village as us, and sometimes, on her days off, she brought ice cream over to the Tachibanas' home.

We lapped up ice cream until our tongues felt funny from the cold. I liked coming over to their house because they treated me like a member of their family.

"Hey, turn on the TV—my anime is almost on," Yayoi said to her mother, who turned the TV on without reply. At my house, asking to turn the TV on at dinner would just start a fight. I was jealous of Yayoi for having a nice mother.

The TV buzzed to life, and after a short while, the picture came up. A picture of a boy filled the screen.

"Not again…" Midori said softly, her voice filled with pity and sadness. "How horrible."

The child, an elementary school student, had disappeared a week before. He was the fifth boy to go missing this summer. The adults all thought they had been kidnapped.

"It's awful," Mrs. Tachibana said. "Look, that town he's from isn't too far from here."

And not just that one. All the supposedly kidnapped boys had been from neighboring prefectures.

"Ken, you'd better be careful," Midori teased, trying to lighten the mood. "You're such an adorable boy, you might get kidnapped too." Her hair, waist-length and silky smooth, flowed in the air as she faked a lunge at him.

Ken nodded and blushed—a common sight when Midori was around.

Laughter filled the room, only to be broken by Yayoi's shout. "Mom, turn the channel! My anime's starting already!"

Mrs. Tachibana, sitting closest to the TV, sighed and turned the dial. "Okay, all right. But just because food and anime are the only things that will keep you two quiet."

The anime was shown in a marathon until six, and by then we'd made our way through the pile of ice cream cups. For some reason, at six, there was nothing on but news programs, and we quickly became bored again.

So we left to go play in the woods behind their house.

✳

At six o'clock in the summer, it's still bright outside. The leaves of the trees formed a ceiling of green above us, and sunlight spilled through the gaps and made patterns on the rocks and the roots that poked up from the ground. The smell of the forest was so enticing I felt like I could suck it in until I choked.

Ken had told us he would come and meet us after he'd walked Midori home, so the two of us decided to climb our tree. It was what we always did when the three of us came to the forest.

Up a few slopes into the forest, there was a clearing with a hill. From the south side of it, you could see the whole village. A single tall tree stood in the clearing with low branches perfect for climbing on its southern face. Ever since Ken found it, the top of the tree had been our secret hideout.

"You mean you can't watch TV while you eat?" Yayoi was asking me. "We don't get in trouble for it in our house."

"Yeah, that's nice. I wish I'd been born in your place."

Yayoi's smile disappeared. She hesitated, then said, "I wish I'd been born in a different family too."

Yayoi jumped onto a rock that rested next to the tree. Ken had rolled it there from nearby to help us shorter girls climb up onto the lowest branch. I bet that hadn't been easy for him to do.

"Why do you say that?" I asked.

Using the rock, I started up the tree after her. Ken had taught us which branches to climb on and in which order to make it the easiest. Our destination was an extra-wide branch that grew near the top of the tree. The view of the village from up there was much better than from the clearing below. You could even see the shrine and the old stone foundation. There was just enough room for the three of us to sit, and just the three of us knew about it.

"Come on, tell me why," I insisted.

"Well, because..." Another pause. "My brother and I could..."

"Your brother?" I looked up at Yayoi in surprise. She'd already made it to the branch and had sat down.

Moving my way from branch to branch, I climbed up as easily as walking up a staircase.

I sat down on the branch and took in deep breaths of the crisp air. It was cooler and more refreshing than the thicker forest air on the ground.

Among the green paddy fields stretching out below us, red and silver tape glistened in the sun, and the yellow eyes painted on the bird-repellent balloons floated in the breeze. There were even some scarecrows—protecting the rice from sparrows, not crows. Occasionally, they let forth an explosive sound I could feel echo through the pit of my stomach and vibrate through my head. Ken had told me that those devices, called "scare-sparrows," were gas-powered machines with a timer-activated noisemaker designed to frighten sparrows away.

Gazing out at the view, I asked Yayoi, "You don't wish you were born in a different house so you could marry Ken, do you?"

Yayoi widened her already wide eyes even farther and turned to look at me. She seemed to shrink inward, and then she nodded. She pouted her lips and said, "Ken's my brother. I wish he were just Ken and I didn't have to call him Brother." Her legs dangled from the branch.

We were fairly high off the ground, but we never worried about falling. The rough bark wasn't slippery, and children are nimble and quick.

"But Ken likes Midori, right?" I offered.

"I know…"

Yayoi had started growing out her hair about a year before, and hearing her confession, I wondered if she had done it to be more like Midori.

Yayoi and I both liked Midori. She treated me no different than she did the rest of her family, and she gave me all that ice cream. Plus she said my sandals, the ones with the flowers on them that my mother gave me, were cute. It was natural that Ken would like her too.

I understood that brothers and sisters couldn't marry, and yet I was still jealous of Ken and Yayoi spending all their time together.

"Oh, you knew?" I felt bad for upsetting her. Thinking it wasn't fair for her to be the only one flushed and embarrassed, I made a confession of my own.

"Did you know that I like Ken too?"

"What?" It sounded more like a little shriek than a word.

Yayoi looked at me in shock. Her eyes burned red, as if reflecting the sunset.

"I…I like Ken too," I repeated softly, intoxicated by the thrill of saying it out loud.

At that moment, I saw Ken walking toward us in the distance.

"Heyyy! Up here!" I called down to him, waving my arms wildly. He saw me and waved back at me with both hands. That made me happy.

After a moment I lost sight of him as he passed under more tree cover. Even though I knew it would be a little while before he came out into the clearing, I strained myself this way and that just to see if I could spot him between the leaves.

"There he is!" I caught a glimpse of him running my way.

That was when it happened.

Through my light jacket, I felt a small, warm hand on my back. *Oh, that must be Yayoi's hand*, I thought, and in that instant, the hand pushed me. Hard.

I lost my balance and slipped from the branch. I saw the leaves rise up around me in slow motion. As I fell I snapped through branches I'd climbed up only moments before and I kept falling. I came down hard on one branch and heard the sound of myself snapping. My body twisted into a wrong shape, and I let out a scream that didn't make it past my throat. And still I fell. In midair, I was sad to see that one of my favorite sandals had come off.

And then, as my back struck the rock at the base of the tree, the one we'd been using as a step stool, I died.

*

Dark red blood flowed from everywhere—from my nose and my ears, from gashes all over my body. Even my eyes cried with it. It was all such a small amount, really, but all I could think was how I didn't want Ken to see me like that.

The snapped tree branches thudded to the ground around me,

and scattered leaves floated down onto my body.

"Hey, what was that noise?" Ken called out, running to the tree. "It sounded like a snapping tree bran—"

Seeing my body, he froze.

Yayoi was climbing down the tree in tears. Since my dead body was currently occupying the stone, she leapt down to the ground from the lowest branch. She stood up, bawling, and wrapped her arms around Ken.

Ken regarded his sister and my corpse with a reassuring smile and, like a parent calming his crying child, asked, "What on earth happened here, Yayoi?"

He came closer to me and said, "Satsuki, you're dead, right?"

That settled, he again cast his smile upon his sister.

"I need you to stop crying and tell me what happened."

Yayoi, seeing him beaming at her, stopped crying and said in a slow, wavering, and pained voice, "Well…we were talking up on our branch…and…Satsuki slipped and fell."

"Oh, so she fell? Well, you couldn't have done anything about that." He spoke in a persuasive, grown-up tone. "You didn't do anything wrong, so don't cry."

He turned back to look at me. "We'd better tell Mom. Come on, let's go."

Ken took Yayoi's hand to pull her away.

But she shook her head forcibly, *no no no*, refusing to budge.

"What's wrong, Yayoi?"

"Well…" She hesitated as she thought of an excuse. "Well, wouldn't Mom be upset if she heard about this? I don't want to make her sad!" She burst into tears.

I could sense that Yayoi was afraid. She was afraid that someone would find out what she had done.

He thought it over. "Yeah, you're right." Almost to himself, he said, "Not just Mom, but Midori too."

His face lit up with sudden inspiration. "That's it! Let's hide Satsuki. We'll be fine as long as nobody finds out that she died here!"

Yayoi looked at her brother with a mixture of sadness and happiness.

My eyes, frozen open, could only gaze at them with envy.

※

"But how are we going to do it?" Yayoi asked. "We don't have a shovel or anything to bury her."

"I know," Ken answered with a kind smile that could dash away all of his frightened sister's worries. "That's why we brought her here, right? Just leave everything to me, and you won't have anything to fear."

He was carrying me over his shoulder, taking care not to let any of my blood dribble onto his back.

We were near the edge of the forest along an empty road that passed through the woods.

Yayoi looked around, puzzled. "What are we going to do here? How can we hide Satsuki?"

Ken laid my body upon the ground and lightly brushed away a patch of dirt, revealing a row of concrete tiles the size of cutting boards that covered a ditch. He bent over and pried up one of the slabs. The ditch appeared to connect to a creek that ran all along the paddy fields. But that day it was dry and contained only empty space. Ken lifted a few more tiles. The ditch was fairly wide, and he was able to fit my body snugly inside.

He then lowered the concrete slabs back into place, just as he had found them. They must have been heavy to move. But Ken silently went about his work.

"Brother, wait."

Ken, just about to lower the last slab, stopped, holding it in place.

The gap was a window, just one tile wide, through which my feet could be seen. On one foot, a sandal. On the other, only dirt. I felt self-conscious under their intense stares.

"I see," said Ken, unconcerned. "I guess we'd better go look for the missing sandal."

Ken unceremoniously lowered the final slab, sealing me in darkness. He then covered the tiles with dirt once again, concealing the ditch from casual observation.

Yayoi and Ken worked together to hide any evidence that the earth had been disturbed, and as they finished, the sun sank beneath the horizon.

✳

Just like any other evening, the Tachibana family was all gathered in their living room. Dinner had been served on the kotatsu-turned-dining table, and the small room was filled with the smells of delicious food. Ken's grandmother and grandfather had just returned from working in their fields, and his father, wearing a sleeveless undershirt, was sitting in the strong cool breeze of an electric fan and watching a baseball game on the TV.

"Dad, change the channel," Ken said. "*Starship Sagittarius* is about to start. You know Yayoi watches that every week." He looked to his sister for support. *Starship Sagittarius* was an anime program about three lovable characters working together to pilot their starship across the galaxy. Yayoi, who hadn't been paying attention to the conversation and had a mouthful of food, frantically nodded her head up and down.

"Yeah, yeah, I know," their father replied, timidly turning the TV dial. "Since nobody seems to care what I want to watch."

"And turn the head of the fan over here. We're hot too."

Their father pressed the button to oscillate the head of the fan without a word. It was one of those older models with a pin sticking out near the motor that you press to start the fan's panning movement.

When her brother said *turn the head*, Yayoi shuddered, remembering the way my neck had been twisted around in the fall.

Starship Sagittarius started without regard to Yayoi's mental discomfort. Her grandparents talked about their fields, how their watermelon crop was growing, how their rush mat was getting old and needed replacing, and so on.

"Excuse me," came a voice from the entryway.

Mrs. Tachibana replied with a loud "Coming!" and went to the front hall.

Yayoi, upon hearing the voice from the front door, began to tremble. Ken had surely recognized the voice too, but he didn't have the slightest reaction. He just kept on quietly eating his dinner and watching the anime.

Before long, Mrs. Tachibana came back into the living room. She had left the caller waiting at the front door and quickly motioned for the two children to come over.

"Hey, Satsuki's mother just came by, and she says her daughter hasn't come home yet. Do you know anything?"

Ken noticed that the hand Yayoi held her chopsticks with was shaking and answered for the both of them.

"No, we split up in the forest. Same as always."

"Oh, I see..."

Leaving further comment until later, Mrs. Tachibana went to the front door to tell my mother. Disappointed, defeated, and on the verge of tears, my mother said only, "All right," and headed back home. It hurt to see her like that. She looked so terribly small as she walked away—nothing like the angry demonic mother who yelled at me not to watch TV while we ate.

Mrs. Tachibana stood there watching my mother leave, then went back into the living room.

"I'm worried about Satsuki," she said, taking another mouthful of white rice. "It's already dark out. Where could she have gone at this hour? And with all these kidnappings? I'm really worried."

Each time her mother said *I'm worried*, Yayoi lost a little more strength and lowered her head a little farther, as though trying to hide from her mother's gaze.

Ken asked his mother, "Is Satsuki's mother going to look for her in the forest?"

"Yeah, it sounds like it. Satsuki was an only child, after all, so I'm sure she's all the more worried. I wonder what happened? She was saying it might be best to tell the police."

"The police?" Ken and Yayoi said in unison. The two looked at their mother—Yayoi with desperation and Ken with something that looked like excitement.

"Well, don't you think this could be related to those recent kidnappings? She was last seen in the forest, right? There might even be a search party out there tomorrow. Even if she hasn't been kidnapped, she could be lost in the woods right now. Her mom said she'd start looking right away."

The two kids hadn't expected to hear talk of the forest, but it was the most obvious place to look for me. Aside from the forest behind their home, there wasn't anywhere else in the area where a child might get lost.

When Yayoi heard that my mother was searching the forest, her expression froze. My body wasn't in a place where it would be discovered, and the two of them had cleaned up all traces of blood. But they hadn't been able to find my missing sandal. Ken had climbed back up the tree to see if it had gotten caught on a branch, and Yayoi had searched the ground until her back ached. But no sandal.

If the sandal weren't discovered, the police would likely consider my disappearance a kidnapping and would focus their search outside the forest. But what if my mother found it? She would recognize it immediately. She would remember how happy I'd been when she gave them to me.

"I'm really worried," Mrs. Tachibana was saying. "Maybe I should help her look."

I couldn't tell if Ken was listening or not. He was sitting there, amused, watching the anime on TV.

※

Ken and Yayoi shared a bedroom. The room was twelve feet long on each side, which was more space than they needed. The night was hot and humid, and the large bedroom window had been left open in an attempt to cool down the room, if only a little bit. There weren't any burglars around to worry about in that area, anyway. A night-light provided the room with dim yellow-orange light, and a blue mosquito net hung suspended from the ceiling, draped down over two futon mattresses spread out in the middle of the floor.

Ken was asleep, breathing quietly. But Yayoi couldn't sleep. When she closed her eyes, she couldn't stop thinking about what had happened that evening.

"Hey, Brother..." Yayoi said, nearly crying. She was wrapped in a towel cloth blanket—we called it a towelket—barely enduring the heat. Her bangs were plastered to her forehead with sweat.

Ken sleepily mumbled a response and sat up. It was so hot he had pushed not only his comforter aside but his towelket as well. He stood and reached up to turn on the light. He had hung a cord down from it so he could switch it on and off without getting up, but the cord was laying on top of the mosquito netting. He tried to tug the cord from under the net, but it kept slipping through his fingers.

"Don't worry about the light, Brother."

"All right," Ken said, still half asleep. "Well, what's the matter, Yayoi?"

"I'm scared. Could I...come over there with you?" Her voice was embarrassed and pitiful. She was sweating so much it looked like she might boil away.

Ken took a moment to respond, then said brusquely, "Oh, sure," and laid back down on his futon.

Even in the heat, Yayoi kept her towelket wrapped around her, as if hiding something, as she crawled over to his futon. She pressed her warm forehead against his back and closed her eyes.

And as the room filled with the peaceful regular breaths of

sleep, the dark curtain of night fell over Ken and over Yayoi, over my corpse hidden in the ditch, and over my mother, weeping as she searched through the forest.

DAY TWO

Early the next day, Ken and Yayoi went to their morning exercise session, a sequence of group calisthenics choreographed by radio and held at the shrine every day during summer break. The shrine felt pleasant in the morning, and the cool, crisp air was revitalizing. As the sun began its ascent into the sky, the few cicadas that had begun singing earlier were joined by a full chorus.

After the exercises were completed, a sixth grader (the oldest grade schooler in the village) made a stamp on the attendance cards of the children present. He commented on how I wasn't there that morning, but Ken ignored him as if it were not his concern. His attention was elsewhere.

Behind him, some of the mothers were whispering to one another. They were talking about me and my mother, saying that she had searched for me through the night and how sad it all was. Even though it had all happened just last evening, word had already spread throughout the village. The police would begin their search of the forest in the afternoon. But since nobody had yet found any evidence of wrongdoing or any clues as to my whereabouts, the women doubted that anything would turn up in the woods. And some were saying that I was another victim of the serial kidnapper.

Ken was eavesdropping on the women, gathering all the information he could. Two facts were plain: the police were coming, and my sandals hadn't been mentioned in their conversations.

Ken stared off into the distance, lost in thought, and Yayoi clung to his arm, gazing up anxiously into his face.

✳

As soon as they got home from exercising, Ken and Yayoi went straight through their back door to the forest. While walking the gravel road as it cut through the dried paddy fields, Ken made a suggestion.

Since the sandal had apparently not been found yet, they just needed to find it first.

That way, Ken's reasoning followed, there wouldn't be any evidence that I was still in the forest. Everyone would surely assume I had been kidnapped and taken somewhere else.

And so they made their way deeper into the forest, searching for my sandal as they went. Ken wanted to look on the steep slope below the tree and so was wearing a pair of baseball cleats instead of his usual straw sandals. But first they checked the area around the ditch where I was hidden. Finding nothing there, the two headed back up the path toward the tree where I died, their eyes focused down along the ground. Ken thought that maybe the sandal had fallen off my foot when he carried me slung over his shoulder on the way to the ditch.

"The slope is too dangerous, Yayoi. Why don't you go on home? Just let your brother handle it from here."

Ken was trying to be considerate, but Yayoi just shook her head, wrapped her arm around his, and stood firm.

"No! I'm going with you!"

"All right." He looked down at her and spoke like a father dealing with a stubborn child. "Go take another look at the area where Satsuki died. You remember what the sandal looks like, right? See if you can find it."

Yayoi's cheeks flushed. "Okay, but if I call for you, you'd better come right away. I mean it."

Ken gave her a reassuring smile and nodded, *yes, yes, I will.*

They had arrived at the place where I died. But still no sandal. Our tree stood above the southern slope, quiet and peaceful, as if the day before had never happened. The rock had been wiped clean and showed no traces of blood. The broken branches and fallen leaves were gone too. Ken and Yayoi had carried them off.

All they had left to fear was a single out-of-place sandal with a single flower on it somewhere in these woods.

Maybe it's fallen all the way down the slope, Ken thought as he gazed down the incline. The village shrine, elementary school, and the faraway cluster of houses looked small in the distance.

Yayoi looked down at the same landscape, thinking the same thoughts as her brother. The slope was probably too steep for her to climb down without cleats. She could slip and get badly injured, or even die.

The two children steadied their resolve for the search ahead.

Then Yayoi cried out, "Oh no! Brother, look!"

She pointed to a small road visible from the slope. The road climbed up into the forest, passing right by the ditch where I was hidden. Cars almost never used that road, but at that moment, there were two.

Ken and Yayoi both realized immediately what the two brown passenger cars must be. Police. Ken had figured they would come around noon to start the search, and there they were.

Ken got a thrill watching the cars make their way up the road.

Yayoi, her face twisted in fear, tightly held on to Ken, following him as he rushed down the hill.

The two cars turned off the road and into the forest, passing—of all places—right over my hidden body. Dust fell onto me through the cracks between the concrete tiles. But I couldn't move aside, and I couldn't close my still-open eyes or mouth.

The cars stopped in a small clearing connected with the forest trail. Several men, all of them dressed for hiking, emerged from the vehicles, and by the way they talked I could tell they had come to search for me. I could also tell, from some scattered laughter, that they doubted I was lost in the forest.

Ken and Yayoi couldn't see any of this from the slope. Ken listened to the sound of the cars stopping. He had probably predicted that they would park in the clearing. He smiled, maybe because his assumption was correct, or perhaps because the irony of the tires crossing right over the ditch in which he had buried me pleased him.

"Change of plans," he said. "We're going to hide. Let's spy on the police from behind the trees." He wanted to find out as much as he could about their search.

Ken gently took his sister's hand and led her off the trail and into the woods where people normally never went. He walked along, carefully choosing a route where Yayoi wouldn't slip or get hurt, where she could walk easily, and where they wouldn't be spotted by the search party.

Ken held the entire layout of the forest clearly in his head, and within a half hour or so he knew how many people were searching, what they were doing, and even where they were at each moment.

The search party, however, was completely unaware that they were being watched.

And as the search party—expert investigators all—began their investigation, and the two children, familiar with the forest, shadowed them, the cries of the cicadas echoed through the summer forest.

✳

By evening, the search party had found nothing, and their search grew half-hearted. I couldn't fault them for it. They didn't know if I was even in the forest or if their efforts mattered at all. As they tired, the search started to wind down.

Throughout the forest, the members of the search party welcomed the announcement that came over their radios. The search was called off for the day, and the teams of detectives headed back to the clearing.

Ken was somewhat disappointed, but Yayoi, pressed up against him, let out a breath of relief.

"They're all meeting back up now," Ken whispered. "We should go too." He hoped to overhear more valuable information when the search party gathered at the clearing, and he pulled at Yayoi's arm to leave. She followed, her shoulders hunched from fear.

As they passed near the ditch that hid my corpse, Ken saw something that made him stop.

Close to the ditch the two children had camouflaged with dirt and mud stood two policemen in matching blue uniforms. The taller one was saying something to his partner, a short man with a cigarette in his hand.

Yayoi paled. Ken grabbed her by the shoulders and hid in the tall grass. They held their breath and listened. Ken took in every word of the officers' conversation without so much as a single drop of sweat forming on his expressionless face.

"Hey, would you just forget about it?" the cop with the cigarette was saying. "We're done for the day, and everyone's waiting with the cars. We're supposed to go out for drinks tonight, you know."

"Don't be like that," the taller one replied. "I mean, that girl…What was her name? Satsuki, right? I know she was probably kidnapped, but…doesn't something about this area strike you as odd?" He gestured at a section of the forest—right in the direction of my body.

Ken's mind was racing. *What does he see? That ditch should be completely hidden by the dirt, like just any other part of the forest.* The boy's face remained confident.

"Not particularly, no."

"Look, see over there? There's a bunch of markings in the ground, like from cleats. Children's cleats. Probably ones for playing baseball."

Ken hadn't thought of the consequences of wearing cleats to climb down the slope. He kept silent as he listened to the two detectives talk, but his eyes began to work back and forth as if he were measuring something in his mind.

"Yeah, but we're looking for a girl, right?" the smoking cop said after a drag from his cigarette. "Besides, the mother said she was wearing sandals."

Disregarding his partner's lack of interest, the taller man walked over to where I was hidden and stooped down to inspect the dirt.

Yayoi, frozen with overwhelming dread, could only stare at the scene unfolding in front of her.

"Whatever, we're quitting for the day," the disinterested cop continued. "It looks like we're all going to have to come out here again tomorrow. Dig all the holes you want then. Come on, everyone's waiting for us."

Ignoring his partner's protests, the man closer to me brushed away a layer of dirt with his gloved hand, revealing the gray slab of stone beneath. "Hey, there's concrete here. A small waterway, maybe? Hidden under the dirt."

"Come on, hidden? Look around you. There's dirt everywhere. That dirt probably accumulated over time until it was just another part of the forest floor. It's part of nature."

But the taller one wasn't buying it.

He slowly lifted one of the concrete slabs.

Yayoi gave a silent scream.

"See? Nothing there," said the smoking cop, flicking ash to the ground. "Well, I don't know about you, but I've had enough of crawling around in the dirt for one day. I'm leaving."

Beneath the slab was only a dried-up empty space. The detective was standing just a little bit down the ditch from where I was hidden. If he had lifted up the tile three to the left, he might have seen my toes.

"Don't be in such a hurry." The taller officer's voice was firm. "We've got decades left to drink before we die."

He moved one tile to the left and lifted. One tile closer to me.

"Bzzzt!"

"Would you shut up!" The policeman at the ditch was indignant. "Go ahead, have your laugh now, and just see if I let you borrow any money from me ever again." He put his hand on the next tile. Just one more after that...

"Brother!" Yayoi was crying now, unable to withstand the

terror any longer. "We need to get out of here! Run!" She tugged forcefully at her brother's arm. But Ken made no signs of moving. His eyes, fixed on the two policemen, were sharp and cold, not those of a weak child.

The cop with the cigarette said mockingly, "Sorry, sorry. Keep going, who knows, maybe there'll be something under the next one!"

"Yeah, yeah. You'll be sorry all right."

The next slab lifted, and a slash of sunlight fell across my big toe, delivering the living warmth of the summer heat to a part of my cold corpse. If the policeman just lowered his head a little, he might have been able to see the tip of my toenail. But his face showed no signs of recognition. Just one more tile and even a complete fool would notice me.

"Brother!" Yayoi implored, almost shrieking, but not loudly enough to be overheard from the clearing.

Ken, giving no response to his sister's cries, picked up a rock larger than his fist from the forest floor. Yayoi watched him move, trying to guess at what he planned to do with it.

"That's it, one more, and we're going," the uninterested cop said. "Not that it'll make a difference anyhow."

The detective at the ditch moved to the next tile. "Fine, this will be the last one. But we'll be back to do the rest tomorrow."

He gripped the edge of the slab. *Lift it. Just lift it and you'll see my feet.*

Yayoi's pulse was racing. The pounding of her heartbeat echoed in her ears.

Ken acted. He took the rock in his hand and swung it upward, bashing it against his own face. Again and again he swung with all his might.

The officer braced himself and began to lift up the concrete slab.

Blood streamed from Ken's nose and started dripping from his chin.

Reflexively Yayoi shouted, "Brother!"

Her scream sounded like a piece of silk fabric tearing right down the middle.

Shocked by the sound, the detective let the concrete slab fall from his fingers. Both officers turned to face the source of the yell.

Ken, his face covered in blood, gave his sister a stage wink and walked slowly out into the open.

He stood in front of the officers, faking loud cries of pain. Yayoi was still clinging to him.

"God, his nose is gushing blood!" the cop with the cigarette exclaimed.

His partner, standing only inches away from my body, called out, "Kid, what happened to you?" and started to walk over to the blood-soaked boy. Away from me. "Come here, let me take a look at you."

The receiver hanging on the back of his belt announced, "We are waiting for you at the meeting point. Report back immediately," and the two detectives exchanged bitter smiles. The day's search had ended.

"Well, the first aid kit is in the car, anyway," the taller cop said. "I'll take the boy over there. You'd better put that slab back on straight, otherwise we won't be able to drive the cars out of here." He took Ken, still wailing, and Yayoi, crying from shock and fear, by the hands and started to walk away.

"Hey, wait a minute!" his partner yelled after him. "You're the one that dropped this thing! Pick up your own damn mess!"

But the taller one just kept on walking, children in tow. Yayoi was worried. *The police have us*, she thought, repeatedly looking back over her shoulder in panic. *What if the other one looks under the concrete? If they figure it out, we'll never get away.*

The other policeman, muttering a string of complaints, slid the heavy tile back into place.

Meanwhile, the detective asked Ken in a gentle voice, "So kid, how'd you get hurt? What happened?"

Ken toned down his crying enough to reply, "I slipped and fell." A sob. "Down the steep hill." He lifted up a hand and pinched his nose together to stop the blood.

Whether the cop was satisfied or not, he didn't ask any more questions.

Ken's clothes were soaked dark red with blood. Drops of blood rolled down from his hand holding his nose and dripped from his elbow.

Yayoi was still clinging to his side, and the blood fell onto her long hair—the hair she'd grown out just to be a little more like Ken's crush, Midori.

❋

Earlier that day, Midori sat on the wooden steps of the shrine, two steps from the bottom and three from the top.

She had stopped in at the Tachibanas' and had been considering if there was any way she could help with the search when she decided to make a detour to the forest shrine.

Her long hair flowed down from underneath a white wide-brimmed hat, and her white skirt rippled in the soft breeze. The skirt was long enough that she had to hold its hem with her small, delicate fingers to keep it from resting on the earth. She looked up at the cicadas noisily chirping away in the trees and remembered that the fireworks show was coming soon—only two more days.

The children bought the fireworks with money collected door-to-door—not much, just a few hundred yen at a time—from the villagers. They couldn't buy the serious stuff, just the smaller fireworks you could buy in any store, but everyone looked forward to the show anyway—even the adults, who came each year to pray to the gods of the shrine and watch the fireworks.

Midori recalled that the collection box was usually positioned right on the steps on which she was sitting. Lost in her memories, she sat and watched the sunlight spill through the gaps between the leaves. The patterns made by the light and shade flowed and changed, never forming the same pattern twice.

Midori traced her finger along the lines of the old wooden steps and wondered aloud, "How many times did I come here to play when I was a child?" The grain of the wood was rough to the touch.

Midori had told me once that she was from here. She even told me about this boy she liked, and how he had rejected her. She had joked about how Ken resembled that boy.

"Oh, is that supposed to be a picture of a dog?"

Midori had noticed the figure drawn in the dirt at her feet—the picture I had drawn the day I died. She leaned down to get a closer look at the drawing, her waist-length hair swaying in the breeze, and said, "I used to make drawings like this, back when I didn't care if I got mud on my fingers."

A dog barked.

Startled, Midori snapped her head up. In front of her, poised to pounce, was a white dog.

"Oh, hello there, Six-Six. It's been a while."

Six-Six, tail wagging, leaped at Midori, licking at her face and covering her white clothes with muddy paw prints.

"I've missed you, boy."

Six-Six rolled onto his back and looked up at her, his tongue lolling out in a dog's version of a grin.

"I guess this is where I used to bring you treats, isn't it? Although I admit it was pretty mean of me to throw them down below the stairs."

Midori had told me once that she was the one who gave Six-Six his strange name.

"By the way," she said, tapping the dog on his nose with a dainty finger, "you've earned quite the bad reputation around here!" Her smile beamed like the sun, as if she had been reunited with a long-lost childhood friend.

"I hear you're a shoe thief now. So where do you keep your stash?"

Six-Six gave a short yip and circled around behind the stair-case. The side of the stairs had an opening big enough for a dog to fit through.

Midori peered in after the dog.

"I knew it, here they are!" she said, satisfied with herself. "But there's so many of them!"

Beneath the stairs was a jumbled pile of unmatched shoes. Once she had recovered from the initial shock, she found herself impressed at the number. The dog had sprawled out among his spoils in a manner both regal and shameless.

Shaking her head, Midori started to straighten up, thinking that maybe she should check back with the Tachibanas. Perhaps something had turned up in the search. But something she saw when she raised her head made her stop—one solitary item at the edge of Six-Six's mountainous collection.

Mindless of the dirt she was getting on her clothes, Midori lowered herself in and reached for the object. Her fingers found their target, and she retrieved it from beneath the steps.

Pulled from the darkness was a single sandal—a sandal with a flower on top. And Midori knew whose it was.

A shadow seemed to pass over her narrowed eyes, and behind them flashed a flicker of foresight. As she gazed in the direction of the Tachibanas' house, a wrinkle of doubt formed between her perfectly shaped eyebrows.

She returned the sandal to Six-Six's cache and left. She headed, not for the Tachibanas', but for her own home.

The day is over, anyway, Midori thought to herself as she walked across the shrine grounds. *I'll visit the Tachibanas tomorrow. Oh, and didn't I leave some new trial flavors of our ice cream back in my freezer? I should just spend the afternoon eating that and watching talk shows. The serial kidnapping can wait for later.*

Walking along under the summer sun, she could feel the heat of the gravel through the soles of her shoes.

✳

Night fell, and the raucous singing of the cicadas faded into silence, and the countryside, bathed in the pale light of the moon and the stars, fell into slumber.

The concrete tile above where I lay was lifted up by Ken's hand. Beside him stood Yayoi, who nervously looked at my corpse.

The search party was coming back the next day, and that clever cop might find me. Ken had recognized that the time had come for me to be moved.

That evening, he had been led back to the two police cars and received treatment for his nosebleed. A large gash ran across his nose where he had bashed it with the rock. He was then asked his name and where he lived. The officers had known that Ken and Yayoi were the last two people to see me before my disappearance, and when Ken admitted his name, they had a lot of questions for the two children.

"Did you see anyone suspicious?" Ken could answer that one honestly. "No, I didn't," he replied. Yayoi had thought it might be possible to make up something, anything, to make the police think my disappearance was connected with the serial kidnappings, but she stuck to her brother's answers. The safest thing to do, Ken had reasoned intuitively, would be to avoid telling many lies, and only cover up what they absolutely had to. Create too many lies, and they could start to contradict themselves.

Standing in the beam of Yayoi's flashlight, Ken lifted me in his arms and carried me out of the ditch. He had a large bandage right in the middle of his face.

"I'm scared, I'm scared," Yayoi said softly, again and again, as she turned her head to look in every direction.

When Ken had woken up in the middle of the night, Yayoi, who had been snuggled up next to him, woke with him. Ken had instructed her to stay in their room, but she was far more afraid of being left alone without him than she was of entering the forest at night. The two children slipped out from under the mosquito netting and tiptoed carefully along the old squeaky floorboards of the hallway. Taking care not to awaken any of their family, they gathered up the tools they'd need.

Ken laid my body, colder than the chilly night air, to rest upon a rush mat that had been spread out on the ground, and straightened out my haphazardly twisted limbs. If I had been standing, I would have been at attention.

"It looks like we might have cut the matting a little too short," Ken said with a dry chuckle intended to calm Yayoi.

He wrapped me in the matting so that Yayoi could help carry it when he started to tire. It must have been difficult for Ken to carry me the day before. Or maybe he'd just had enough of my dangling, lifeless limbs.

Ken had salvaged a discarded rush mat, and before leaving the house, he had used a pair of sewing scissors to trim the matting to match my height. Only he had misjudged the size, cutting it short, and now my toes poked out from one end and my hair spilled out the other.

He then tied up the bundle tightly with string so that it wouldn't fall open as he carried me.

When they were leaving the house, Yayoi had been unable to find any string and was in a panic. Their mother always saved the wrappings and string from when she went shopping, saying that they'd come in handy one day. But the children didn't know where she stored it all. They obviously couldn't wake up their mother and ask her, and the string, though needed at long last, would have to remain unused. Instead, they took the cord that hung down from their bedroom light. Ken and Yayoi would just have to stand up when they wanted to turn their light off.

Ken slid the concrete tile back into place and hoisted me over his shoulder like a piece of timber.

"Brother, where are we taking Satsuki?" Yayoi asked, afraid of what the answer might be.

Ken, walking back toward their house, answered, "To our room. From what I saw watching the search party today, I think that's the safest place now."

I was rolled up neatly into the matting, my limbs cooperating and not hanging down.

"We'll hide her in the closet," he explained, "and we'll keep watch in there all afternoon. But we won't be able to keep her in there forever. So we'll have to find another hiding place, and fast."

Yayoi kept the flashlight pointed downward, lighting the path in front of her brother. His face, barely visible at the edge of the light, was awash in excitement.

Ken and Yayoi brought me into their room and placed my body in the closet. They closed me inside there—Ken, as if hiding a valuable treasure, just a naughty child pulling a prank, and Yayoi, as if to hide away her terror and her unease, to keep her sin far from God's eyes.

The paper door of the closet slid silently shut.

DAY THREE

Ken and Yayoi were not prepared for what they saw when they returned home from the morning exercise class. Not only was their mother preparing breakfast, but she was also getting everything ready for the kids to go to school.

"Quit dawdling, you two," she scolded them, setting their breakfast on the dining table. "You know there's school today."

They had completely forgotten.

The summer morning sun was glaring down, and the world outside the window was blindingly bright.

Ken dropped his rice into his soup, miso with seaweed and onions. "Mother," he asked, "where are you going?"

She was headed for their bedroom.

"I'm putting away your futons. And the mosquito net. You two aren't tall enough to bring the net down from the ceiling hooks."

Yayoi looked at Ken, frightened. Their futons were always

stored away in their closet, where I had been hidden. If their mother opened the closet door, she'd discover what they had done. Yayoi's worry showed on her face.

But Ken remained calm. He answered coolly, "Don't worry about it, Yayoi and I will do it. It'll build character, right? So just eat your breakfast and let us take care of it."

"That's awfully grown-up, coming from you," his mother replied skeptically, but she was clearly happy to have one less chore to do. She walked into the kitchen.

Ken and Yayoi shoveled down their food and went back to their room.

"Brother, what are we going to do? She could come in here while we're at school!"

Yayoi was on the verge of tears. Ken had climbed onto a chair and was deftly detaching the blue mosquito netting from the corners of the room.

"We'll be fine, Yayoi." He smiled at his sister reassuringly. "If we fold up the futon mattresses and stack them on top of Satsuki, Mom won't notice anything."

Ken folded the mosquito net into a small bundle and placed it in the closet. The closet was divided into two sections, top and bottom. My body lay in the upper level, where their futons were usually stored. The netting was on top of me.

In the bottom section of the closet, there were old floor cushions, winter clothes, an outdated vacuum cleaner, and so on.

"But, but..." Yayoi protested.

"We'll be fine." Ken's smile had a funny way of being reassuring, even when no proof was there to back the words.

Yayoi wiped away her welled-up tears. She folded the yellow towelket, a gift from Midori, that she wrapped herself in every night.

Ken folded up the two futons and carried them to the closet. Lately, Yayoi had been sleeping next to Ken, but they were still in the habit of setting both of them out.

One futon was piled on top of me and then the other. I felt the oppressive weight pressing down on my body. Had I still been alive, in this hot, humid weather, it would have felt so awful that I would have died.

"Darn," Ken said. "Her feet are showing."

The futon didn't quite cover my feet. And neither did the rush mat, which had been cut too short. My feet—one wearing a sandal, the other barefoot—were plainly visible. I felt self-conscious under their stares. Had I been alive, I would have blushed.

"Here, use this, Brother." Yayoi held out her yellow towelket.

Ken took it from her and placed it over my feet. He stepped back and looked at the closet, making sure I was completely hidden. "Perfect," he said, happy with their work. Seeing Ken's satisfaction, Yayoi felt glad too. Her face flushed a little.

The two children took one last look, making absolutely sure that no part of my body was visible, and then slid the paper door shut.

They filled their backpacks, unused for over a week, with their notebooks and finished homework.

"School only goes through the morning today," Ken reassured his sister, packing the last few things for school. "So there's really little chance that anyone will find Satsuki."

They walked out the front door together, the voices of the cicadas already chirping around them. The brilliant green rice fields, still dry, basked in the warmth of the sunlight. The arms of the trees seemed to reach up, grasping at the clear blue sky.

Upon everything but me, morning came, and everyone but me was alive.

✳

Our grade school had only one class for each grade, so Yayoi and I, being the same age, were in the same class. It was time for the morning homeroom.

"Teacher, Satsuki isn't here yet," the girl in the seat across the aisle from my empty desk reported to our teacher. I had been missing for only three days, and none of my classmates knew about it. Well, none of them except for one.

Yayoi paled and began to tremble. She strained not to look at the girl who spoke or at my empty seat.

The teacher hesitated, then replied, "Satsuki is…home sick with a cold." She faked a smile. "Take care not to get sick now, all of you." She must have heard from my mother.

The class replied cheerfully in unison, "Yes, Teacher." The children's beaming faces were full of brightness, as if the future had been promised to them—and if it hadn't, you'd want to promise it.

"Brother…" Yayoi softly cried out to herself, quiet enough so that no one would hear. She shrank down into her chair, and her legs were shaking. She thought that maybe if she just said "Brother," he'd come to save her.

His words replayed in her head. *We'll be fine. Nobody will find her. Nobody but us knows*. She stared down at the scribbles scratched into the surface of her wooden desk until her racing heart calmed down.

Patience, she thought to herself. *It's only one morning*. Then she noticed that the teacher was staring at her.

And walking slowly toward her.

What did I do? Did she notice me? She certainly had been shaking enough to be noticed.

Yayoi's heart started thumping in alarm. She began to sweat all over.

The teacher stopped next to her desk. A hand reached down to her tiny shoulder.

She wanted to run. She wanted to run straight to Ken's classroom.

She must have figured it out! She'll capture me and take me to the police! Yayoi couldn't banish the thoughts from her mind.

The teacher put her mouth to Yayoi's ear and whispered so that none of her classmates could hear.

"You know that Satsuki is missing. How hard this must be for you, being her best friend." The teacher's face was filled with pity.

"But please, don't tell any of your friends. Do you understand what I'm saying?"

Yayoi's head snapped up to look at her teacher. It took a moment for the girl to grasp the meaning of her words, but when she did, she nodded furiously.

"Yayoi…" The teacher grasped Yayoi's hands consolingly and then left the classroom before she drew the attention of the rest of the class. It was time for the short break between the first and second hour.

To Yayoi, her classmates seemed to rush around her, dancing and spinning.

And she realized, to her relief, that she was saved.

A cool breeze drifted into the classroom, and I could sense all her sweat being carried away.

※

"We're home," Yayoi called out as she walked through the front door. Ken followed her in.

After the scare in first period, the rest of the morning passed uneventfully. Yayoi's class was let out early, but she gloomily waited a half hour or so for Ken to get out so they could walk home together.

"Mom, where are you?" Yayoi asked. "I'm hungry!"

Hearing no response, the two children went to their room.

"Mom!" Yayoi cried sharply.

Their mother was inside their room. She had opened the door to their closet and was searching around for something inside.

Ken casually asked, "Mother, what are you doing?"

She was digging around in the closet, taking things out and putting them back in, not from the upper section where I was hidden, but rather from the bottom level. But the futons and towelket had been nudged aside a bit, and my hair and toes were just barely visible.

"My vacuum machine is acting up," she answered. "And just as I was thinking I'd clean your room for you. I was going to drag out that old one I had. I know I put it in here somewhere."

"You don't have to, we'll clean our own room," Ken said. "Why don't you go watch that show you like. You know, *Laugh On?* Right, Yayoi?"

Yayoi looked at her mother with wide, surprised eyes and nodded rapidly.

"You will?" Mrs. Tachibana closed the paper door, stood up, said, "Well, that would be nice of you," and left.

Yayoi, realizing that she had been holding her breath, let out a sigh of relief. Ken set his backpack down unceremoniously on his desk.

Yayoi opened her mouth to ask where they'd hide my body next. "So, Brother, what—"

Their bedroom door slid open, and their mother's face peered through the crack.

Yayoi's mouth was frozen open, but Ken asked, "Did you need something else, Mother?"

"I forgot to tell you. Your lunch is ready, so come and get it. You can clean later."

"Yes, fine." Ken's brusque answer must have been enough for her, and she shut the door.

Yayoi unfroze and exclaimed, "That was scary!"

Again the door slid open, and again through the crack popped the face of the persistent Mrs. Tachibana.

"What was scary?" asked the face.

Yayoi whipped around to look at the door and froze again, once more on the verge of tears.

"Well," their mother said, "I don't mean to bother you."

"Mother, what is it?" asked Ken. "You're being a pest."

"Well, I don't know what you mean by that. But you've been an awfully good boy lately, Ken. Putting away your futon and doing your cleaning, you're like a kid on an after-school special."

Ken curiously tilted his head to the side. "Now I don't know what you're talking about."

"You've been getting along very well with your sister. It's like you two are hiding something from me. That's all I wanted to say."

The door closed. Ken strained his ears, listening to their mother's footsteps walk down the hallway.

Fearful, Yayoi asked, "Is she gone?"

Ken nodded, then turned to Yayoi and smiled.

Their mother's last words still on their minds, the two children opened the closet door to make sure I hadn't escaped.

✳

Ken and Yayoi finished their lunch and went back to their room to discuss their next move.

"Brother, what are we going to do?" Yayoi, barely holding back her tears, sounded distressed. "I don't think we can leave her here any longer…"

But Ken already had a solution. Wearing a self-assured expression, he replied, "I've been thinking. Maybe you've had the same thought too, even if you weren't quite aware of it." He shrugged. "We could just throw her down the hole in the stone foundation at the shrine. No one would ever find her. And then everyone will think that she was just another victim of the serial kidnapper."

Yayoi nodded in agreement.

One of the stones on top of that old foundation on the edge of the shrine grounds had fallen loose, revealing a pit shaped like a well. The boys used it like a trash can, throwing away candy wrappers and empty bags. And Ken meant to dump me in there with the rest of the garbage.

We should have thrown her in there from the start, they were thinking.

"Okay," Yayoi said. "But when are we going to carry her there?"

"That's a good question. We should do it as soon as possible. We don't know when she's going to start to stink in this heat."

Yayoi, picturing my body rotting and smelling, scrunched up her face in disgust.

In just a number of hours, it would be two full days since I had died.

"We'll do it tonight," Ken stated. "Tomorrow is the fireworks show, right? I bet there'll be a lot of people around there tomorrow night."

The festival, even as small-scale as it was, was attended by over half of the village.

Yayoi, finally seeing an end to all this, appeared relieved. "Sounds good to me, Brother. We'd better go to sleep early. A nap would be good too."

Ken looked at his sister, pleased. But part of him was disappointed to have it end. He was enjoying this.

As Ken tore the bandage from his face, he wondered if that clever policeman from the day before was just then lifting the concrete tiles from over the ditch and if his loudmouth partner was having a good laugh. Ken's cut had closed over, forming a scab. He tossed the bandage into the trash and opened the closet door to start cleaning like he'd promised his mother. That old vacuum cleaner should be in there somewhere.

"Come on, Yayoi, let's clean up the room before we nap. Mother will be suspicious if we don't."

"Oh, right."

"I'll help too." The door slid open, and the two children were startled, eyes wide and bodies stiff, at the sight of the unexpected visitor.

"Midori!"

"Hiya! I brought you a brand-new kind of ice cream today." Midori looked proudly at the children, white plastic sacks dangling from her hands. Droplets of water had formed on the plastic. "It's not even in stores yet, so you'd better thank me!"

"Sure, Midori," Ken said, sliding the closet door shut behind his back. "Let's go eat in the living room." Yayoi nodded her support. But Midori didn't go along with it.

"No, Mrs. Tachibana—your mother is passed out in the living room. Let's eat here. Hey, I'll even help out with your homework."

Yayoi looked nervously at Ken, who, seeing no way out of it, nodded.

"Oh, well, I don't see why not," Ken said. "Hold on, I'll get the floor cushions out." As he opened the closet door, Yayoi held her breath. He took a cushion from the lower compartment, handed it to Midori, and then took one for himself and one for his sister and laid them on the straw tatami mat floor.

Midori looked up at the fluorescent light.

"Hey, didn't you used to have a string attached to the light?"

"It broke off," Ken said quickly. "It was pretty old."

"Yeah? That's funny, usually that kind of string is a lot tougher than that."

They all reached for the ice cream at the center of the table.

"Wow," Yayoi said. They hadn't seen that style of ice cream before. The containers were tall and transparent, and the ice cream looked extravagant, like a chocolate parfait you'd get at a nice restaurant.

They took the attached long wooden spoons, also something of a novelty, and started eating.

"It's delicious!" Yayoi exclaimed.

"Of course it is, it's from our factory. Be sure to tell all your friends. But this ice cream is special. It costs more than our usual products."

The three continued to talk as they ate, and when Yayoi had finished hers, she scraped the insides of her cup for any precious remains with her spoon and licked it with her tongue. They chatted for a while and then moved on to Ken's and Yayoi's homework.

"Let's see, *A Summer Friend*." Midori picked up Yayoi's summer workbook. "Some friend! These workbooks haven't changed a bit since I was your age. Now, what's your assignment for today?"

On the front of the book were the words *A Summer Friend*, and below that, *Grade 3*. I had been given that same book when the spring semester ended. It was still sitting on the desk in my room.

"Hey, nice work, Yayoi. You've done very well. Ten years ago I fed this stuff to my dog. Just kidding."

Ken looked at Midori and asked, "You turn twenty this year, right?"

Embarrassed, she scratched her face and admitted it.

Midori looked through Ken's workbook and said, not without amazement, "And it looks like you're doing even better, Ken."

Ken and Yayoi started their studies, asking Midori, who was lounging behind them, whenever they had a question.

After that had gone on for about thirty minutes, Midori became bored. She started to talk about me.

"Really, I wonder what happened to Satsuki. I hope she's all right, but..." She looked at—no, observed—their studying figures.

In stark contrast to Ken, who hadn't shown any movement, Yayoi's shoulders twitched.

The motion was not overlooked by Midori. Her dark, emotionless eyes bore down on the two children.

"Yeah," Ken said. "I just hope she wasn't killed by that serial kidnapper."

"Oh?" Midori's perfect lips formed a half-amused smile. Her expression and voice were filled with interest. "You think Satsuki was kidnapped? They haven't said anything about that on the news."

"Could it be anything else? The search party hasn't found anything, so it must have been that kidnapper. The news was saying they never found any clues with the other kids either. And the kidnappings were all in prefectures near here. Mother was even saying how it was odd that none of them happened in ours."

"Hmmm. You have a point. But maybe the kidnapper had a reason for staying away from the children in this prefecture. Still, I didn't know you were such a smart boy, Ken." Midori meant the praise.

Ken's face turned a deep red. Embarrassed, he blurted out, "Um, I'll—I'll get some coffee," and left the room.

Midori watched him with a smirk and turned to face Yayoi.

The girl had slumped onto her desk, asleep.

Midori giggled. "Oh, did you fall asleep? You must be so tired."

Careful not to wake her, Midori gently laid the child down on the tatami floor. When she saw the pencil-mark math equations imprinted in reverse on the girl's cheek, it took an effort to keep from laughing.

She sat there fondly watching Yayoi sleep, but after a moment Midori quickly rose.

"I'd better cover you up with something before you catch a cold. Where's that yellow towelket I gave you?" Walking softly so as not to wake the young girl, Midori moved toward the closet.

Slowly, quietly, she slid the closet door open.

"There it is!"

She saw it right away. Right in front of her face lay Yayoi's yellow towelket. Well, I should be a little more precise. It wasn't just lying there—it was hiding my feet, which stuck out from the rush mat, a thin, fragile barrier between me and discovery.

Midori grasped the edge of the towelket and started to pull.

The towelket gently slid toward her, and the light pressure against my leg slowly lifted.

Just as the far edge of it was about to slip off, it caught on my toenail.

Midori was suspicious. She pulled harder, and the towelket broke free, and she held it completely in her hand. My feet were uncovered. But at that very instant...

"Aaah!"

Ken had fallen down, knocking into Midori. She went tumbling to the woven-straw tatami floor. The boy collapsed on top of her, dropping the small round plates and the cups of iced coffee that rested on them, spilling their contents everywhere. The glass coffee cups didn't break, and the three of them had somehow avoided the flying splash of coffee, but it was still a terrible mess.

Yayoi was awakened by the clatter. Rubbing her eyes, she looked up and saw my pale blue feet.

Her breath caught, and she snapped completely awake, but she wished it was all a dream.

"Ow ow ow ow…" Midori looked around at the floor and said, half angry, half laughing, "Ahh, the floor is soaked. But at least I'm still dry. Ken, I know you want to cool off in this heat, but that was really too clumsy of you."

She hadn't seen me.

While Midori was still inspecting the floor, Yayoi rushed over to the closet and shut the door. Midori didn't seem to notice that either.

"I'm so sorry," Ken said as he gathered up the dishes, the cups, and the ice that had been in them. "My foot must have caught on something. I tell you, it's been causing me nothing but trouble lately." When Midori wasn't looking, he signaled a thumbs-up at his sister.

Yayoi brightened and chirped, "I'll go get a washcloth!" As the girl ran to the door, Midori called to her.

"Yayoi, wait."

She froze and looked uneasily at Midori, who was helping Ken pick up the spilled ice.

"Careful not to wake up your mother. If she saw this mess, she'd freak." She raised her pointer fingers to her forehead, making little devil horns to illustrate her point.

"I won't!" Yayoi said and ran out the door.

※

Night fell. It was time for those still living to rest.

Once the roads had emptied of the villagers, Ken and Yayoi started to transport me out toward the shrine. They took care not to be seen. It was crucial not to be.

Yayoi rubbed her tired eyes, savoring her lingering dreamlike haze, and asked, "Brother, what time is it?"

Ken was carrying me over his shoulder. His voice was sharp and sober. "Half past three. We need to hurry if we're going to make it by dawn."

The two of them—or should I say, the three of us—had just

left their home, which was quite far from the shrine. Even the normally unflappable Ken was daunted by the distance.

No matter how much he talked like an adult, he was just two years older than me. It was hard work to carry me by himself.

"Are you okay?" Yayoi asked, holding the flashlight aimed at the gravel road in front of them as she walked by his side. "Do you want me to carry her legs? Brother, are you okay?"

The round light of the flashlight spilled over the sides of the road, bringing the long slender green shapes of the rice leaves to dim light.

The shrine was still far, and Ken was slowing down.

"Yeah, let's do that. Thanks, Yayoi." He held my legs out to her. She transferred the light to her brother and took my legs with both hands, a look of distaste crossing her face.

Ken was struck with an uncharacteristic regret. *I should have brought a wheelbarrow from the shed.*

For the first time he truly understood how far away was the shrine, and how heavy my corpse.

The light of the moon and the stars was faint, and the two children walked through the darkness. Occasionally they would stop, rest, say a few needed words of encouragement to each other, and then start again.

"Brother, I'm tired." She paused, out of breath. "Can't we just finish this tomorrow?"

"Tomorrow?" He considered it. "Well, the fireworks are tomorrow, but I suppose by this hour everyone should have gone home. But where would we hide Satsuki tonight?"

Yayoi's youthful face scrunched up in thought. Ken took a moment to come up with an idea, waving away bugs that were drawn in by the flashlight. But he had set out to carry me to the stone foundation and throw me into the hole that night, and that was what he still meant to do.

"Come on, Yayoi, we're almost there. Just a little farther, and we'll be able to make sure that no one will ever know what happened to Satsuki."

He summoned every last bit of his willpower to move forward. Yayoi, who had sat down on the gravel, stood back up.

If they threw me into that pit, would anyone ever find me? The stone foundation was as big as a warehouse. No matter how much trash all the boys threw down there, the vast, empty, black space within would never fill. The structure had withstood the wind and the rain. It had lasted long after the people who built it, and it would last long after the memories of the kids who played on it faded away.

But just as they had gathered the resolve to carry me again, they saw it.

"Brother, look! Over there!"

Ken had noticed it at the same time. Far off, near the end of the road, from beyond a row of houses, came a light. It was a flashlight, and it was being carried. It was too far to see if a person was holding it, but if it wasn't a person, what else could it be?

Ken and Yayoi's flashlight, which they had set down on the ground as they rested, illuminated them from below. Did the other person notice it? Even if their figures weren't visible, surely the light was.

"Brother, what are we going to do?!" Yayoi cried out in complete panic. "Brother!"

Ken was focused in thought and didn't respond.

"Brother!"

The light was approaching them. It was drawn to their flashlight, no different from the insects.

Ken, having come up with a plan, quickly looked at their surroundings to make sure it was without fault.

The figure of the person carrying the flashlight was not yet visible. And there weren't any places to hide. The road was surrounded only by the expanse of rice fields.

"Yayoi, over there!" Ken grabbed his sister and pushed her into the dark green carpet of leaves behind them. Next he picked me up, and taking care not to obstruct the light of the flashlight, he ran in after her.

They ran through the field until they could barely see their flashlight, and then they sat. The rice, reaching up to receive the life of the sun's rays every summer day, had grown just enough to hide us as it swayed in the breeze.

They held their breath and silently watched the light approach. The night was hot, and soon Ken and Yayoi began to sweat. The fresh scent of the young crops was stifling.

Their timing had been good. The fields were being dried and the earth was bare. Otherwise, their feet might have gotten stuck in the mud as they ran. If the field had been submerged, Ken may not have even thought to hide in it.

"Brother," Yayoi started to whisper, but Ken cut her off with a clipped *shush*.

They could now make out the figure that was walking toward them, and they recognized him at once. Old Man Thunder. That was what all the kids called him, partly because he looked like a character from a manga called *Mr. Thunder*, and partly because he often yelled at us when we played too much. He and several of the other elderly residents of the village met at the shrine each morning before the radio exercise to play gateball. I think he might have even been in charge of the group.

Old Man Thunder walked up to the flashlight the children had abandoned in the road and inspected it with a tilt of his head. Keys jangled on a key chain hung at his waist. They were the keys to the shrine's storeroom, where the gateball equipment and various other things, including farming implements, were kept.

Ken and Yayoi watched him, rapt. Yayoi pressed up against her brother to stop herself from shaking. The wind was still that night, and the two were dripping with sweat. Their sweat mingled together as it dripped onto the rush mat that covered my body, which lay on the dry earth.

Yayoi was barely keeping herself together.

Old Man Thunder lifted the flashlight from the ground. His thoughts were plain to see in his puzzled expression. Why would a switched-on flashlight be lying in a place like this?

From that expression, Ken knew that they hadn't been seen. His assumption had been correct—if all they could see of him was his light, then he couldn't have seen anything but theirs.

But they weren't safe yet.

The old man switched off their flashlight and panned his own over the area. He was thorough, as though searching for a fleeing rat. Thunder felt like he had seen something running into the field as he had picked up the flashlight, and he carefully passed his light back and forth over that direction. Ken and Yayoi stiffened, and each time the rice in front of them was bathed in the bright light, they feared that their shadows would be projected onto the plants behind them. *Why does he keep pointing the light over here?* they both thought, feeling like escaped convicts under a searchlight's pursuit. Each time the light passed over Yayoi, she could feel the police on her trail.

After a time, Old Man Thunder noticed something. In the direction he thought he had seen someone run, the rice was waving back and forth. But the rest of the field was still in the now windless air.

He stepped into the field, and as he pushed his way through the rice plants, he felt the dry earth crumble into dust beneath his feet.

The children sensed him drawing nearer and froze completely. Ken's mind raced.

Even if he finds us, as long as he doesn't find the body, won't we be fine? But if he tells our parents, how will I explain it?

The old man was walking straight at them, and soon he was only one row in front of them, reaching his arms to push a path through it.

Yayoi's eyes were filled with tears, and she had to bite her lip to keep from screaming.

It's now or never. I have to stand up and lie to him and say that he caught us pulling a prank. And I have to do it now.

That was his only plan. If he'd had a weapon to kill the old man and keep his mouth shut forever, it would have been different.

And just as Ken was about to stand up, a voice called out to Old Man Thunder.

"What are you doing out there?" It was the old man's wife. "We need to set up for gateball. Everyone will be there soon."

Old Man Thunder scratched his head in embarrassment. "Well, I just..."

He walked back to the gravel road and away from the two children and me.

He showed her the flashlight. "Look, I found this on the road here."

"Oh," she remarked. "I wonder whose that is, dear."

She was curious, but not curious enough. She took her husband's hand and started walking in the direction of the shrine. Old Man Thunder kept looking back at where we hid, but he went with her.

"They're probably all there by now," his wife said as they walked away. "You know we have to get everything ready and start practice soon, before we lose the space to the kids on summer break and their radio exercises."

They kept talking as they disappeared into the distance.

"That was close," said a relieved Yayoi. She felt light, even giddy. All her tension had been hanging by a thread, and the thread was cut. Ken couldn't help but laugh at the unforeseen turn of events.

But quickly his expression darkened.

"What do we do now though?" he whispered. If the gateball club was already at the shrine, they might be seen lifting me up onto the stone foundation. Had they missed their chance?

Worry returned to Yayoi's eyes. "Brother..."

"Well, it doesn't matter." Ken smiled reassuringly. They had lost their flashlight, and dawn had not yet broken the darkness of the night, but Yayoi could tell he was smiling without having to see it.

He continued, "We can just leave Satsuki here for now. Nobody bothers with the fields when they're dry."

During field-drying time, no one came to tend the fields. The flow of the water wasn't restricted at the site of each field, but rather controlled at one location higher upstream. That way the water could be stopped for all of the fields simultaneously.

"So let's just go home," Ken said. "We'll come get her after the fireworks are done tomorrow. Or maybe even the day after. We'll have plenty of time."

They moved me even deeper into the field where I would be less likely to be seen and started to walk back home. They didn't have a light, and Yayoi had to struggle to make the long walk back in the darkness.

But soon, from the east, the sky began to slowly brighten. The light looked like it was shining into a deep blue sea and lighting the way back to their home.

"Wow..." Yayoi said with heartfelt awe. It was the first time in her life she had seen a sunrise.

Not two hours had passed since they had left their house with me. As the sun reddened the morning sky, the path they had left to walk grew shorter and shorter.

DAY FOUR

The next morning passed uneventfully, as if the events of the past few days had never happened.

Ken and Yayoi had gone back to their room to get what little sleep they could before their mother came to wake them. Then, just like any other day, the two children left for the morning exercises. They walked along the road they had carried me down hours before, passing by the field I was hidden in with feigned indifference. The funny thing about Ken was that when he pretended not to care about something, he started to actually feel apathetic toward it. Yayoi was gripping his shirt as she walked alongside him.

After the radio exercises, Ken said to his sister, "You can go on home. You won't have anything to do here, anyway."

On a normal day, they would get their booklets stamped and go home together, but today was different. The older boys were to stay at the shrine to get ready for that night's fireworks show. The preparations were fairly simple—taking the wooden benches and the collection box from their resting places in the storeroom and making sure all the fireworks they had bought were in order.

"No, I'll stay here," Yayoi said, smiling at her brother. "It shouldn't take very long, and I can wait."

She followed her brother as he walked around the shrine looking for the storeroom key. Two radio exercise attendance booklets dangled from a string around her neck.

Ken approached a group of the elderly gateball players who had gathered by a corner of the shrine. Yayoi stood behind him, hiding herself.

"Excuse me," Ken said in a raised voice. "Could I borrow the key to the storeroom?"

"For the fireworks show, is it?" a relatively athletic senior replied. "I had almost forgotten."

He nodded to Ken and said to the man standing beside him, "You've got the key, Tanaka, don't you? Give it to the kid."

Yayoi peeked out from behind Ken. When she saw the face of Mr. Tanaka, she snapped back behind her brother and buried her face in his back.

The man named Tanaka, with gray hair and thick eyebrows, had almost seen the two kids early that morning. It was Old Man Thunder. But the old man showed no sign of recognition.

"Yeah, yeah, I've got the key," he said. "We might as well put away the gateball equipment while we're at it. Help me out, Kobayashi, will ya?"

"Sure," the able-bodied senior replied. "That's it for today, everyone."

The rest of the elderly left with their gateball sticks, while Old Man Thunder and Kobayashi, carrying the U-shaped gates for the gateball game, went with the children. The seniors kept the gates in the storeroom, taking them out each morning for their practice games.

Ken hadn't reacted when confronted with Old Man Thunder, but Yayoi was visibly nervous. She clutched at the back of her brother's shirt and kept him directly between her and the old man as they walked.

"Aren't you the Tachibana boy?" Old Man Thunder asked. "I forgot your name."

"Ken. And this is Yayoi. Say hello, Yayoi."

At her brother's insistence, Yayoi bowed to the two men, her eyes pressed shut as if she expected her head to be bitten off.

The two older men smiled at her, but quickly their faces darkened.

Kobayashi looked at Yayoi and asked, "Were you friends with the girl who went missing the other day?"

She shrank inward and nodded dejectedly. Her reaction was that of fear and unease, but the two men didn't read it that way.

"Oh, I'm so sorry," Kobayashi apologized. "I shouldn't have brought it up. But you need to be careful now, we wouldn't want you to be kidnapped yourself." He looked at Ken. "Take care of your sister, young man."

"Yes, sir!" Ken answered boldly, and the two men nodded in approval. Yayoi knew he was putting on a show for the seniors, but that didn't stop her from feeling a little happy to hear the words. Neither did it stop her cheeks from turning a bright red.

The four of them stood in front of the storeroom door, which looked to be the only sturdy part of the structure. The door was made of metal and looked extremely heavy. Old Man Thunder set his armful of gates on the ground and removed the key ring from his waist. He inserted a key marked STOREROOM into the lock and turned it.

"There, the lock's open," he said.

Ken tried to move the door with all his strength, but it wouldn't budge.

"What's wrong?" Ken asked the two men. "I can't get it to move."

Kobayashi answered, "Sometimes this door can be a bit stubborn. It worked fine when we got everything out this morning, though. The pulley might be jammed. I told them to come take a look at it, you know."

Kobayashi set down the gates he had been holding and joined Ken at the door. Yayoi and Old Man Thunder stepped up to help too. But even with all four of them pulling together the door only jiggled in place. It looked like they'd need a little more strength to open the door.

A voice called out to the struggling, red-faced foursome. "Hey, there! What's wrong? You guys seem to be having trouble!"

It was Midori. She was in jeans, strolling over to them a little more leisurely than they would have liked.

"Help us out," Ken said to Midori, who had stopped to watch. "You're right, we are having trouble here."

"You're getting ready for the fireworks show, are you? Keep up the good work, and all that." She laughed. "Since you're trying so hard, I suppose I can help you out. You'd better thank me."

She joined them at the door, and with her added strength, the gate screeched its way open.

Ken whispered. "You're crazy strong, Midori."

She gave him a pat on the head and strutted into the storeroom. The others followed.

The room was dark and humid and reeked of straw. Haphazardly piled inside the large room were farming implements including hoes and spades, cardboard boxes with contents unknown, bits of lumber, and countless other objects. Motes of dust drifted through the sunlight shining in through the open door like microbes floating in the deep sea.

"There's all kinds of things in here," Yayoi whispered with genuine interest, looking all around the room.

Kobayashi set down his pile of gates, their blue paint peeling here and there, in a corner of the room and said to Old Man Thunder, "Tanaka, while we're in here, we might as well replace that old pulley on the door."

Without waiting for a response, he pulled a wooden box down

from the top of one of the piles of stuff.

Inside the box were several unused, shiny dark gray pulleys. They were very large, each with a hole near the top for metal fittings to pass through. The two men gathered the box of pulleys and a selection of tools and went to the door to take it down and repair the pulley.

Ken, leaving them to their work, went to retrieve the wooden collection box from the rear of the storeroom. The box was small and used only during public events such as the fireworks show that evening, but it was still too heavy for Ken to lift by himself.

"I'll help you," Midori offered. "Really, whatever would you do without me?"

Midori and Ken dragged the box to the middle of the room. They stood at opposite ends of the box and lifted it up to carry it outside. Since there wasn't enough room for Yayoi to help carry it, she just walked alongside her brother, watching him and Midori with an uneasy boredom.

As the three passed through the storeroom door, they thanked Old Man Thunder for his help. He responded with a yell, "Hey! Careful, we're taking the door down here!"

The kids carried the box over toward the wooden shrine. Setting it in place was Ken's only task for the morning. After that he'd say goodbye to the older boys and would be free to go home.

"So when are you two coming to the fireworks?" Midori asked. "You are coming, right?"

They both nodded. They intended to forget about me during the fireworks show. Besides, they certainly couldn't move me to the stone foundation during the event. It would be too risky with all the potential witnesses around. I was safely hidden in the rice fields, and they could take one evening and not think of me.

"Well, then I guess I'll come too," Midori said. "Did you hear? The other kids are doing something interesting this year."

Yayoi asked, "What do you mean, interesting?"

"They're taking some string, and they're running it all along some of the fireworks they bought, so they'll all light up at once.

They're calling it Niagara Falls." Midori laughed. Her face was radiant, like a sunflower in the morning light.

Yayoi's eyes lit up. "Really? Really?" She pictured it in her mind. All the beautiful sparkling flower petals of light bursting into bloom in unison, then the dazzling waterfall cascading back down, powerful, fantastic, and fleeting.

"Really," Midori said. "So don't be late."

Yayoi gave several enthusiastic nods.

Midori said, "You'd better stop that before you make your eyes spin!"

Yayoi was elated. She had been so depressed lately that I'd forgotten what she looked like happy. If I were to compare her expression to a season, it would be summer.

Midori looked down at Yayoi, her eyes a mixture of happiness and pity.

Ken, still carrying one end of the collection box, was listening to their conversation, prepared to answer Midori quickly if she asked him a question, but his thoughts were elsewhere.

And as they set the box down on the wooden steps of the shrine, he thought, *How are we going to lift Satsuki up to the top of the old foundation?*

"Ken, you should come too," Midori said. "It's not summer without fireworks. And you might even get to see me wearing a *yukata*."

He gave her a bashful smile as he gazed over at the stone foundation across the shrine grounds.

Ken had been putting the problem off until later, but looking at the old foundation again, he realized it was a long way up to carry my body.

But he had no other choice. He couldn't think of a safer place to hide a corpse.

Having completed his duty, Ken climbed the stones of the old foundation to report to the older boys. One of the boys gave him permission to go home, adding, "Don't be late. We're not going to wait for you."

Ken took a moment to look around before going home with Yayoi. On top of the structure was a wooden board the boys used to cover up the hole and keep anyone from falling in. One of the boys shifted it aside and tossed in a candy wrapper with the words BIG KATSU written on it. I wondered if I would soon be thrown in there the same way.

Ken looked up. A wide tree branch jutted out above the stones, blocking the sunlight and keeping the top in cool shade.

✳

Ken walked in the front door. His mother was lying on the floor of the living room watching TV.

"Mother, you've been saving all that string, haven't you? Where do you keep it?"

"The string? What on earth do you need string for?"

"That string on the light in our bedroom broke. I need a new one, so where is it?"

His mother, somewhat irritated at the disturbance, stood up and walked into the storage room. After a short time she returned, holding a round metal cookie tin with the word *Tyrolean* written in cursive lettering across the top. In the Tachibana household, the cookie tins of that brand were well known as Mother's sewing boxes. One time, Midori brought over a box of Tyroleans, and Yayoi took one look at it and said dejectedly, "What, another sewing box?"

"Here, you can pick one of these," said Mrs. Tachibana, proudly displaying the tin. "Just leave the box here when you're done. See, I told you these would come in handy one day."

"Yeah, one day in how many years? That's some ratio."

Ken's mother, appalled, said flatly, "You're still in fifth grade, right? And you've already learned ratios?"

"Well, I'd better take this up to our room. If I chose one without Yayoi, she'd get mad at me."

Without waiting for a reply, Ken took the tin and started walking back to his room. Judging from its weight, there must have been quite a lot of string inside. He opened it and took out a handful of the sturdy string, used at stores to bundle up purchases, that had been sitting unused for years. As he walked, he idly played with the string in his hand, and thought.

With all this string, I should be able to lift Satsuki up somehow…

He would move me the next day. That would give him plenty of time to test out his rig.

Ken's grandmother and grandfather waved at him from their room. He stopped and asked what they wanted.

"Ken," said his grandfather, "the fireworks are tonight, aren't they?"

"Yeah."

"Maybe we should go." He turned to his wife. "Don't you think, dear?"

That seemed to be all they wanted to ask of him, so Ken said, "Yeah, you should both come. It'll be fun," and headed for his room.

Behind him, Ken heard them talking.

"That's right," his grandmother said. "It's tonight, isn't it?"

"Yeah. We'll check on it in the morning."

"Okay, dear."

"It's always right around the fireworks show when they turn on the water. It'll take a while for it to reach our fields though."

Ken pondered the new dilemma as he walked into his room. It seemed like he wouldn't be able to relax and enjoy the fireworks this year.

Our time together was almost over. Just one more night.

✳

As the world turned the color of night, Ken held Yayoi's hand and ran down the gravel road toward the field where they had left me early that morning.

The fireworks show was about to start, and there was little

time left before the fields would fill with water. Once they collected my body and took it to the hole in the old foundation, it would all be over.

"Hurry, Yayoi!" Ken yelled. A black backpack hung from his back, jolting from side to side with each step. Yayoi didn't know what all was inside the bag, aside from the pieces of string tied into a decent length. The two had spent the afternoon in their room tying all of the string in the cookie tin into one long piece. The work had taken a long time—too long, perhaps—and now the kids had to rush.

The water coming into the fields and soaking me wouldn't be fatal to Ken's plan, but they did have reason to keep me from being submerged in the water.

Fireworks sounded from the shrine in the distance and burst high above in the sky.

"Brother, it was around here. Satsuki has to be around here somewhere."

"Yeah…"

Ken and Yayoi stood on the gravel road, looking in my direction. But they couldn't remember exactly where they had left me.

The two children were holding flashlights. Yayoi had been worried about running into trouble as they had so early that morning, but Ken told her it would be fine. Even if somebody spotted them, they would just say they were on their way to see the fireworks, and nobody would doubt them.

Yayoi said to herself, distressed, "Maybe it was a little up ahead."

Ken, appearing similarly agitated, surveyed the field. "I forgot where we left her."

Neither one was looking my way.

Above the shrine, the sky shone in faint colors as fireworks began to spray fountains of light.

"Come on, Yayoi," Ken said, walking into the field. "We need to go look for Satsuki."

She followed after him.

The field was quite large, and even more so for two children. They split up and moved methodically through the area, keeping their flashlights pointed down at the ground as they pushed through the green rice.

But it wasn't easy to find me. Several times they unknowingly walked right past my corpse.

Yayoi's panicked voice cried out to her brother. "Ken! The water's coming!"

Her shoes were wet and half covered with mud. The ground beneath me was still dry, but the water was spreading.

"We have to find her, Yayoi!" he called back to her. "If we start getting bogged down in the mud, it'll only be harder!"

The night was filled with darkness, and the deep green fields were thick with rice plants fed by the summer sun, plenty tall enough to hide a child. The rice blocked Yayoi's view and encircled her as if preventing her escape.

Between that oppressive feeling and the sensation of her feet sinking into the wet earth, the girl was terrified. With a trembling, almost wailing voice, she cried out.

"Brother!"

She sprinted to Ken to embrace him, if only to keep herself from shaking.

Water spread underneath my cold back. In minutes I would be half buried in mud.

Yayoi ran like she was fleeing from a wild beast. Deep in her heart, she felt she could see the shadow of the monster that chased her.

Ken had aimed his flashlight at her and watched her run, unsure of how to react.

The figure of his running sister rose up in the light, then promptly disappeared into the rice.

"Yayoi!" Ken screamed, sprinting to where she had vanished.

Yayoi had tripped and collapsed on the ground and now lay on a pile of rice plants she had knocked down. She was crying.

Her fall had broken the last thread of resolve she had left. When Ken reached her, she clung to him fiercely, sobbing.

"There, there," Ken said, comforting her. "You did good." He pointed at the object that she had tripped on—me.

My body had twisted from the impact of her foot—not that I could offer any protest. My toes and my hair poked out from the ends of the rush mat that wrapped around me like seaweed around a piece of sushi.

"Come on, Yayoi, let's get Satsuki to the shrine. We can't leave her here—there might be people coming to check on the water in the fields."

Ken lifted me from the ground. Yayoi wiped the tears from her eyes and took my feet.

As I was picked up, droplets of water dripped off my back. The water had spread through most of the field, and as they walked I weighed them down and their feet sank into the mud. To the two children, it felt like hands were reaching up and grabbing their feet to prevent their escape.

Water poured into the field (now properly a paddy) and filled it completely, but the children were just paces from the road, and soon they stumbled out, almost collapsing onto the gravel. They were caked with mud and looked as if they had spent the whole day doing farm work in the field.

But the two didn't stop moving, and at last they made it to the concrete wall that ran along the shrine grounds. Since the stone foundation was far from the shrine's entrance, they decided to climb over the wall at the rear of the grounds.

Not only could they now clearly hear the sounds of the fireworks coming over the wall, they also saw the smoke and even heard the voices of the villagers who had come to watch. Hearing them made Yayoi more nervous. The more people there were, the greater the chance that they would be seen.

"All right, Yayoi," Ken said. "Once we climb over this wall, we'll be inside the shrine grounds. We'll have to run to the foundation. We have to be careful not to draw the attention of anyone who's come to see the fireworks."

Yayoi listened intently to her brother's reminder and cautiously nodded.

Ken turned to face the concrete wall. It was just a little taller than his head, but tall enough that Yayoi wouldn't be able to reach the top.

"I'll have to lift you over the wall," Ken said, just loud enough for his sister to hear. "So you'll be going in first. I'll throw Satsuki over next, and then I'll be last in."

Yayoi meekly nodded again.

"Okay. Think of this as a raid. We have to move fast, and the hardest part will be making sure we're not seen. And when you drop down from the wall, be careful not to twist your ankle."

He lifted her up the wall.

The fireworks show was about half over. The fireworks were more elaborate than the cheaper handheld Roman candles and fountains, and some were even rockets that launched up into the sky (although still only of the size a child could buy). The children were there to provide entertainment for the people who came to worship in the shrine, and they even handed out smaller fireworks to the younger children who came with their parents. It was our village's tradition, and it kept worship of the shrine's gods alive in the hearts of our people.

Yayoi jumped down the other side of the wall, where the pungent smell of gunpowder assaulted her.

But that shock was trifling compared to what she saw. Just paces away from where she landed stood a large group of people. No, not a group—a crowd. The crowd faced the center of the shrine, where the fireworks were being set off, their backs to Yayoi. But any of them could turn around at any moment. And if they did, and they saw my corpse, what could she do?

Fighting the terror welling up in her chest, she turned to the wall and raised up on her shaking toes to tell Ken on the other side. She tried to cry out to him. *Don't come over. There are people here. Don't throw Satsuki over.*

But the words never tumbled from between her trembling lips, because when she turned it was me that came tumbling down.

As I flopped to the ground, pink and green light spilled between the people watching the fireworks, splashing vivid colors across Yayoi's back and the rush mat that covered my body.

"Brother!" she said in a harsh whisper, but neither the crowd of people nor Ken heard.

But they might have heard the sound of my body thudding on the gravel. With tears in her eyes and despair and terror on her face, Yayoi looked up at Ken as he leapt down from the wall.

He landed next to me, saw the crowd of people, and raised his eyebrows a fraction of an inch.

"Yayoi, don't cry," he comforted her, thinking they had to get moving before anyone noticed them. But someone already had.

"If it isn't Ken and Yayoi," a woman in the crowd said, looking right at them. Yayoi stiffened, clutching at her brother's arm.

The woman was backlit by the fireworks, and they couldn't see her face in the darkness, but the two children immediately recognized her voice. Squinting at her, they could see a tinge of sadness in her expression.

"Hello, ma'am," Ken greeted my mother. His voice had sympathy in it, but I knew it was an act. Ken hadn't given up yet. "Where's Satsuki?" he asked. "Isn't she coming to see the fireworks? Hasn't anyone found her yet?"

She shook her head mournfully. She looked like she would lose her composure and break down at any moment. She had come to the fireworks festival to relive the memory of her only daughter. The memories were all she had left.

My mother and I came to the fireworks show every summer. I'd watch the show with Ken and Yayoi, and we'd even set off some of our own. Even now, the memories were too much for me.

And there I was, with Ken and Yayoi at the fireworks again.

Ken spoke hesitantly, choosing his words carefully. "I...hope you find her soon."

My disappearance hadn't been on the news yet. The police, having been unable to find me anywhere, had just begun to treat my case as a kidnapping. The next day, the media would be all over the town.

"Thank you, Ken," my mother said. "You know, when I watch these fireworks, I can't help but think of her. It feels like she's right here next to me."

Yayoi tightened her grip on Ken's arm. She started to tremble. I was lying on the ground right behind her. Even with the faint light of the fireworks, it must have still been too dark for her to notice me. But Yayoi was becoming so nervous that she couldn't think straight. How much longer until my mother saw me?

"You'll find her, I'm sure of it," Ken said with an innocent smile. "So cheer up." It was a perfect smile, and for a minute I thought it would be enough to convince my mother that she would find me, or that maybe I'd walk right through the front door the next day.

She looked at Ken for a moment, with no words left to say, only tears spilling out the corners of her eyes. No one else in the crowd seemed to have noticed us. They were watching the fireworks bursting above the shrine, oohing and ahhing in appreciation.

"Thank you..." my mother managed, bathed in the colored light. Her eyes shone with gratitude. "Thank you, Ken."

Yayoi looked like she was about to cry too. Was she remembering all the times we played together, all the summers we came to the shrine to watch the fireworks? Had she realized the vastness of her sin?

Ken was only waiting for a chance to break away and deliver me to the stone foundation.

"There, there," he tried. "Don't cry. Crying won't bring her back. Hey, look, they're about to start the finale."

Ken pointed over to where the fireworks were being lit. One of the older boys from the village was setting a large tube down upon the ground. It had cost a few hundred yen—fairly pricey compared to the rest. The crowd's attention was focused on it as they waited expectantly.

"You're right," she said, looking over at the center of the shrine. "I shouldn't be crying."

The village boy stood a few steps away from the firework tube, and slowly, carefully, stretched out his arm to light the fuse.

That was the chance Ken was waiting for.

Without missing a beat, he shook his arm free from his sister's grip and lifted my head from the ground. He whispered at Yayoi to lift up my feet. They stood at each end, blocking my hair and my toes from view.

"Well, we'd better get going," Ken said to my mother. If he had left without saying anything, it would have been suspicious. Yayoi was completely focused on hiding my toes.

"All right. Thank you, Ken." She turned to look at them and showed a little surprise at seeing the oddly shaped rush mat tube in their hands. "By the way, what are you two carrying?"

Since the children were standing at each end, she could only see the ambiguously lumpy midsection. She couldn't have known that I was inside.

Ken's reply was quick. "Fireworks. The older boys sent us to get them."

My mother either believed the lie or was not interested enough to press it.

"Well," Ken said, "goodbye. Don't give up hope. Yayoi, let's go."

They started walking toward the old foundation, careful not to let any part of my body show out the ends. Yayoi walked stiffly as she tried to fight off panic.

It was a losing battle. Soon her grip loosened, and I tumbled out of her hands.

Ken was still holding my head, and I arced downward. My feet slammed against the ground and I slipped further out of the matting. Now not only were my toes showing, but my feet—all the way up to the ankles—as well.

Yayoi gasped and Ken turned back to face her.

"Quickly, hide it, Yayoi!"

They might not have been seen yet. By the time her brother had given the instruction, Yayoi had already begun to hurriedly stuff my feet back into the matting. Tears welled up in her eyes.

Ken looked back at my mother. She was walking toward them and called out, "Hey, Ken!"

Had she seen? The two children tensed and looked at her like two defendants awaiting a death sentence.

"Hey, Ken," she repeated. "Satsuki liked you. Did you know that?"

Relief filled Yayoi's face. My mother hadn't seen me. She had still been watching the fireworks.

Ken's expression softened a little. "Yeah, I knew."

My mother sobbed a few more times and said goodbye. Ken and Yayoi resumed their walk to the old foundation even more cautiously than before.

All Ken had to do was get my body to the top of the stone foundation and toss it down the hole, and the game would be won. He could see victory right in front of him.

The fireworks show was nearing its climax, with the majority of the fireworks now the more expensive kind. The boys, not eager to be so quickly parted from their haul, tended to save the most expensive ones for the end.

A particularly large tube of fireworks ignited, and a fountain of grain-sized spots of light burst forth. The shrine grounds, from the stone foundation to the wooden shrine itself, were illuminated by the dreamlike light, glittering in brilliant silver and gold. Many of the spectators would doubtlessly remember it for the rest of their lives. With time, the memory would only grow brighter, forever radiant.

Finally, Ken and Yayoi stood at the base of the stone foundation. Had it not been for my mother's interruptions, they would have reached their destination sooner.

Looking up from the base of the structure, it seemed to tower high enough to touch the stars above. Clearly, they weren't going to be able to just carry me to the top.

They were out of the view of the spectators, and out of the reach of the light. But there was still a chance that someone would happen by.

They set my body down on the ground, and Yayoi asked her brother in a wavering voice, "What do we do now, Brother?"

"I need you to listen carefully. We're going to lift her to the top of the foundation. There's a few things we need to do and I'll explain them in order."

Yayoi nodded, and Ken went over the plan in simple terms.

From his backpack, he removed the string they had spent the afternoon tying together and passed it under the cord that was holding the rush mat closed around me. Ken would climb up to the top of the foundation holding both ends of the string in his hands. Then, using the string, he'd lift up my body, which would still be resting on the ground.

"Okay, I'm going to climb up there now. You stay down here and keep lookout."

Ken slung his backpack over his shoulder and found a foothold in the dry stone wall. Holding the string in his hands, he adeptly worked his way up the side of the foundation. Any of the boys in the village would have no trouble climbing it—it was their secret hideout, after all.

The rocks that formed the wall were just larger than a human head and were stacked about as high as the roof of the shrine's storeroom. Patches of moss grew on the surface of the old stones. Below, Yayoi paced as she watched her brother climb. Her attention was focused above her, and she stumbled on a tree root that protruded across her path. She regained her balance and chastised herself for forgetting her brother's instructions to stand watch.

The rear of the old foundation, out of the reach of the fireworks' light, was enshrouded in foreboding gloom.

Ken reached the top of the wall and raised himself up to the stone platform. The foundation was deserted, its rocks cold to the touch. He could see across the entire grounds. The fireworks sparkled brilliantly above.

Ken tugged at the string in his hands, making sure it was still secure around me. He set down his backpack, and from inside it he removed two objects.

The first was one of the U-shaped iron gateball gates, and the second an unused pulley made for the storehouse door. He must have sneaked them out of the storehouse before saying goodbye to the old men.

Ken placed one side of the gate's U through the hole in the side of the pulley, and hung the other side over a thick branch of the tree that protruded over the top of the foundation.

He threaded the string over the top of the pulley's wheel. The plan was to hold the end of the string and jump down from the top of the foundation wall. He'd slide down, and I'd be pulled up.

And then I'd be tossed down that hole, and that would be that.

Below, Yayoi watched my mother intently, worried that their crimes would be revealed if she came back and noticed me.

Just as Ken had finished his preparations and was ready to jump down, a voice called out from behind Yayoi's back.

"Oh, if it isn't the Tachibana kids. What are you two doing over here?"

Yayoi spun to face the voice. Ken had heard it too.

Old Man Thunder and Mr. Kobayashi were passing by, looking up at Ken with puzzled expressions. If they had been looking down and not up, they would have already seen me wrapped in the rush mat.

After a moment, Ken found his voice. "Good evening."

He was holding the string in his hands, still poised to leap. He looked completely ridiculous.

But the old men kept walking past. It wasn't that unusual to see kids playing on the old foundation, and it wasn't like they had anything in particular to talk about anyway. Yayoi silently prayed that nothing would happen.

"Careful up there, Ken," Old Man Thunder said. "Some kid got hurt up there just this year, you know."

They kept walking toward the crowd and the fireworks.

Yayoi's heart cheered.

And that was when it happened.

"Oof! What's this now?"

Kobayashi tripped over my body and stumbled.

Yayoi's body went stiff, a shriek escaping through her mouth but not finding voice.

Ken watched from above.

Kobayashi eyed the object that had tripped him. "What on earth is this? And what's it doing here of all places?"

There was little light behind the foundation, and I lay half in shadow. He couldn't quite make out what I was. But it was only a matter of time—moments, even—until he would.

Yayoi wanted to run. She wanted to run more than she had ever wanted anything in her life. But without Ken, where could she run? And who could she run to, if not Ken?

Mr. Kobayashi started feeling out with his hands.

"Hm? Is this...rush matting?"

Just a few more seconds and he'd surely see my body poking out from the end of the mat.

Yayoi shook uncontrollably, about to collapse into tears.

But Ken called down from the foundation.

"Hey, you two guys had better hurry. They're about to light the fireworks waterfall!"

"Really?" Kobayashi withdrew his arm. "Tanaka, let's go. The kids put in a lot of work for that one."

The two old men looked over at the fireworks.

Ken moved quickly. The instant they turned their gaze over to the show, he leapt down from the foundation with the string wrapped around his hands. Pulled by his weight, I rose silently up into the air. The thin string strained, threatening to snap at any moment. The gate, balanced precariously over the tree branch, was barely able to stay in place under the weight of two children.

The pulley jolted with the passing of each knot in the string, jiggling the tree limb and shaking loose its green summer leaves one by one.

"Well, we'll be off, then," said Old Man Thunder. "Careful not to hurt yourself, Ken."

When the two men turned back to say their goodbyes, Ken

had already landed on the ground, still holding the string in his hands, pulling on it to keep me from lowering.

"When did you get down here?" Mr. Kobayashi asked, tilting his head to the side. "And where did that bundle of rush matting go to? Someone could trip on that and hurt themselves, you know."

Yayoi watched the exchange unable even to breathe.

Ken answered, "Don't worry, I'll find it. And when I do, I'll take care of it." His words sounded like a bad joke. I remembered that he had made a similar joke when Midori had almost discovered me. I would have laughed were I able.

Ken smiled a genuine smile at the old men, and they were deceived by it just like all the others had been.

"Thanks, kid," said Kobayashi.

And just as the two men were about to leave, the string that was suspending me in the air began to creak. I was only nine years old, and my body couldn't have weighed much, but the string, unable to bear it any longer, was crying out.

And then, the cord that had once hung down from the children's bedroom light snapped without a sound.

I fell through the air and landed with a thud. The rush mat dangled above me, half open.

"What was that?" Kobayashi looked up to the source of the noise.

I had landed on top of the old foundation, only inches from the edge. Only inches from a longer fall down to the earth. Only inches from being seen.

"It was nothing," Ken said. "I'll take care of it. If you don't hurry, you're going to miss the waterfall."

Ken immediately understood what had happened when he felt the tension of my weight on the string disappear. But the realization didn't register on his face. Yayoi exhaled and thanked God for hearing her prayers.

"You're right," Kobayashi said. "Tanaka, let's go."

They went.

Yayoi stood, watching them leave. When the two men had passed around the edge of the foundation, she let out a sigh of relief.

"That was close, Brother!" It couldn't have been any closer.

Ken looked down at his sister, who was once again her normal, cheerful self, and smiled. "Yeah, it was."

It's over, Yayoi thought to herself, allowing her smile to spread wide across her face. *Once we climb to the top, there will be no one to stop us. I won't have to live in fear any longer. And I can say goodbye to Satsuki and keep only the happy memories of when we were friends.*

"Come on, Yayoi," Ken said brightly, "climb on up here. All we have to do is throw Satsuki into the hole. Don't you want to say goodbye to her?"

Yayoi nodded back to him energetically and climbed up the wall. Ken pointed out the path to her as she went, just as he had done the time he showed her how to scale that tree.

And for the first time, Yayoi stood atop the stone foundation, Ken by her side. From there, they had a perfect view of the fireworks show. The Niagara Falls had just been lit.

The fireworks, strung together and hanging from a string, burst into light, red and blue and green and pink, and all the millions of colors in between. The streams of color ran together, creating a waterfall of sparks that shone in their eyes. It was an impressive display coming from a group of kids. The spectators, dazzled by the show, would remember it for the rest of their lives.

"Why..." Ken whispered regretfully, mournfully, "why are you here?"

Waves of pain swept across his face, his expression shouting as loud as his voice had been soft. *You, of anyone. The last person I'd want to see here.*

"Didn't I tell you not to be late? I've been waiting here all night. I even wore my yukata for you."

As she fanned herself with a paper fan, Midori chuckled.

Midori sat watching the fireworks from the edge of the foundation, cradling the rush mat bundle, myself wrapped inside, in her arms. Her deep red lipstick shone in the darkness of the summer night.

Lit by the waterfall of fireworks, perhaps half over yet still bright, Midori smiled a smile so beautiful and seductive it was almost inhuman.

Ken and Yayoi stood dumbstruck, staring at Midori.

"Ever since I was a little kid," she said, "I've always wanted to watch the fireworks from up here."

His voice wracked with pain, Ken said, "Midori, give that to me."

She gave the boy a glance and returned her gaze to the fireworks. "I know what you're doing. You're thinking that you're going to dump Satsuki down that hole, aren't you?"

She watched the light of the fireworks as it colored the summer night. Her eyes squinted in the light, and memories of her childhood filled her thoughts.

Somehow, thanks to my deceased state, I became aware that she had suffered a tough childhood. Her father had passed away when she was young, and her mother bullied her. Underneath her smile lay years of pain and torment.

She began to unwrap the rush mat in her arms. The string tying it together had broken, and the mat was half open. My face would be visible once she had lifted the lower flap.

"No!" Ken screamed. "You can't! Don't open it, Midori!" Beside him, Yayoi was bawling.

But Midori's hand gently spread the rush mat open, consolingly, and as if she were showing the fireworks to me.

And as the rush mat spread out across the stone surface of the foundation, my face seemed to look up at her.

Midori gazed into my face, already tinged with rot and discoloration. My eyes, open from the moment I died, took in the light of the moon and the stars.

Midori gently closed my eyelids and whispered, "It's over now," to me, and to Ken.

The cascade of fireworks stretching up into the sky were

reaching their conclusion as well, and suddenly, like the end of a fleeting and vibrant life, the last light scattered into the night, to linger on only in the hearts of those who had witnessed it.

And as if on cue, darkness spread its wings across us.

Beneath the dark, starlit night, Ken and Yayoi heard the far-off crackling sound of decay, and then, the sweet song of Midori's laughter reaching out to them.

KAGOME, KAGOME

The rice in the fields was painted with yellow and ripe for harvest, and the old stone foundation at the shrine was being demolished.

Around the dry stone structure were several bulldozers accompanied by busy men in construction vests.

"Hey, come check this out," one of them said. "There's something over here." He was pointing at the foundation, which sat sliced open like a cake. Along the edge was a single vertical fissure shaped like a well.

"What the hell?" another responded, agape. "Look at all that garbage!"

At the bottom of the well was a human-sized pile of trash. The garbage had accumulated and congealed together as if part of the foundation from its construction.

But near the top of the pile, some of the garbage, mostly plastic bags and candy wrappers, had not yet decomposed.

"Look, there's even some spinning tops, and what are these, Pogs? What a waste!"

The toys were bundled up in a plastic bag. Perhaps they had been accidentally dropped down the hole, or perhaps someone had thrown them away to say goodbye to his childhood.

A little farther down was a large pile of papers, some written on with brush and ink, some yellowed with age, some so damaged by rainwater as to leave their original form indiscernible. It was as if all the memories of childhood had fused over the lifetimes into a single object.

And then, one of the workers saw something odd.

"Hey, look…"

It was a clump of hair. And judging from the length of it, it seemed to him as if someone had thrown a young girl into the hole.

The worker cautiously pulled at the hair.

The hair slipped easily from the pile of garbage, and from beneath it the rotted face and body of a child slid out onto the ground at their feet.

The man gave a frightened shriek and slumped down on his knees.

One of the others laughed at him. "Thank God it's not the real thing, 'cause who knows what you would have done then!"

What had appeared from the pile was a life-size Japanese doll. Before it had been thrown away, it must have been very beautiful. Even though it had been rotting in the garbage pile for years, just looking at it, you could still tell it had once been a girl doll.

The two construction workers, standing at what was to have been my grave, roared with laughter over the events of that peaceful autumn day.

❋

"See, aren't you glad you listened to me?"

Midori and Yayoi sat on either side of Ken, three abreast on the shrine's wooden steps as they watched the workers demolish the stone foundation. The three of them reminded me of how we used to sit on the branch of our secret tree.

The tree leaves that had protected the shrine from the harsh rays of the summer sun had turned to shades of yellow and were drifting down one by one to the ground. The stone pavement that stretched out before the three was covered in browns and yellows.

"We are glad," said Ken. "If we hadn't, there'd have been a lot of trouble right about now."

Midori, happy to hear his words, broke into a smile.

"That's right. Never underestimate the resources of a nineteen-year-old! There's been talk of tearing down that foundation and building a community center in its place for a long time. Of course, some people wanted it preserved because the foundation was all that survived when the castle burnt down in the war. But you heard about the kid who hurt himself up there earlier this year, right? Well, when that happened, they decided to move forward with the demolition. Adults are selfish creatures, aren't they? Destroying the places we like to play and then turning around and complaining about how 'kids these days never go outside anymore.'"

She affectionately looked down at Ken sitting next to her. *Another five years, maybe six,* she thought, *and he'll be about my height.*

With admiration in his voice, Ken said, "Really, Midori, you saved us. When I first saw you up there, I didn't know what to do. I never thought you'd come to help us deal with Satsuki."

He gazed up at her with eyes full of respect, and she looked right back at him. She was happy.

"It's all taken care of. Getting rid of bodies like that is something I'm quite used to by now. And don't worry, I won't turn you in to the police or anyone else. Your secret is safe with me."

Midori's red lips formed a smile, and she gently traced her finger along Ken's cheek, her red-painted nail sliding sensually down the curve of it.

Then, as if awaiting his next words, she looked into his eyes.

"You're really something," he said brightly.

Midori pulled him into her arms, thankful for and delighted by his admiration. She held him tightly, pressing his face against her chest so firmly that he couldn't even breathe.

She felt his body turn warm, and thought, *Maybe now I can finally stop...*

Yayoi listened to them talk, her eyes pressed shut. She would never have to say that she had murdered me. If she kept on lying, saying that I had only fallen from that tree, no one would ever doubt her innocence. She hadn't been able to tell her parents that lie because she had felt guilty and afraid. She had been worried that she would get caught.

The autumn wind blew through the temple grounds. It was cold, and winter would come soon. As the wind swept through, yellow and brown leaves shook free of the trees and drifted down upon the three sitting on the steps.

As she tenderly plucked the dead leaves from Ken's hair, Midori smiled like an angel. She recalled all of her dreadful past sins and felt aware of the boyish demon sleeping somewhere in the bottom of her soul.

Was that hole the result of shoddy workmanship of the builders of old? The stone structure, once the foundation for a great castle, was no more. Another era had passed.

The memories of the children that rested within the foundation over all the generations were carried away in the autumn wind, vanishing like a fleeting summer dream.

Sitting on the wooden steps before the sacred shrine, above where my sandal still lay hidden, the three sinners smiled at the future that awaited them and the childhood they had left behind.

CODA:

Midori brought me to this cold place.

She took me to the back corner of a refrigerated storage room in the ice cream factory where nobody but her ever sets foot.

It's a place with no seasons, only winter all year long. If a living person were in here, they would freeze to death within the day.

But I'm not lonely at all.

In fact, since I came here, I've made all sorts of friends.

They're all boys, and their faces all look like Ken's. They even play "Kagome, Kagome" with me.

Their faces might all be a pale blue, but we can still have lots of fun.

Me and my kidnapped friends sing "Kagome, Kagome," and the song echoes hollow and forlorn through the room.

YUKO

That day, when Masayoshi arrived at the gate to his home, the first thing he saw was Yuko wrapped in flame. He ran to her screaming and put out the fire, but it was already too late.

Weeping, he cried out, *I'm sorry. I'm sorry.* His heart was too full of guilt to experience the sadness of losing her.

He was thinking of a story that his mother had told him long before.

The story of a mother and child who came to Torigoe Manor many generations ago.

The story of a flower the child had been holding in her hand.

Clutching his Yuko to his chest, Masayoshi looked up at the sky and saw no moon.

1. KIYONE

It was soon after the Second World War had ended.

Kiyone had been at Torigoe Manor two weeks, and she was starting to become familiar with the layout of the house and the specifics of her duties. And though it was the first time in her life she had worked, she hadn't found it particularly difficult or painful. Rather, Kiyone felt gratitude toward the master of the house for giving a woman like her a place to work.

She stood by an old gate in a corner of the house's spacious garden, thinking. *What should I make for dinner tonight? I wonder what kind of food the master likes to eat?* Beside the gate grew a few lonely hydrangea bushes and a shrub with round, pitch-black berries.

It was the summer rainy season, and clouds hung above, threatening rain. Kiyone was admiring the hydrangeas when the pleasant *clop clop* of wooden shoes came to her from outside the gate. She looked down the narrow stone path that continued beyond the gate—it seemed like it would be crushed by the bamboo trees along its length—and saw the master of the house walking toward her. *Clop clop.* His footsteps echoed down the path to her, and as he approached he looked at Kiyone with gentle eyes.

When he passed through the gate, she politely bowed her head and greeted him. "Welcome home, sir."

"Thank you, Kiyone. It's good to see you."

He stopped next to Kiyone, his gaze lingering on the hydrangeas behind her. "The hydrangeas are in bloom. Is it that time of year already?"

He crossed his arms, slipping them within the opposite sleeves of his kimono, and smiled. For a moment, Kiyone was transfixed by his youthful face.

Every time she saw it she thought, *He looks so feminine. If he grew out his hair and put on lipstick, he might be as fetching as a* hina *doll.*

His name was Masayoshi. He was a writer, and Kiyone couldn't help but think what a shame it was for his white and slender fingers to be so calloused from his fountain pens. Masayoshi was a friend of her father's.

Masayoshi turned his eyes to her and asked, "Have you grown accustomed to your duties? You're still young. It must be tough for you to manage the house all by yourself."

It wasn't. She was filled with gratitude but couldn't find the proper words to express it. All she managed in response was an awkward smile. With only one exception, she loved being at Torigoe Manor.

Just then, Kiyone noticed that Masayoshi was not carrying the thick brown envelope he had left with, and she realized that he must have gone to the village's only post office.

"If you'd told me," she said, "I could have gone to the post office for you."

"No, it was nothing. I have to get out of that room every now and then, you know."

"Oh. Is it really all right that I don't ever clean your room?"

"Yes, it's fine. Yuko can do the cleaning for that one room."

Kiyone gave a start when she heard the name, just as she did every time she heard it.

"Ummm, is the lady feeling well?"

She could see his face cloud over. *Just like the sky today*, Kiyone thought.

"No, she's not well and may not be for a while…"

But Kiyone didn't hear the ring of truth in the master's remark. It had been two weeks since she came to Torigoe Manor, and she had yet to see his wife's face. All Kiyone knew was that she was nearly bedridden in Masayoshi's room. *I wonder what kind of woman his wife is*, she thought to herself whenever Yuko's name escaped his lips.

"The hydrangeas," Masayoshi said, walking over to the flowers. The smell of his clothing wafted toward Kiyone as he passed. "Those aren't the petals of the hydrangea. Did you know that?"

He pointed a finger at a pale blue hydrangea. "These blue parts here that look like petals—they're actually sepals. They're only imitating the real petals."

Kiyone's heart began to race, although she didn't know why.

"Hydrangeas seem to sparkle in the rain." Masayoshi noticed the black berries growing next to the hydrangeas and tilted his head. "Now what on earth is this plant with the black berries?"

He bent over, putting his nose to the berries. For some reason, seeing his odd pose gave Kiyone a sense of relief.

Berries, pitch black and glossy, about the size of the tip of a little finger, dotted the bush.

"What a pretty black color they have," Masayoshi said and then walked to the house, the *clop clop* of his wooden shoes echoing through the garden.

Kiyone took a deep breath. Her lungs filled with heavy air that smelled of a forest just before the rain, and she coughed.

She looked over to where Masayoshi had walked. Torigoe Manor stood outstretched like unfurled wings. She couldn't believe that she worked in such a large house. She had never before seen a gravel garden or stone paths and stepping-stones like those that led all the way from the gate to the front door.

Kiyone stood there, thinking of a woman named Yuko whom she had not yet seen.

＊

Masayoshi always took his meals in his room with Yuko. For each meal, Kiyone set two servings on a tray and carried it to their room through a dim hallway with windowless earthen walls set with flanking rows of sliding paper doors. The black floorboards were old and worn smooth and complained beneath her footsteps, *creak creak*.

That was probably how Masayoshi could always tell when Kiyone had come with their meals. Before she could speak up and inform him that she had arrived with their food, he would say from behind the sliding door, "Thank you, just leave the tray there, please."

She set the tray down in front of the doorway and left. She had never seen into his room.

The master and his wife are such odd people, Kiyone thought. Masayoshi and Yuko went to great lengths not to open the door in her presence, and it gnawed at her curiosity. Thinking of how intently they listened for the *creak creak* of the floorboards sent shivers down her spine. Many times since she came to Torigoe Manor she had the creeping feeling of a dreadful gaze watching her from the shadows pooled at the ends of the long corridors in the mansion. She walked quickly past the demonic masks of *hannya* and *tengu* that hung from the walls. Their expressions seemed to change whenever she glanced back at them.

※

One day, soon after Kiyone had begun to work at Torigoe Manor, she was walking down the hallway to Masayoshi and Yuko's room to retrieve the tray with their dishes. When the two had finished eating, they always left the tray in the hallway in front of their room, exactly in the same spot Kiyone had set it, and she would pick it up without a word and bring it back to the kitchen.

On this day, Kiyone had prepared a side dish of tempura along with their meal. When she was a child, her father had once taken her out to eat tempura, but she hadn't had it since. Now, she had been nervous trying to cook it all by herself.

Is this all right? Does it really taste like actual tempura tastes?

Kiyone had spent some time looking at the tempura, comparing it with the image in her memory.

Kiyone always went to a house in the neighboring village to buy the vegetables, and she often asked for advice on how to cook. She had followed the instructions to make the tempura, but she had no way of knowing if she had done so correctly or not. And when she saw the tray on the floor of the hallway with half the food uneaten, she felt deeply abashed.

Kiyone picked up the tray and stood in front of the door to their room, unsure of what to do. *Should I say something? Should I ask what was wrong with my tempura?*

Masayoshi's kind voice came from inside the room. *It feels so awkward to have a conversation through the closed paper door,* she thought.

"Kiyone, do you have a minute?"

Here it comes, she thought.

"From tomorrow," he went on, "could you only make half the food for Yuko and me?"

Why only half? Is my cooking that unbearable? Do they not even want to eat it anymore?

"We're both light eaters. Because neither one of us moves around much, you see. So starting tomorrow, we'd like you to cut our servings in half."

"Um…" Kiyone fearfully began. "Um…is it because of my cooking? If that's the case, I'd be happier if you just told me so."

She heard Masayoshi's pleasant laughter from behind the paper door. "Your tempura really was delicious."

Kiyone felt her cheeks quickly warm, and she hurriedly left. Not until she lay alone tossing in bed that night did she realize that she had heard Masayoshi laugh, but not Yuko.

※

The house's pantry was just off the kitchen. Among the objects that sat on its white dried-earth floor were several cardboard boxes and a dust-covered stove. The strong, stale odor of wet straw filled the room.

Kiyone kept potatoes, carrots, and other vegetables bought from the next village in the boxes, but one day, she looked inside only to find them empty.

What should I do? I can't make lunch like this. Kiyone methodically went through the boxes one by one. The cardboard had softened in the humidity, but the dirt clinging to the sides had long dried. As her hands moved through the boxes, her fingers started to turn white with the dry mud and began to grow cold.

Each box she opened was empty, and soon it seemed that none would contain any ingredients at all. *What should I do?* Kiyone cursed her carelessness. *Why didn't I notice that we were running out of food earlier?*

But Kiyone kept searching. She lowered her head to the dusty earthen floor in search of anything she could cook, and behind the legs of the stove she spotted a single cardboard box.

Kiyone let out a sigh of relief and pushed the stove aside to get at the box. The stove was heavy, and as she lifted it she could feel the kerosene sloshing around inside.

Inside the box were a few old, yellowed daikon radishes and onions, maybe just enough for Masayoshi and Yuko's meal.

But not enough for me, Kiyone thought. *Well, I can just make do with some berries or something.*

Kiyone looked up and saw a row of crates lining a shelf high on one of the storeroom walls. The word DOLLS was written in kanji across the rough wood of the crates. Both the writing and the wood itself looked quite old.

She was drawn in by the word DOLLS. Kiyone had never learned how to read kanji, but her father had been a dollmaker, and she remembered the meaning of those characters.

Do all those crates contain dolls? If they do, that's certainly a lot of dolls. Maybe some of them are my father's handiwork.

Unable to contain her curiosity, Kiyone stretched her arms up and carefully pulled down one of the crates from the shelf.

She was surprised by its lightness, and when she set it down and opened the lid, she discovered the reason.

It was empty. She opened all the other crates, and they were all empty. Among the many crates, there wasn't a single doll.

＊

That afternoon, Kiyone decided to go to the neighboring village to restock the vegetables. When she informed Masayoshi, he gave her a generous amount of money and said, "I don't have a car, but there is a cart in the shed you can use. Will you be fine going by yourself? If it's too heavy, please have someone there help you bring it back."

Kiyone thanked him, said she'd be fine, and left. The cart, even though empty, took a considerable amount of strength to pull, but once she got it rolling, it moved along without needing much further effort.

She pulled the cart through the gate of Torigoe Manor and along the narrow stone path that cut through the bamboo grove.

I don't understand why he sends me all the way to the next village to buy the groceries. Why does he want me to avoid doing the shopping in our own village?

As she thought about it, Kiyone noticed that the neighbors she passed on the street were watching her with rigid gazes. As she pulled the cart along, she attempted to greet some of the villagers, but they only looked away, as if to them she were nothing but a nuisance.

Between the two villages, an expanse of rice paddies stretched as far as she could see. Kiyone pulled the rattling cart down the long, straight road that led to the neighboring community and to the home of a family who occasionally helped out the Torigoe household. Kiyone loved to visit there. They sold her vegetables, carefully and meticulously taught her how to cook, and treated her with warmth and kindness—like she was a person.

Beneath the clear sky, uncommonly cloudless for the rainy

season, Kiyone was pulling the cart down the gravel road when she noticed a three-wheeled truck driving toward her from the next village. The road was narrow enough to make passing difficult for the cart and the truck, and the driver pulled his vehicle to the side of the road in front of her and waited for her to pass.

Kiyone thanked the driver and sped up to get out of his way as quickly as she could, and as she passed, he called out to her.

"Hey, you wouldn't happen to be running errands for Torigoe Manor, would you?"

"Yes, I am."

The driver scratched his chin in thought, then said, "Well, good luck."

His words were brusque, but there was some warmth behind them. Kiyone got the impression that he was from the neighboring village and knew exactly why she had to go all the way there to do her errands.

Next to the road, a harvested wheat field fell into shadow. Kiyone looked up and saw a single cloud floating across the sky, hiding the sun.

2. THE ROOM

Masayoshi sat on a legless chair in one corner of his spacious ten-mat room, his fountain pen gliding across sheets of paper.

In another corner of the room stood an old three-panel dressing mirror. The left and right panels were tied closed with red string wrapped clockwise around the handles to keep the doors from falling open. Along the opposite wall, a large number of dolls were lined up on display, almost all of them Japanese dolls with long smooth hair and white, expressionless faces all aimed at the center of the room. Anyone who entered the room would be encircled by the dolls and surrounded by the blank faces of the nameless children.

A futon was spread out on the straw tatami flooring in front of the rows of dolls.

Masayoshi's hand paused, and he looked over at the futon, where he saw the figure of the woman he called Yuko.

Yuko was lying in the futon, staring in Masayoshi's direction.

Her voice, thin and soft, barely discernible, came to his ear, and he could hear every word. *I caught a glimpse of Kiyone's face, dear.*

"She's an intelligent young lady."

Yes, I just saw her through the crack of the door as she walked by. She's young. I hope the work isn't too tough for her.

Masayoshi stood, went to the side of his resting wife, and gently placed his hand on top of her comforter.

When she was gone, I went to the kitchen and found a piece of paper with recipes on it. But it was written entirely in simple hiragana—no kanji.

"Yes, she never went to school, and she never learned how to write kanji."

Still, that's quite a feat, learning hiragana on her own.

To Masayoshi, Yuko's voice sounded dim, precarious, as though it might vanish altogether.

"I hired her because I felt sorry for her, left all alone when her father died of tuberculosis. But I'm lucky to have her here. By the way, did I ever tell you that she brought one of her father's dolls when she came here? It was a little girl doll."

Masayoshi gently brushed three fingers down the curve of her smooth, white cheek, and he thought he saw a faint smile touch the cold colors of her inanimate face.

✳

Masayoshi was troubled by Yuko's occasional catatonic spells. She would stare off at nothing in particular and seem oblivious to his attempts to talk to her. He felt it was as though she were in another world, and it worried him greatly.

Usually, Masayoshi and Yuko knew that Kiyone had brought their meals when her footsteps came *creak creak creak*ing along the hallway. Masayoshi would thank the young woman and listen for her to walk away down the hall before he slid open the paper door to take the tray into their room.

But when Yuko was having one of her spells, silently sitting on her futon, she made no response and showed no recognition. Even when he placed chopsticks in her delicate fingers, she made no attempt to eat.

One such time, Masayoshi became so frightened that he cried out, "Yuko! Yuko!" He shook her slender shoulders, and her long smooth hair waved violently in the air.

What's wrong, dear?

Masayoshi was relieved by the sound of her voice, and when he looked at her face he saw it filled with affection. He always felt as if her face, its features so perfectly assembled as to appear otherworldly and the purest white skin, would swallow him whole.

What's wrong, dear?

3. THE OPENING

The garden at Torigoe Manor, dotted with aptly placed stone lanterns and large, well-shaped rocks, was as expansive as the grounds of a shrine. A fence of roughly bound bamboo encircled the garden. Outside the fence grew a bamboo grove, and Kiyone often listened to the rustling of the trees when the wind blew through them. In the evening, the setting sun painted the sky behind the trees a vibrant orange, and the bamboo loomed large and black. When the bamboo bent in the breeze, they seemed like some far-off howling beast.

I wonder what path this is.

Kiyone was walking around the back of the house where she usually never went when she noticed a narrow path snaking through the bamboo grove. She had been about to start preparing dinner.

What is it?

Kiyone tilted her head, peering into the bamboo. The path

wound through the trees, and she couldn't tell where it led. But the young woman still had work to do, so she went back into the house to start peeling sweet potatoes with thoughts of the path lingering in her mind.

The next day, Kiyone walked down the path. On either side the bamboo trees stretched straight up into the cloudy gray sky. When Kiyone looked up, the trees converged at a single point above her and seemed to enclose her on all sides.

Tall, wild grass grew on either side of the path, and the long blades brushed against Kiyone's nose as she walked. The path continued unbroken through the grove. At the end of the path was a single grave.

It was a fine grave, not just a lone marker left among the trees but a tombstone that stood upon an arrangement of large rocks. A name was engraved on the stone.

It didn't look to be that old.

Kiyone approached the grave. A snake was winding its way through the small gap between the tombstone and the bamboo.

Whose grave is this? I can't read this kanji.

A flower placed on the grave had long since turned black, and a bamboo sprout left in offering lay rotting beside it.

※

As Kiyone returned to the garden, a gentle rain began to patter on her head.

Oh no, I need to bring in the laundry. Kiyone ran lightly over to where she had left the laundry out to dry.

A faded bamboo drying rack was suspended by a string from the roof next to the kitchen door, and a line of laundry hung along the rack.

Kiyone swiftly pulled off an armful of the clothes and carried it into the house, then repeated the process once more. There had been constant showers lately, and Kiyone had taken to hanging out the laundry even on cloudy days in a fruitless attempt to dry them.

As she brought in the second armload of laundry, she noticed that the outside door to Masayoshi and Yuko's room had been left open a crack.

Once all the laundry had been brought inside, Kiyone felt relieved. But the image of that opening in the sliding door lingered in her mind. It had been one month since she had come to stay at the manor, and yet she had not once seen the inside of their room. And not only that, she had not had a single glimpse of Yuko. From time to time, Kiyone had washed Yuko's white pajamas, but they had been nearly pristine—so clean that she doubted they had been worn at all.

She found it difficult to believe that a woman named Yuko even lived in the house.

She's bedridden, so of course her clothing wouldn't get dirty so easily. That's why the laundry is always so clean. Kiyone tried to dismiss it at that, but she couldn't help but think it peculiar that she hadn't met Yuko even once.

Masayoshi's wife must be beautiful, Kiyone thought. *Because she's his wife.*

Because she's a wife.

Kiyone couldn't stand it any longer. She put on her sandals and went outside.

The air was hazy with misting rain.

She looked over at Masayoshi and Yuko's room. The door was still open a crack, but she couldn't see inside.

With steady, controlled breaths and careful footsteps, she walked toward the door.

I'll just pass right by it, like nothing's unusual.

The closer she got to the door, the faster her heart raced. A narrow wooden porch ran along the outside of their room, and below the walkway was a long, flat stone. Atop the stone, a thin layer of water had pooled around a single straw sandal.

I'll just stroll by. Just one glance inside the room, that's all.

As Kiyone walked awkwardly past the door, she noticed out of the corner of her eye that the paper of the sliding door had started to turn a faint yellow, and through the tiny opening of the doorway she saw a three-panel dressing mirror. She also made out a legless chair, although no one was sitting in it.

Her clothes were damp in the rain, and the palms of her closed fists were moist with sweat.

Through the opening, she saw that one wall was decorated with a great number of white-faced dolls, and in front of them a futon was spread out on the floor. The coverings on the futon were filled out, as if someone were lying in it. But what Kiyone saw in the futon as she passed the opening of the doorway was the expressionless face of a doll looking right back at her.

※

The next day, when she had a break between chores, Kiyone went to visit Shizue, a young woman who had also worked as a maid at Torigoe Manor and had quit six months earlier, after marrying someone from the neighboring village. Kiyone was always welcome in Shizue's home, and she sometimes went there for advice with cooking and sewing.

"What's wrong?" Shizue asked her. "You seem down today."

Kiyone tried to smile, but it soon vanished.

The two women sat drinking tea on the wooden porch. Kiyone looked up and saw the hydrangeas in bloom. She thought the pale blue flowers looked much like the cloudy gray sky.

"Hey," Shizue said, "look at what I found." In the palm of her hand rested a tiny short-haired kitten.

"Oh, it's cute," said Kiyone, looking at the cat with wonder. "That's really something. Is it a little kitty doll?"

Shizue narrowed her eyes at Kiyone. "Don't be silly, she's the real thing. She got lost. She must have had a home somewhere, otherwise she wouldn't be so used to being held like this. If I see a lost animal, I always take it in."

Kiyone took a sip of her tea and asked, "Is your husband around today?"

Shizue laughed. "He's in the fields."

"Why did you laugh?"

"Because he's funny, that man. 'You stay at home,' he says."

Kiyone tilted her head, unsure what was funny about that.

"Because I'm pregnant."

"You're pregnant?"

Kiyone looked at Shizue's stomach, but it hadn't yet begun to swell. All she saw was the kitten rolling around on her friend's knees.

Kiyone was delighted. "That's great!"

"Well, thank you. But how are things with you? How's your work? I hope you're not finding it too difficult."

"No, it's going well. My father and I are very grateful to Masayoshi. It's just—" Kiyone hesitated, but Shizue kept drinking her tea, patiently waiting for her to continue.

In front of the porch was a small field with several thin poles wrapped in green vines blooming with tiny flowers. Off in the distance, a slouching figure of a man was slowly walking by.

"Ummm..." Kiyone hesitantly asked, "Have you ever seen his wife?"

"His wife? Yes, I have."

"What?"

"She was beautiful."

Kiyone looked at Shizue with a surprised expression. When she hadn't seen Yuko through the opening of the door the day before, Kiyone had questioned whether or not Yuko actually existed. She had gone all the way to Shizue's house just to talk about it, and now she felt silly.

Shizue gently brushed the cat from her knee, got to her feet, and walked over to a tree that was growing in front of them. Its trunk was thin, but it was almost twice as tall as Kiyone. Small, shiny red fruit grew on the tree, and Shizue picked one of them and put it in her mouth.

She picked a few more and offered them to Kiyone. "Would you like to try one of the goumi fruit?"

Kiyone put one into her mouth and bit down on it. Tart, sweet juice spread over her tongue.

"What do you think? It's good, right? This is the time of year they're ripe. But some of the trees have bitter fruit, which can taste especially nasty if you're expecting it to be sweet."

Following Shizue's lead, Kiyone spit out the seed, then said, "That happened to me the other day. I only took one bite, and I spit it out immediately, but the terrible taste stayed in my mouth forever. I rinsed out my mouth with water, but it didn't help. That night, I felt nauseous and dizzy, and I couldn't sleep. It was so awful, I thought I'd die."

Kiyone put one more goumi fruit into her mouth and bit down on it.

With Shizue smiling in front of her, Kiyone felt enveloped by a serene happiness. She was without fear or doubt.

Kiyone rolled the remaining fruit around in the palm of her hand and whispered to herself, "Thank goodness."

Master Masayoshi wasn't seeing hallucinations or anything like that. Of course he wasn't. I've just been caught up in some foolish notion.

Kiyone asked, "Could you tell me more about his wife?"

Shizue tilted her head slightly, taking a moment to search her memory. "She had white skin."

"You mean she was white, like Caucasian?"

Shizue narrowed her eyes and laughed. "No, don't be silly. She was fair-skinned and slender. She and her husband always sat side by side on the veranda. I always wished I could have a marriage like they had."

Kiyone felt slightly jealous of her reminiscing friend.

"I was such a fool," Kiyone said.

Startled by the statement, Shizue asked, "Why?"

"Because I had been thinking she wasn't even there in Torigoe Manor. I haven't seen her this whole time. But really, what a foolish thought."

Now Shizue looked even more startled. "What are you talking

about? His wife died two years ago. I've never seen anyone take the loss as hard as he did. It was frightening, the way he was crying and raving."

It took a moment for Kiyone to understand the meaning of the words she was hearing. As they sunk in, one by one, Kiyone set her teacup down on the porch.

She rose to her feet and found them shaky. She felt dizzy, and she turned around to see Shizue's puzzled expression.

"What's wrong, Kiyone?"

What should I do? Should I tell her everything? Should I tell her about Masayoshi's behavior, about the doll I saw through the opening of the doorway, about Yuko, the woman I haven't seen? What would happen if I did tell her? If the rest of the village found out, how would they treat Masayoshi? The thought was unbearable. The *clop clop* of his shoes echoed in her mind, and she could see his figure bent over the hydrangeas as he talked of flowers. She had no idea what to do.

"Kiyone?" Shizue repeated.

The cat meowed.

But Kiyone didn't hear either of them.

The tart, sweet fruit dropped from her hand and fell noiselessly to the ground.

✳

"I'm going out for a while, Kiyone."

When Kiyone saw Masayoshi off she made up her mind. Masayoshi was out of the house. Her emotions raged. It was the resolve borne of a terrible uncertainty.

With a *creak creak* she passed through the constant gloom of the hallway and stood before Masayoshi's room. Inside should be only Yuko. Kiyone knelt before the sliding door and sat in the formal *seiza* position with her legs folded beneath her thighs. Drawing strength to still her trembling shoulders, she said, "Par—"

Her voice cracked. *How relieved would I be to find that Yuko really is there on the other side of the sliding door before me.*

"Pardon me, it's Kiyone. Ma'am, ma'am, it's Kiyone, please answer. Please, could you answer..."

She waited a long time, but Kiyone never heard the slightest response.

"Ma'am! Please answer me! Ma'am!"

After a short pause, Kiyone, summoning all of her courage, put the fingers of her right hand upon the sliding door. As she tentatively slid the door open, the opening grew ever wider, and at last she could see the entire room.

From where she still sat seiza, Kiyone slowly scanned the room from corner to corner. Faint yellow sunlight bleeding in through the paper door leading outside lit the room only dimly and created pools of darkness within. Girl dolls were there, half melted into the shadows, and when she tried to count them one by one, she realized the total would be more than fifty. Their blank bloodless faces seemed to be crying or laughing. Stranger still was the white futon spread out in front of the dolls. There Kiyone saw a white doll with long hair, like the one she had seen the day before, lying peacefully in the futon. Indeed, that doll had a strange and mysterious aura compared to the rest, and when she looked into its slender white face, she felt she was being drawn into a dreadful yet somehow dreamlike illusion.

In a panic, Kiyone drew her eyes away from the doll and turned her head to look at the opposite side of the room.

She saw nothing that could be called Yuko.

On the opposite side of the room was the sliding door of a closet with Mount Fuji painted on it in blue and a legless chair that Masayoshi probably sat in to write. Before the chair was a glossy wooden desk, on top of which quite a number of fountain pens were lined up waiting for their master's return. The sight made Kiyone feel somehow sad and lonely.

In one corner of the room, she saw an odd three-panel dressing mirror. Both side doors were closed, and for some reason a red string was fastened clockwise around their handles. But what made it odd was that compared to the rest of the objects in the room, it was old. Nothing was carved upon it, and the wood had no luster. But why, despite its age, hadn't it been replaced, remaining instead inside Torigoe Manor?

Kiyone removed the string and quietly opened the doors. The mirrors inside had splintered into a weblike network of cracks. Only in the corners of the panels were there small patches of uncracked mirror she could look into and see her face thrown straight back at her.

Just then, in one of those minute corners of uncracked mirror, Kiyone thought she saw the pale face of a woman. Kiyone let out a tiny scream and spun around, and at that moment, her right elbow bumped against the three-panel mirror, and several fragments of the glass shook loose and fell to the floor. But no matter how hard she strained her eyes to look, she could see no pale woman—or anyone else, for that matter—in the room. Terror welled up within her like a cold snake crawling along her spine.

She hurriedly gathered up the shards of broken glass and closed the doors of the mirror. She wound the red string around the knobs on the doors, and without stopping to look over her shoulder, she fled into the dark hallway.

Crying from fear, she went to her room and cowered small in the corner, clutching the doll her father had made her.

4. THE MIRROR

"Yuko, I'm home," said Masayoshi as he opened the sliding door to his room. "Did anything out of the ordinary happen while I was gone?"

No, nothing out of the ordinary happened.

"I see, that's good. Nobody came in here, right? That's a good thing."

But when Masayoshi happened to glance at the mirror in the

corner of the room, he noticed something curious. He walked up to the mirror, and when he drew close to it, he let out a cry.

"What happened here? It's not good to lie, Yuko. Somebody came in here today, didn't they? And they opened this mirror, right? You can't lie to me like that, Yuko."

Why? Why don't you believe me? Nothing happened.

"That's not so, Yuko. Look at the string on this mirror. Since the mirror's old, it sometimes falls open. I keep a red string looped around the two knobs to keep it from opening."

What's the matter, then? Isn't it like that now?

"No, Yuko, you're wrong. I always wrap the string around clockwise, and here, look, today it's wrapped around counter-clockwise. Why would that be?"

Oh, that's because I opened it, dear. I opened the mirror.

Masayoshi opened the mirror and let out an even more surprised cry.

"Yuko, the mirror is broken. The shards should have fallen to the floor."

Dear, wasn't the mirror already broken?

"No, Yuko, you're wrong. The mirror was cracked, but none of the pieces were missing. But look, there are pieces missing here, and here. They should have fallen somewhere, but I don't see them anywhere, Yuko."

Masayoshi approached one of the many white-faced dolls, smoothly brushed its hair, and spoke gently. "Come, tell me the truth, Yuko. Kiyone came in here today, didn't she? You've been lying to cover up for her."

Yes, you're right. Kiyone was here.

"I see. But what were you doing then? Didn't you tell her that she couldn't come in? Didn't you caution her not to touch that mirror?"

Oh, I'm sorry. When she came in here, I was in something of a daze. But luckily I awakened, and I told Kiyone to leave the room right away. I told her that. But please, dear, don't scold her.

"All right, Yuko, I won't. I'd just like her to return the pieces of the mirror."

The sliding door to the outside glowed red from the sunset. Only at that time did the faces of the dolls warm to a rosy color, almost as though they were flesh and blood babies.

5. YUKO

Kiyone couldn't take it anymore.

The night before, when she had gone to retrieve the dishes from outside Masayoshi's room, she had noticed something strange.

The many bowls on the wooden tray had been emptied as usual. The two pairs of chopsticks and two teacups had also been used. But why was there one dish that neither of them had touched, both their portions uneaten? Kiyone, unable to contain her curiosity, spoke to Masayoshi through the closed door.

"Master Masayoshi, may I ask you something?"

His reply came from inside the room. "What is it, Kiyone?"

His voice was as gentle as ever, and hearing it made Kiyone feel like her heart was being squeezed.

"Master Masayoshi, was there something wrong with the boiled horse mackerel I served tonight? Please be frank with me."

"No, there was absolutely nothing wrong with your dinner. It's just that Yuko and I cannot stand to eat horse mackerel. I never told you. I know it was incredibly rude of us, but neither Yuko nor I could eat any of it."

"But, but, both you and the lady dislike horse mackerel? Both of you hate it so much that you can't stand to eat a bite of it?"

"Yes, Kiyone, that's how it is."

Now that she thought about it, Kiyone remembered another time they both had left their food uneaten. At that time, she was inexperienced and hadn't known up from down. Unaware that they both had small appetites, she had made them a large meal.

Kiyone was struck by a sudden thought. They had each left

half their meals. *Then, the master told me to cut both his and his wife's meals in half. What on earth did that mean? According to him, they both only ate half of what a typical person eats. Didn't that mean that both of their meals added up to precisely the amount for one person to eat? What did that mean? If what he said had all been a lie, then…*

No, it couldn't be. I don't want it to be. But if the woman called Yuko has already passed from this world…

Kiyone pictured Masayoshi posing as Yuko and eating both their meals.

First, Masayoshi, as himself, took a bite of his food with his chopsticks. Then, Masayoshi ate in Yuko's place. Next he whispered something to Yuko, who wasn't there, and mimicking her voice, he replied to himself.

Dinner continued like that until, unable to eat any more, he left half of each meal.

Of course the horse mackerel that Masayoshi couldn't eat remained on Yuko's plate as well.

Yuko was Masayoshi.

The doll that had been in the futon must have been sitting in front of Yuko's dinner tray. But Masayoshi believed that Yuko lived in that room with him. *What a nightmare.* Kiyone felt dizzy.

Master Masayoshi, didn't your wife Yuko pass away two years ago, and isn't she buried in the bamboo grove?

As Kiyone was walking back to her room, she couldn't hold back the tears any longer. Her tears fell into the bowls on the tray she carried, and the floor of the hallway *creak creak*ed away.

❈

The next day, Kiyone came to a decision, triggered by Masayoshi's sudden departure.

"Kiyone, I have to make a bit of a trip after lunch. I probably won't be back until late."

Masayoshi was dressed in his finery, and he carried a large

black briefcase he almost never took with him.

"Kiyone." He gazed straight into her eyes and said, "You are not to enter Yuko's room. Do you understand?" Kiyone was startled. "All right? You are not to enter that room. Promise me."

"Yes, I understand." Her voice had the slightest quaver. "I won't enter your room."

After hearing her answer, Masayoshi left the mansion. He hadn't been wearing his sandals, and Kiyone, watching him leave from the front gate, was soon alone without even their familiar *clop clop*.

I will end this today, Master Masayoshi, Kiyone vowed in her heart. *When you come home today, the woman who lives inside your head will truly be gone from this world. Oh, you will probably hate me for it. You'll probably resent me for it. But I cannot bear it any longer. It's time for me and for you to stop dreaming. I believe that when you wake up, a magnificent, clear morning will await you.*

✳

"Ma'am, ma'am. I've brought your dinner."

Kiyone called into the room, but of course there came no reply. Just in case, she set Yuko's meal down in the hallway in front of the door. If the food was gone when she came back for the tray, she would know that Yuko had eaten it, and that Yuko really did exist.

✳

I'm betraying the master, Kiyone thought as she used a funnel to transfer the kerosene that had been left in the stove into a two-liter bottle. A bare lightbulb dangled from the storage room ceiling, swinging its weak orange glow back and forth, and the kerosene glimmered darkly as it flowed into the deep green bottle. When Kiyone glanced up, she could see on the shelf above her the row of wooden crates that had held the dolls, and each time her eyes came upon the word DOLLS she hastened her work.

When she had finished transferring the kerosene into the bottle, she brought it and a match to the center of Torigoe Manor's large garden.

From there, she wouldn't have to worry about the fire spreading, no matter what she burned.

The sun had already hidden itself, and as the world settled into darkness, Kiyone could no longer see the line dividing the bamboo grove and the sky. The moon and the stars would not show themselves that cloudy night.

I will remember this darkness for the rest of my life. This bottomless pit of darkness, this darkness blocking out the bamboo and the stone lanterns that are right over there—the dark of this night will torment me for the rest of my life.

✳

Kiyone carried a lit candle as she went to get Yuko. The flickering light danced across her face.

She *creak creak*ed down the hallway to Masayoshi's room. He was away, and no one would be inside. If what he had said was true, then Yuko would be in there alone. But when Kiyone inspected the tray in front of the door, she felt dejected.

The meal was exactly as it had been when she left it there. There was no sign that anybody had even laid a finger on it.

Master Masayoshi, if a woman named Yuko really lived in this room, shouldn't even a small portion of this meal have been eaten? Yuko died two years ago. Aren't you just seeing an illusion of your departed wife inside that doll?

Feeling like she was about to cry, Kiyone said, "I'm coming in," and slid open the door. But even after she turned on the light, she didn't see anyone there—only the rows of white dolls. When the warm light of the lightbulb fell upon the dolls, their puffy white cheeks and softly flowing black hair floated in the darkness, and Kiyone gasped.

How many years has it been since I was surrounded like this by white-faced dolls? Kiyone thought back to the time she spent the night in her father's doll workshop.

Kiyone was afraid of dolls. She found it creepy the way the girls seemed to stare at her. *Are they about to start moving? The second I take my eyes off them, will they discard those expressionless masks and grin? Will they leap onto my shoulders in their disheveled red kimono like bawling children?* Kiyone was terrified. The thoughts were enough to make her want to flee from the room.

Two futon mattresses were laid out inside the room. One must have been where Masayoshi slept. The other should have held Yuko.

But however Kiyone looked at it, the white face atop the futon looked not like a human, but like a doll.

This doll is "Yuko." Kiyone was convinced.

My father may even have made this one.

Kiyone removed the comforter and saw that the figure was wearing white pajamas. She realized that she had been washing clothes worn by a doll, and she couldn't keep the thought of it from her mind no matter how hard she tried.

All this time, haven't I just been a puppet for that doll?

But I'm not the only one she's been manipulating.

Kiyone picked up Yuko.

On her way out of the room she turned out the lights, and the rows of dolls were covered in darkness.

Could they have been laughing just then?

Or crying?

※

Kiyone laid Yuko face up in the center of the garden and lit her candle. The flame wavered and jostled shadows across Kiyone's face and Yuko's expressionless visage. The candle's single dim light seemed to surface in the garden.

This doll is blinding Master Masayoshi. He calls it by the name of his wife who now rests in her grave and cares for it as if it were a woman.

Without hesitation, Kiyone splashed the kerosene over Yuko. The oil seeped into Yuko's white clothes, turning them vaguely transparent. Kiyone tipped the bottle until nothing remained, and then she set it gently on the ground.

Yuko's body, lying on the ground soaked in kerosene, reflected the candlelight. Kiyone thought, *This doll really is pretty—prettier than any woman alive.*

Quietly she lit the fire.

Yuko's white oil-soaked clothes were instantly engulfed in flame, and the flames flared high. The fire around Yuko was hundreds of times larger than the light of the candle, and the garden flooded with light. *It's as bright as day*, thought Kiyone. She watched the flames and felt their heat on her eyes.

The doll is burning away. The doll he loved is burning away. The words echoed again and again inside her mind, and she took one step back from the flames.

Even after fully enveloping Yuko, the fire continued to torment the corpse with its unceasing fury.

Embers floated up and whirled high into the windless sky. From far heights the embers appeared as red points in the sky dark with no moon or starlight.

※

Suddenly came Masayoshi's violent cry.

"What's happening? Yuko! Yuko!"

He tossed aside his briefcase at Torigoe Manor gate and desperately dashed to the edge of the fire.

"Ahhh, this is—! This is—!" he screamed again and again, unable to find any other words. In one swift motion, he swept off his kimono and laid it over the fire. He threw himself on top, and the garden was left with only the light of the candle and that of the flames that still burned where the kerosene had soaked into the ground.

"Master Masayoshi! That's a doll! There is no Yuko! Come to your senses, master!"

But as if Kiyone wasn't even there, Masayoshi kept crying out, *Yuko, Yuko*, as tears streamed from his eyes.

"Master Masayoshi! Look at me, master!"

Masayoshi, having extinguished the flames with his own body, tightly embraced Yuko, who had lost all traces of the beauty she'd had before the flames burned her. He pressed his cheek against hers and apologized over and over.

"Oh Yuko, I'm sorry, I'm sorry!"

From every corner of his being, he yelled until his voice wavered and finally shattered as if his soul itself had broken away. It pained Kiyone to see him so pitiful.

Masayoshi wept over Yuko in his arms, and Kiyone clung to his back and began to sob.

The fire of the candle she had thrown to the ground dwindled, and the few patches of flames on the earth reflected their flickering light in the tears that ran down her cheeks.

6. BELLADONNA

The hospital's old wooden door caught before grudgingly sliding open at Masayoshi's touch. Inside, a miasma of medicine and must hung in the air, and an unpleasant feeling took hold in his chest. The brown hospital slippers were also old, and he searched for but did not find a pair without some amount of damage.

In contrast to the dim, dank interior of the hospital, the world outside the windows was bright with the early summer light.

Masayoshi passed through the waiting room with its black leather chairs that had patches of yellow stuffing poking out here and there, walked down the aged wooden hallway, and was led to a room where a doctor sat waiting.

The doctor was young, his face serious, and he met Masayoshi with a gaze that felt ominous.

Masayoshi was nervous, unaware he was squeezing his hand-kerchief.

✳

"Oh, I'm glad. I really am. I'm sure you are too, Father. Master Masayoshi is going to be released from the hospital very soon. He just has to have a little talk with the doctor first, and then he'll be free to go. I was worried, so I asked the doctor about it. That's when he told me. He said, 'The most important thing for him now is a calm place where he can relax.' That's what he said. The master's talking with him right now. You know him, don't you, Father? You were friends with him."

When Kiyone heard that Masayoshi wouldn't have to stay in the hospital, she was overjoyed. To her, the best news was that though he still was in severe shock, he would soon be able to return to his normal life.

✳

"Shall we talk about it?" said the doctor as Masayoshi took a seat on the stool.

At Masayoshi's slightest movement, the stool let out a high-pitched grating slash of a sound.

"Yuko was…Yuko was burning. When I came home, Yuko was in flames. Oh, I can still see it now."

Masayoshi realized his voice was quavering. He closed his eyes, and on the back of his eyelids he saw the flames dancing around Yuko. The flames never stopped.

"Oh, Yuko…Doctor, when will Yuko return to me…"

With a furrowed brow the doctor answered, "No, it would be best for you not to see her again. The body is in a terrible state."

A drop of sweat slid slowly down the middle of Masayoshi's

back. He wiped sweat from his forehead and it clung to the back of his hand.

"I understand how you must feel," said the doctor, pity in his face.

"Yuko was my second wife. After my first wife died, all I had left of her was a three-panel mirror."

Masayoshi slouched forward, and the stool made a loud screeching that quickly faded into a corner of the room.

"It was cracked and utterly useless, but I'd kept it to remember her and how she was before she died of tuberculosis. So when Kiyone lost a piece of the mirror, I was saddened."

"When did your first wife pass away?"

"Two years ago. I gave her a proper burial and made her a fine gravestone. When she was alive, the villagers treated her unreasonably."

"I see. So that's two wives you've lost in succession…"

Masayoshi paused. "It was fate."

"Fate?"

"I never thought that Yuko would die in such a way…"

Masayoshi and the doctor fell quiet. The long silence lay over the room, and for a moment Masayoshi wondered if all sound had vanished from the earth.

Finally, the doctor broke the silence.

"I've spoken with Kiyone." His face went pale. "There are quite a few differences between your stories. Tell me, why would that be?"

For a short time, Masayoshi was silent. He set down his folded handkerchief on the wooden table as if he were letting go of something heavy, and then he looked the doctor in the eyes and spoke.

"You might not believe me."

"What won't I believe?"

Masayoshi didn't reply. Instead, as the doctor watched, he quietly unfolded the handkerchief with trembling fingers.

Inside were two small, glossy, pitch-black berries that seemed to swallow all light.

They were the berries of the plant that grew next to the gate of Torigoe Manor.

The doctor looked closely at the black berries on the table and asked, "What are these?"

"I found those berries on the floor of Kiyone's room. You see how they are small and glossy? They're from a plant that grows on the grounds of Torigoe Manor. It's called a belladonna."

"Belladonna?"

"Yes…" said Masayoshi, his lips violently trembling and his face pale as though he were struggling not to retch. "Belladonna. The poisonous berry used in the murder of Hamlet's father."

The doctor, who had begun to reach out for the black berry, froze his hand, his face a dreadful color.

Masayoshi continued. "I had a friend of mine in one of the publishing houses look into it for me."

"But what do these berries have to do with what happened?"

Masayoshi wrinkled his sweaty brow, unsure of where to start. There was quite a bit left that needed explaining.

"This story doesn't have a direct connection to the tragedy, but…"

The doctor nodded and urged him on.

"I'd heard it from a friend. Something that happened—no, a rumor, I should say, of something that happened decades ago at the base of a mountain."

Masayoshi and the doctor both were sweating, yet they looked cold.

※

Several decades ago, a group of men had gone deep into the mountains to gather plants for food. It was just before nightfall when the men discovered a bush they didn't recognize.

On it grew small but delicious-looking berries.

The men wondered what they tasted like. Figuring they couldn't find out just by looking, one of the men grabbed a berry and ate it.

That was his undoing.

The other men circled around the one who ate the berry and asked what it tasted like. But the man didn't answer. Instead, he dropped to his hands and knees and ran off like a wild beast. They said his bloodshot eyes had glittered.

The dumbstruck men watched him vanish into the mountains.

After a time, an eerie howl, not that of human or wolf, echoed three times through the mountains.

Wind blew in through an open window.

"After that, they went farther into the mountains from where the howl had come, and they found the dead body of the man with foam running from his mouth."

The doctor frowned and drew his body back, and his chair gave a sharp creak. "After he ate the poisonous berry, he thought he was a wolf, and then he died? What does that have to do with Kiyone?"

Neither Masayoshi nor the doctor could avert their eyes from the black berries on the table. They could hear the far-off sound of someone running through the hallways, but it sounded like it came from an entirely different dimension from the room Masayoshi was in.

"I believe that she ate the belladonna berry, fatal at even a tenth of a gram."

The doctor's eyes jumped wide open. "If the berry is fatal, shouldn't she be dead? Yet she's still alive."

"Just because some amount is called a fatal dosage, that doesn't mean that it has been measured and tested on humans, so it's an imprecise amount. And maybe she spit it out after biting into it, or it just affects some people less than others. The fact is that she is still alive. She survived it."

"I see what you're getting at. You mean to say that Kiyone is in a state similar to that of the man who ate the poisonous berry and became a wolf."

"No, not quite. I don't think her condition is a symptom of consuming the atropine, the primary active agent in belladonna.

Rather, I believe it is the aftereffects of the fierce shock when she ate the 'devil's cherries.' In other words, she ate the fruit of the belladonna plant and survived. But the price she paid for her life was a state of chronic delirium. That's what I believe happened."

"And in a state of delirium, the line between delusion and reality blurs, and consciousness becomes clouded."

"Exactly. How horrible!" Masayoshi moaned, his grief escaping. "Once, when Kiyone was a young child, she was locked inside her father's doll workshop for an entire night. I heard that for a time after, she had a terrible fear of girl dolls. That terrifying experience intertwined with the delirium caused by the devil's cherries, and Kiyone could no longer easily distinguish dolls from humans. Now the line between humans and dolls is hazy to her."

The doctor opened his eyes wide. "Kiyone became convinced that Yuko was a doll all because of that?"

"It was all the fault of that black berry."

Without Masayoshi so much as pointing his finger, the two turned their eyes toward the small berries atop the table.

"Belladonna is the devil's herb. And the devil's cherry made Kiyone see a fantasy. Incredible. The belladonna planted a fantasy in her head—that Yuko the person didn't exist, but that she was instead a doll."

"And, under the spell of the devil's cherry, Kiyone set the doll on fire."

Masayoshi drew his hands to his face and started to cry through gritted teeth. "I still can't believe it!"

"A hell of a thing. Such a tragedy—for both Yuko and Kiyone. Kiyone was unknowingly possessed by belladonna. Was she nothing more than its puppet?" the doctor wondered.

"But why didn't you let Kiyone in your room? Why didn't you introduce her to Yuko? It makes no sense to me."

"Yuko also…" Masayoshi spoke in a nasal voice. "Yuko also had pulmonary tuberculosis. I didn't want Kiyone to get too near, in case she were to be infected. Her own father, her only relative, had died from the disease just before she started working for me.

So I alone did all the nursing. I kept Yuko's tuberculosis a secret from everyone. Even Kiyone. You probably understand—the icy looks from closed-minded villagers. I didn't want to tell anybody about my wife's illness. I didn't want them hurling at her the same terrible abuses that had been thrown at my first wife."

The room filled with silence, and Masayoshi felt as though he were being crushed under some heavy weight. The ground grew soft beneath his feet; he felt like he might sink down into it at any moment.

His arms were covered with cold sweat. When the doctor sighed, Masayoshi straightened up in his chair. It creaked.

"Please listen to me," said the doctor. "That night, Yuko didn't eat the dinner Kiyone had prepared. And Kiyone said she didn't respond when she called out to her. Yuko didn't resist when Kiyone picked her up, and she didn't try to flee when the kerosene was being poured on her. Is there an explanation for that? Why did Yuko let Kiyone do anything she wanted to her?"

Masayoshi thought it over. He felt sick. It could have been due to the room's poor ventilation or the heat. But he was hopelessly sad—disconsolate.

"Yuko often had these dazed spells. She would just blankly stare off at a point in space, motionless. Yes, just like a doll. When she got in such a state, it was difficult to rouse her from it. Sometimes I could roughly shake her shoulders or shout her name right next to her ear, but it was rare for her to snap out of it on her own. So even if she were laid down on the ground..."

He closed his eyes and saw Yuko's burning figure.

I'm sorry. Every time he saw her he had a need to apologize.

I'm sorry.

I am the source of tragedy.

"Oh, the belladonna berry." The doctor breathed the words as if letting out a sigh. "This thing here on the table set a trap for Kiyone and Yuko. There's no other way to put it. But why was such a dreadful plant, a plant capable of obliterating the line between humans and dolls in the mind of a young woman, growing on your land?"

Fingertips still on his forehead, Masayoshi lowered his head in anguish, but finally, in a somber tone, he spoke.

"Torigoe Manor has a long and famous history. It's a long history, but the truth is, Torigoe blood does not flow through my veins."

A slight tremor entered his voice. "My mother told me a story that happened some generations ago. A woman and her young daughter collapsed in front of Torigoe Manor. That was the beginning of our doom."

"Your doom?"

"Yes. The master of the mansion back then should never have aided that woman. My mother never said it in so many words, but I think that woman was trying to gain favor with the master of Torigoe Manor. No, I'm certain of it. And if you wonder how, why else would she have collapsed in front of that particular mansion?"

Masayoshi was forlorn.

"The master of the house had a wife at the time, but she died soon after that woman and her child came to the mansion. And then he made that woman his new wife."

"His new wife..."

"Yes. But that wasn't the end of it. Soon after that woman became a member of the house, the master died too!"

The doctor gulped.

"That woman and her child took over Torigoe Manor. I'm a descendant of the child and have no Torigoe blood in me."

Masayoshi could no longer hold back his tears.

"The sudden deaths of the master of Torigoe Manor and his wife. Oh, my heart could just burst! My ancestors poisoned them and seized the house, of that I have no doubt. My mother told me the child was holding a flower when they came to the mansion. Now I know what that flower was. The girl had been carrying a belladonna flower. The tuberculosis isn't the only reason the villagers look coldly on our house. No, I fear they must know that it was my ancestors who took Torigoe Manor."

The doctor tried to calm Masayoshi, but the writer stood up and shook his tightly clenched fists.

"It was fate. A cursed destiny passed down from one generation to the next. Revenge of the Torigoe line! There's nothing I can do. I fear that the person who killed Yuko was me, the descendant of those who made a deal with the devil! No, not just Yuko! My first wife…Kiyone—I am the root of all their misfortune!"

Masayoshi looked up at the ceiling and screamed, and as the tears streamed from his eyes, he didn't wipe them away. The doctor sat, his eyes closed and his brow creased, silently waiting for Masayoshi's tears to dry.

*

Was it inevitable?

His eyes upon the black berries, unaware that he was standing now, he quietly spoke, his heart stripped of all color.

"Had all this been decided from the moment that mother and her child with the devil's flower began their act at the gates of Torigoe Manor?"

The doctor was quiet for a time, but when Masayoshi wrapped his handkerchief back around the berries on the table and started to lift them, he grabbed the writer's hand. Masayoshi could feel the doctor's hand tremble.

"Burn them immediately," said the doctor. "Not just these berries, but all of the belladonna growing on your land. And then, come to get her. I will cure her. No, even if I can't cure her, you will come to get her. Aren't the two of you alone now? Once your heart has calmed, have a long talk with her. I know it will be tough, for both you and Kiyone, but in time you will need to find acceptance. End this curse, and everything else with it, with your generation."

The doctor released the belladonna berries, and Masayoshi gripped them tightly and slumped down to his knees. Even after the doctor quietly slipped from the room, Masayoshi's sobs could be heard inside.

※

Somewhere far off inside the hospital, a baby cried.

Hey, Father, aren't you listening? I've found someone I like. A fine person. You like him too.

Kiyone was talking to a doll, her father's, that sat beside her in her bed. Bright sunlight shone in through the open window, casting its gentle rays upon her, and the white hospital curtains billowing in the breeze seemed to beckon to her.

Father, it's warm out today. When we get back home, I'll have to hang his laundry outside to dry.

But when the doll didn't talk back to her, Kiyone tilted her head.

She felt a little lonely.

BLACK FAIRY TALE

THE EYE'S MEMORY

1

The raven was able to speak human words because his nest had happened to be in the eaves of a movie theater. When he was a chick, he had watched the movie screen through a hole in the wall as he ate the food his mother brought him. He loved movies, even though his siblings weren't interested in them. He enjoyed reciting the lines he heard and after a while had learned how to speak like a human.

The raven met the girl after the theater's demolition had sent him flying from his home. He was now fully grown, a fine young bird. His parents and siblings had already moved on to other places; alone, he flew aimlessly through the town.

Near the base of a mountain stood a mansion with blue walls and a large garden with a stately fence around it. Next to the house grew a tall tree with a branch perfectly shaped to perch upon, and so one day the raven landed there to rest.

Within wing's reach of the branch was one of the home's second-floor windows. At first the raven didn't notice the young girl sitting by the window. Usually when he came this close humans would shout, startled. But this girl had no such reaction. She didn't even seem to notice him.

The raven sat on the branch for a while to observe her. He had never before been able to watch a human up close. She had petite features and strawberry lips and sat in a chair near the window, staring off into the distance.

The raven thought about flapping his wings to draw her attention but rejected the idea. He knew of a better way to get humans to notice him.

"Ahem!"

The girl gave a start and, with a mixture of fear and confusion, asked, "Who's there?"

The raven finally understood why the girl hadn't noticed him sitting right in front of her. Normally, this close his black form would be plainly visible to the eye. But sadly this girl had nothing resembling an eye in either of her eye sockets—just two open holes in her little face. She wasn't able to see anything.

This is my chance, thought the raven. *If she can't see what I am, she might talk to me.*

Ever since he had learned to talk, he'd attempted conversing with humans a number of times. But even though he wanted to try out the words he'd learned from the movies, he preferred to avoid people—he knew of the tragedy of his fellow fowl doomed to become fried chicken.

But if she can't see what I am, then surely she'll talk to me.

In an affected voice he asked, "Hello, miss, how do you do?"

"Who is it? Is somebody there?"

"Don't worry, I mean you no harm. I just want to talk to you."

The girl rose from her chair and walked toward the center of the room. She reached her arms out, trying to locate the source of the voice. "Where are you?"

The window was open, and after a few beats of his wings he was inside. It was a nice room, with flower-print wallpaper, a soft bed, and many pretty dolls. A round table occupied the center. The raven landed softly on the top of the chair by the window.

"You have such a strange voice," said the girl, "unlike any I've ever heard. But you don't have any manners. A gentleman is supposed to knock before entering a lady's room."

"I must apologize. Sometimes I forget what I've learned about manners. Why, I'm not even able to hold a knife and fork."

"Well, then, how do you eat?"

"By pecking at the food with my beak, of course."

"You're a strange person, you know." She smiled, showing off her dimples. "Whoever you are, I'm grateful you came. I don't have anyone to talk to here."

From that day forward, the raven came to visit her whenever he had spare time. At first he had no purpose other than to try out his human words, but after a week he came to enjoy speaking with her.

The raven saw something different about her. Most other humans flocked in groups of their own and would throw rocks at him. But this girl always stayed alone in her room, sitting on her chair by the open window, enjoying the feeling of the breeze on her cheeks. To the raven, staring at her from the tree branch outside her window, she looked somewhat lonely.

The raven greeted her. "Hello, miss."

Her expression brightened, as if she'd felt a sudden warm breeze on a cold winter day. "You're hopeless!" she said, not in an angry voice but rather one reserved for greeting a dear friend. "You forgot to knock again!"

The raven hadn't experienced anything so delightful since hatching from his egg. His mother had never sung for him, only fed him caterpillar after caterpillar, and his siblings were just typical birds with no individuality.

Drawing from the many movies he'd seen, the raven made up stories to entertain the girl. His conversations with her consisted only of these stories—he'd decided not to talk about himself in order to keep his true nature hidden. Before long, he'd built a false life with an elaborate, nonsensical history.

One day he asked her, "Miss, why don't you have any eyes in your head?"

She tried to sound casual as she told her unusual story: "It happened when I was little. One Sunday, my parents took me by the hand and brought me to church. The church had a beautiful stained glass window and I spent the entire service admiring it. It was really beautiful and I stared right at it, my eyes wide open. That was my mistake, because suddenly the window shattered into a thousand pieces. We never found out why. Maybe somebody threw a rock into it. Maybe a meteorite happened to crash through it. Whatever the reason, the window shattered and I didn't have time to react. All I could think was how beautiful all the shattered pieces of colored glass were as they fell."

Her story reminded the raven of how the floating motes of dust had twinkled, illuminated by the beam of the theater's projector.

"The next instant," she continued, "two pieces of glass pierced my eyes—blue in my left eye and red in my right. I was rushed to the hospital, but all they could do was take out my eyes to stop the bleeding. The last things I saw were the many-colored shards of glass, glittering in the light as they fell upon me. It was a wonderful sight."

Someone knocked at the door.

"Miss," the raven said, "thank you for talking with me, but I must go now."

Ignoring her protests, he quickly took flight through the window. He didn't go far, rather perched on the branch outside her room where he wouldn't be seen but could still listen to the conversation inside.

He heard the sound of the door opening. Someone walked into the room.

"I thought I heard you talking. Was someone here?"

The voice sounded like it belonged to the girl's mother.

The raven couldn't see it, but he could tell that the girl was having trouble coming up with an answer. His voice had come into her room with no warning, leaving as soon as someone knocked on the door. He wondered what she thought he was.

He spread his wings and flew high up into the sky. Above him were clouds, below him the gray city.

I want to show her everything. Until then he hadn't realized it: the girl had come to fill his heart.

She had told him how she had lost her sight as if it didn't matter to her, as if she accepted it as just the way things were. But when the raven told her stories of vast prairies and fantastic creatures, he had seen a dreamlike look on her face that said, "I want to see that."

He recalled that she had once said to him, "My dreams are all dark now."

She'd tried to hide her sadness from him by changing the subject, cheerfully talking about her favorite things to touch—for just as you might savor the flavors of a fine wine with your tongue, she found pleasure in touching the objects around her.

He'd asked, "Are you afraid of the dark?"

She thought for a moment, then gave a tiny nod.

The raven flew beneath low clouds heavy with rain and thought, *If it meant that she could see light and color again, I'd paint the world with blood.*

It took eyes to see. And so the raven flapped his shiny black wings and flew to the city to collect eyes.

2

The raven landed on the roof of a bakery and surveyed the scene below.

A green, bushy tree grew in the backyard of the bakery, its thick branches stretching out like the flexing arms of a bodybuilder. From one of these arms hung a rope, a tire dangling from its end. The owner of the bakery had tied it there one Sunday afternoon for his five-year-old son, a boy with rosy cheeks and curly hair. This child was now hanging upside down with one leg inside the tire swing.

The raven was still perched on the roof of the bakery, staring at the boy, when the voice of the boy's mother came from inside:

"It's time for your nap! Quit playing and get upstairs, young man."

The boy sprang down from the swing and went inside the house.

The raven glided over to the tree branch that held the swing. From there he could see into the second floor of the bakery. He watched the boy enter his room and lie down on his bed.

All right, let's take his eye. Just to be safe, the raven waited for the child to fall asleep. Soon the bird's dark eyes saw the gentle rising and falling of the sleeping boy's chest.

He flew quietly through the bedroom window. The scent of freshly baked bread filled the room. The boy was still asleep, unaware of the shadow-black raven at his bedside.

The raven, careful not to crush his gift for his friend, plucked the boy's right eye out from under his eyelid.

The boy awoke, saw the raven with his one remaining eye, and screamed.

"Mom! A raven is eating my eye!"

The boy flailed angrily at the raven, trying to capture it; the sound of his mother's footsteps rose from the stairway.

The raven beat his wings and fled through the window while he still had the chance.

With the eyeball clutched in his black beak, he soared high into the sky, heading toward the mansion where the girl waited.

When the raven flew in through the open window of her bedroom, the girl was slumped at her desk, crying.

The bird thought to say something to her, but his beak was still holding the eyeball. He rested the bloody eye upon the round table in the middle of the room and said, "Miss, why are you crying?"

Shoulders trembling, she turned her head to face him. She knew where he was just from the sound of his voice. "I didn't want you to see me crying like this."

The two holes in her face were filled with lovely tears, and when she gave a slight turn to her head the tears spilled from her eye sockets like water overflowing a filled cup. The raven found it beautiful.

"Something sad happened to me today," she said. "You see

that round table in the middle of the room?"

The raven looked over at the table where he had deposited his bloody gift.

"On the table," the girl continued, "there's a vase with flowers in it. I thought the flowers were blue and fresh."

The flowers in the vase were red and starting to wilt.

"My mother lied to me. I thought the flowers were blue because that's what my mother told me."

"Do you like blue flowers?"

The girl nodded. "But she could have just told me they were red. I only found out when my father came into my room and said, 'Those red flowers are starting to wilt.'"

The raven didn't want to see her cry any longer.

"Please stop crying," he said. "I brought you a present today."

"A present?"

The girl wiped away her tears. She had memorized where everything in her room was and walked straight to the table with the wilted flowers and bloody eyeball, taking not one step too far nor one step too short.

She moved her hands along the top of the table and found the eyeball of the baker's son.

"What is this?"

"Well, what is it shaped like?"

She ran the tips of her fingers across the surface of the eye.

"It's round. Round and soft."

"Try putting it into one of those holes in your face."

Slowly, nervously, she raised the soft, round object to her face. She paused and asked, "The right one or the left one?"

"It doesn't matter. Go on."

The girl pressed the eyeball into the cavern on the left-hand side of her face. Since she had done it without thought, the eye pointed off in an unnatural direction. But it rested firmly inside.

"Well," said the bird, "how does it feel?"

"It feels...calming. But what is it? It feels like a plug—like a stopper or something."

"It's our secret. You can't let anyone know that I gave it to you. Not even your mother or your father. You can't let anyone see you with it either. Keep it hidden safely underneath your bed when other people are around. Put it back in when you lie down in bed, when you're tired of crying."

The girl nodded and yawned, rubbing at her new eye with her hand. The eyeball rolled halfway around in its socket.

"Good night, mister. Thank you for your present."

The girl lay down in her bed and soon fell asleep.

"Good night," said the raven and flew out the window and into the town in search of a second eye.

＊

The next day, the raven returned to the girl's room with a new present. He stopped on the branch outside her window, making sure that the girl was alone. Seeing that she was, he flew into the room.

He placed the new eyeball on the table in the middle of the room, and said, "Hello, miss."

"Mister, you have to listen!" the girl cried out joyfully. "Last night, I saw a dream! A real dream, with pictures and everything! It's been so long since I've seen any color at all. And this dream was so pretty. In my dream, I was a child living in a bakery."

She closed her eyes and described in detail everything she had seen in her dream. The raven realized that even after she had taken his present out of her head, the images the eye had once seen remained in her memory.

"I was a boy. My father was kneading dough and my mother was shaping bread. Customers who came in smiled at me and spoke to me as I played inside the store. And then I was hanging upside down with one of my legs in a swing in the backyard. It was a tire swing, hanging from a tree branch."

After living so long in a world of only noise and darkness,

she was thrilled to have had such a color-filled dream, and the raven was happy for her.

"It was so beautiful a dream," she said, "that I kept your stopper in for a really long time. Even after I woke up. But don't worry, whenever I hear someone coming up the steps, I quickly take it out and hide it. I keep it in a glass jar under my bed. But when I'm alone in here, I put the stopper back in and practice dreaming. At first I could only see the wonderful world of the bakery when I was asleep, but now I can see it when I'm awake, daydreaming. I'm getting better at it already."

"Miss, I brought you another present today."

"You did?"

The raven told her he had put another "stopper" on the table and that it too was filled with dreams. Her face beaming with anticipation, the girl took the bloody, beautiful thing into her hand and placed it inside her empty eye socket.

"I can see it, mister, I can see it!" The girl clutched her hands at her chest, whispering as if in thankful prayer. "It's like bright aqua blue paint spreading across the world. It's a flood of color! It's as if this stopper was full of blue color that's spilling into my mind."

The eyeball the raven had brought that day had belonged to an old woman who lived in a house on a hill surrounded by fields and fields of flowers. When the girl had said she liked blue flowers, he'd remembered her words.

I want to show her all her favorite things. I must find someone who spends all day looking at blue flowers.

As he'd flown around the city, he chanced upon the field of blue flowers. In the center of the field was a house and in the house was an old woman who spent her days knitting. She had many grandchildren and knitted handmade clothes for each.

The raven had perched in a tree with a clear view of the inside of the house. The old woman was wearing glasses, knitting in a rocking chair. A canary chirped in a birdcage next to the window.

After a time, the woman's hands stopped their work and she set her glasses down atop a side table, rubbing the bridge of her nose to relieve her tired eyes. Soon she fell asleep.

The raven came in through the window, landing softly upon the arm of her rocking chair. His weight rocked the chair slightly, but the old woman kept on dreaming a pleasant dream. As the canary in the birdcage began to stir, the raven had gently slipped his beak around the woman's eye—

The girl said, "What a gorgeous blue field of flowers! And this stopper has me knitting too! Even though I've never knit before in my life!"

More! More! thought the raven. *I want to find more eyes. I want to show her the world! I'll fly everywhere and bring her the eyes of people near and far, just to see her happy like this.*

And as the raven watched the girl crying tears of happiness he swore, *I'm going to fill that jar she keeps under her bed. I'm going to fill it to the brim.*

PART 1

1

I've had to piece together the events of that day from the recollections of other people. I don't remember it myself.

Snow had been falling from the dark gray sky since morning. The snowflakes drifted lazily between the tall buildings; below pedestrians scurried along with their umbrellas.

Within the crowd I was on my hands and knees, my face inches from the ground. I was searching for something. My umbrella lay near me where I had discarded it.

The sidewalk was teeming with people and as they passed by, they glanced down at me for just a moment before looking away. Nobody wanted anything to do with me.

But after some time, one kind man—a businessman on his way

home from work—took pity on me and approached. In one hand he held a black briefcase, in the other a black umbrella. He spoke to me. *Young miss, are you looking for something?*

I seemed not to have heard him and made no response.

You lost a contact lens, did you? Could I help you look?

Still focused on my search, I responded despairingly, on the verge of tears, *No, not my contact. Something else.*

That was when the man finally noticed something was wrong with me.

I wasn't wearing any gloves and I was pressing my palms into the snow. My fingers were turning red from the cold, but I wasn't showing the slightest concern for frostbite.

I don't know how long I had knelt there, but snow had begun to pile up on my back. I was oblivious to my surroundings, focused only on my search.

My voice was shrill with panic. Where could I have dropped it?

Then, he noticed it. Specks of red were on the snow all around me. Blood.

Are you all right? he asked me and I raised my head to look at him with what I was later told was a dumbstruck expression.

No matter how long I look, I can't seem to find it. My left eye should be somewhere around here...

Blood ran all the way down to my chin from where my eye should have been. I collapsed, unconscious.

My left eye was found a little way down the street, a grotesque blob mixed with snow and mud. It had been crushed beneath the shoes of the passersby and no longer held its original shape.

The city was white with snow that had been falling since the day before and the crowds with their umbrellas had jostled about. I had been among them when by chance one of the umbrellas jabbed my face. Its tip had pushed around the edge of my eyeball and severed my optic nerve. My eye was torn from its socket and fell to the ground. I'd panicked, dropping to my knees to search for it.

I learned all of this afterward, from the reports.

I was taken straight to the hospital, where I received treatment. A high school ID in my wallet gave my name: Nami Shiraki.

And that's the story of how, in the middle of the month of January, I lost my memory.

❋

When I first opened my eyes, my vision was blurry. I was in a room with a white ceiling and white walls. I lay in a bed with a blanket over my body.

Next to me a woman sat in a chair, reading a magazine. I looked at her for a while. I didn't say anything or move aside from opening my eyes to see.

After a while, the woman looked at me as she turned the page of her magazine. She leapt to her feet, dropped the magazine to the floor, and cried out, "Someone, come quick! Nami's awake!"

A doctor came to ask me questions, along with a nurse. The woman who had called for them stayed to listen.

"What's wrong, Nami?" the woman asked. "Stop looking around and pay attention to the doctor."

I looked down at my hands and saw them wrapped in bandages. Another bandage slashed a diagonal across my face and I couldn't see out of my left eye. I tried to remove the bandage from my face, but the doctor and nurse pulled my hand back.

The woman inclined her head and said, "Nami?"

I understood that Nami was a name, but I had to explain that I didn't know who that was.

"Your name is Nami," the doctor said. He pointed at the woman next to me. "Do you recognize this woman?"

I studied her face, then shook my head no.

"This woman," he said, "is your mother."

I looked at her again. She raised her hand to her mouth and drew back.

The doctor told me that I had hurt my left eye and that I had lost my memory from the shock.

*

I was taken to a car. I sat in the back seat, next to my mother. A man was behind the wheel. He told me he was my father.

My mother tried to talk to me about various things, expectantly awaiting my replies. But when I had none—because I didn't know what she was talking about—she looked disappointed.

"You've become so quiet," my father said.

I didn't remember my house. A nameplate by the door said SHI-RAKI, which I had been told was my last name. I took off my shoes and went into the foyer, but I didn't know where to go from there.

My mother took my hand and led me to the living room and then to the kitchen. "You remember here, right?"

I shook my head.

She took me to a room on the second floor. There was a piano. It was a girl's room.

"What do you think?" asked my mother.

I thought it was a nice room. I said so, and she told me that it was my room and had been my room since I was a little girl. I was tired and asked if I could lie down.

"It's your room," she said, "so do what you like."

I hadn't noticed until then that she was crying.

Later my father came to my room with photo albums and trophies. The bases of the trophies had plaques commemorating victories at various piano competitions.

"Don't you remember anything?" he asked.

I shook my head.

In one of the photo albums there was a picture of a little girl sitting in a sandbox with a plastic scoop in her hand and tears in her eyes. I pointed to the picture and asked if I had been teased a lot as a child.

"That girl was a really close friend of yours. You're the one laughing behind her."

After that, he showed me several more objects, but I didn't remember any of them. He brought me a flower vase I had made, but it was the first time I'd seen it. I had forgotten the name of my favorite stuffed animal, one my mother had given me. I had forgotten the title of my favorite movie.

✳

At first I had to ask my parents all sorts of detailed questions just to get through day-to-day life at home. I didn't know where anything was. Initially I asked permission before doing anything, but my father told me this wasn't necessary.

I got confused every time I tried to do something. One night I tried to turn on the lights to go upstairs, but I couldn't remember where the light switch was. Even when I'd found the panel, it held a number of switches and I didn't know which to flip. Finally I went to my mother in the living room and asked her which switch lit up the stairway.

She snapped at me, "Come on! It's this one, of course!"

I'm sorry, I apologized.

✳

My mother worked harder than my father at trying to bring back my memory. Every day she told me stories of how I was before the accident. Most were stories about me and her.

"Do you remember when you caught a cold and had to stay in bed?"

I don't remember.

"Don't you remember how I cared for you, how I grated that apple so you could eat?"

I'm sorry. I don't remember.

"Why don't you remember?"

I don't know. I'm sorry.

"Why are you apologizing? You used to be such a cheerful girl. When you were in preschool, we'd go shopping together. You carried the bags of bread home for me, remember?"

I shook my head. *I don't remember.*

"Why are you crying? It's not something to cry over!"

Whenever I forgot my manners or did something wrong, my mother would mutter, "Nami would never have done that. Nami was better than that."

For a while I just stayed at home, but eventually I started taking walks into town. Sometimes the neighbors would say something to me.

One day at dinner, my father said to me, "Yesterday Mr. Saitou said hi to you. Why didn't you greet him back?"

I was trying to remember his face.

"People are starting to talk about you, how it's creepy the way you just stare at them. You could at least bow."

"It's embarrassing me," my mother said, displeased. "The people around here know you lost your memory in an accident, so they should understand. But people are watching you and you need to be on your best behavior. You really stand out with that bandage wrapped around your face. I hope you get your memories back soon. But until then you could at least act like the old Nami."

✳

In the middle of the night I heard my parents talking:

"Don't you think you're being too hard on her?" my father said.

"It's just too much." My mother was crying. "It's like she's not even our child."

✳

One night after dinner my father said, "You were in a public high school. You probably don't remember what your classmates look like."

I shook my head.

"I spoke with your teacher on the phone. She said that she's ready to have you back in your same class and you're welcome to come at any time."

He decided that I would go to school on Monday, in two days.

He told me I was in eleventh grade.

I went to my room and tried on my school uniform. I opened my notebook and my textbooks. I didn't remember any of it.

Small notes were written in the textbooks, words I had written in the past. For all they meant to me, they could have been written by a stranger.

※

Monday came.

I put my schoolbooks into a white tote bag I found in my room. When my mother saw me leaving for school with the bag, she raised her eyebrows and said, "Nami always took her black backpack to school. You should too."

I apologized and she took the bag out of my hands.

Since I didn't know how to get to school, my father walked with me.

The school was large. My father led me to the school office, where the teachers prepared their work for the day's classes. I had to walk quickly to keep up with him.

In the office I met my homeroom teacher, a man named Mr. Iwata.

"It's good to see you back," he said, then closed his mouth, remembering something. "Well, I guess for you it might as well be your first time here."

My father bowed to Mr. Iwata, then left for work. All the teachers in the office were looking at me.

"I know all this attention must be awkward for you," Mr. Iwata said between furtive glances at where my left eye would have been if there were anything but emptiness beneath the bandages. "But please forgive us. We've all heard about how you've lost your memory."

I asked, *What kind of student was I?*

"You were a determined student, and you did well in both your studies and at sports. You were the heart and soul of your class.

So don't look so worried. Now come on, morning homeroom is
about to start."

I followed him out the office and down the hallway. Afraid
that I might get lost, I walked closely behind him. He stopped
outside a classroom marked 2ND YEAR, CLASS I, and turned to
me and asked, "Are you all right?"

I nodded my head.

As I entered the bustling classroom it fell silent. All of their
eyes were on me. Mr. Iwata pointed to a single empty desk in the
center of the room. I sat at it.

The teacher explained my situation to the class—the accident
and the condition it had left me in—but everyone already seemed
to know.

When the homeroom period was over, my classmates circled
around me. They had faces I didn't recognize but were talking
to me as if we were friends. I didn't know their names, but they
knew more about me than I did myself.

"Nami!" said one. "We were so worried about you!"

"Are you okay?" asked another.

I didn't know what to say, so I didn't say anything. It didn't
take long for their enthusiasm to turn to disappointment.

"Why aren't you joking around? Where's your laugh, Nami?
Why do you look so gloomy?"

I'm sorry.

A girl sitting in the desk in front of me asked, "Do you really
not remember anything?"

No, nothing.

"Don't worry, I'll fill you in. I owe you for letting me copy
your homework. Why are you looking at me like that?"

I don't know your name.

"Get out! We're best friends!"

I'm sorry.

"Okay, whatever. I'm Yuri Katsura. Just hurry up and remember, okay?"

Thanks.

She told me about myself. The girl she talked about could have been an entirely different person. Yuri told me how wonderful I was, and I could tell she had a lot of respect for who I had been.

"It was like you were the center of everything. When you smiled, everyone relaxed. Do you remember Mr. Kamata? That horrible English teacher?"

I shook my head.

"You beat him in an argument—in English! It felt so good seeing him put in his place."

I went to the rest of my classes that day, but I didn't understand any of them. My teachers all came up to me, beaming, talking about how good a student I'd been. Then they'd give me a question and I wouldn't know the answer. I'd hear them mutter something like, "She even forgot how to solve that."

I rode the train home. I had to use notes I'd been given—I couldn't remember the names of the stations or the address of my own home.

＊

I had a grandfather on my mother's side whom, I was told, had once held an important position in some major company and knew a lot of people in a lot of places.

He adored me like no other, and he was distraught over my condition.

One day, my father was talking to him on the phone. Lowering the cordless receiver, my dad said to me, "Nami, your grandfather says he's going to do something about your left eye. He's going to find a donor eye."

If I had a left eye, I'd look like the normal me again. My father explained that they could repair the optic nerve and I'd even be able to see with the eye.

✳

"Nami, you've become so moody. You should talk more."

That was what everyone said to me at school. As the days passed, fewer and fewer of my classmates tried to talk to me.

One came up to me, saying something about some TV show she'd watched the night before. Another girl took her hand and pulled her away from me and, thinking I couldn't hear her, whispered, "Nami isn't the old Nami anymore. She's a bore."

Soon Yuri was the only one who would still talk to me. She wistfully told me stories of my past self. No, not of myself, but of some person I didn't know. When Yuri looked at me, she wasn't seeing me.

And not just Yuri, but also my teachers. I could tell, whenever I failed to answer another simple question, that they missed Nami Shiraki, model student.

"Unlike you now," Yuri said once, "the old Nami could do anything."

Really?

"And she was just so cute. I mean, your face is the same, but your expression is lacking something. Even talking with you, you're just not interesting at all. It's like talking to the air."

I'm sorry.

✳

Everyone saw the current inept me and the past adept Nami as two entirely separate beings.

I noticed that the warmth had gone out of my mother's eyes when she looked at me. My father told me that my mother and I used to be close, like sisters.

I was studying in my room when he came to see me.

"I've never seen you studying before," he said. "And yet your grades were excellent."

If I study hard and become like I was before, will Mother love me?

My father answered uncertainly, "Well, I wonder. Now wipe those tears away."

※

The day before the surgery my grandfather came to visit.

"Nami," he said, "would you play the piano for me? Even if your memory is gone your body should still remember how."

He sat me down in front of the piano. Everyone—my parents, my grandfather and grandmother, my uncle, and my cousin—circled around me. Their stares were fixed upon me, their expectant faces waiting for my performance.

But even with the piano keys spread out before me, no music sprang forth. I sat motionless; soon I could sense their disappointment.

My grandfather sighed.

I was mortified and I felt my face turn red. I wanted to run.

They started to praise the old Nami. That Nami wouldn't have disappointed them. She would have played the piano beautifully. They talked about the differences between how I was then and how I was now, my mother reciting a list of my faults.

I couldn't raise my head. I wished I could just disappear. I felt the same way whenever I was at school. Everyone wanted to be with the me who still had her memories. There wasn't a place for the current me. Even the ones who still talked to me weren't anyone I knew—they were people Nami knew.

※

The next day I was taken to the hospital. It wasn't the one I always went to, but rather a small hospital outside of town.

I asked my grandfather why they didn't take me to the usual hospital.

He said, "In order to get you a new eye, I couldn't go through all the proper channels, so we have to go to a small hospital. But don't worry, you have a real doctor."

Just before the operation I saw the eyeball in a glass container, floating in clear water, looking at me.

I was put under anesthesia and they performed the transplant surgery.

It was over quickly.

2

Someone else's eye was put into the hole in my head and the optical nerves were connected with tiny threads. For three days after the operation I wasn't allowed to touch anywhere near my eye, not even through the bandages. I was even told to avoid excessive eye movement.

For a time, the left side of my face felt off, unnatural. It felt heavy, like something was pressing against it. Sometimes I noticed that my head was tilting to the left.

Four days later I was allowed to remove the bandage from my face, although I was still confined to my room. By that time the unnatural feeling in my left eye had almost completely disappeared.

The doctor said to me, "Even with the bandage gone, you may not be able to see very well at first. The connections between the optical nerves are still fresh. But they should soon acclimate to your body, and you'll be able to see normally again. Be absolutely sure you don't rub your eyes for a while."

What I first saw through my left eye was hazy and washed out, as if I were looking through a pane of frosted glass. And everything was too bright. My eye must not have been able to adjust to the light yet.

There was a calendar on the wall of my hospital room. On its lower half was a grid of the days; a photograph was on the upper half. The picture was of an empty swing in a daylit park.

Since the calendar hung on the wall opposite my bed, it was all I looked at. When my bandages were first removed, the edges in the picture blurred together and I couldn't see much. But after two days, I was able to make out even the chains of the swing.

One week after the operation it was time for me to go home again.

My mother came to pick me up. It was the first time she had come to the hospital. Only my grandfather had come to visit me, and that was only once. And even then we hadn't had much to talk about, and he'd quickly lost interest and left.

"Can you see out of your left eye again?" my mother asked. "When you only had one eye you didn't look much like the Nami I used to know, but now that you have both eyes again I'm sure that will change."

I looked into the mirror and noticed that the irises of my eyes weren't quite the same color. I looked closely at my left eye. It was clear and brown.

My mother appraised my completed face and gave me a satisfied nod. "At least you look like the old Nami again. You look lovely." Then she crossed her arms and admonished, "But hurry up and get your memory back. It's like you're not Nami anymore. How did you get this way? There's nothing more horrible than having your own daughter forget all her memories of her mother."

She left the room to finish the paperwork for my release.

I stayed seated at the foot of my bed and stared at the calendar on the wall. I could sense that the optic nerve between my left eye and my brain had connected properly. And yet, the calendar's picture was slightly blurry. I was crying. I took a tissue from the side of the bed and, careful not to rub it against my eye, wiped away the tears around it.

My chest was so filled with sadness that I thought I would burst. I thought over the things my mother and my classmates had said. They'd loved the old me deeply. But the new me couldn't do anything right. Most of the time somebody tried to talk to me, I didn't know what to say. I knew that while they watched me try to stammer something in reply, in their heads they were comparing the me they had known with the me now standing before them. Even when I tried not to notice it, I could still feel it. And then I'd think about how much happier they would all be if they still had the model student Nami instead of the good-for-nothing me.

As I sat there thinking, I looked over at the calendar and the picture of the girl on the swing.

I decided to get my things together before my mother returned, and I started to shift my eyes from the calendar in order to begin.

But an uncertainty came to me—just a small doubt at first—but when I realized what had caused it, the feeling turned to dread.

The photograph on the calendar had been of an empty swing. Now a girl was sitting in it.

I groaned and touched my hand to the left side of my face. It felt hot. My newly transplanted eye was warm—not hot enough to burn, but my optic nerve seemed to be twitching.

I thought I saw the swing in the photograph move. And when I tried to tell myself that was impossible, it moved again.

Bewildered, I closed my eyes, expecting to see only darkness. I was wrong. Even with my eyelids closed, the girl remained. If anything I could see her more vividly. That was when I noticed that the girl and the swing were semi-transparent. Only my left eye could see the image. I closed my right eye and opened the left; the image was still clear.

I tried to convince myself that it was just some daydream.

The picture grew before me, enveloping me, filling the sight of my left eye, replacing the hospital room with a park I had never seen.

As the vision swept over me, I clutched at my bedsheet to make sure I was still in the hospital room.

The girl lowered herself from the swing. She was young, not even old enough for grade school, and had long hair that bounced as she moved.

The chains of the swing had started to rust; behind the park was forest.

The dream in my left eye started to sway and my body seemed

to shift, although I knew it hadn't really. The girl approached me, a smile filling her face.

Then, like a wave receding into the distance, the dream gently vanished. My left eye saw the calendar as it had been before—an empty, still swing.

I felt slightly nauseated. What had that been? A dream. A hallucination. An illusion. I had only thought I'd seen the swing move, and my left eye had begun to dream.

I looked again at the calendar. Some of the details were different from my dream. The chains of the swing had no rust. In the background was the ocean.

The door opened and my mother came in.

I left the hospital filled with strange thoughts. I had wanted to take the calendar home with me, but couldn't find the words to ask.

The smile of the little girl in the dream of my left eye kept replaying in my mind. It was a smile that took me in and accepted me—all of me. A pleasant warmth filled my chest. Since the day I'd lost my memory, nobody had made me feel so happy.

As we left the hospital, my mother noticed me crying. She gave me a suspicious look and asked, "Why are you crying?"

I didn't know how to answer. When that girl smiled at me, I'd felt content, and for the first time I realized how tense, how uneasy, and how miserable I was.

✳

After I left the hospital I returned to my normal daily life. I went to school, I took my classes. I didn't talk much with anyone. I was alone.

When I first awoke with all my memories gone, I'd spent much of my time in confusion. I'd listened to the conversations around me passively. I'd just been nodding, not thinking, not feeling.

But after the transplant I began to understand how I was feeling each moment.

Sitting at my desk in class, I asked about the model student I had been. Even with my new eye and the bandages gone, I was still in exactly the same situation as before.

"Unlike you, the old Nami used to talk to everyone and entertain them."

That doesn't sound like me at all.

"Yeah, like a different person. And she was better at everything too. We lost that last volleyball match in gym class because of you. The old Nami would have nailed that spike."

I felt alone on the volleyball court. I messed up so many times that no one let me near the ball anymore. My teammates looked at me with irritation. I was out of place.

The classroom was noisy. It was the break between periods and excited voices rang in the air. I sat alone at my desk waiting for the next class. The breaks were the loneliest parts of the day for me. I felt pitiful.

I closed my eyes and recalled the dream from the hospital room. The girl who smiled at me. The swelling in my chest. I could feel her, abandoned in the darkness, afraid, her hand reaching out to me and softly gripping mine. Whenever I felt lonely, I could remember that dream and find calm.

What was that little girl? Was she just a dream? Ever since I'd awoken in that first hospital, useless and hopeless with no left eye and no memory, I hadn't had a single dream. If that daydream in the hospital room had been reconstructed from my old memories, then that girl was a part of those memories.

I asked my mother, *Do you know anything about a girl with long hair or a swing set surrounded by woods?*

She shook her head. "No, I don't."

That wasn't what I'd hoped to hear. If my memories came back, I wouldn't need to be sad anymore—the me I was now would disappear and the Nami everyone loved would return.

❋

I was at the train station on my way home from school when I experienced my second waking dream.

I was standing by myself on the edge of the platform, nudging the raised yellow bumps of the tactile warning strip with the toes of my shoes as I looked down at the tracks. Around me swarmed a crowd of students and other commuters on their way home. Groups of high schoolers talked and laughed as they passed by. I worried that they were laughing at me.

There was still a short wait before my train came.

I faintly felt my left eye growing warm. At first I thought I was imagining it, but the feeling grew hotter and hotter. Blood pulsed through the capillaries of my eye, so much so that I felt as though a heart had been transplanted there instead of an eye.

I froze and focused my mind on what I saw. I was still looking at the railroad tracks. The rails had been shiny and silver, but the ones I saw now were covered with brown rust.

A dream was coming. Confident, I closed my eyes, knowing from my experience in the hospital that I would see the dream more clearly that way.

The rails slid downward, as if I had tilted my head up. But before my eyes was not another platform set against the evening sky. What I saw was a forest, and it filled my vision with green.

The ground was covered in green grass. A single train car sat deserted there, almost buried among the trees of the forest. From its shape it looked like a type that hadn't been in service for a decade. Its window frames were bent and without glass, and grass grew atop its roof. The unmoving train car was becoming a part of the forest around it. Sunlight dappled the leaves of the plants. It must have been summer.

The view was so beautiful my breath caught. I had no memories of a deep forest, no memories of a limitless horizon. I couldn't remember any of the things I had seen in the first seventeen years of my life. The scene was entirely new to me, engraved deeply into the blank slate of my mind.

The dream was semi-transparent. I opened my right eye and

turned my head to look around. As I'd expected, it seemed like no one else could see the rusted train. Through my right eye I saw a businessman reading a newspaper.

No matter which direction I turned, the image of the train in my left eye followed. I looked up, I looked back, and the train was still in front of me. It was like my left eye and my right eye were in different locations.

Suddenly I noticed the figures of several children in the windows of the train. Had they been using the train as a playground? I saw other children whacking the body of the train car with sticks, but it made no noise. There was only image. And yet I felt as if I could hear the sound of the wind and the insects.

The point of view in my left eye swayed. It rocked up and down at a steady pace. I stood motionless on the train platform but felt as if I were walking. I had to be careful to keep my balance and not fall from the platform.

As I approached the dream train, it grew large in my vision. The children were looking at me. My line of sight was low, and I realized that in the dream I was a child too.

I stopped at the side of the train, looking up at one of the windows. The train loomed frightening and large to my child-self. Bits of paint clung to the surfaces not covered with rust.

An aggressive-looking boy gazed down at me from the window. A small arm with the small hand of a child rose up from the lower right edge of my view. It was my own arm, connected to the child I was in the dream. My hand reached up for the window, but the window was too far.

The face inside the window drew back. After a moment it returned, and the boy threw a small rock at me.

Standing on the train platform, I gasped, startling the man next to me.

Inside the dream, a boy who had been hitting the train with a stick turned and threw the stick at me. My child-self reflexively raised an arm to cover my face.

On the train platform, I realized that I had struck the same pose.

A train glided along the tracks, stopping alongside the platform. The dream ended and my eyesight returned to normal.

❋

When I got home I documented my dream at the train station on a sheet of loose-leaf notebook paper, including sketches of the scene and the children I'd seen. I even recorded when and where I had the dream.

I suspected the dream at the station wouldn't be my last.

First was the little girl on the swing. Second was the train car overgrown by forest. I didn't know what would come next. Maybe the dreams were of places I'd seen before I lost my memory. Maybe they were scenes from movies I'd seen.

But I'd noticed that the dreams had certain peculiar rules to them. For example, both dreams came when I had been looking at an object that matched something in the vision—the first, a swing and the second, train tracks. The instant the two semi-transparent images coincided, a film reel within my left eye was stirred to motion.

I saw the dreams only in my left eye—my newly transplanted left eye. I started to think of the eye as a little jewel box filled with dreams. Most of the time the box was locked, and it worked just as a normal eye does. But with the right key—a key like the swing or the train rail—the box would open and a dream would pour out.

I kept the records of my dreams in a three-ring binder.

I replayed the sights of the train dream in my mind. My child-self had reached up to the boy in the window, only to be hit by a small rock...

I could only guess at the meaning, but I must have been trying to join in their games and been rejected.

What I saw in the dream stirred my heart. It stuck with me, like a memory from my own childhood long ago. Thinking of the dream filled me with sadness. I had never seen the abandoned train car playground or the group of playing children keeping me out. With no memories of my own, it was all new to me.

I was starved for memories. I had none since I first awoke in the hospital not that long before. I was like dry, barren sand. Without memories, I had no roots, no foundation on which to stand.

But then came those mysterious dreams. Visions of places and experiences I hadn't seen poured deep into the corners of my heart and provided me comfort.

✳

One week after my dream at the train station, my dream diary had grown twenty pages long. Just as I'd hoped, I'd seen many dreams.

The analogy of the keys and the locked jewelry box had proven correct. Things I happened to see, even on TV or in books, became keys that freed images that had been locked into my left eye.

Anything could be a key—a milk carton turned on its side, the surprised face of a little kitten. Each time I saw one of the keys, my left eye would grow warm. I couldn't choose when or where—the instant one of the keys caught my left eye, it just happened.

And then the box of dreams inside my left eye would open. The films were only fragments. In one I was standing alone, looking down at the shards of a broken window. In another I was being chased by a dog. In yet another I had been left behind in what looked to be an empty, lonely schoolyard. And so on.

With each passing day, the dreams came more frequently.

One day I was by myself, sitting at my classroom desk, idly staring at my eraser. My left eye began to feel hot. My chest filled with anticipation of the dream. I know this may be a strange way to say it, but I felt excited—like I had found an old photo album of myself I had never seen before.

Before long the eraser had flipped the switch on the film projector in my eye and the dream began to play, the semi-transparent tableaux of my left and right eyes overlapping. I closed my eyes and the playback of the dream was all I saw.

My dream-self was in a classroom. The other children in the class looked like middle-schoolers, so I probably was one too. In each dream so far I had been a different age.

It appeared that we were about to take a test. A man who looked like a proctor walked down the aisles placing problem sheets on each desk.

In the dream, my right hand gripped a wooden pencil. It was a boy's hand—I could tell by the black sleeves of my school uniform. I was always a boy in the dreams. With the pointed tip of the pencil, I began to write my name on the test paper. The sloppy lettering read "Kazuya Fuyutsuki." Next to the space for my name were the words ENTRANCE EXAMINATION and the name of a high school.

My viewpoint panned over to a window beside my desk. The outside was dark with rain, and the face of a young boy reflected back at me in the glass. I had never seen the face before, but I knew it belonged to me in the dream.

And with that the dream faded.

Kazuya. I wrote the name down on a sheet of my notebook paper so I wouldn't forget it. I added the date I'd seen the dream and the name of the high school printed on the test paper, then put the sheet of paper into my binder.

That night, as I sat watching TV in the living room, I thought about the daydreams my eye had presented to me.

My father had not yet returned home from work. My mother and I were alone in the house. We had not become close. She looked at me like I was a stranger. And when she talked to me, she never called me by name, only "you." Even in the way she spoke, she kept me separate from Nami.

After dinner I wanted to go straight to my room but decided to keep my mother company so as not to be rude. I felt guilty about only seeing her during meals. Maybe I couldn't be Nami, but I could still spend as much time with her as possible.

A special program on missing persons was on the TV that night. Displayed across the bottom of the screen was a telephone number for anyone who had seen or heard anything to call.

Any memories I'd once had of television shows—even famous ones that had run for years—were gone from my mind.

As the picture of a boy who'd gone missing some months before appeared on the screen, I recalled the face of the boy I'd seen reflected in the window in that dream.

In my dreams, I was a boy named Kazuya, and the images were all from his viewpoint. There was no sound, only visuals, and they flowed past as if seen by his eyes. Every dream had taken place from somebody's distinct point of view—the view rocked from side to side as I walked forward, and occasionally everything would go dark, as if I had blinked.

It was not a third-person view looking down from above.

My heart began to race. I had seen dreams where I had been talking with other people, but because there was no sound, I hadn't been able to hear what name others called me. Now that I had found it—Kazuya—the dreams suddenly felt concrete.

My mother stood up and said, "I'll clean up the dishes. Are you going to keep watching TV?"

No, I'm fine.

A picture of a girl appeared on the screen. She could have been in grade school, or maybe middle school. In the picture, she was outside, cooking with several other girls, possibly at a summer camp. The faces of the other children were blurred out.

Suddenly, heat burst through my left eye. It was like the warmth that came before each dream, only this time far more fierce. My eye pounded like a heart immediately after a full-out sprint, and the nerve connecting eye and brain began to scream.

I was so startled that I didn't know what to do. I couldn't even close my eyelids. I was motionless, my eyes affixed to the girl in the middle of the screen.

The box inside my eye opened. A bead of sweat trickled down my spine. Something terrible inside the eye was about to emerge. I felt it coming, not a dream, but a nightmare.

Abruptly the screen went dark, and the picture of the girl

vanished. The fever in my eye faded rapidly and my body was released. As my breath escaped from my lips, I looked up at my mother. She had the remote control in her hand.

"Did you want me to leave that on?"

I shook my head.

3

Saori and the owner of the café were talking. I—that is to say, Kazuya—was leaning on the counter, head resting in my hands, watching them. Beside the counter was a vase with white flowers. As Saori turned, she knocked over the vase. The water within silently ran across the counter.

The dream ended there. I opened my eyes and closed my magazine. I took a sheet of notebook paper from my backpack and recorded the dream:

Day dream was seen: March 10
People appearing in dream: Saori, café owner
What triggered dream: Reading a magazine in my room.
Left eye responded to white flowers in an advertisement.
Content of dream: Saori was talking with the owner of the café. As she was working, she knocked over a vase of flowers and became upset. The flowers fell to the floor and the water from the vase spread across the counter. A pool of water formed around the base of my coffee cup.

The dream had taken place in Melancholy Grove, a coffee shop.

I placed the sheet of paper in my binder. Two weeks had passed since I had started keeping a diary of the dreams, and over that time the binder had grown thick and cumbersome to carry.

Saori was Kazuya's older sister. She had a part-time job at the café.

The same people appeared many times in my eye's dreams. Because I couldn't hear any of the conversations, most of their names remained unknown to me, but Saori's name had been on her bedroom door.

Saori often showed up in the dreams within my eye. I became vaguely aware that she and I—well, she and Kazuya—were brother and sister.

Sometimes she was a child and other times she was grown up. My viewpoint grew taller and shorter along with her. We weren't always children in the dreams. But whatever our ages, she always looked at me with the same kindness. She had been the girl on the swing in that first dream.

Her hair and fashion changed along with her age. One time, her hair was long and braided; another, straight and shoulder length. But one feature was uniquely hers, and whenever I saw it I knew I was seeing her. With few exceptions, her nose was red. Whether it was some disease she'd had from birth or just a bad case of allergies, her nose was constantly runny. She blew her nose until it became irritated and red.

In my left eye, I often saw her blowing her nose. I saw her buried in a pile of wadded-up tissues. I saw her out shopping, a box of tissues under her arm. I saw her blowing her nose while waiting on customers at the coffee shop.

Aside from that, she would have been beautiful, but she spent her life with tissues bunched up under her nose, unconcerned with the gaze of others.

In the dreams we walked together, we played cards together. In one, we were children arguing through tears. Between the tears and the snot, her face was a total mess.

Most of the time Saori was taller than me, but I had dreams in which Kazuya had outgrown her. Those times, his viewpoint was taller than my own, and I saw the world from higher than I ever had.

The world I saw in the dreams was always the same. There were no sudden wars, no voyages into space, just moments from a normal, regular life. I took in those dreams with all my effort. They were memories—footprints of the past—and having none to call my own, I took all I could from them.

❋

Day dream was seen: March 12
People appearing in dream: Saori, our parents
What triggered dream: Saw a cotton swab on my bookcase.
Left eye responded to the white cotton at its tip.
Content of dream: Saori and I (probably in our grade
school years) were taking turns lying in our mother's lap
to have our ears cleaned out with cotton swabs. When it
was Saori's turn, I started playing a short distance away. I
held a toy locomotive in my hand. Saori seemed not to like
having her ears cleaned and held her head stiff. Her snot
ran down onto our mother's lap. Behind them, our father
walked by.

Day dream was seen: March 14
People appearing in dream: My (Kazuya's) father, his coworker
What triggered dream: Left eye responded to a truck idling
at a traffic light. Waiting for the dream, I missed my chance
to cross the road.
Content of dream: My father was working at a lumber
mill, work gloves on his hands. Judging from my viewpoint,
Kazuya was still a small child. Blotches of machine oil dotted my father's work clothes. Felled trees were piled up on
the bed of a large truck, and a young man was working
alongside the vehicle. He was wearing the same clothes
as my father, so he must have been a coworker. I started
walking over to my father, but he raised his hand to stop
me. I think it was a signal saying, "It's too dangerous over
here, stay away."

Day dream was seen: March 15
People appearing in dream: Saori, a middle-aged couple
What triggered dream: Left eye responded to the butt of
my father's cigarette.

Content of dream: Saori and I were in a man's home. The man was drunk and he slapped a tray out of a woman's hands. The dishes on the tray scattered across the floor. Saori wore a stiff expression.

*

The world of Kazuya and Saori Fuyutsuki lay deep in the mountains. Many of the scenes of my dreams took place on mountain roads, with tall peaks on one side and a cliff protected by a guardrail on the other.

Kazuya and Saori lived with their parents, making a family of four. I hadn't seen their grandparents in any of my dreams. After Kazuya's viewpoint reached a certain height, his parents stopped appearing in the dreams. Maybe they had moved out.

I gathered up the countless settings that unfolded in the dreams. I enjoyed the task.

Inside the dreams, my parents held me warmly in their arms. It felt pleasant when they did so, but it also filled me with guilt toward my real mother. It didn't feel right to be more at ease around the parents in my dream than around my actual mother.

At school and at home I lived in a state of constant unease. Thinking of the world inside my dreams made that feeling fade. Sometimes I'd discover myself escaping from reality into the dream world, and it saddened me.

Whenever my mother or my friends talked about Nami, I felt a pain in my heart. When Mr. Iwata or any of my other past acquaintances spoke to me, I couldn't look them in the eye. I'd start to worry about how I would fail them next, then my legs would begin to shake and I'd want to run away.

"Nami, it's your turn to erase the blackboard today."

Oh, yes, okay…

Even that much of a conversation with one of my friends made my heart feel like it would burst. I lived each day in anxiety and fear. Did I pronounce my words strangely? Did I smile right? Did I do anything to displease them?

Whenever I looked at my piano, I remembered how I had disappointed my family, and I wanted to cry. Every little thing became a terror, until I could no longer move my body.

Even though I knew that wasn't how I should think, I couldn't help it. I wished I could live in the world in my eye—Kazuya's world—not my own.

I couldn't become Nami. No matter how hard I tried, I couldn't play the piano and I couldn't pass my lessons and make my teachers like me again.

At some point I had stopped seeing myself as Nami.

But it wasn't just that. I was becoming different from when I had first lost my memory and hadn't understood the things around me. For someone who had reset, who had started from zero with no memories, I carried too many scenes inside—too many memories that couldn't have belonged to Nami, an only child raised in the city.

I was afraid of dogs. I kept my distance from them for fear of being bitten. At first I didn't understand why.

My mother once commented, "And you used to like dogs so much…"

Later I realized the fear came from one of the dreams inside my left eye.

One of the dreams recorded in my binder was as follows:

Day dream was seen: February 26
People appearing in dream: A large dog
What triggered dream: On my way to school. Left eye responded to a dog being walked.
Content of dream: I ran, chased by a large dog. Just as it was about to bite me the dream ended.

I think that was when my wariness of dogs began. The things I had seen as Kazuya had affected who I was in real life.

During class, Yuri said to me, "It's like you've become a completely different person lately. But you still can't seem to do anything right. You'd better get your memory back—and fast—or you're going to fall behind everyone."

I nodded. I really was incapable of anything. Everyone was piling Nami on me until I wanted to die. I could never be even an imitation of her.

My mother showed me a video tape of a time when I still had memories—that is to say, a video tape of Nami. She hoped it would awaken some of my memories, but it didn't work.

When the video began to play it showed Nami, dressed in a lovely outfit, standing upon a stage. She bowed to the audience, then sat down at a piano and began to play. It was a beautiful melody. I closed my eyes and let the sound flow to my eardrums, and a semi-transparent world opened inside my head. Nami's fingers moved confidently across the keys. It was like a miracle.

Another tape captured the image of her at a birthday party as a young girl. The party was in our living room. Nami was surrounded by friends, talking in an uninterrupted stream. In ten minutes she said more than I did in a week of school. She chatted, flashed her dimples, and occasionally smiled broadly to the delight of the crowd around her.

An aura seemed to shine around her. The girl on the tape may have had my face, but she was a different person.

I felt shut away in the dark.

✳

Day dream was seen: March 21
People appearing in dream: My parents, people working at the lumber mill
What triggered dream: Left eye responded to a circular saw in a hardware store.
Content of dream: My father and my mother had an accident.

I went to the hardware store to buy a compass for school. Inside, I got lost trying to find the office supply section and ended up in the area where the construction tools were kept.

On one of the shelves was a small circular saw. As soon as I saw it my left eye warmed. I stopped, focusing my attention on the saw's round blade.

Although nobody had touched it, the blade started to noiselessly spin. In the center of my vision, the real-life circular blade viewed by my right eye overlaid the circular blade seen by my left eye. The dream was beginning. I closed my eyes.

Within the dream, the circular saw sprayed wood shavings into the air. Its round blade spun quickly, sucking in white boards and cutting them into pieces. I was at the lumber mill where my father worked.

The dream was only a visual experience. But the image was so clear I thought I could hear the sound of the wood being cut, that the scent of fresh-cut wood was filling my nose.

The workers at the lumber mill were using electric saws to cut the timber, and I stood beside a building watching them. I could see a large loading bay for the trucks. From the height of my viewpoint, I'd say I was still a boy.

Then my view shifted and I saw my parents standing together. My mother often brought me to visit my father at work.

My parents were standing next to a large truck. Several large tree trunks were piled in the bed of the truck and secured with rope.

My father waved me over. I started to approach them.

Without warning, one of the trees fell from the bed of the truck and onto my parents.

Standing in the hardware store, I screamed.

In my left eye, I saw the two of them crushed beneath the tree. I wanted to stop the dream, but I had no control over it. I opened and closed my eyes, but the dream played on. And even when I turned my head to look away, the vision was still in front of me.

My dream-self stopped still and remained motionless until a crowd of workers ran over to me. From a short distance, I silently watched the figures of my parents trapped beneath the tree. The tree was quickly lifted from them, but I could see that they weren't moving. Maybe that was why I hadn't ever seen Kazuya's parents in dreams that took place when he was older.

My father lay broken upon the ground, blood pouring from his head.

The memory in my left eye cut off, and its vision returned to normal. I lay slumped on the floor in the aisle of the hardware store. An employee had heard my scream and ran toward me.

※

At the end of March I returned to the hospital where I had undergone the transplant surgery for a scheduled follow-up exam. Directly after I'd first been released from the hospital, I'd made several return visits, but this was the first in the month of March. Because I remembered how to get to the hospital, I turned down my parents' offer to drive me there and took the bus by myself.

Standing outside the hospital, I gave its facade another look. It was a small hospital, hidden outside the town. I hadn't given it much thought before, but the building had an unusual atmosphere. For one thing, there wasn't a sign. Second, the entrance was obscured by a growth of trees. I would bet that most people walked by without ever knowing what it was.

Inside I changed out of my shoes and into the standard green hospital slippers. I tried to find a pair that hadn't been torn or had a hole in one or the other, but there were none.

I saw no sign of any outpatients other than myself. At the reception desk sat an expressionless nurse whom you could call old and almost get away with it. Not only was the waiting room dimly lit, but the whole inside of the building was too.

When I had been staying in a private room on the second floor, I hadn't noticed it, but now I sensed a dubious air to the place. Maybe that was a sign of the changes inside me.

The nurse at the desk directed me to an examination room. It was a drab room with only a changing screen, an examination table, a desk, and a chair.

The doctor, mustached and just past middle age, was at the

desk filling out some documents. I bowed to him.

His eyes went to me, then back down to the papers in his hand. "Please lie down on the table," he said.

I did so and waited for the examination to start.

I stared at the ceiling for a time. When I looked to my side, I noticed a large mirror on the wall. In the center of the mirror I saw myself, lying flat on the exam table.

I thought back to the eye transplant operation. I had been lying on a similar table in the operating room. That was when I had first met the eyeball that was now in the left side of my face.

Before, I'd only had one eye and a hole where the other should have been. After the surgery my appearance matched Nami's, but that hadn't really changed anything aside from how I looked, and I had been disappointed.

At first my mother had been happy to see my new, complete face.

She'd looked at me straight on and said with a pleased expression, "That's my Nami's face." She beamed at me, pinching my cheek between her fingers. I was so surprised I think I almost jumped. And I was overjoyed. It was wonderful to see my mother happy like that.

But before long, it became clear that I was still not Nami. Whenever I did something wrong or made some mistake that Nami wouldn't have made, my mother's mood worsened. With my face now like Nami's, I think my mother found it even harder to forgive me.

The doctor, finished with the documents, set them down in a neat pile on the desk. The examination was about to begin.

As I looked over at the mirror on the wall, I felt my left eye grow warm, the usual indicator of a coming dream. The reflection in the mirror was a key, triggering a dream.

But as long as I waited, the dream didn't come. I didn't see the young Kazuya or Saori or the forest. In my left eye I saw only myself, flat on the exam table, looking up at the ceiling.

No, wait. I felt my pulse quicken. Something was off. And

then I realized that what I was seeing was unnatural: impossibly, my reflection was looking up at the ceiling. *If I'm looking at the mirror, shouldn't my reflection be looking back at me?* It was strange to see my own profile in the mirror.

As I pondered it, I noticed another peculiarity. My eyesight was somewhat blurred, as though I were underwater, and the edges of my vision were distorted.

Suddenly, I realized what was happening. *I'm not seeing the examination room—this is the operating room. That's me on the operating table moments before my surgery.*

Confused, I closed my eyes. My vision had felt out of focus, but now it became distinct, and the operating room projected sharply onto the back of my eyelid. *Why is this vision being shown to me like one of the eye's dreams? This isn't Kazuya's world.*

I strained my memory for the events just before the surgery. *Yes, beside me there had been a glass jar with the eye in it. This matches what the eye would have been seeing.*

The realization pierced through me. *The edges of my vision are distorted because I am looking out from inside the glass jar. It's blurry because the eye was suspended in water.*

This isn't a dream. It's what the eye saw. The visions I'd been seeing weren't illusions or daydreams. They were undeniably the eye's memories. Locked inside the jewelry box of the eye were sights of the past that had burned into its retina.

"Sorry to make you wait. Now, shall I start the examination?"

The doctor was standing next to me. I shook my head and sat up on the table.

In my left eye, I still saw myself lying flat. My uneasy expression turned away from the ceiling and across at me.

I had been looking at my right profile. Looking at myself head on, I saw that my left eye socket was a pitch-black hole.

4

After having realized the true nature of the images shown to me by my left eye, my medical exam passed by in a daze. I think the doctor asked me some questions, but I don't know how I answered. After a time, the checkup was over and I left the hospital.

On my way home, I stopped at a bookstore and looked through the shelves for books on high school entrance exams. I found a thick book listing every high school in the country and searched for the name of the school on Kazuya's test. I found it almost immediately. The high school on Kazuya's test paper I had seen in my left eye really existed.

Before seeing the vision in my left eye, I had never heard of the school. I had assumed the visions were not real, that they were only dreams of another world unrelated to my own. But this school was real, and it existed in my world.

If everything I've seen in my eye has been dreamed up by my own imagination, how do I explain this? Did I hear the name of the school somewhere and incorporate it into my dream? No, that doesn't sound right. If anything, this is proof that the visions I've seen in my left eye are events that actually occurred.

Before making its way into my head, the eye had once belonged to a real person named Kazuya. Everything it had shown me were memories of scenes Kazuya had witnessed. I had given my "Dream Journal" the wrong name—to name it correctly, I'd have to call it the "Scenes-the-Eyeball-Witnessed Journal."

The discovery left me with mixed feelings, but what I felt most was confusion.

I'd thought that my dream world did not exist. I had thought that when I entered the oddly familiar fantasy world I transformed into a fictional character named Kazuya Fuyutsuki. I had taken in the images from the eye and stored them in the void my memories had left behind. My mind, once a blank sheet of paper, had become filled with things Kazuya had seen. Through the eye, his experiences had become mine. I felt like I was more Kazuya than Nami.

But Kazuya wasn't just someone I had imagined. Saori and everything else I'd seen in the eye were not from some fantasy world of my own creation. It was all real. That was what caused my confusion. Suddenly I was afraid. When it had all been a dream, Saori hadn't been anything more than a character in a movie. But now that I understood that the visions were recordings of the past, everything and everyone I'd seen took on actual weight.

But I felt more than fear alone. Rather, a feeling of fevered anticipation spread within my chest.

The people and places I'd seen in the dreams had given me courage when I had no memories of my own to lean on, and as I thought of the fact that everything I'd seen actually existed in some other place, I was filled with excitement.

The earth I stood on connected with scenery I had thought existed only in my imagination. The sky that spread above me was above Saori too, and at that moment she could be looking at the same point in the sky I was.

In the eye I'd seen fragments of Kazuya's world—schools, train stations, and place names; every glimpse caught at the periphery of my dreams was recorded in my journal.

The day after my examination I researched them all, one by one. It wasn't that hard, and within a day I'd determined which part of the country Kazuya and Saori lived in.

It was about a half day's ride on the bullet train from my town. I looked up the area in an atlas and found, printed in tiny letters, a name I'd once seen in my left eye. The town was up in the mountains and far from the sea. I stared at the page for some time.

I wanted to know what had brought Kazuya's eye to the hospital and decided to ask my grandfather.

I went to the phone. Several times I started to press the buttons of his phone number, but during each attempt I became scared and set the receiver back in its cradle. I'd only spoken with my grandfather once, when he came to visit me in the hospital. I couldn't remember what we talked about, only the feeling of shame I was left with when I couldn't hold up my end of the conversation.

After a number of rings, my grandfather answered.

He sounded happy to hear from me. "How is your eye? Has your memory returned?" His cheerfulness calmed my nerves.

My memory hasn't returned, but the eye is fine. We talked about my parents and other things before I brought up my question.

"You want to know where I got the eye?" I heard caution in his voice. "Nami, that's not something you need to know…"

He didn't tell me exactly, but I got the understanding that he hadn't obtained the eye through proper channels.

The eye donor had applied to donate his organs and after his death, with the permission of his family, his usable organs were removed from his body. The organs were harvested by an organization overseeing such donations and transplanted into recipients.

My grandfather had secured the eye unlawfully from an important man in that organization. There was a long list of people requesting an eye transplant, and the wait for one numbered in years. And beyond that, people who had lost both their eyes were given priority over those who, like me, were missing only one. If my grandfather hadn't gone outside the legal channels, I would not have received an eye.

The eye was supposed to have gone to somebody else. I felt guilty. I had stolen the eye unfairly from someone who needed it to see.

"Are you angry with me?" my grandfather asked.

I'd never…But I think you shouldn't have done that. I felt thankful for the good fortune that had brought Kazuya's eye to me, but in my conscience I knew he'd done something wrong.

Then I had an idea. Nervously, I put the receiver against my face. *To help me make things right, there's one more favor I have to ask of you…*

"Anything I can do for you."

I thought it was a good idea, but I was afraid he might refuse.

I'll donate my organs. When I die, the eye can be passed on to someone who needs it.

For a second, the phone went silent and I regretted saying it. Then my grandfather's laugh came through the line.

"I like it! I'll seriously consider it."

I felt my cheeks flush with surprise, and a warm, peculiar feeling welled up inside me.

Even after I hung up the phone, a happiness remained with me. Inside my heart, I thanked my grandfather again and again.

✳

Kazuya was dead. That was a fact. He must have signed a document declaring that, after his death, his eyes could be donated. Some tragedy had occurred and he'd passed away. His eye was then taken from his body and transferred into mine.

I watched the memories of his childhood, taking in the times of sadness and times of cheer. I was at his side through his many experiences. I even shared his emotions.

They were only images, but somehow, his feelings showed through. They became a part of me—his happiness, his sadness, all of it.

I loved Kazuya. I loved seeing the world as he saw it. So when I learned of his death, I felt sad.

What does Saori feel now that she has lost her parents and her little brother? I opened the atlas to the page I had bookmarked. I couldn't count how many times I had done so. And every time I did, I lost track of the time.

I want to meet her. Not that I'd know what to say, but it would be enough just to see her face. Thinking about it weighed on my heart.

Even after I learned that the visions weren't dreams, I continued to see them every day. As many as five times in a single day, my left eye would grow warm and the film inside the box would start to spin. Events witnessed over the course of a single human life projected into me at random.

Sadly, once shown to me, the same scenes never came again. Each film played only once. If I didn't pay attention, there wouldn't be another chance. I observed each scene carefully, committing every detail to memory.

I never grew tired of the visions. If anything, I thirsted for more. I wanted to learn everything I could from them, and with each passing day my love for Kazuya and Saori grew.

But as it did, I felt my own parents and my school life fading from my thoughts.

One day my mother confronted me. "What's wrong with you?" she asked. "I got a call from school today. They said you haven't been showing up."

I'd been reading books in coffee shops. And dozing off in libraries. And spending an entire afternoon on a bridge over a pond in the park, watching the ducks swim.

Guilt filled my heart. But I was too frightened of going to school. And even when I tried, when I reached the schoolyard gate my legs would become too weak to take another step.

I was sure Nami could have passed right through those gates without a single thought—she would have jogged into the class-room where her cheery friends were waiting. But there was no place for me there. Or anywhere.

"Why aren't you going to school?" my mother demanded. "Didn't you used to like it before?"

I noticed that I cringed as she spoke. I had betrayed my mother and it hurt me.

My mother hadn't forgotten Nami, and she resented who I had become. She thought that if she accepted who I was, Nami would truly be lost.

"Don't you like school? Look at me and answer!"

I felt like my heart was being squeezed, but I gathered my re-solve, looked my mother in the eye, and said, my voice shaking from worry and sadness, "I'm sorry I didn't tell you I didn't go to school."

I tried to study and I tried to practice my piano, but I couldn't do it like I used to. I even practiced how to smile. Everything I've tried I've been inferior at, and I know everyone is fed up with me. I feel completely worthless now.

But I help around the house and I love you, Mother, and I hope that you can love me again. I told her all of this.

My mother gave me a cold look and left the room without a word. She stopped talking to me after that. The rift between us was beyond repair.

The next day I rearranged my room. I shifted the furniture to how I wanted it. I moved my TV and my bed; I even bought new curtains and tore the posters from the walls. I made the space Nami had created my own. No trace of Nami's room remained.

My father, hearing the racket, came to see what was going on. Pointing a finger at my bookshelf, he asked, "What happened to Yoikoro?"

Yoikoro was the name of a stuffed pig.

"I put it in the back of my closet."

"I can't believe it! I never thought you'd even think about putting your little piglet away." He shook his head. "I can't say I'm happy to see this happen."

Unnerved, I started to wonder if I should just put the room back to how Nami had wanted it.

As I tried to stammer out some response, my father picked up a binder from my desk. He flipped through the pages and asked, "What's this?"

It was the binder in which I'd recorded the scenes from Kazuya's life.

Inside I panicked, but I managed to say, "Um, well, it's sort of homework."

Disinterested, my father placed the binder in my hand. The weight of it gave me courage. Recalling the memories I had seen in my eye, I looked at him and said, "Father, I want to make this room how I want it. I'm not concerned about what things I might have cared for in the past."

He nodded, considering my words. "I suppose that's fine."

✳

That afternoon, I went to the library to look for newspaper articles mentioning Kazuya's death.

I didn't know anything about how he died. I didn't know when he lost his life or how it had happened. I didn't really expect rummaging through old newspapers would help me find articles mentioning the death of a man like Kazuya, but I couldn't just do nothing.

The city library kept copies of newspapers from the last three years. But even though they had the old papers, I didn't know how to go about searching through them. I stood in front of the bookcase that held the rows and rows of newspapers, overwhelmed by their number. When had Kazuya died? I considered it.

I'd heard that donor organs were transplanted relatively quickly after they were obtained. My eye wouldn't have been stored somewhere for even a few months. Therefore, I reasoned, it would be best to search the newspapers that were published just before I underwent the transplant surgery. I had to look back weeks or months, not years.

The operation had been on February 15. Starting from that date, I carefully searched backward through the newspapers.

I slowly scanned the pages for names in traffic accidents and obituaries. As my eyes passed over the printed type, I noticed that each name was followed by a number in parentheses: their ages.

I wondered how old Kazuya was when he had died. In the memories, I'd never seen a wrinkle on Saori's face. The eye hadn't witnessed her in old age—or even middle age. That meant that he might have died young.

In fact, even at the oldest I'd seen her in the eye's visions, she couldn't have been past her late twenties. If my logic was correct, then Kazuya had to have died in his twenties.

For two hours I hunted through the library's newspapers. I found a bundle of newspapers that looked to be from the right period. I pulled it down from the shelf, took it over to a desk, and began to search through the columns. The work was hard on my eyes, and after a time I took a break to give them rest. Thinking about it from my left eye's standpoint, I was forcing it to look through articles in search of the death of its own body. It was a cruel task.

I kept looking, but I never found the name of Kazuya Fuyutsuki. There was a chance I had overlooked it in one of the newspapers I had already checked, but I was sure I hadn't. After all, he had lived in a different region. That was why his name wasn't printed in any of our local papers. Reluctantly, I gave up.

I gathered the papers and went back to the bookshelves. The papers were stored in order, and I had to look through the shelves for their rightful place.

That was when I saw it. My eyes had stopped on one of the bundles of newspapers lined up on the shelves, in the section where last year's issues were kept. A picture on the topmost paper in the bundle had caught my eye.

It was an article about a missing girl and included a portrait of her face. The article wasn't particularly prominent on the page; fate must have moved me to discover it.

In large printed letters, the headline read, FOURTEEN-YEAR-OLD GIRL MISSING. The article itself began, "Yesterday, Hitomi Aizawa, age fourteen, disappeared after leaving a friend's house..."

I looked at her photograph. Her face stared in color straight at the camera. It looked like a class photo. I felt like I had seen her somewhere before.

Suddenly, pain burst through my left eye, turning it into a throbbing ball of heat. I felt like my eye might explode at any moment.

Something similar had happened when I'd been watching TV.

That program had also been about missing children.

I remembered. *The girl in the newspaper is the same girl I saw on TV.* The girl in the picture stared right at me. I couldn't turn my eyes away.

My left eye twitched. The capillaries constricted, and it felt like my bloodstream reversed course.

Something dreadful lay inside the jewelry box in the eye. The memory of it was trying to get out. *No,* I thought, *I have to look away from the picture.*

But my left eye, as if magnetically locked onto it, stared at the picture of the girl.

She had a youthful face and large eyes.

The eyes blinked.

It started. The box of memories opened, images pouring from my left eye. Hitomi's picture had been the key, and it had brought forth the semi-transparent images stored within. This time, as always, I couldn't look away until the projected film reached its natural end.

I closed my eyes and images filled my head, enveloping me in the memories of what Kazuya had seen.

A girl's face was a short distance from Kazuya. It was Hitomi. She was lying on the floor on the other side of a window. She stared blankly in his direction, then blinked again.

The scene panned around, passing over his surroundings. He was standing next to a large house deep in a forest. The walls of the Western-style house were made of blue bricks. Kazuya was either at one of the sides or the rear of the building.

His view shifted back to the window between him and Hitomi Aizawa. The window was at his feet, low to the ground. It must have been the window to a cellar. It was rectangular and small and the glass was dirty. He looked through the window, down at the girl on the cellar floor. The room was dark, so he couldn't see much. Only the girl's face was illuminated by the light from outside.

In the library, I watched the dream in disbelief. *Why was the missing girl inside the cellar?*

Why was Kazuya looking at her?

At first, I didn't know what to make of it, but soon a hypothesis floated into my head. Maybe Hitomi Aizawa had been kidnapped by someone and confined in the cellar. If so, then Kazuya had witnessed something important.

I stood frozen in the library, unable to move.

The view in my left eye turned from the window and focused on the surrounding bushes. He was nervous, and I felt like I could almost hear his breath. He must have been afraid that the owner of the house would find him.

Was the owner of the house the one who had shut Hitomi Aizawa inside the cellar?

The space between the bushes and the walls of the house formed a small path. The house had two floors. Leafless trees clustered around the house. It was winter, or at least near it.

At some point Kazuya had taken a large flathead screwdriver into his hand. Perhaps he had been keeping it inside his jacket pocket. He kneeled on the ground and started to inspect the edges of the window frame.

I know what he's doing. He's there to save her.

The window was built into the wall, and he couldn't see any screws to remove. Taking one more cautious look around, Kazuya wedged the flat tip of the screwdriver in between the window and the wall. It looked like he was going to try to pry it open.

But his hand stopped. He'd noticed something. One second later, I noticed it too.

Hitomi Aizawa, lying on the floor of the cellar on the other side of the window, was looking at him with the side of her face flat against the floor. There was something peculiar about her clothes as well. She wasn't actually wearing clothing, just a cloth sack. She had been put into the sack in such a way that her body only showed from the neck up. The end of the sack was tied shut at her neck with a string.

The size of the sack was wrong. An ominous feeling came over me. The room had been too dark for me to notice at first, but the sack the girl had been put into was clearly too small—not nearly big enough for a person's body to fit inside. I supposed she might have been able to scrunch her knees up to her chest, but I quickly rejected the theory, because if that were true, the bag would have had more of a bulge. The body of the girl in my left eye could only have been the size of a torso.

Could it be? I rejected the thought. *If she had no limbs, then she could fit into that sack.* I felt immediately disgusted with myself for even considering it. I drew my hand to my mouth.

The viewpoint in my left eye moved violently. The vision rocked up and down as Kazuya ran from the window. He turned the corner of the house and hid himself there. He pressed his body against the blue brick wall, seeming to listen for a sound. For me there had been only silence, but I knew Kazuya had heard the sound of footsteps and fled from the window.

The blue bricks of the house filled the upper half of my vision. The corner of the wall was just before my nose, beyond that was where Kazuya had been standing. A shadow fell across the ground. Someone was there.

I was too terrified to breathe.

Kazuya stepped backward to escape the shadow. My vision moved, and he looked down to put the flathead screwdriver back into his jacket pocket.

That was when he met his misfortune. The large screwdriver caught on the edge of his jacket and slipped from his hand. I watched the tool as it fell through the air.

A concrete gutter lined the base of the outer walls. The gutter was open, lidless. Rotting leaves formed a layer at the bottom. If the screwdriver had landed in the leaves, it might not have made a sound. But it struck the exposed concrete edge before rebounding inside. The dream was silent, so I heard nothing, but the sound of metal colliding with concrete rang inside my head.

My viewpoint rocked violently. Kazuya broke into a run toward the forest behind him and down a tree-lined slope. The earth was piled with leaves. He ran through them.

He took a swift glance over his shoulder. In the center of his choppy, shaking vision I saw a figure in pursuit. I couldn't make out its face or its height. But it was there.

Shuddering, I clutched at the newspaper shelves.

Kazuya ran through the gaps between the tangled trees, ducking under branches and scrambling over exposed roots. Twigs caught at his clothes as he sprinted past, and he shook them free without breaking his stride. The trees were endless. Just as he'd pass one, another would take its place. It felt like it would go on forever.

After a time, the trees changed. The shorter, barren trees gave way to tall, upright, pillarlike conifers. He wove his way between the trees and ran on.

The image in my left eye flipped top over bottom. The slope had suddenly turned steep, and he must have lost his footing. He rolled down the hill, scattering fallen leaves into the air. Suddenly, he broke through the edge of the forest. Kazuya rose to his feet. Beneath him was asphalt. A road. Right in front of his eyes was the rapidly approaching bumper of a white car.

In the library, I screamed. My left eye pulsed fiercely.

Kazuya was struck down by the car. How hard, I couldn't tell from the images. But the view remained motionless on the pavement. After rocking and shaking so much, the viewpoint was still, as if drained of its power. His eyes were still open.

The fever faded from my eye. The image dimmed, and the memory ended like the lifting of a fog. But in the last moment, on the slope Kazuya had tumbled down, I thought I saw a figure hiding among the trees, out of sight of the car's driver.

The scene in my left eye ended completely. I was crying. That had been the moment Kazuya had died. He'd been hit by a car and died. But it had not been a normal death.

He saw her, the kidnapped and captive girl. Unless I had been mistaken, Hitomi looked as if she had no limbs. In the picture I'd seen on the TV, she had been whole.

Kazuya had witnessed where she was being held. He'd tried to save her but had been discovered by the kidnapper.

I despised the kidnapper. Whoever it was might just as well have murdered Kazuya. But Kazuya's death was probably assumed to have been a traffic accident. The thought was unbearable.

How devastated was Saori? How many dreams had been cut short?

I stood frozen in place. After the memory had finished playing, my left eye returned to normal, just another part of my body, as if the fever that had come over it hadn't been real.

I have to go to where he died. In that house nearby, Hitomi Aizawa is still trapped.

PART 2

1—AN AUTHOR OF FAIRY TALES

Miki had a dream in which people rained from the sky.

He stood atop a building in a city where he could look out far into the horizon. He saw clearly the figures of the raining people.

They wore black suits, every one, men and women alike. From high up in the sky they poured down endlessly. Above him, people formed black stars against a cloudless purple sky. The people, possibly asleep, showed no signs of fear.

Miki looked at the city below. Countless bodies had struck its roofs and streets and soaked them in red. Bodies, twisting on impact, piled up throughout the city. But none had fallen upon the roof where Miki stood.

He awoke. He had fallen asleep at his desk while revising his manuscript. Sheets of printed copy paper were scattered on the carpet. He started gathering them up.

"Are you awake?" the young girl on the couch asked with a tilt of her head. "You were asleep for an hour. I got bored."

Miki neatly stacked the papers on top of his desk. It was an antique, with solid wood and intricately carved detail work, left in the house by the previous tenant.

He looked out the window. The sun had already begun to set.

The forest spread black along the base of the crimson sky. He shut the curtains. They too had been left behind by the last person to live there. They were black and thick like a theater curtain.

"Tell me a story," the girl said as she wriggled on the couch. "And not that one about the raven bringing eyes to the girl. I'm tired of that one, so tell me another."

She was talking about "The Eye's Memory," a story of his that had been published some time before. He often read it to her when she grew bored.

"Tell me about when you were a child," she continued. "Don't you think that's a splendid idea? It's been a while since you brought me here, and yet I still don't know anything about you." The corners of her mouth turned up into a smile. "Is Shun Miki even your real name?"

He shook his head. Miki was only his pen name.

He sat down on the couch and put his hand on the girl's head. He adjusted her hair and she closed her eyes. Miki thought back upon his past.

✳

He was born the son of a doctor. His father was a surgeon and a large hospital was their home.

The first thing Miki always remembered when asked about his childhood were the patients who had been hospitalized in his home. Young Miki liked to run his toy cars up and down the hospital hallways and he frequently saw, through the open doors of the rooms, patients lying on the hospital beds, staring out their windows—some with their bodies wrapped in bandages, others with their limbs suspended in slings. When they noticed him playing with his toys, they stared at him with eyes that might as well have been hollow pits.

When he was in grade school, Miki often went bug catching with some of the neighbor kids. Near his house was a piece of land overgrown with weeds and left vacant by whoever owned it, where the children would search through grass up to their eyes for crickets and grasshoppers.

When he was in fourth grade, one of his friends came up with an idea for a new game: killing grasshoppers by sticking them with needles. His friend impaled countless numbers of the insects onto a wooden board and showed them to him. The legs of the freshly pinned grasshoppers twitched for a time, then stilled.

Miki wanted to try it for himself. He put a captured grasshopper onto a board and stuck it through the abdomen with a sewing pin he'd brought from home. But the grasshopper didn't die.

He didn't think anything of it, assuming that by pure chance he'd missed the vital parts of the insect's anatomy. And so he'd stabbed some more pins into the bug.

He stuck three pins into it—one in the head, one in the thorax, and a third in the abdomen. Yet the grasshopper continued to move, its six legs scrambling at the air as good as new. Its antennae waved about and bodily fluids leaked from where the pins stuck into it, but its squirming didn't stop.

With the piercing of the twelfth pin, the grasshopper finally died. Stuck onto the board, it no longer resembled an insect—just a clump of pins.

Miki tried it with other insects and got similar results. He threw a stag beetle against a wall over and over, but it wouldn't die. Even with its legs detached and its exoskeleton fractured, its horns kept moving.

He assumed that this was just the way insects worked. With a pair of scissors he cut a cicada into two halves, and he grabbed a beetle by the horns and plucked its head right off, but for a time, their legs and wings continued to move. They just wouldn't die. *Insects are stubborn creatures*, he figured.

But eventually Miki came to learn this wasn't normal, that none of the other kids thought as he did. *Maybe I just happened to catch bugs that were tougher than the rest*, he reasoned. But when he looked down at his hands, he had the feeling that something else was occurring.

I have a mysterious power.

＊

One time, a girl Miki's age was admitted to his parents' hospital. Their eyes happened to meet through the open door of her hospital room, and from that point on, Miki often went to visit her.

Miki didn't have very many close friends. Even the friends who used to catch bugs with him had found more interesting playmates and then grown distant. So each day when he came home from grade school, he went to talk to the girl.

When Miki would enter her hospital room, her face would light up, and she'd wave a bandaged arm.

Both of her arms ended at the elbow. She'd lost them playing alongside some railroad tracks. Just as an express train passed by, she had thrust her arms out onto the tracks.

"I just wanted to see what would happen," the girl explained, looking at her bandaged arms. "The instant the train passed, it burst open my arms from the elbow down."

Miki enjoyed their conversations. He made up stories from his father's speeches and his mother's lectures.

＊

One day, Miki had been telling one of his stories to the girl when an emergency patient was rushed to the hospital. The two children stood in front of the door to the operating room and peeked inside to see how bad the patient's injuries were.

Miki's father and several nurses were preparing for the surgery. After a moment, the children caught a glimpse of the patient on the gurney. He was a young man, with no discernible injuries, and he looked asleep.

But during the operation he died.

"He was hit in the wrong spot," Miki's father said to his son, explaining that the patient had only fallen from his bicycle and hadn't suffered any external injuries.

"What's the wrong spot?" Miki's amputee friend asked. "As long as that spot is okay, could someone keep living?"

Miki asked, "Is it possible that somebody could have the subconscious ability to avoid the wrong spots while injuring someone?"

"Gosh, I wonder," his friend said, trying to cross her arms. Since they ended at her elbows, the gesture wasn't very effective.

＊

Miki captured grasshoppers and tried to discover which injuries killed them. At first, they died quickly, comparatively speaking. His subjects, pierced with a great number of pins, died within a minute. But as he repeated the experiment, he felt they were staying alive longer.

A group of stag beetles, the lower half of their bodies crushed, lived for a week. But squishing or cutting off their heads killed them immediately.

He dissected a frog, and he cut open the belly of a fish and removed the organs from its body. He returned them to the water, and for a time, they went about just as they had before. The frog kicked through the water, pulling an increasingly lengthy trail of guts behind it.

He also tested mammals. With a trail of food, he lured a stray cat to an unfrequented area behind the hospital, and when the feline came close, he chopped it neatly in half.

The cat kept on living and Miki learned something new. His test subjects didn't seem to feel any pain from the injuries he inflicted on them.

The cat hadn't noticed that it had been cut into two pieces. Even though there wasn't anything below its stomach, it still tried to lick its back paws. There wasn't much blood, and it still experienced thirst and hunger. The food it ate passed right out of its exposed stomach. Over a period of a week, it gradually lost its strength, eventually dying as though it had lain down to sleep.

He tried it on another cat. That time it lived for two weeks, and without any food or water.

Miki wanted to share his findings with his short-armed friend. She had been released from the hospital and lived in another school district a thirty-minute bicycle ride away. Miki often went there to play and talk with her.

Miki parked his bike in front of her house, went up to the door, and rang the bell. Her mother answered the door and said, without much sadness apparent in her voice, "She died the day before yesterday."

The mother went on to explain, "She fell down the stairs. She used to love sliding down the banister, so I'm sure that's what she was doing. If she slid down it and lost her balance, she wouldn't have had a way to grab on. She must not have realized that until it was too late. She was always forgetting that she didn't have anything past her elbows."

❋

In the fall of his junior year in high school, Miki committed murder for the first time.

It was a cold and cloudy day. Miki was riding his motorcycle along a mountain road not far from his home, headed nowhere in particular.

The road widened near the mountain's peak, providing space for cars to pull over. There were even a couple of vending machines.

As Miki approached the parking area, he noticed there weren't any cars around. He stopped his bike and went to look at the view of the mountainside below. The edge of the overlook dropped steeply into an exposed rock face, almost a cliff. A gap in the guardrail opened to a path of stairs leading down the cliffside.

He stood there for a while, gazing at the autumn view. The clouds tinted everything gray, and even the vibrant colors of the fall leaves seemed dull.

Miki turned at the sound of a car pulling into the lookout. A young woman stepped out of the driver's side of the car. She was alone. She wore a business suit and was holding a map. She was walking toward Miki.

Her shoulders bunched up as if she were cold, she said, "I'm sorry, I'm trying to get to the city. Do you know the fastest way?"

She looked at his motorcycle.

"That's a cool bike you've got there. But isn't it too cold to ride this time of year? Maybe it's just me—I've never been very good with the cold, you know." She touched her hand to the guardrail, then drew it back with a shiver.

Miki pushed her from behind. She toppled over the rail and down the side of the cliff. He looked around—only after he had done it, not before—to see if anyone had been there to witness it.

He looked to see where she had landed and saw her long hair in the shadow of a tree quite far down the rocks. He took the cliffside stairway down to her.

Even after hitting the ground, she still lived. Her limbs were twisted in unnatural directions. Blood seeped out from her eyes and her mouth. The woman, unaware of what had happened, stared up at him with a dumbstruck expression. Her map had fallen to the ground at her side. Miki picked it up.

He looked at the nearly vertical cliffside. He saw the exposed rocks she had slammed against in her fall and, small in the distance above them, the silver glimmer of the guardrail.

Miki dragged the woman deeper into the woods, where she wouldn't be seen from above. The whole time her mouth moved feebly, but a large tree branch had pierced her chest in the fall and she could no longer speak. He withdrew the branch, leaving a large hole in her body. Broken ribs and shriveled, airless lungs peeked out from the edges of the cavity. Miki could see her red, beating heart.

She didn't look to be in any pain, and her face was without even a frown. But it seemed that she wasn't able to move her body. The impact of the fall must have broken nearly everything inside her. Her eyes and her mouth were all that moved.

Miki instructed her to blink twice for yes and once for no. He asked her if she understood.

Two blinks. That meant her ears worked too.

He asked if she was in pain. One blink. No.

He asked if she was frightened. She made an odd face and her eyes went to the map in his hands.

Miki spread the map open in front of her and showed her the fastest route to the city. Then he asked if that was all she wanted. She blinked twice.

Miki said goodbye, and as he started to leave, she looked at him with a question in her eyes. She seemed to be asking, *What should I do now?*

Miki ignored her, went back up the stairway, and climbed onto his bike. The woman's car was still running. He opened the passenger-side window, turned off the ignition, and wiped the fingerprints off everything he'd touched.

The next day he returned to the lookout. The woman's car was still there, just as he had left it. He descended the cliffside stairway and went to see how she was.

She was still alive. When she saw Miki, she gave him a relieved smile.

He asked if she was all right—telling her one blink for no, two for yes. She blinked twice.

He looked at the cavity in her chest the branch had made. Her heart was still beating. There was very little bleeding—some, but hardly any at all.

Miki noticed something strange. It wasn't cold enough yet to call it winter, but the temperature was lower than it had been the day before. But the woman didn't show any signs of feeling it. Her lips and her face had gone pale, yes, but they didn't look cold.

He asked her if she was cold. She thought it over, then blinked once.

He took the wallet from her pocket and found her name and address.

The next three days he came and spoke to her. Each day as he left her expression turned lonely. On the third day, her car was gone.

Some of the people in the area had been concerned over her disappearance, and the search party had discovered her car at the overlook.

When she saw him come on the fourth day, her eyes fixed intently upon him. Then, as if to say she had something to show him, they turned down.

Miki followed her gaze down to the hole in her chest. When he looked closer, he thought he noticed something concealed inside and almost immediately saw it was a snake. It was coiled around her broken ribs. The snake stared up at Miki, flicking out its red tongue. Her body must have still been warm. The snake had nestled its scaly body up against her beating heart and was settled in for its winter slumber.

Miki pulled out the snake. He told her goodbye, and then he stabbed the knife he had brought through the hole in her chest and into her heart. As if drifting to sleep, the woman closed her eyes, and her breath stopped.

Some time later, he read an article in the newspaper about the discovery of her body. Her bones had been found under the melting snow.

Miki never thought much about why he pushed the woman from the top of the cliff. He had done it for the same reason he'd stuck pins into those insects. He had done it because he could.

That and because he'd wanted to see what would happen.

✳

The girl had fallen asleep listening to Miki talk.

A bell sounded in the study. The phone on his desk was ringing. He lifted the receiver and heard the voice of his editor.

"I'm looking forward to your next story."

Miki considered it less a demand for a manuscript and more a check to see if he was still alive. In the first place, Miki wasn't exactly the fastest pencil around. Being an author wasn't really his job—his fairy tales were only products of his spare time. And he didn't keep up a diligent correspondence with his editor, instead remaining mostly silent. Whenever he happened to finish another manuscript, he'd send it in and that was it.

Miki had written an award-winning fairy tale when he was in twelfth grade. He had simply transcribed one of the tales he'd told, back when he was a child, to his friend with the arms that ended at the elbow.

His first work was the story of a raven who gathered eyeballs from people and flew off with them.

His second tale was about a doctor who put a zipper in his patient's back to make it easier to perform surgery. The doctor was able to open the zipper to get at the organs inside without having to make an incision every time. But when a nurse forgot to zip the patient back up, all of the organs spilled out and only a husk of skin was left.

His third work was a book entitled *The Collected Black Fairy Tales* and had been well received by the reading public.

He'd never intended to become a writer, and he'd assumed that once he'd exhausted the stories he'd told as a child, the writing would stop. But the stories never ceased to pour out from within him.

"Could we meet and talk in person next time?"

Miki replied to his editor's words with silence. He rarely met with anyone associated with his publishers. Nor did he give interviews or attend parties. He wrote fairy tales and sent them away. On the other end they were accepted and published, with money deposited into his bank account. That was the extent of it.

He had even heard that some doubted a fairy-tale author named Shun Miki even existed. That was fine by him.

He hung up the phone, took the girl on the couch into his arms, and left the study. Her body was light—around twenty pounds.

He had met her in the city. She was distraught, separated from her friends, and he had taken her with him. She said her name was Hitomi Aizawa.

Miki still remembered when he had removed the blindfold from her eyes in the cellar.

She'd tilted her head and asked, "What are those mannequin arms and legs over there?" She was looking over at the scattered appendages in the corner of the room. It didn't take long for her to notice that the limbs that should have been attached to her shoulders and hips no longer were.

"Are those...mine?"

He had used a handsaw for the amputation. There hadn't been an anesthetic, but no signs of pain had shown on her blindfolded face. He hadn't applied any tourniquets either, but there hadn't been much blood. And her wounds still hadn't healed; the stumps remained a fresh red color.

Hitomi couldn't wear normal clothing anymore. Miki made a sack to fit her body and put her torso into it. He made other sacks, with flower prints and checkered-patterned fabric, but she didn't like them.

"I don't like how the top scratches my neck," she said.

Finally she picked one he'd made from pale blue cloth. It opened right at her neck, and he tied it shut with a red necktie.

He carried the sleeping child downstairs. Her cheek was damp against his chest. Sometimes she thought of her parents and cried.

The entrance to the cellar was behind the staircase at the rear of the first floor. The doorway was the same color as the wall, and it was hard to notice from only a glance. Miki had rented the Western-style home in the mountains because he liked the cellar.

He flipped the light switch on and went down the stairs. The underground space was made of exposed brick. It was cold—cold enough that Miki's breath steamed white. The ceiling was low, but not too low to walk upright.

The cellar formed a large rectangular space. The lightbulb was weak for the size of the room, and the corners of the cellar were deep in shadow. There were several freestanding shelves, left in the cellar by the home's previous tenant. Boxes of tools and old clothes lined the shelves.

Hitomi's bed sat in front of the small forest of shelving units. He rested her inside it.

From behind one of the shelves came Shinichi Hisamoto's voice. "Hey..." he said.

Miki looked up from Hitomi in the direction of the voice. In the tiny gap between two boxes on the shelf was Shinichi's eye. It was looking at Hitomi.

From the dark space on the other side of the shelves came the sound of a massive body moving. Shinichi's eye vanished from the tiny gap, only to be replaced by another one. It belonged to Yukie Mochinaga.

"Something's wrong with the Old Man," she said. "Take a look at him."

The Old Man was a nickname for one of the people who lived in the cellar. His real name was Tadashi Kaneda. Miki nodded, and Yukie's eye disappeared from the gap. He heard her let out a deep breath.

From the darkness behind the shelves she said, "It's hard work, lifting my face up to that crack."

Miki covered Hitomi with a blanket. He was aware that the people he injured didn't feel much warmth or cold, but he covered her anyway.

It wasn't only that they became insensitive to changes in temperature—their bodies were unaffected by it altogether. They wouldn't freeze to death. They were also freed from hunger and disease. The people he injured lived on, as if the flow of time toward death had ceased.

It was the power to sustain life. It was a pair of scissors that severed the magnetic force of death. He understood. This was his gift.

Yukie Mochinaga started to sing in the darkness. It was a sorrowful song, its lyrics English. She had been an English teacher and her pronunciation was beautiful. The cellar filled with her delicate, wavering voice.

Hitomi moaned, troubled by something in her dream. Her lips moved, forming the shapes of words. Miki lowered his ear to her mouth.

Her sleep-talk was unintelligible, except for two words.

"The raven..."

2

The raven swayed. The key chain with its cutesy black-feathered bird hung from the car's rearview mirror; it swayed in front of my eyes to the motions of the car.

"Do you know somebody who lives here?" asked the young man in the driver's seat.

I nervously shook my head. It had taken a lot of courage to climb into the car of someone I knew absolutely nothing about. But there were only two buses a day that went near my destination—the town of Kaede—and even though it was still early in the evening the second bus had already left. So I'd resolved to find a ride from somebody headed that way.

I moved my eyes from the raven on the key chain and looked out the window at the expanse of gray sky. The mountains were close, the road winding alongside. Seeing the slopes covered with a blanket of dead white grass made me feel gloomy.

We stopped once at a place surrounded by cedar trees. The black and yellow arm of a crossing gate lowered before my eyes, and the continuous ringing of a bell drilled through my ears. There was a crossing in the road in front of the car, and after a moment, a single red railroad car passed by. The driver said it was a municipal train.

He was making an effort to talk to me, but I was afraid. I didn't know how to interact with strangers.

But because he was letting me ride in his car, I thought it would be ungracious of me to hurt his feelings. I scrambled to think of something to talk about. But I didn't have any stories to tell. Having lost my memory, I was without a past and without experiences. I didn't have a life worth talking about, and if he were to ask me about my past, I wouldn't have an answer. If I could avoid it, I didn't want to tell anyone that I had lost my memory.

Anybody I met wouldn't know anything about me, so I figured I could just make up whatever lie popped into my head. But I wasn't able to come up with one on the spot. Under the oppressive strain of anxiety and worry, my words faltered until I could hardly speak. Whenever the man driving said something to me, I responded with simple nods.

My high school was on spring vacation—not that school was relevant to me anymore. I had been skipping class since well before the ceremony that marked the end of the school year. Still, I did feel guilty whenever I skipped.

On days that I legitimately had off I felt a little more at ease. And somehow, when I told myself that I too had the right to be a bother to others, I'd been able to make the leap and run away from home.

I left a letter for my parents. In it I wrote that I would be leaving the house for a while and I would call them once a day to tell them I was all right.

A few days before I had withdrawn Nami's entire savings from her bank account. On that weekday afternoon I'd gone to the bank with the bankbook that had my own name written on it. It had been hidden in the back of my desk drawer. Before I lost my memories, I had been steadily saving my money.

I didn't know my PIN. Everyone forgets their PIN sometimes, but I really had forgotten mine. I thought about speaking with one of the bank clerks to explain the situation. I had my student ID and my bank seal, which was certainly enough to prove I was myself.

But I felt like Nami's bankbook wasn't mine to have, and I would be taking money that belonged to somebody else. I didn't want to attract any attention.

I decided to see if I could withdraw the money by entering some possible PIN codes into the ATM. I started with my birthday. My parents had told me what it was and I remembered it:

1021.

No good. I started to worry that the security guard was going to question me.

I tried another number.

Yon-ichi-go-roku. 4156. Like Yoikoro, the stuffed animal I'd stuck in the closet.

That did it.

With a vaguely apologetic feeling, I withdrew all the money that Nami must have saved so carefully before the memory loss. Somehow I just couldn't rationalize it as money that had been mine in the first place.

I got dressed and waited for my resolve to come. I studied maps of the area and of railroad lines and tried to figure out what route I should take.

Kaede, where Kazuya grew up, was nestled in the mountains at the edge of the prefecture. I doubted very many people lived there. The name of the town was written so small on the map it could easily be overlooked.

As I'd made my preparations to leave, the visions had continued to come to life inside my left eye, and in them I saw Kazuya's childhood. But ever since I'd witnessed his death in the library, no matter how happy the memory, as soon as the fever in my eye subsided I wanted to cry.

"Why do you want to go to that hick town?" the driver asked with interest.

I hesitated, then said, "Someone important to me is there."

"Didn't you say that you didn't know anybody in Kaede?"

"Well, that's..." Unable to think of a good answer, I let the sentence trail off.

The landscape outside the car window gradually became more like what I had seen in the images of my left eye. I felt myself drawing nearer to where Kazuya and Saori had lived.

The conifer trees and the transmission towers that now pierced the sky had appeared in my eye's memories from time to time. My skin crackled as if charged with static electricity. I was on edge. It was spring, but the landscape was the dead of winter. I saw not the vivid green of plant life but only barren trees, dead grass, and the nearly black needles of the conifers. Cold air leaked through the cracks around the glass of the windows—cold enough that I wouldn't have been surprised to see snow falling.

The car stopped at a light. I didn't see any other cars around.

On the left-hand side of the road stood an open space of dried white earth where rusted semi-trailers and old tires had been left to sit. Beyond the clearing was thick forest. Next to the traffic signal, a giant sign towered over the road.

My left eye began to warm. *Oh, this is...*

I found the courage to say, "Could you please stop the car here for a minute?"

A look of suspicion came to his face. The light turned green. I saw it with my right eye.

"What's wrong?" asked the driver. "Is it allergies?"

I wiped the tears from my eyes and closed the lid on the box of memories in my left eye.

"May I step outside for a little bit?" I asked. "I'll be right back."

I opened the passenger-side door and got out. The air outside was freezing cold, not like inside the heated car.

I approached the base of the giant sign. It was held up by two metal poles. As I stood directly beneath it, it rose up like a perfectly vertical cliff.

In the scene painted on the sign, clouds soared across a brilliant blue sky. With the real sky covered by dark gray clouds, bright summer seemed to have come only to the square cutout of the sign. It must have belonged to some business.

I spent some time there, crawling beneath it, tapping on its metal supports, and looking at it from the reverse side. And then I noticed that I was smiling.

The man in the car was watching me from the driver's seat. Thinking that I shouldn't be making him wait like this, I returned to the car.

"A long time ago, the person I know used to play beneath that sign, back when it was still being built..."

In my eye's memories, a man in work clothes had been painting the blue sky onto the sign. Kazuya, staring up at the sign, had accidently tripped over a paint can. Since his viewpoint was fairly high up, I guessed that he must have been nearly grown.

But when he knocked over the paint can, he fled like a little child.

I couldn't keep from laughing as I recalled the scene. But for some reason it evoked sadness as well.

The car began to move. I took the binder from my backpack and recorded the vision. I had been standing on the same spot that had been in my left eye's memory. Joy welled up inside me. When I stood in front of the sign, I had felt the real-life scenery perfectly line up with the scenery of my vision. If you thought about how Kazuya and I were two completely different people who were raised in two distant places, it was a miracle.

The man driving the car said, "We're in Kaede now."

I was transfixed by the view that spread out beyond my window.

"By the way, there's a place I want to stop at," he said. "Do you mind if we go there first?"

I didn't object to the request. After all, I didn't know where to go from there anyway. My goal had been to get to Kazuya and Saori's town, Kaede. I hadn't really thought much past this point.

I have to find a place to stay. From there I'll base my search for Saori. She should still be alive. Kazuya died only two, maybe three months ago. Saori must still live here.

Then I'll find the house with the blue bricks, I thought.

At last, the small mountain town was outside my window. The highway ran like an artery through the center of it. Traffic was light and the road was quiet.

I saw no tall buildings through the windows, just a few small businesses and homes between stretches of wilderness overgrown with dead grass. A scraggy stray dog lifted its head to sniff at some garbage.

A large flatbed truck loaded with a pile of felled conifers passed by in the opposite lane. The man told me there was a cedar tree farm up in the mountains, and the town had grown up to support it. Absentmindedly I wondered if that kind of place would be hard on someone with allergies. I had hardly any of my memories, and yet I had some half-useless knowledge regarding cedar allergies. *Maybe Saori has allergies and that's why her nose is constantly running.*

I saw a supermarket that made me worry if it ever had any customers. The paint on its sign was a depressingly drab color. An old man with a towel wrapped around his neck was wearily unloading cases of alcohol from the back of an old rusted mini-truck.

In this lifeless town the air felt thin, and under the cloudy sky everything looked drab. Even the paint of the road markings had almost completely faded away. It seemed very barren for being only twenty minutes from the train station.

Several times as we drove through the town I almost spoke up. Places I'd seen in my left eye—shops, landscapes, streets—passed by my window.

I had no doubt that this was the town Kazuya had lived in. Each time I saw a familiar sight I wanted to stop the car and go to it. But I didn't want to annoy the man driving, so I resisted the urge. I pressed my face and my palms against the glass window and took in everything I could see of the town.

"There's this business just a little ways out," said the driver. "I've got something I want to deliver there."

Soon the car left the highway. The buildings became fewer and I stopped recognizing things from the images of my left eye. Just as I was starting to feel a little disappointed, the car stopped in a parking lot.

The man got out of the car, picked up a box from the back seat, and said, "Once I'm done here, I'll take you where you want to go."

But I had already realized that wouldn't be necessary. I climbed out of the car and looked at the building the man had entered.

It was a café. Built from round logs, it looked like a mountain lodge. A sign read MELANCHOLY GROVE. It had been in many of the visions of my left eye.

Saori worked there.

❋

I pushed open the wooden door and stepped into the café. At once I was enveloped in the warmth from a heater. To the left of the entrance was the counter, to the right were the tables. I recognized all of it.

With each footstep, my shoes struck the floorboards with a peculiarly pleasant sound. I sat at the counter.

The owner emerged from the rear of the store and said, "Welcome."

My pulse quickened. The man had appeared in a number of my left eye's visions. A mustache grew across his bearlike face. He was as large in real life as he had appeared in the visions—enough so that I worried that he was uncomfortably cramped in the space behind the counter.

"What's wrong?" he asked. I had been staring at his face.

"Nothing, I'm sorry." Feeling self-conscious, I averted my eyes. I looked around the café's interior and saw familiar things—vases, flowers, decorations, wooden tables and chairs. The café was filled with a warm yellow light, the same color I had seen in the visions of my left eye.

"Can I take your order?" asked the owner.

I hastily opened the menu and said the first thing I saw.

"I'll have a café au lait, please."

The man who had given me the ride came from the back of the store. His delivery must have been for here. He and the owner seemed to know each other, and they were having a friendly conversation. Maybe the owner had asked him to pick up some supplies as a personal favor. The man who drove me glanced around the room. He seemed to be looking for someone.

There were two customers. One, a gray-haired woman, I figured to be around sixty. She was seated by a window, taking sips from her coffee cup as she read a hardcover book. She turned a page with a wrinkled hand. Her clothes were elegant. I wondered if she lived nearby. I got the impression that she was a regular here.

The other patron was at the back of the room. At first, I hadn't noticed someone was there, as the seat was mostly out of the light. The person appeared to be male; his black clothes made him melt into the darkness.

The man who had driven me from the station looked at me sitting at the counter and told me he was ready to leave.

I thought for a second, then made up my mind.

"I'll stay here. Thank you for the ride."

The man waved goodbye and, looking back over his shoulder at me with a concerned expression, left the café. I felt like I'd seen his expression before. Maybe he'd been in one of the memories of my left eye. It seemed he was a regular, so the chances were high. Given how thick my binder had become, there were bound to be many faces I wouldn't remember straightaway.

The owner returned with my café au lait and said, his voice just as I'd imagined it would be, "Here you go."

This was my chance to see him close up. I couldn't believe he was right there in front of my own eyes.

Kazuya had frequented the café—probably because his sister worked there. I was sure of this because the place often showed up in the memories of my left eye. He had even been present when the store first opened. He would have been around middle school age then. The store had had a different owner at the time, a slightly older man.

I had seen that memory back home, when I'd looked at a coffee cup and my left eye had grown warm. The coffee shop was brand-new then, like a fresh pair of clothes ready for a night out. Kazuya had skipped school and, still dressed in his school uniform, sat at the back of the room. The gray-haired man behind the counter had been imprinted into his eye.

Everything has a past, I realized anew. *This café has one too. Maybe I'm the only thing in here that doesn't.*

I felt odd. Here I was, walking around with that binder inside my backpack, carrying the fragments of the past of these people and the town. But in reality they were all strangers to me. "Excuse

me..." I said to the owner. But as I started to talk, I couldn't think
of what to say next. To me he was someone I had seen many times
before, but to him I was just another customer.

He raised his eyebrows as if to say, "Can I help you?"

"I know it's strange to ask this all of a sudden..." I resolved
to ask—it was something that had been bothering me. "Please
tell me your name."

Since speech hadn't been recorded in the visions of my left eye,
his name had long been a mystery to me. More than anything, I
had wanted to ask what it was.

He was taken aback. "It's Kimura, but..."

"Th-thank you." I felt like I had embarrassed myself, and I
sensed my cheeks reddening. At the same time, I was moved—*I
see, Kimura, then.*

Kimura leaned his elbows on the counter and peered into my
face. He was a large man, and that alone was intimidating. A
smile spread like a bear showing its teeth. He didn't laugh, maybe
because other customers were around, but I was frightened enough
that I almost screamed.

"Why did you want to know my name?"

I didn't have an answer.

"Well, you see...I've been here for coffee before, and I'd heard
someone say your name, and I just wanted to make sure I had it
right..." Along the way I'd stopped comprehending the words
that were coming out of my mouth, and my voice tapered off.

"You say you've been here before? How long ago was that?"

I hesitated. "About two years ago."

It was all a lie.

Kimura crossed his arms and regarded me suspiciously. "You
shouldn't tell lies. I remember all of my customers' faces."

In a panic I blurted, "It's not a lie."

"Well, then..." Kimura thought for a moment. "There's something that's just recently been brought in here. See if you can
spot it. Everything else should be about the same as it was two
years ago."

Just then the elderly woman sitting at the table by the window spoke up. "Now, Kimura, that's too much. It's impossible. I wouldn't be able to answer that myself."

I hadn't noticed her eavesdropping. I was overcome with embarrassment.

Kimura looked over at her and said, "What, you were listening, Kyoko?"

The woman he had called Kyoko closed her book and gave Kimura a reproachful look.

"She's right," Kimura said, "that question was too—"

"I can answer it," I declared. I pointed to a painting that hung on the wall. It was a painting of a lake, a sparkling lake in the middle of a black forest. It hadn't been in the memory of my left eye, so I figured it must have been hung recently. In my binder, I had detailed records of the café's interior that I could have checked. But I didn't need to check.

Kimura's round eyes widened in surprise. I knew I had answered correctly.

At the back of the room, the man shrouded in darkness stood up. I hadn't seen it earlier because he had been in the shadows, but he had a pretty face. He had long hair and wore glasses. His black coat flowed past me. The man moved so quietly I couldn't hear the sound of his footsteps on the floor. He stood at the register to pay.

"I'll be damned," Kimura muttered, scratching his head as he moved to the register. He took the money from the man in black and returned the man's change.

As the man left the café, I had the feeling that he looked in my direction, and I knew that he had been listening to our conversation.

"The man that just left," Kimura said, "he was the one who painted that. Have you heard of Shiozaki, the painter?"

I shook my head.

"No memory of him?"

I felt those words particularly fitting for me.

"I wonder why he moved all the way out to a place as remote as this. By the way, what brings you here?"

I thought about how to answer. Should I just tell the truth? *A girl has been kidnapped.* Maybe I should get his help.

But would he believe me? I wasn't sure. If I said that my transplanted left eye showed me visions that had been burned into its retina, would he think it a lie? If I said that a girl was being held captive, would he laugh at me?

"I'm looking for someone," I explained. It wasn't incorrect. I was looking for Saori and Hitomi Aizawa—and the killer. "Oh, is there a woman who works here?"

Kimura said with a grin, "Did you come here looking for Saori too?"

I was startled for a moment. It was the first time I'd heard her name coming from another's mouth.

"Looking for—too?"

"That girl has a fan—that jackass who gave you a ride, he comes here to see her. When I told him she was home sick with a cold he took off. You'd think the bastard could've at least ordered something first."

He cursed.

When I heard Saori wasn't there, I was both disappointed and relieved. I wouldn't have known what to do, suddenly faced with her. I wasn't ready for it yet.

But I had confirmed that she still worked at Melancholy Grove, just as she had in my left eye. She hadn't quit her job after Kazuya's death.

Gentle music played inside the café, so softly as to be nearly unnoticeable. As I listened to it, I held a sip of my café au lait in my mouth. I wondered if Kazuya had experienced the same taste.

I brushed my hand along the counter. The seat Kazuya had once sat in. The chair he had touched.

I stood up, I bent over, I leaned around, filling in the rough sketch of the café I had seen in my left eye. Kimura and Kyoko watched me curiously. I told myself to keep quiet and sat straight up in my seat, sipping my café au lait.

A woman came from the back of the café and announced to the owner, "I took out the trash."

She wiped her hands on the front of her sweater. She had long hair in a ponytail, and probably because she had been outside, her cheeks—and her nose—were red.

"I lied to that guy from before," Kimura told me.

The woman pulled a tissue from behind the counter and blew her nose into it. She noticed I was watching her and looked embarrassed.

"Sorry, my nose has been bad since I was born."

It looked like it hadn't been allergies after all. This was the first time I'd heard her speak. Just as I'd imagined, her voice sounded stuffed up, and yet it seemed to suit her.

"Saori Fuyutsuki…"

She tilted her head as if to ask how I knew her name.

I continued. "It's nice to meet you. I'm…"

I couldn't stop, and the words tumbled out: "I'm Kazuya's friend."

Saori and Kimura drew in their breath.

The truth is, this isn't the first time we've met. I've known you for a long time. I feel like we've been together since we were little. On the outside, I kept my composure, but on the inside, I was crying.

3

"Come over to my house," Saori said, after I told her I didn't have a place to stay that night. I had the money to rent a room for the night, but there wasn't really a proper hotel in Kaede. Though I felt bad for the imposition, I took Saori up on her offer. Truth be told, a part of me had hoped she would offer, and I was eager to see her home with my own eyes.

"Could you wait until we close for the night?"

I nodded. She wasn't too busy with work, so she talked with me. I still only half believed I was seeing her moving and talking. I

stared at her face. It must have been the same feeling as reuniting
with a long-lost relative. With my almost nonexistent memories,
she was the closest thing to a relative I had.

But to her, I was a person who had appeared out of nowhere.
I started to forget that fact.

After Kyoko paid her bill and left, Kimura said, "That's enough
for today. I don't think we'll be getting any more customers
anyway. Take the girl and go on home. Since she's Kazuya's
friend..."

There was concern for her in his voice. I realized that Kazuya's
death had badly bruised their world.

Saori and I left the café. For the first time, I walked at her
side—although in my memories I'd done it many times before. I
remembered how it had looked.

The outside was cold, and as soon as I'd exited the café I felt
my body begin to chill. My cheeks, having relaxed in the warm
air of the heater, tensed up as if I'd been slapped. The lighted
walls and the sign seemed to float in the darkness. The road cut
through a cedar forest and was quiet and dark.

Sniffling, Saori said, "Where we're going—it's actually my
uncle's."

"I heard about that from Kazuya."

After they lost their parents, the two children were taken in by
a man who lived in the neighborhood. I'd seen it in my left eye.

"The two of us are living together now."

"What about your aunt?"

"Just a little before Kazuya's accident, she caught pneumonia
and died."

I hadn't seen that in my left eye. I realized that there was a lot
I still didn't know. The visions I'd seen were only fragments of
what Kazuya had experienced in his life.

The area around us was lonely, with few homes. Saori had
said that it was about a fifteen-minute walk to her house from
the café. My teeth chattered from the cold. There were many
trees on either side of the road. I saw a pile of abandoned cars

formed into a giant clump of rust. Deserted shacks emerged from the darkness.

There was the sound of a bird flapping its wings. It was dark so I couldn't see for sure, but a bird that looked like a raven was flying near the tops of the conifers.

I thought back to my first conversation with Saori in Melancholy Grove.

"Kazuya isn't here," she had said. For a moment those words had felt strange to me. They gave the impression that her brother had just stepped outside for a moment. Her voice was flat, with only a faint tinge of sadness.

"I know about the traffic accident."

"Oh..." Her eyes lowered.

"Please, could you tell me what happened after he died?"

And that was how I learned how his death had been handled. Two months ago Kazuya had been struck by a car on the road. The driver had called for an ambulance, but Kazuya had died by the time it arrived. Saori had seen his body in the hospital. It hurt to try to imagine what that moment must have been like. After their parents had died, Kazuya had been Saori's only family.

I asked her what day it had happened. It was right before I underwent the transplant surgery. The accident took place on a mountain road about a ten-minute drive away from Kaede.

The blue house of Hitomi Aizawa's kidnapper wasn't far from the site of the accident. If anyone was to blame for Kazuya's death, it was that kidnapper.

I had to go to the scene of the accident and I had to find the kidnapper. Since only two months had passed, I thought that Hitomi might still be alive. According to the newspaper, she had been kidnapped a year earlier, but Kazuya had seen her two months ago. This I knew from the date of his death. If the kidnapper hadn't taken her life in ten months, I could assume she still lived.

I composed myself. To save Hitomi I needed to find the house and I needed to obtain evidence; then I could just report it to the police.

As I walked alongside Saori I decided that the very next day, I would take real steps to find the kidnapper. I was afraid. I was worried that I wouldn't be able to do it.

Soon I saw Saori's house.

My left eye had shown me the day Saori and Kazuya had moved into their uncle's place. A sign reading ISHINO was next to the front door. That was their uncle's last name.

Kazuya's viewpoint had been low to the ground, so he must have still been a child. Saori pulled him by the hand into the house. His feeling of helplessness was conveyed through my left eye. Desperately gripping his sister's hand, Kazuya turned his eyes upon unfamiliar walls and furnishings.

Saori looked into my—that is to say, Kazuya's—eyes and smiled. *Everything's fine, don't be afraid.* Saori was a young child too—she had to be afraid herself. But still she lent her brother courage.

Their new life with the Ishinos had just begun. Mr. Ishino was indifferent to the children. I saw him driving a truck and assumed he was a truck driver. But Kazuya's eye held no memories of him smiling and talking with Saori and Kazuya. It was Mrs. Ishino who looked after the two.

Saori said, "This is my uncle's home. Where Kazuya lived."

She entered ahead of me, probably to explain to Mr. Ishino.

I waited at the entryway. I wasn't bored.

I walked back to the front gate and looked at the house. I felt excited. The newspaper box. The small gate. It was a typical house.

I don't remember much from when I awoke in the hospital and returned to my own home. I don't think I felt much. But standing at the front of the house where Kazuya had lived, I was so overwhelmed with nostalgia I could hardly breathe. Even though it was my first time there, it was as if I'd known it forever.

I had many memories of the front of the house. I'd experienced them through my eye.

Kazuya walked past here on his way to grade school. On his way back from high school, he'd stopped in an arcade and come home late at night. His sister had stood angry at the front door.

"Nami, you can come on in," Saori said from the doorway. The memory of her scolding her little brother with her hands on her hips overlapped with the real her waving me inside. "Is there something funny?" she asked.

I thought I'd be nervous going into someone else's home, but oddly enough, I wasn't. For the first time, I felt in my heart the comfort of being in a familiar place. I went through the small entryway and down a hall. There was a fairly steep staircase—above it, I knew, was Kazuya's room.

The living room was a modest-sized Japanese-style room, with straw tatami-mat flooring. A kotatsu table was in the center of the room; scattered magazines, satsuma mandarins, and a TV remote formed a mess across it.

A gray-haired man in a tracksuit looked at me and bowed his head. He sure looked like an uncle.

"Hello." His voice was higher than I'd imagined it. He was probably around sixty years old. Before I actually met him I had perceived him as a frightening man. In Kazuya's memories he was always yelling at his wife.

But the man bowing his head before me was smaller than I'd expected. His hair had turned gray and his smile seemed weak. How old were the memories of him in my left eye? He was different now—not just older, but drained of spirit and left dry.

It seemed like he still worked regularly and took care of Saori every day. He had even prepared some rice for her.

"I apologize for the mess. Nami, you haven't eaten yet, have you?"

He invited me to sit at the kotatsu and I did.

Usually I felt that wherever I was, I was an inconvenience; whenever I did anything I felt vaguely ashamed of it. Maybe it was because I thought I was inferior to Nami. Here that feeling was faint. My eyes would land on something I'd seen before—on a shelf or in a cabinet—and I'd be struck with an impulse to brazenly pick it up and examine it from all sides.

At Saori's insistence I ate dinner with them. While she was

preparing the meal, I talked with her uncle.

"Did you come here to visit Kazuya's grave?" he asked.

"Yes, I know I'm late, but..."

I had thought up the reason before I'd left on the trip.

"Saori can take you there."

From the kitchen, separated from the living room by a sliding door, came the sound of Saori getting out the dishes.

"You know," I said, "I've heard a lot about you and Saori from Kazuya."

"You have? Kazuya never said a word about being friends with someone like you."

"Well, that's..." I trailed off.

"I'm glad you came," he said and lowered his head. I thought it odd. In the memories of my left eye, I'd never seen him give Kazuya a single smile. But his words sounded like they came from the bottom of his heart.

I never imagined I'd be sitting around a dinner table with Saori and her uncle. I didn't know if I should feel moved or just plain confused.

I wondered what they thought of me. *Do they think it was rude of me to show up all of a sudden?*

If they did, they didn't show it. They didn't talk much over dinner. It was almost as if they weren't even aware of each other's presence. Even with the three of us, I still felt alone.

In my memories dinnertime had been merrier. Maybe it had just felt that way because Mrs. Ishino had still been in good health and all four of them had been around the table.

The remaining two now seemed tired and worn out. I was nervous and could hardly taste the food, and as I watched them silently eat their meals, I grew sad.

Within the thick silence I found the courage to ask what kind of person Kazuya had been.

"He was a coward," Saori said, "and he was lazy. He was bad at school, and he wasn't athletic. There really wasn't anything good about him."

After Kazuya graduated from high school, he had enrolled at a college. But the courses were too difficult for him, and he had dropped out. He had spent the year leading up to the accident in Kaede doing nothing.

"But," she added, "he was a kind boy."

I nodded, but I realized that I didn't really know anything about him. In the visions of my left eye, the eye was his own. I had only seen his face when by chance it had been reflected in a mirror or glass. But I did know from the fragments of his memories that Kazuya hadn't been an exceptional student. And I knew that he'd never had enough friends for the eye to have recorded him in the midst of a group of people. I had the vague impression that as a child he'd been the exact opposite of who I had been when I had my own memory—when I had been Nami.

Besides, couldn't you get a good idea of who most people are based on what they look at? Even when a number of people took pictures of the same scenery, their photos would be different from one another's.

What did Kazuya choose to look at? I didn't have an immediate answer.

I went to the bathroom. While I was there, I washed my face and looked into the mirror above the sink. Did Kazuya's eye, having somehow escaped the grave, feel any nostalgia for being back in his home? Kazuya's toothbrush was next to the sink, where it had probably remained for the past two months. I hadn't seen any memories of such trivial details, but for some reason I thought the toothbrush had been his.

When I returned to the living room the two watched me with curious expressions.

"Nice job finding the bathroom," Saori said. "Most people who come over end up getting lost."

✳

They let me stay in the guest room, Saori bringing me a futon from the closet. But before I went to sleep there was something I had to do. When I had trouble finding the right words, Saori asked me what was wrong.

I decided just to say it.

"I want to see Kazuya's room."

Saori stared at me for a moment, then smiled.

Kazuya's room had been preserved just as I had seen it in the visions of my left eye.

"I still clean it," Saori said as I looked around the room. "I know there's no reason to, but I still air out his futon."

There was a large jigsaw puzzle. The picture on it was of a boy sitting on a motorcycle holding a stuffed sheep. My left eye suddenly grew warm. The box of memories opened and what Kazuya had seen came back to life.

"This puzzle..." It took me a moment to realize I had spoken. "A piece of it was missing and there was a huge fight..."

Saori nodded. "I found it in the vacuum cleaner. I'd gone into his room to clean without telling him."

So that's why they're fighting, I thought. In my left eye I was in the middle of an argument with a still youthful Saori. I couldn't hear our voices, so I hadn't known what the fight was about.

Saori took a tissue from a box in the room and blew her nose. She looked lonely.

"My brother told you all kinds of things, didn't he?"

As the memory of the puzzle ended, another vision began to play in my left eye. An uncontrollable succession of memories came to life. The many objects in his room—his desk, his books—became keys to unlock the visions. His experiences, both happy and sad, took root deep within me.

The visions were not fleeting flashbulb illuminations—they played at the same speed as real life. I watched time go by in the past just as time passed by in the present. In my left eye, I saw a young Saori smiling; in my right, she looked lonely.

Saori sat on Kazuya's bed.

"Who told you my brother had died?"

I was at a loss for words. *Who should I say?* As I searched for an answer that would sound natural, she continued:

"The police think it could have been suicide."

Did I hear her right? I had assumed it had been treated as a traffic accident, but I hadn't thought it through any further.

"The driver who hit him said that my brother had suddenly leapt out into the road. And Kazuya had been acting strangely since a little before the accident. Something was weighing on his mind—he kept getting lost in thought. He seemed unwell." Saori gave me a beseeching look. "I thought that maybe you knew something about what was bothering him...?"

My heart ached for her. I did know something about what was bothering him. He had seen the kidnapped girl.

Kazuya's eye had shown me his memory of Hitomi Aizawa. He had fled and been struck by a car. In the days leading up to his death he must have been thinking about the girl held captive in that house.

Apparently he hadn't told anyone about Hitomi. Maybe he, like me, had wanted to find solid evidence that Hitomi was here before going to the police. And that was why he had been acting strangely.

I told her plainly, "It wasn't suicide."

She looked into my eyes. For a moment she appeared startled, but that quickly vanished.

Saori let out a deep breath. She lowered her gaze and said, almost in a whisper. "Of course it wasn't. I...I don't know why, but when Kazuya died, I didn't cry. And even now, I'm not sad. When everyone else is crying, why am I—his own sister—fine? Why?"

Saori had started to play with something in her hands. I looked to see what it was—it was Kazuya's precious wristwatch. It was gold-colored, with a broken strap.

Saori, noticing that I was looking at the watch, said, "I gave this to him on his twentieth birthday."

I hadn't known that, but I did know the watch was important

to him. Even after the strap tore he had still carried it with him in his pocket.

"It broke in the accident, stopped at the time he died." She held it out to me. "Will you take it?"

I shook my head. "He'd want you to keep it."

I knew that was what he'd think—it was what I thought. Besides, I already had an important keepsake of his.

Saori stood.

"Shall we go visit his grave tomorrow?"

I nodded. I wanted to see it.

We left Kazuya's room and went back downstairs. On the way she said, "Something surprised me when I looked at your eyes earlier. They look just like his."

✳

Kazuya was buried next to his parents in a graveyard outside of town, an hour's walk from the house.

"If you'd rather take a car there," Saori offered, "I can ask a friend of mine who has a driver's license."

She didn't have one herself. I told her I wanted to walk.

Countless rows of gravestones rested at the base of a mountain with a magnificent view. There were so many markers that I couldn't tell where Kazuya's was at first.

Gravel paths passed between the evenly spaced gravestones. Without hesitation, Saori chose one of the paths and started down. Though there were no signs, she knew the way. I followed after her, not wanting to get left behind.

The Fuyutsuki family grave was at the edge of the graveyard. Saori cleaned it up and brushed off the fallen leaves.

We put our hands together and offered a prayer.

I gave Kazuya my heartfelt thanks. *Thank you for giving me your eye.*

I couldn't comprehend how completely his memories had redeemed me. I had had almost nothing; they were nearly the entire world to me now.

I thought back to the tragic memory I'd seen in the home improvement store, the memory of their parents' death.

On the way back from the graveyard, Saori blew her nose and said, "Mom and Dad were unlucky. The rope holding the logs on the truck just snapped."

We were heading to Melancholy Grove. On the way, we cut across the highway that passed through the center of town. We went by many places from Kazuya's memories.

"I heard that Kazuya saw the accident happen," I said.

Saori halted and looked at me in shock.

"Did Kazuya tell you that?"

I didn't understand her reaction, but I nodded.

"That's what the other people who were there said. But he didn't remember it. He insisted that he never witnessed it. I think it was just such a horrible memory, he forgot it to protect himself."

I thought her reasoning made unusually perfect sense. After all, it had happened to me too.

But even if his mind had forgotten what happened, the images had remained seared into his retina.

"The accident was apparently caused by a boy who had just started working at the lumber mill that season."

"A boy?"

"He was barely out of high school, and he tied the rope. But he didn't know the proper knots..."

No resentment colored Saori's voice. If anything, I'd have said she pitied the boy.

The walk from the graveyard to Melancholy Grove took about an hour.

I remembered the rows of stores and houses, even though I'd never been there before. The storefronts of the stationery store and the rice shop were unchanged from Kazuya's memories.

We found a candy shop. The inside was quite dark and I wondered if they were open. Bags of candy lined the shelves in the window, so I knew it hadn't gone out of business, but I thought I could see a thin layer of dust on top of the bags.

"Do you want to go inside?" Saori asked. "Kazuya used to

come here all the time, back in the day."

When we stepped through the door, an old woman emerged from the rear. She had been watching TV in the back room.

"You haven't changed a bit," Saori said with a contented smile. When she smiled like that she looked just like a cat.

The old woman's face hadn't aged a year from when Kazuya was a little boy.

I bought a lollipop and licked it while we walked.

Saori blew her nose, her shoulders shaking. She tossed her used tissue onto the ground.

"Is it okay to just throw it away like that?" I asked.

"I believe it's all dust in the end."

I tried to make sense of her words but eventually realized that it was just too much of an inconvenience for her to carry the tissue home.

I gazed out to where utility poles made a line through the dead grass. Occasionally we passed people on the road, and as we did Saori would bow her head to them. They all looked at me with eyes that said, "Who the hell is that?"

I felt like I had lived here for the longest time. Everywhere I looked, I saw places I recognized. But when the people made those faces at me, it made me realize that to the town I was only a visitor.

Visitor. The word sank deep into my heart. I felt like a traveler who had come to this world by mistake. I was Nami and yet I wasn't. *So what am I? Where did I come from?* Those were the thoughts that came to me at times.

Through some working of fate, I'd arrived in this world and now was in the town of Kaede. I was a visitor.

The sky was cloudy and the sun's light weak. It was dark for afternoon. I thought it might start to snow at any moment.

The whole town was quiet. The air hung cold over the dried-up streets. A thin wind blew through the wire fencing and shook the limbs of the lifeless trees. Few people were out and fewer still were smiling.

It felt like the town was dying. Its vitality gone, it slowly marched to death, a gray town on the verge of oblivion.

Five minutes away from Melancholy Grove, Saori stopped.

"Let's take a detour," she said.

We took a side road toward the mountains. The road sloped gently, and as we went up it the city appeared lower and lower below us. On one side of the road was the edge of the cedar forest. On the other side was a guardrail and beyond that more trees. The scent of the trees was rich in the air. When I looked up, the cedars on each side of the road were pointing straight up at the gray sky.

After we had walked a little while, Saori stopped. She looked down at the asphalt pavement, silent.

I understood. This was where Kazuya's life had ended.

Saori was expressionless. I couldn't tell where on the road her eyes were fixed. I thought back to when she'd told me that she hadn't cried, not even when she saw his body. Although everyone around her was sad, she was the only one who couldn't cry.

To me, her heart was like a vast hole—a dark, bottomless void where nothing remained. Maybe she hadn't recovered from the shock of her brother's death.

She seemed weak, like she might just disappear into nothingness on the spot. I squeezed her hand, and she looked at me in surprise.

I didn't know what about it was making me sad. Whether it was Kazuya's death or Saori, I couldn't say. But my heart hurt so badly I could barely stand it.

I looked up toward the mountains. Somewhere up the slope from where I stood would be the blue brick house. That was where it had been in the memories of my left eye.

We stood quietly next to each other, neither of us saying a word. The oppressive presence of the cedar trees enveloped the place where Kazuya had lost his life.

❈

212 BLACK FAIRY TALE

When we opened the door to the café, a bell inside rang. To our relief, the warm air of the space heater was waiting for us.

Saori bowed to the owner and said, "Suddenly coming into a warm place from the cold really melts my sinuses."

"Sinuses can melt?"

"Well, it all comes out like water."

Saori blew her nose. In the café at least she threw her refuse into the wastebasket.

Sitting at the counter was the man who had given me the ride the day before. When we first came in he was slumped over his coffee, but when he saw Saori he quickly sat up straight.

"Saori!" He waved at her, his face beaming.

"Oh, welcome back," she replied.

Later I learned his name was Sumida. He had been friends with Kazuya.

Because they'd been friends for only a year, there were few visions of Sumida burned into my eye. A little later I did see a memory of them hanging out.

They had met the year before. Sumida had carried Kazuya—who'd passed out drunk in front of the train station—into the coffee shop. Apparently they'd met at a pub earlier that same day and really hit it off.

And even after Kazuya's death, Sumida kept going to the coffee shop.

"How's college?" Saori asked him.

"Well, good now that I'm on break."

His face turned bright red. He was easy to read.

"Thanks for yesterday," I said. Now that I knew he had been friends with Kazuya, I felt closer to him.

He turned an affable smile my way. "Kimura told me all about you."

I sat at a table and watched Sumida and Saori talk across the counter.

The bearlike Kimura brought a glass of warm milk over to

my table. As I drank it, I felt the chill from the long walk leave my body.

Saori, talking with Sumida, seemed like a different person from when we'd stood by the road together. Her voice was bright, as though she'd completely forgotten about her brother. I sensed it was a little more complicated than that, but maybe it was a good thing.

Shiozaki, the man who'd sat in the back of the café the day before, wasn't around, but Kyoko was in the same seat as before. Our eyes met and she smiled and motioned me over.

"Were you Saori's brother's girlfriend?"

"What?"

"That's what Kimura said."

Oh. So that's who people think I am.

"I just said that I was his friend..."

I couldn't look her in the eye. I could feel my cheeks blushing and I didn't want anyone to see.

"I just moved to Kaede," she said. "I only started coming in here a few months back. So I never got the chance to talk with Kazuya much."

I wondered if she had been in any of my left eye's memories. I couldn't remember the faces of each and every one of the vast number of people Kazuya had met in his lifetime. The only ones I could recall without much effort were the people close to him, like his uncle and the owner of the café.

Kyoko took my hand. The skin of her fingers was tough and wrinkled. "Poor thing. Keep your spirits high. I had a child your age once too."

I stayed inside the café for a while, drinking my milk. When I had finished, I went to pay.

"Don't worry about it," said Kimura. "It's on the house."

"Nami," asked Saori, "where are you going?"

"Just on a walk."

"Don't get lost."

She was truly worried for me. I smiled and nodded in response. She had told me I could stay at her uncle's house as long as I wished.

I went outside. The warmth the heater had provided me began to fade.

I headed for the site of Kazuya's accident.

On the way I thought about him. I had a memory of him, alone in the large playground of his grade school, crying. The sight of the beautiful skies and flora he had seen replayed in my mind.

I loved Kazuya. All of the light he had seen streamed into my heart. *How many things are burned into a person's eyes over the course of a life?*

I must find the kidnapper. I want to teach him. I want to show him the value of the life he stole.

The air where Kazuya had died felt colder than everywhere else. The sky was cloudy and the shadows of the cedar trees reduced the world to silhouettes. The sound of flapping wings came intermittently from deep within the forest.

I felt my body begin to tremble. Two months ago, Kazuya fell to the road where I stood. And I'd seen the moment of his death. I'd seen the kidnapper hide himself in the shadow of a tree, where he watched Kazuya get struck and die.

I was afraid, but I gathered my courage. I took a right angle from the road and stepped onto the slope of the cedar forest. I headed up the mountainside. The ground was soft with a layer of fallen cedar leaves. In his memory, Kazuya had fallen down the slope and onto the road. I followed the reverse of the path he had likely taken.

I searched in front of me but couldn't see the blue brick house. The view ahead was obstructed by countless cedar trees. The trees seemed like row upon row of pillars. I walked between them.

I had expected my body to warm, for the freezing cold to fade, but it didn't. With each step I took, the cold air snatched away more of my warmth. The noiseless cedar forest seemed to swallow my body heat.

I stuffed my gloved hands into my coat pockets, my fingers

finding the disposable camera that was in one of them. I planned to use it to get photographic proof I could take to the police. Maybe Hitomi Aizawa was still visible through that cellar window.

But just then, I was struck by disbelief.

I had expected to find the kidnapper's house straight up the mountain from the site of the accident. But ahead of me stood a ten-foot-high concrete wall. I could see a guardrail atop it. There seemed to be a road up there. I looked left, and then right, but the wall continued far in each direction.

I was confused. What had happened in Kazuya's memory? He'd entered the forest at the house, and as he was trying to flee he fell down the slope and emerged at the road. Had he crossed another road somewhere in between? Had he jumped over a guardrail and down the side of a concrete wall? No, neither of those things were in his memory.

Where am I?

Mystified, I walked along the concrete wall, searching for a place I could climb.

This wasn't supposed to happen. I was gripped with frustration. The house was gone and in its place was a concrete wall. I couldn't think of an explanation.

After I had walked for another ten minutes, the wall began to shrink as the road atop it approached the ground.

The road snaked through the woods. Had I kept following the road from the site of the accident, I would have ended up on the road above the concrete wall.

When the wall had lowered to my hips, I jumped over it and landed on the asphalt. I slipped under the guardrail.

I had lost the kidnapper's house. As time passed, I became more and more aware of how grave the situation had become. Unless something changed, I would never reach Hitomi.

Finding the site of Kazuya's death and backtracking along the path he had taken to get there had been my only plan for locating the house. That should have led me straight to it.

But that wasn't what happened. I was confused. With no other plan, I walked back down the road toward the town.

I decided to wander around. I thought that maybe I could discover the blue brick house purely by chance.

I strolled around town until nightfall. Several times, such as when I saw an old, broken-down vending machine, my left eye grew warm, and visions of Kazuya's childhood came to life. But I didn't come any closer to finding the kidnapper's house, and I still hadn't found any believable explanation for why reality didn't match Kazuya's memory.

One thing—a rumor I overheard from a group of elementary school students in the candy aisle of the supermarket—stuck with me. It was a strange rumor.

"I swear!" said one boy, clutching a bag of candy. "A long time ago, my cousin really did see it!"

The disbelief of his friends was obvious.

I had been trying to decide what kind of chocolate to buy when I happened to hear his energetic voice.

"Even though the back half of its body had been crushed by a car, it still kept on living!"

"You're full of it," one of the other kids said. "There's no way."

"But he told me he saw it. He said the dog's face looked like nothing was wrong, and it walked with only its two front legs. Its insides spilled out in a straight line on the road, but even with only a head and a heart, it lived for two whole hours. But then a motorcycle came along and ran over its heart and it finally died."

4

I awoke to footsteps in the hallway. I crawled out of my futon. The only things in the empty tatami-floor room were the futon and the backpack I'd brought.

I wiped my eyes and went into the living room. Saori's uncle was there.

"Good morning, Mr. Ishino," I said and then felt vaguely embarrassed. I had come to think of him as my own family.

For an instant wrinkles of surprise formed on a face that looked like it was permeated with cigarette smoke.

"I thought you were Kazuya, wearing that thing." He pointed at my jacket. It was Kazuya's jacket from seventh grade. Saori had given it to me to wear.

We ate the breakfast prepared by Saori, and the old man left for work.

He worked hauling felled cedar trees from the mountains down to the lumber mill. Each morning he put on his work clothes, worn soft from long use, and drove a minicar to work.

As he was getting in his car I called out to him.

"There's something I want you to look at for me."

I took out Hitomi's photograph and showed it to him. I'd cut it out (without permission) from the library's copy of the newspaper.

"Have you ever seen this girl around here?"

He pulled his eyes from the picture to look at me. "Are you looking for her?"

"Yes."

He scratched his head, shaking it from side to side. "No, I haven't seen her."

Saori's response was the same. She had left the TV on in the living room as she cleaned up after breakfast. She didn't remember ever seeing Hitomi's face before.

"What are you doing today?" she asked.

"I'm going to visit all the places Kazuya told me about."

"Well, you can stay here as long as you want. You know, you don't feel like a stranger. It's like Kazuya is here. Even the way you walk and how you eat your rice, it's like him."

"Are you working at the café today?"

She nodded and turned on the kitchen faucet.

"Ever since Kazuya died, I've done nothing but go between this house and the café every day. Nothing else. Once a week I deliver coffee beans to the houses that order it, but I never leave Kaede."

She stopped her work and stared at the flow of water from the tap. A morning show played on the TV in the other room. When the show's horoscope segment came on she turned off the water and hurried to the TV.

She blew her nose. "Oh no, it's a bad day for Virgos."

She gave me a copy of the house key and left for the coffee shop.

"Do you really trust me with this?" I asked as she handed me the key.

"If you steal something, I won't allow it."

I watched her leave, wondering what the heck she was talking about. Probably some quote, not that I'd know it. I sat myself under the kotatsu and thought about why I hadn't been able to find the house from the scene of the accident.

Again I tried to recall the vision I'd seen in my left eye at the library. It had started when I saw the picture of Hitomi Aizawa's face and it had ended when Kazuya was struck down by the car. Already ten days had passed. I took my binder from my backpack and rechecked my notes on the vision.

It began with Kazuya looking through the ground-level window into the cellar. That was when he saw Hitomi. He looked around, and I'd seen that the house was built of blue bricks.

I never saw the entire shape of the house—I didn't know what the roof or the front entrance looked like.

Kazuya had attempted to open the window with a screwdriver but realized that somebody was approaching. Knowing that he had been discovered, he ran into the forest next to the house.

That was where the account got problematic. Had he jumped over that concrete barrier that stopped me yesterday? There wasn't any record of it in my notes.

He'd gone straight from the house into the woods, and as he ran through the forest he'd fallen down a hill, finally emerging where the car had run him down.

I thought it over for a while before realizing another possibility.

Maybe the kidnapper, for whatever reason, had moved the body. If so then the place I saw in my left eye would be different from what I'd been told was the site of the accident.

No, that wasn't it. I was disgusted by my own stupidity. The driver of the car that had hit Kazuya stayed there to call the ambulance. Surely he would have noticed something like that. I couldn't believe that the kidnapper would have been able to emerge from the shadows and move the body.

So had the concrete wall not been there before? Had it been a plain slope two months ago when Kazuya had died? That way he would have been able to run straight through the woods...Then, after his death, first the road was built and then, where the asphalt and the guardrail passed through the cedar forest, the concrete wall.

I could find out quickly enough if my theory was correct just by asking around. All I had to do was ask if the road had been there two months before.

Gathering my thoughts, I headed for the café to find my answer. The only people around town that I knew were there.

I looked at the clock and saw that more time had passed than I'd thought and it was already almost noon.

I went to Melancholy Grove, thinking I might as well get lunch.

Inside I found the café as warm as ever. I felt happy and just for a moment my thoughts of the kidnapper and all the rest of my worries vanished. With a smile, I sat at the counter.

Kimura was alone. "Saori's out on an errand right now," he said.

I ordered lunch. As I waited for my meal to come I looked at the countless tea sets decorating the room. None had any dust that I could see. Was someone meticulously cleaning them? Kimura had thick fingers, so I got the impression that Saori had to be the one doing it.

"I do all the cleaning myself," Kimura said, watching my face. His tone accused me of being rude. He must have read my mind.

When he brought the tray with my lunch, I asked my question.

"That road where Kazuya was in that accident—it snakes up the mountains farther up. When was that part of it built?"

He hummed in thought, trying to remember. His answer was unexpected:

"A long time back. I can't remember. But before I was in my twenties, that's for sure."

Feeling slightly dejected, I showed him Hitomi's photograph. "Have you ever seen this girl?"

He looked at me and said, "What are you, a cop now?" He shook his head. "I don't know her."

"I see...Well, has anyone gone missing around here?"

"Well, I heard about this one guy, an older man who suddenly disappeared. No relatives."

He told me the man's name was Kaneda. Kaneda had lived near town, but no one had seen him for some time.

"People didn't like him much," Kimura explained, "and he owed some folks money, so my guess? I think he ran off to somewhere far away."

It didn't seem like Kaneda had anything to do with me.

"All right, well, do you know of any brick houses around here?"

"That Kyoko, who you were talking to before? If you're looking for a brick house, she lives in one."

"I'm talking about a blue brick house."

"Blue, huh..." He gave a thoughtful nod. "Yeah, I might know something about that."

I was shocked. I hadn't expected he might. "Really? Please tell me!" I leapt from my stool. He tried to calm me down.

"What's so special about that house?"

I thought for a moment and decided there wasn't an easy way to say there was a chance a little girl was being held captive there. "I heard about it from somebody. It sounds like an unusual building and I'd like to see it for myself."

"Shiozaki should be here soon. He always has lunch here. He

knows about the place, so you should be able to get him to take you there."

I looked over at the painting of the lake on the wall that was Shiozaki's work. In it the forest reflected across the still surface of the water.

I never thought I'd find the blue brick house this way. *Shiozaki will take me there, but then what?*

No, it would be too dangerous for him to take me all the way to the house. I have to go around it, where I won't be seen, and then I'll get photographic proof. If we drive up to the house, the kidnapper will realize that I'm after him. I can't let that happen.

What would the kidnapper do if he knew someone suspected him? If Hitomi is still alive it could put her in danger.

The door opened and Shiozaki came in. He went straight to the back of the room and sat at his table in the dark corner. He moved like he didn't even notice any other table in the place.

The manager brought over his food. I'd heard that Shiozaki always came to the café at the same freakishly precise time and always ordered the same meal. Kimura specially prepared his meal without meat. The painter had said that meat tasted of blood; he was a vegetarian.

I became aware that Kimura was talking to Shiozaki about me. I had been watching them when Shiozaki looked over at me. Our eyes met. His gaze was sharp and I grew nervous and lowered my head.

Kimura turned to me. "He says he'll drive you there after he's done eating."

I guessed it would take about an hour for Shiozaki to finish his meal, so I decided to read some of the café's magazines in the meantime.

I had read several novels since losing my memory. After I stopped going to school the printed word and I had become close friends in various cafés. I read indiscriminately, and not just novels but manga and magazines too. Of course, everything I read was new to me.

What kinds of books had I read before I'd lost my memory? Had I read exquisite novels that made me cry? Had I memorized poetry well enough to recite it?

I felt guilty for casting aside those beautiful memories. I knew that it wasn't my fault, knew I didn't need to feel guilty. And yet, when I'd rearranged my room and parted with Nami I had betrayed and abandoned that past.

With these thoughts in my head, I looked through a number of magazines. I decided to try reading a new book. When I rummaged through the bookcase, I found a mysterious-looking one. It was thin and small. It felt new in my hand. I noticed it was a fairy tale book.

The title read *The Eye's Memory*. Smaller and above the title were the words *The Collected Black Fairy Tales*, Volume I.

I flipped through the book and saw there were illustrations every few pages. The pictures were drawn with thin, pitch-black lines and had an eerie feel.

In one of the pictures a raven was using its beak to pluck an eyeball from a child's face. An ominous feeling came over me, making me want to put the book right back on the shelf. And yet I couldn't take my eyes off it; it was as if it had cast a spell over me, drawing me in.

Just as I decided to read it from the beginning, Shiozaki finished his lunch. I returned the book to the shelf.

"Shall we?" he said brusquely as he put on his black coat.

I stepped nervously into his car. I sat in the front passenger seat. Kimura stood outside the café, sending me off with a wave. For some reason he was smiling. I didn't know why he was, but I returned the smile and the wave.

The car started quietly. It was a black car, and while I didn't know much about cars, the seats were spotless and of good quality. A pleasant scent tinged the air.

"Do you mind if I stop to buy something in town first? It won't take long."

I shook my head.

"So you came here to visit Kazuya's grave?"

"Did you know him?"

"I'd seen him a few times."

"You moved here recently?"

"Last year."

He talked to me about art. I knew as much about paintings as I knew about cars. Was he famous?

Apparently he'd painted the piece on display in the café when he had been overseas. Gripping the wheel he said, "I don't know, I just felt like giving it as a present to that café."

How much was that painting worth? And why had Shiozaki decided to move to Kaede? I wanted to ask him, but I kept quiet. He wasn't much of a talker and I worried I would annoy him.

The car stopped in the parking lot of a farm supply store.

He told me he wouldn't take long, so I stayed in the passenger seat. I rested my head in my hands and absentmindedly stared out the window at the side mirror. In it Shiozaki was loading his purchases into the trunk of the car.

He returned to the driver's seat. "We'll go to the house from here."

I nodded nervously.

The kidnapper and Hitomi are there. As soon as I see the house, I'll ask to be let out of the car. As long as I know where I am and what road leads there, it should be enough.

After a short drive we were on the highway that cut through the town, and a little while later we turned onto a side road and headed for the mountains.

"What did you buy?"

His eyes still on the road, he replied, "After that last earthquake, I noticed a crack in one of the walls of my house. So I bought some things to try to repair it."

I hadn't heard of an earthquake. He said it had happened the day before I'd come to Kaede. Now that I thought about it, I hadn't felt anything that could be considered a real earthquake since I had awoken in the hospital.

Staring absentmindedly out the window and watching the scenery pass by, I suddenly saw something I had seen before.

"Stop the car!"

Shiozaki hit the brakes, giving me an inquisitive look.

"There was a park!" I ran from the car. Half buried in the center of a small grove was a clearing. A rusted chain crossed the entrance to this park and from the chain hung a sign reading NO TRESPASSING. The park seemed to have fallen into disuse for whatever reason. Weeds were growing wild. But the slide and jungle gym remained. And though all traces of its original color had rusted away, so did the swing.

I knew immediately that it was the same swing as the one in the calendar picture—the key to the first memory after my eye transplant.

I stood in front of the swing. Shiozaki came up to me.

"A long time ago," I explained, "Saori and Kazuya played together here." I looked at the swing from every angle. "No doubt about it."

Happiness bubbled up inside me. Since I had come to Kaede I had discovered any number of places I had seen in the memories of my left eye. But when I found that swing where Saori had sat smiling, I was especially happy.

I jumped up on the rusted swing. It was only after I'd done so that I realized Shiozaki was watching me. Feeling more than a little undignified, I became embarrassed. I told myself to behave in a more ladylike fashion.

"You've been acting strange all day," Shiozaki said. "At least it's interesting."

He looked into my eyes. At first he did so casually, but then he seemed to notice something and froze.

"What's wrong?" I asked.

"So I haven't just been imagining it. I'd thought your eyes were two different colors. Although it's a subtle difference, barely perceptible..."

I brushed it aside with a laugh. If he found out that I'd had surgery—that one of my eyes had once belonged to someone else—it would be too much trouble to explain. We got back into the car and drove away. Even then I could tell that Shiozaki was still thinking about my eye. *I'm sure it's an artist thing. They're bound to be interested in unusual appearances.* I dismissed it and relaxed.

After a time we came upon a road I had seen before. With its cedar trees lining both sides the area was dark even in the afternoon.

"Is this where Kazuya..."

Shiozaki nodded, his hands on the wheel. We were on the road where Kazuya's accident had been.

I was relieved to find that the blue brick house was down this street after all. The visions of my left eye hadn't been that far from reality—there were only a few trivial differences.

We drove past the site of Kazuya's accident. It wasn't a nice feeling, being in a car and passing over the spot where another car had hit him. The moment we did so I closed my eyes. I felt a shiver run down my back.

As we drove farther the road curved to the left, and soon we were facing the opposite direction we had been going before.

On the left-hand side of the car was a guardrail. The concrete dropped off on the other side and I couldn't see the ground, only cedar trees poking up from below. That was where I had come the day before.

I asked Shiozaki the same question I had asked Kimura. "When was this road built?"

"I don't know, but it was here when I moved here."

We passed a side street.

"Kyoko Kurozuka lives down that way," said Shiozaki.

This time the road curved to the right.

After a while, Shiozaki stopped the car and instructed me to look outside.

I was positioned just perfectly to look up the slope. I put my face to the window and looked up the mountain from below.

The forest of cedar trees crowded my view, but between the trees' vertical trunks I saw the color.

Blue. But not the bright blue of the sky. A deep blue that looked almost black.

At the other edge of the cedar forest stood the house I'd been searching for. My skin tingled with apprehension. As far away from the house as I was, I couldn't tell for sure if it had been built from brick. But the blue color was the same as I remembered it from the vision.

The kidnapper is there. And he's hiding Hitomi. I wondered what kind of person the kidnapper was.

Although I had been trying to keep her image out of my mind, I thought again about the figure of the girl I had seen in the memory of my left eye. Maybe I had seen it wrong, but it had looked like she didn't have any limbs.

What had happened to them? *If that was the kidnapper's doing, then how dreadfully cruel he must be.*

I asked Shiozaki, "Do you know much about that house?"

He told me what he knew and I got out of the car.

"I'm just satisfied knowing that the house actually exists," I said. "I'd made a bet with Kazuya. I didn't believe him when he said it was real."

"If you're going home, I can take you back to the café."

I declined the offer. "Thank you very much, but I remember the way, and I'd like to walk back."

I bowed to him. He gave me a skeptical look and drove off. *Did he notice the trembling in my voice?* I'd acted as naturally as I could.

He had told me about the house:

"Kimura said you wanted to see it, so how about coming up for some tea?"

Then he had looked me in the eye and said, "There's no need to be polite. I live there."

✳

Shiozaki's car drove away and I went into the conifer forest alongside the road to wait awhile. I thought it would be best not to go up to the house immediately. I wanted to get there after he had already gotten home and was settled inside.

He's the one who lives in the blue house. He's the kidnapper. I sat in his car, not knowing anything. We talked! I couldn't believe it.

I thought about the smile on Kimura's face when we had left the café. He'd been hiding the fact that Shiozaki lived in the house. I was enraged by his prank even though I knew I was being unreasonable.

After a half hour had passed I headed for the house. I had spent the time mentally preparing myself for what was to come.

Cars passed rarely along the road—there was one maybe every ten minutes or so. Farther down the road had been the site of Kazuya's accident. For him, at the end of the chase, to be struck by a car that just happened to be passing by—that had to be some really lousy luck.

I had trouble deciding whether to approach the house from the street or from within the trees. In the end I figured that if I were to take the road and Shiozaki were to happen to drive back down it, it would be too much trouble to come up with an explanation for why I was walking up the street. So I went with the forest.

As at the scene of Kazuya's accident, the cedar trees along the road were on a sharp incline. All the roads passing through the mountains seemed to be similar—on one side a steep slope, on the other a guardrail and a small drop.

Taking care not to slip, I climbed up the slope. The layer of dead leaves on the ground made it easy to fall. As I continued up, the incline started to level out.

The closer I got to the blue house, the more a different type of tree joined with the cedar. Their leaves had fallen and their limbs seemed to reach out like feelers. I had seen them in my left eye's memory: as Kazuya fled into the forest he had struggled against their branches.

The cold was fierce. My breath exhaled white and vanished among the trees. I counted each tree I passed by and slapped its trunk with my gloved hand. By the time the count reached fifty, I had grown tired of the game.

Before much longer the blue house towered before me. It was two stories tall and, as I'd expected, was made of brick. The building seemed like a giant curled-up monster clutching on to darkness. It lurked at the back of the forest, gazing through gaps between trees at the humans in the world below, an ominous creature inspecting the world with narrowed eyes. Seeing the house close up, I felt like I was being watched with grim intentions.

Frozen on the spot, I stared up at the walls of the house. They seemed to breathe. Like an animal about to swell its lungs to take in air, the brick walls gave the illusion of smooth contraction.

My legs wouldn't move. I had become aware of the danger I was in. *If I'm discovered, what will happen to me?* I imagined the worst and found myself unable to draw any nearer to the house.

Closing my eyes, I waited for courage to come. I thought about Kazuya, and I thought about Hitomi.

I pulled the camera from my pocket. Barely hidden among the trees, I looked for signs that anyone else was around, satisfying myself that Shiozaki was nowhere near.

I moved through the shadows of the trees to emerge from the forest. I pushed my body snug against the wall of the building.

Touching my hand to the wall, I knew I hadn't been wrong—it was the same wall I had seen in my left eye's vision. Even through my glove, its surface felt cold enough to freeze my soul.

I looked up. The house rose high into the gray clouds.

I moved along the wall of the house, looking at the ground as I walked. The cellar window had to be somewhere.

The house was surrounded by woods. But between the wall and the trees was a gap just wide enough for a person to pass through. The ground was bare earth, its surface smooth. The wall and the earth met at a right angle and at their intersection sat a number of planters of the same blue brick as the house, but nothing grew in them except dead grass.

Only the front side of the house was not fringed by the forest. But I didn't want to be anywhere I might easily be seen, so I stayed away from that side of the building.

I thought back to the vision of my left eye. The cellar window wasn't at the front of the house. Also, Kazuya had used a corner of the building to hide himself. The window must be near a corner. And where Kazuya ran into the forest, the ground sloped down. He had to have been at one of the corners at the back of the house.

Soon I found a place that closely matched what I had seen in my left eye. It was the southwest corner.

The surroundings were almost the same. But maybe because some time had passed, the shape and the shadows of the nearby plants felt slightly different.

But I still couldn't find the cellar window. There was nothing like it in the wall. The spot where I thought Kazuya had found the window was only a brick planter filled with thick dead grass at the base of the wall.

Maybe Shiozaki had constructed the planter there to hide the window. It wasn't a stretch to believe that it could have been built in the two months that had passed since Kazuya's death.

If I broke through the planter, it might reveal the window on the other side. But the bricks looked sturdy.

The window had been covered up. I wouldn't be able to find any evidence to take a picture of.

It was frustrating, but in the end I decided to withdraw for the day. I would need stronger nerves before I could go walking around the house in search of evidence.

I looked around the rear of the building. Attached to the wall was an old wooden shed. Now that I thought about it, Shiozaki had bought some things from the farm supply store that day. Something to repair a wall, he'd said. They might be inside the shed.

I decided to look inside the shed before I left and walked toward it.

From the second floor came the sound of a window opening.

Immediately I froze, and then, pressed up against the wall and careful not to make any sound, I moved away. I thought Shiozaki might poke his head out the window at any moment.

I ran into the forest, perhaps on the very same path that Kazuya had taken. I looked back over my shoulder, but I saw no signs that Shiozaki had followed me. Still, inside I felt a shadow chasing after me.

At last I cautiously emerged from the slope and onto the road. Free now from my terror, I cried a little.

5—AN AUTHOR OF FAIRY TALES

Miki looked at the half-crushed fly in the palm of his hand. It had been bothering the limbless Hitomi as she sat on the couch in the study.

"I couldn't stand it," she said, relieved. "I couldn't do anything to shoo it away."

It wasn't that her wounds had grown rotten and attracted the fly. Wounds inflicted by Miki didn't rot. The fly had just happened to be nearby.

When it landed on her sack, he'd crushed the insect, its bodily fluids leaving a small stain on the fabric.

He looked at the smashed fly stuck to the palm of his hand. It still moved.

"That has to be annoying," Hitomi said. "You can't even kill a single fly easily."

Miki had two options: crush the pest completely until its movements ceased altogether or throw it outside while it still barely squirmed. He moved to the window.

"So that fly too will be eaten alive by ants," said Hitomi.

Just as he opened the window, Miki froze.

Cautiously, he stuck his head outside to look around.

"Is someone there?" asked Hitomi.

The study was on the rear side of the house. He'd thought he'd heard a noise from the area between the house and the surrounding forest.

But no one was there. Maybe it had just been his imagination.

"I just know somebody's come to rescue me. They must have figured out that you're a kidnapper."

Miki walked out of the study, leaving Hitomi in the room.

"Where are you going?" she asked. Then, after a pause, she answered her own question. "Oh, that's right, you're going to bury the Old Man."

✳

Kaneda had died in the cellar a short time before.

As Miki had been carrying Hitomi to her bed, Yukie Mochinaga said from behind the shelves, "Something's wrong with the Old Man."

By that time, Kaneda was already near death in the corner of the cellar.

Miki took his new shovel and went outside. He walked along the brick walls to the back of the house.

He looked around. Whatever he had heard from the second floor window was no longer there.

The still trees spread out around him. Pushing aside the layers of leafless branches, Miki stepped into the forest. After a short walk, he found a suitable place to bury Kaneda. He stuck the tip of the shovel into the ground. The earth had frozen, but with a little effort he was able to dig.

✳

Miki first met Kaneda shortly after he had moved into the house—two weeks before he dragged Shinichi and Yukie into the cellar.

At that time, Miki had not interacted much with any of his neighbors. Because his house was up in the mountains, nobody bothered to come calling on him unless he first sought out company. He secluded himself there and lived as if nobody resided in the home.

Consequently he didn't learn until later that Kaneda lived in the area.

The man had come to the house and looked at Miki as if he were inspecting a strange creature.

"I didn't think that anybody lived here," he said.

Miki invited him in. He wavered for a bit before passing through the front door.

"Do we leave our shoes on? This house is like a castle."

Kaneda was a shabby-looking man. He was short and he walked with a stoop. Half his hair was gone. He seemed very interested in both how Miki lived and how Miki made a living.

Outside, rain began to fall. Miki moved his attention from the old man and went up to the study to shut a window he'd left open.

Just then a scream came from the first floor. While Miki had been away, the old man had gone rooting around in the refrigerator. Inside he'd found rows of ears and fingers lined up one by one like eggs in a carton. Miki had brought these with him when he moved.

Kaneda was slumped onto his knees when Miki plunged the kitchen knife into his stomach. He bound the old man with a roll of nearby packing tape and led him down to the basement.

Kaneda looked down at the kitchen knife still sticking out of his own stomach. "I feel strange," he said in an reverent whisper. Happiness shone in his eyes. He seemed to have forgotten to wonder why he didn't feel any pain.

Miki leaned the old man against the wall of the cellar and asked him what he wanted to do—live or die?

If he wanted to die Miki could cut off his head. From his previous experiences Miki had learned that when he separated the brain and the heart, death was soon to visit. Or the old man could wait for his wound to close. When wounds that Miki inflicted closed, the life force that had come into the body left as well. Then the man could be left for hunger or old age to overcome him.

Kaneda chose to live.

Miki made a vertical opening in his stomach. He cut through the skin and split the muscle, revealing the ribs and organs inside. After that the man wasn't able to say a single word.

Miki turned Kaneda's body inside out.

He cut the old man open and emptied him. He took everything that had been on the outside and switched it to the inside, and everything that had been on the inside to the outside.

Kaneda's hands and feet were put on the inside, with his skin and muscles covering them. Miki severed the man's bones one by one and then, using screws, secured them back in place facing the opposite way. He decorated the bones with Kaneda's organs, and secured the organs with wire to keep them in their new places.

During all this, Kaneda didn't die and he didn't pass out. There was very little blood—almost subconsciously, Miki avoided the arteries as he worked the scalpel he had brought with him from his parents' home. Even when blood did start to flow, it quickly ceased. Miraculously, Kaneda's organs, now exposed outside of his body, retained their fresh sheen and never dried.

In the end everything from Kaneda's neck down had been flipped inside out. His exposed organs drooped weakly from the wires where they had been fastened so they wouldn't fall.

Kaneda was no longer able to support the weight of his own body, and without any support he would have collapsed. Miki suspended dozens of fishhooks with fishing line from the ceiling of the cellar and on them he hung Kaneda's organs and wires to force the old man upright. The tips of Kaneda's fingers and toes poked out from where they had been stuffed into his lower torso; from time to time, they moved with froglike hops.

Kaneda was still conscious and Miki could read his feelings

from his eyes. Awe was in those eyes. Tears were flowing from them, but Miki knew they were tears of euphoria.

As he evaluated his handiwork Miki realized that Kaneda's nose and mouth were no longer necessary. He made a vertical incision in the old man's face and gathered the skin and muscle into a ball at the back of the head. The bones of the man's skull were now bared, within them only his thoughts and his eyeballs. Only a few troublesome bits of flesh, like the gums, still remained to be shaved off and reattached at the back. Kaneda's eyelids had been removed, and the two exposed orbs in their eye sockets followed Miki's movements.

The old man's body, suspended by the fishing lines, was able to stand. But the parts above his neck limply slumped into a permanent nod. There hadn't been anywhere on his skull to hang any of the hooks.

Miki hammered a nail into the crest of the man's skull. He knew that even if the nail pierced the brain, Kaneda wouldn't die, so he used a long nail. The old man's head shook from the force of each strike of the hammer. After the nail had been driven into the man's skull, Miki tied one of the fishing lines around it to prop it up.

Miki decided he had done enough.

Although Kaneda could no longer blink, his eyes retained their moisture. He couldn't speak, but he could communicate his thoughts through the movements of his eyes and his emotions through the twitching of his limbs beneath the organs.

There was nothing shabby-looking about Kaneda's new form. Within the clump of organs that hung from the ceiling was a mass as red as the sun. It beat at a steady rate, delivering blood throughout the body. Miki had repaired the severed veins and covered Kaneda's entire body with them. His exposed heart was imbued with a divine light.

When he searched the man's belongings Miki learned that Kaneda had lived nearby.

✳

After Miki had finished digging the hole, he left the shovel and returned to the house. He still needed to carry Kaneda's body to the grave.

He heard the flapping of wings and looked up to see a black bird on the roof of the house. From beneath the skeletal branches of the leafless trees, he felt the raven's icy stare.

Behind the house was a shed. The person who had lived in the house before him had left it there. Miki hooked his finger into a dent in the sliding door and muscled it open. That was the only way he could get it to open, probably due to the rotting of the wood.

The door creaked as it slid aside, sunlight falling onto Kaneda's feet and hands. Thinking it would be too heavy otherwise, he had stuffed the rest of the Old Man into a garbage bag. He had brought all of it up from the cellar and stored it in the shed.

The cause of death was a cellar mouse. The rodent had run up Kaneda's body and gnawed at his exposed heart. By the time Shinichi and Yukie noticed something was wrong, Kaneda's breathing had already ceased.

Miki started to drag the garbage bag full of Kaneda's organs out of the shed.

But then he saw something out of the corner of his eye he hadn't seen before and stopped. It rested in the dirt a short distance away.

Miki picked it up. It wasn't his. He recalled the presence he had sensed from the window in his study.

Someone had been there after all. He was sure of it. He trusted his intuition.

It wouldn't have been the first time somebody had figured out his crimes—or at least suspected his actions. They secretly snooped around the places he lived. Miki called them visitors.

A young man had come looking around the house before.

Then, as now, he had gotten the feeling he was being watched.

Did the visitor discover proof of my crimes? If so I'll deal with it. Just like I dealt with the last visitor who came snooping around.

THE EYE'S MEMORY
CONCLUSION

3

One day, the girl sat in the chair at the window and said, "I'm afraid..."

She placed two of the stoppers the raven had given her into the two holes in her face and began to tremble. The two eyes were oriented in separate directions; regardless, she seemed to be taking in the sights the round objects had observed.

"What are you afraid of, miss?"

He had given her two new bloody presents straight from his beak.

"The stoppers you bring me—when I use them like this, wondrous dreams fill my head. It's a marvelous experience for someone like me, someone who can't see anything. But the stoppers you bring me always show the same frightening thing. I hadn't noticed it until recently."

"A frightening thing?"

She nodded, and one of the eyes she had placed in a socket plopped out to the floor. She picked it up and put it into the glass jar where she saved all the eyes. The jar was already filled to the brim.

The raven asked what the frightening thing was. But the girl only shook her head.

"I don't know. I only see it for a split second. It looks like a monster, and somehow I know I should be afraid of it. But..."

She changed her fearful expression into a smile and turned toward the raven.

"Don't think anything of it. Your presents are always wonderful. I'm alone in the darkness, and the light and color you bring me are the only things that give me comfort. I can never express how much you have done for me."

The girl held out her hands to the raven perched on the table. He realized she probably wanted him to hold her hand. There was a scene like that in one of his favorite movies. But her face and her hands were at a slight upward angle. If the raven had been a human and not a bird, her hands might have been around his face.

"Won't you tell me your name, mister? Are you really real? I've never touched your hands…"

The raven's heart felt like it was about to break. He couldn't let her touch him. He was a bird. If the girl ever learned that he wasn't a person, it would only hurt her.

"I'm sorry, miss. I cannot hold your hand. Several years ago, while traveling in a foreign land, I caught a terrible illness. If you were to touch me you would become infected. Miss, the second you touched my body you wouldn't be able to stop hiccuping."

The raven flew out the window. The girl said something behind his tail feathers, but he kept on flapping his wings. A sadness clutched his avian breast. The raven couldn't understand the feelings inside him.

He turned toward the town in search of a new present for the girl. He had to work cautiously. Lately, the humans had become wary of ravens.

Many had witnessed the raven's attacks, and it was known throughout the town that a black bird was picking eyeballs from people's faces.

Townspeople were shooting ravens with rifles, and the children, fearful of attacks, all ran to school with their hands covering their eyes.

The raven himself had even been shot at once, but he'd been lucky—the rifleman had had poor aim. But ever since, whenever he flew above the town he flew high enough that he couldn't be seen from the ground. And in order to safely obtain presents for the girl, he traveled to faraway towns where the rumors had not yet spread.

He had even thought of a few contrivances to help him extract the eyes. By chance he had found a wall with a hole in it in a residential area. The hole's size was just right for a human to peep through. The raven hid on the rear side of the wall and whenever a person walked by he said in a human voice, "Heyyy! You! Stop right there! Please take a look in this hole. If you do it now, you'll see something beautiful and wonderful on the other side."

The raven kept rapt attention for the moment the tricked human put an eye to the hole. Then he thrust his beak deep into the hole from the other side. An hour after the black, pointed tip of his beak dug into the face of a victim, the raven would be rewarded with the girl's smile.

Even after they tried to beat him to death with sticks or chase him away by throwing sharp heavy rocks, the raven still went to the humans and dyed his beak red.

From the tops of trees and the roofs of buildings he observed the humans below, swooping down upon them whenever the opportunity presented itself.

Suddenly the raven would stand directly before them, spreading his large black wings. The instant their eyes widened in surprise, he jumped at their faces.

Once, at the end of a long fight, he'd obtained an eyeball while only half conscious.

He'd accidentally crushed an eyeball in his beak when he had been struck. Another time, he'd swallowed an eye before he'd been able to deliver it to the girl.

One day, she inserted an eye he'd just brought her and was happier than ever before. Apparently the owner of the eyeball had done a lot of overseas traveling. The girl said that all kinds of fascinating visions flowed into her through the stopper.

After he left her mansion the raven happened to pass over a graveyard at the top of a small hill with no houses around it. The sun was fast asleep, and the land was bathed in moonlight. Only the lines of gravestones below were white.

Someone was being buried. A gravedigger was digging into the earth with a shovel. The raven stopped on a withered tree to watch him work.

A person covered by a cloth lay on the ground next to the grave. The raven recognized the bit of clothing from under the edge of the cloth. It was the body of a person he had stolen an eye from a little earlier. The person must have died from the shock of having his eye taken out.

After the corpse was buried in its grave, the raven flew from the tree, beating his black wings. It had already grown dark and only the pale moon was out.

With each passing day the humans grew ever more vigilant.

4

"Hey, guess what?" said the girl one day. "I'm getting surgery."

Previously there hadn't been any techniques capable of restoring the girl's eyesight, but medical knowledge had advanced at a surprisingly rapid pace.

"When I can see again," the girl said happily, "I'll be able to see what you look like."

"That's wonderful, miss," said the raven. "Congratulations."

But his true feelings weren't so clear. If the girl's sight returned, she would be surprised to see that her friend was not human.

And she'd find out that the things she called stoppers were eyeballs taken from others.

The raven didn't care who died if it was for her sake. He knew that his deeds were evil, but sadly, no feelings of guilt formed inside his bird heart.

But surely the kind young girl would be sad to learn that people had died for her. And she would condemn what he had done. He couldn't bear it.

What would I do if she hated me? The fear of it left him sleepless.

Oh, if only I had been born a human and not a bird! thought the raven, as the girl before him took in the visions of the stoppers in her eye sockets.

Suddenly she screamed.

"What's wrong, miss?" asked the raven in surprise. The girl answered in a wavering voice.

"I saw the monster—the frightening thing that always appears at the end of the dreams. It's black, a black monster. Whenever it appears the vision cuts off. A monster that signals the end. At the end, the black beast leaps toward me. A dreadful face."

Her small shoulders drew inward and her face was pale. Her strawberry lips had turned pure white.

The raven realized what she had been seeing. *The black monster she fears so deeply is me! The demon she's seeing is myself recorded in the eyes!*

What should I do? Soon the girl will have her surgery and her eyes will see again. My partner in conversation will discover that I am the black monster that terrifies her to her core.

If only she wouldn't have the surgery! thought the raven, although he couldn't say it to the girl so happily awaiting the day she could see again.

"I'm afraid of the surgery," she said. "But I'll get through it, just to see you."

Her courage bolstered by her desire to meet her mysterious caller eye to eye, she resolved to undergo the operation.

"Tomorrow night," she said, "I'll have to go to a distant town for the surgery. So come again before I leave. I want to talk to you again."

As he heard her words, the raven put the mansion behind him.

It's finally come. The raven's tiny brain was filled with thoughts of the young girl. So many times he had decided to say goodbye to her and fly to southern lands—how many he didn't know. He wished he could just not say anything and never visit her again.

But he wouldn't do that. If he suddenly vanished the girl would be sad. And more than anything else, it would have been painful for the raven himself.

Even after he learned of the girl's upcoming surgery, the raven kept searching for presents for her as he had before.

But it was harder than ever to obtain eyeballs. The humans were carefully guarding their eyes—some even wore specially made protective goggles.

The humans couldn't tell one raven from another. Many innocent black birds had been indiscriminately dispatched by human bullets. Perhaps his own parents or siblings were among the fallen.

The recurring terrors had made the humans vigilant, and he almost never saw an opportunity to harvest eyes anymore.

The day before the girl's surgery was to be performed the raven flew without resting to find her an eye. He went to towns farther away than he had ever gone before.

Soon it grew dark and then dawn came, bringing with it the day of the girl's departure. But still he had not found a chance to collect an eye.

When the surgery was over his presents would no longer have any meaning; still, all the raven was capable of doing for the girl was to offer her yet another eye.

All he could do was give her an eyeball to make her happy. That was his everything. Just one more time before her surgery he wanted to make her happy. If he did that, he could die. That was his strongest wish.

Some humans threw rocks at him and hit him, and his beak cracked. He was caught unawares, and they grabbed his wings. He narrowly escaped, but his feathers had been torn from his wings. As he was beaten by their sticks his prized talons had chipped. Still he tried hard to find an eye, but to no avail.

He moved his ravaged wings to fly. He had to concentrate to keep from falling.

In the end, he hadn't been able to get her an eye. His own pair brimmed with tears as he thought about the pitiful failure he'd become.

The sun had already set, and the girl's departure was closer than ever. The sky grew dark and the moon started to shine its white light upon the world.

That was when he saw it, lit by the moonlight—a corpse about to be buried in the graveyard. The raven passed over the gravedigger in the middle of his digging.

The raven had an idea.

From a small distance away he called out to the gravedigger in a human's voice. "Heyyyy! There's still dead people over here!"

With a surprised expression, the gravedigger set down his shovel and turned to the direction of the voice. A moment later he left the corpse and walked toward the raven suspiciously.

The raven waited for the right moment and then flew into the air from where the gravedigger couldn't see him. He passed over the man's head and landed upon the corpse on the ground beside the open grave.

Using his beak, the raven removed the cloth that covered the corpse, revealing the body of a woman. The raven didn't care how she had died. There were countless scratches upon her face and her body. Her nose and her mouth had been shaved off and one of her eyes had burst and was gone. But the other eye seemed to be in perfect shape.

The raven pushed his beak, stained red with human blood from his wicked deeds, into the face of the corpse.

※

"I was worried you weren't going to come, mister," said the girl to the raven when he came into her room. She was fully prepared for her trip and told him she would soon be getting in the car and driving far away for her surgery. "I won't be back for a while. But I will be back."

The raven placed the corpse's eyeball on top of the round table.

Along with the vase of flowers, a glass jar was on the table. It was filled with all of the eyes the raven had brought her. The girl apparently intended to bring the jar with her as a keepsake on the trip.

"I'm sure the operation will be a success, miss. Good luck."

Cute dimples formed in the girl's cheeks. "Thank you."

"I've brought you one last present. It's on the table. Please put it in and watch the dream."

The raven's heart felt like it would burst. But he made up his mind. As he flew out the window he would say it.

Miss, I won't be coming back.

And he could never think of her again.

The raven turned his back to the girl and poised to fly out the window.

"Miss—" His farewell was cut short by the girl's scream.

At the end of her long, shrill shriek, the girl tore at her face with her fingernails, vomited, and collapsed to the floor, her arms and legs writhing. Her hair was a tangled mess. Her hands were enmeshed in her hair and she yanked it out like she couldn't bear it any longer.

The glass jar with all the eyeballs broke open, the eyes scattering all over the floor. The girl was surrounded by eyeballs, some rotten and squishy, others new and still elastic.

Finally, with a cracked sound from her mouth, like the death rattle of a dying beast, the girl stopped moving.

The raven approached the girl and pressed his ear to her chest. Her heart had stopped beating and she seemed to be dead. Her face was distorted in terror. Her black satin hair and her strawberry lips had turned a ghostly white.

The raven hadn't known. He hadn't known that the corpse whose eye he took had been tortured and maimed, that the sadnesses of the world had been burned into her eyes.

The girl had seen it all. She saw the hell the eye's previous owner had lived and she saw the moment of the woman's death.

The raven kept his head pressed against the girl's chest. For the first time he had touched her body. It had already started to grow cold.

When the girl's mother came into her room to announce that it was time to leave she found the body of her dead daughter, surrounded by countless eyeballs, and the carcass of a raven, its head pressed against her girl's chest, growing cold along with her.

THE END

PART 3

1—AN AUTHOR OF FAIRY TALES

Miki had a dream in which he molded humans into balls.

The dream went like this: The place was a small room, somewhere around nine feet by twelve, with a closet and a TV. Miki stood in the center of the room facing another person.

The person's arm was injured, with a gash a few inches long.

Miki grasped the arm and massaged the wound. Strangely, the skin he touched was soft and moldable, like clay. The surface of the arm smoothed and the cut vanished as if it had been painted over.

Amused, Miki looked at the person's fingerprints. When he rubbed at the minute grooves they too smoothed, as though he'd gone over them with a putty knife.

Feeling like a potter kneading clay, Miki removed all the bumps from the person.

He tightly squeezed together the person's fingers and what had been five were pressed into one. When he applied more force and started kneading at the flesh, the person's body yielded under his hands and its features and limbs were smoothed out.

The person remained conscious the whole time. It didn't speak, but it watched him with thoughtful eyes.

Soon the person had lost almost all its protrusions and had become a smooth, waist-high sphere. It was white and terribly round. As if to indicate it had once been a person, black hairs poked out here and there. On its even surface, a single eye remained, it alone not having been worked into the sphere.

The eye still blinked, and it tracked Miki as he walked about.

The person, having been completely transformed into a ball, had lost the ability to move. Even when Miki left the room, it could only watch him go with its small staring eye.

When Miki awoke, Hitomi said, "You were sleeping again."

To pass the time, she had been flexing her stomach muscles to make her torso hop on the couch. The springiness of the couch helped her small body bounce. She seemed to be enjoying it.

Miki straightened up the papers of his unfinished manuscript and looked out the window. The sky was cloudy. It might snow soon. Miki turned up the heat of the stove and used a steaming tea kettle to make coffee.

"That coffee looks delicious," said Hitomi. "Hey, why are you leaving the stove on? It's not like it's cold in here."

He explained to her that those whom he injured—whose injuries didn't heal—no longer felt changes in temperature.

"Are my injuries not healed?"

He explained to her that her wounds were still a fresh red, just as they had been when he had severed her limbs.

Miki stood by the window, coffee in hand, gazing out at the spot where he had buried Kaneda's corpse. The leafless trees blocked his view of the ground, but he could see far out across the forest to where the barren trees gave way to cedar.

On the next mountain over stood a brick building similar to his. Even its roof was the same shape, but the difference—the only difference—was its color.

"Did you sense someone there again?" Hitomi asked.

Four days had passed since he buried Tadashi Kaneda in the backyard.

Miki stepped back from the window and opened the drawer

of his desk. Inside was the object he'd found next to the house.

"You're being investigated. That's the proof right there. It belonged to somebody; it wouldn't have just suddenly appeared out of thin air."

But it's not like I saw anyone there. I have to find out if someone is harboring suspicions of me and searching around my house.

He looked inside the desk drawer and thought about the person the object belonged to. *Is it someone I know?*

"What are you going to do? I want to see my mother. I want to go home." She turned her head to speak to Miki. Her long hair hung down, covering her entire face. "You should turn yourself in. I'm sure the police will forgive you."

He explained to her that he wasn't going to turn himself in.

"So then," she said in a sunken voice, "I can't go home, can I?"

Miki offered to tell her a story.

"What story?"

He brought over a few suitable books from the bookcase, including one he had written.

"That's *The Collected Black Fairy Tales*, isn't it? You already read it to me. The story was a lot like what happened with Shinichi and Yukie."

She was talking about a tale called "The Human Knot." Several people were forced atop a plate, where a giant demon crushed them on both sides with his powerful hands. That kind of story.

After the demon crushed them, the people were all tangled together. Their arms and legs were knotted, their torsos stretched, and their necks and heels twisted into one large clump. They spent the rest of their days writhing, struggling to disentangle their jumbled limbs.

It reminded Hitomi of what had happened to Shinichi Hisamoto and Yukie Mochinaga down in the cellar.

"Tell me a different one. There, that paperback. No, the one in your right hand."

The book she wanted read to her was a collection of old science fiction short stories. She rested on the couch and listened to Miki read the title story.

It didn't take very long to finish.

"That ended a bit sad." Hitomi's face had paled in shock. It hadn't been a happy ending.

She asked him, "If you were the hero of that story, what would you have done?"

The conditions of the question were basically as follows:

Conditions:

- You are piloting a small spaceship.
- You are bringing cargo to another planet. The cargo is blood serum, and if you don't deliver it quickly, a great many people will die.
- In order to carry the most cargo, the ship has only the minimum amount of fuel necessary. In other words, just enough to accelerate and to brake for landing.
- If there's a stowaway on board, you'll have to eject her into space, because her weight will add to the spaceship's fuel consumption and there won't be enough fuel to brake. You can't eject the stowaway's weight in supplies and you can't remove mass from the spaceship itself.

Question:

If the stowaway is a young, pretty girl, do you have to throw her into space?

"You can't turn back, either. There are a lot of people waiting on that planet for those supplies. If you don't throw the girl off the ship, there won't be enough fuel left to slow down and land properly. Just like that story. Is there any way to save the little girl?"

Hitomi closed her eyes and thought.

Miki also considered the problem for a little while, then explained that he could save the girl, depending on the circumstances.

Hitomi's face brightened and she said excitedly, "Could you really? Can you save both the girl and those people waiting for the blood serum?"

He explained that if the ship had the right equipment and the right controls, and if the girl's weight and the pilot's weight were just right, they could be saved.

First, he'd need something with which to cut off the girl's limbs. It could be anything as long as it could cut through bone.

"The ship doesn't have an axe or anything like that," said Hitomi.

Remove the girl's limbs and make her as light as possible. Throw the severed parts into space. Use the fact that the stowaway is a child to your advantage. The best case would be if the stowaway were diminutive and light and you, the pilot, were stout and heavy.

Cut parts off your own body equal to the weight of the head and torso of the girl, throw them into space too, and you'll have it. The weight of the entire spacecraft will be reduced to the planned weight capable of landing on the planet with the minimum amount of fuel.

"But if you cut off parts of your own body," Hitomi said, "you won't be able to pilot the ship—even if you only have to get rid of your legs to match the girl's weight, you couldn't step on the brakes." Still, her face showed approval of his answer. "But there's one more thing you're forgetting. You couldn't do it that way because you don't have any anesthetics. If you cut off her arms and legs, she might die of shock. And you might not be able to pilot the ship through your own pain. So don't go around thinking every girl out there can have her limbs cut off and be all nonchalant about it."

She looked at her body and added, "Except for me."

*

Miki picked up Hitomi, who had fallen asleep, and took her down to the cellar. The room was dark and humid. Condensation formed on the brick walls and reflected the lightbulb's dim light.

In a corner of the cellar hung several dozen fishing lines, and stuck on the hooks at the end of the lines were pieces of red meat—the rest of Kaneda Tadashi's organs. Soon they too would begin to rot.

When Miki laid Hitomi down in her bed, she wriggled the sack that held her body and whispered in her sleep, "Mother..."

He turned his back to her and went to leave.

Just then, from behind one of the shelves, came Shinichi's voice:

"Has she ever told you about her family?"

There were several racks of shelving in the cellar and Shinichi and Yukie always kept their body hidden somewhere in the shadows behind them.

Miki went to the pair and was faced with Shinichi's head. He couldn't see Yukie's head because it was hidden in the shadows, but Yukie seemed to be asleep.

"She talks to us across the shelves," said Shinichi, "about her past. Like the time she went camping with her family. Or how she always placed first in the long-distance races in gym class. Or how, whenever she went on a picnic, her mother always ended up packing these sausages she hated in her bento box."

Hitomi often spoke of her past. She seemed to miss her everyday life from when she still had her arms and legs—the mornings she would comb her messy bed-hair by herself, holding a cup in her hands and drinking the milk within, playing footsie with her friends under the school desks.

When Hitomi talked about her memories she worked her nonexistent limbs, mimicking the movements.

Hitomi, sitting on the couch, had once said to Miki, "Guess what I'm doing." She was looking right in front of her. Her left shoulder moved busily up and down inside her sack.

"Do you give up? I'm making an omelette, of course!"

She flicked the frying pan she held in her nonexistent left hand and Miki had understood she was trying to flip the omelette.

"Hitomi grew up loved," said Shinichi. "Have you ever loved anyone?"

Miki said he didn't know.

"You talked to me before. About how you had a close friend when you were a kid. Maybe you loved her?"

Miki tilted his head.

Shinichi's face looked lonely and he whispered, "My heart aches. When I think of her, I don't know what to do. I'm helpless and I feel like I just want to die."

He was in love with Yukie. But he kept it an absolute secret from her. He bared his feelings for her to Miki quietly, and only when Yukie's head was asleep.

Shinichi moved his giant body. His torso was longer than an average person's—more than five feet. On different ends were attached the heads of Shinichi and Yukie. Miki had operated on them to create a shared torso. Originally they had been two completely separate people.

"You put us into this shape to test your bizarre powers. I don't know if I should thank you or curse you for it."

Shinichi let out a cry of grief.

To find the answer to the question, *What would happen if I tried to connect two individual people?* Miki had performed the surgery.

First, he had amputated Shinichi's right arm at the elbow. He did the same to Yukie's left arm and connected the two where their arms had been. He set their bones with metal fittings and joined their blood vessels and muscles with thread. Miki had little knowledge of medical care, only what he had read in some of his father's books. But in the end the seam closed and their arms were connected together. Even their blood vessels seemed to heal perfectly. Shinichi's blood pumped from his heart toward his right elbow. At the seam, the blood flowed from his veins and into hers, their two bodies sharing the same blood. Miki had never considered if their matching blood types might have had something to do with the result. Had their blood types differed, the result might have been the same regardless.

And although it happened slowly, their bodies—their muscles and their nerves—began to meld together at the seam. The boundary between their bodies was fading.

They were both still conscious. They were aware of each other's existence and knew what their bodies were doing. They had met for the first time in that cellar. One Miki had found near his house; the other had sent him a fan letter that hinted at suicide and had been invited here.

Again and again Miki cut at their parts and stuck them together.

The bodies of Shinichi and Yukie now looked like one bizarre lump of flesh. Miki had sliced their torsos into two or three pieces each and rejoined them. Their stomach was an inflated sack just big enough to hold their intertwined organs; their limbs were sutured on at abnormal locations.

Next he transplanted the arms and the legs he had removed from Hitomi to their body. There hadn't been a proper place to connect the bones and muscles, but he did connect the large blood vessels on the limbs with theirs for their blood to flow through.

Those Miki mutilated were delivered from a fate of decomposition, but the leftover parts disconnected from the mind and the heart—which Miki believed contained the will to live—were different. In time these parts would begin to rot and, as is only natural for a normal human being, turn to dust.

Hitomi's limbs should have been the same. But when they were connected with the body of Shinichi and Yukie, when their body's blood circulated into them, the limbs lived. At first the transplanted parts were immobile, but soon, whether by

Shinichi's or Yukie's command, they gradually began to move.

After a time, solid bonelike material formed inside their collective body and formed connective joints with the bones in Hitomi's limbs. The joints had similarities with typical ones, but their shape was entirely new. Muscles and nerves also grew within their body like a plant grows its roots. In every way the limbs became one with the lump of meat.

At first, the limbs' movements were sluggish, but eventually the two could move them with complete control—all the way down to the tips of their fingers and toes.

When Miki once asked them which of their brains moved Hitomi's limbs, Yukie had answered with an expression as if she'd dozed off under the afternoon sun.

"I don't know. It could be me or it could be him. I feel so muddled I can't tell anymore."

Neither had clearly delineated control over the lump of meat. And strangely, neither seemed to be bothered by it.

"We're always talking to each other," said Shinichi. "About how desolate and lonely we were when we were separate."

He had been an orphan, with no one to depend on, and felt comforted by Yukie's constant presence. Yukie had once given up on living and decided to kill herself, but now Shinichi, closer to her than anyone, gave her the will to live.

"But you're so cruel," Shinichi accused Miki, appearing on the verge of tears. "If you'd only stitch our necks a little bit closer…"

Their necks were attached on the opposite ends of their torso.

The massive clump of flesh in front of Miki wriggled. Their shadow rocked across the walls of the cellar.

Shinichi's head, still in front of Miki, said, "Are you awake? I thought you were sleeping."

A voice came from the shadows on the opposite side of their body.

"Hey, I still haven't found it." It was Yukie's pained voice. "There just isn't a right way to be in this shape."

They were constantly searching for a way to position themselves comfortably.

When Shinichi's face was upright, Yukie's cheek was pressed against the floor. And when she oriented herself comfortably, Shinichi's protruding elbow had to bear the painful weight of their combined bodies. They spent much of the time wriggling around, trying to find a position that was comfortable to both. But it seemed like one always had to make a sacrifice and bear their weight.

Hitomi had probably been referring to that behavior when she likened them to the people in "The Human Knot."

Shinichi spoke again to Miki. "I wonder what your power is. Normally we'd be dead. You must be a son of the gods. When you injure a person, in that moment they escape from death. I can feel the torrent of life overflowing from the wounds. That terrible paradox. You're keeping people alive. You free us from the cycle of life and death…"

Miki turned his back to them.

As he left the cellar, he looked over at the lumber and brick piled in the back of the room.

I may have to cover the cellar door. I have what I need to do it. There are still some bricks there, probably leftover from when the house was built.

If I don't catch the visitor, I'll have to.

Several days later there was a knock at the door.

2

Even if I were certain that Shiozaki was the kidnapper, I didn't have the proof to accuse him. I don't know how many times I started to phone the police. Each time I'd lift the receiver, set it back down, and lift it up again. If I were to explain what I'd experienced and the conclusion I'd reached—well, I didn't think they would believe me. I had no proof to convince anyone of it.

For a week I gathered information about Shiozaki. But I couldn't come out and ask people to tell me about him directly. I had to avoid drawing attention to what I was doing. If he realized I had any suspicions about him, it might put Hitomi in danger.

One day in Melancholy Grove, Sumida said, "I heard Shiozaki used to be married." As usual he was seated at the counter, watching Saori intently as she poured his coffee.

Saori, her tone that of one speaking to a delinquent child, asked him, "Sumida, shouldn't you be in class?"

Chagrined, he replied, "Which do you think is more important—that I come here or that I attend college?"

Whenever he gave a reply like that, Kimura would smack Sumida's face with a round silver-colored tray. Of course, he wasn't actually mad—Kimura did it with a joking smile on his face.

"Shiozaki had a wife?" I asked. Sumida pointed to the painting on the wall.

"Look closely. There's a red dot nearly too small to see on the shore of the lake. Do you see it?"

I moved my face close to Shiozaki's painting. I hadn't noticed it before, but just as Sumida said there was an out-of-place spot of red color.

"Well, I thought that dot looked like the figure of a woman staring out across the lake. I said so to Shiozaki and he told me a woman he'd married long ago was standing there in the picture."

Compared with the size of the painting the spot was incredibly small. If I hadn't put my face right up close I wouldn't have noticed it at all, but I too saw it as a woman standing. Dressed in red, she was drawn about the size of the tip of a fingernail.

And in that instant, the forest and the lake inside the painting vanished. I was transfixed by the woman in the red dot. The rest of the landscape seemed to have been painted for her. The forest and the lake formed a vast garden dedicated to the woman confined inside the painting.

Sumida shrugged. "I don't know if he really was married or not. It's just what he told me."

I didn't have any reliable information about Shiozaki, his family, or his past. *Who brought him to that house? Doesn't anyone know why he moved to Kaede?*

During my investigation I stayed at Mr. Ishino's house. I ate breakfast with him and Saori. We passed each other in the halls and kicked each other's feet under the kotatsu.

Sometimes I felt like I was imposing on them, but in other moments I felt a familiarity, like I had taken Kazuya's place inside their home.

I called my parents every day. I apologized to them and thought of how wrong it was of me to leave.

"The old you would never have run away," they'd tell me.

My father never knew what to say on the other end of the line, and I still couldn't talk to my mother, not even over the phone. Both she and I would just remain silent until she finally handed the phone to my dad.

"Come home soon," he said. "You need to go to your regular checkup at the hospital."

When my thoughts left the matter of Shiozaki—when my feelings allowed it—I passed the time helping Saori wash the dishes. At the café or at her home, we stood side by side in aprons, idly chatting as we rinsed plates and cups.

Once when her hands were full of dishes Saori yelled, "My nose is running! It's running!"

But she couldn't free her hands to blow her nose.

"Here, is this all right?" I put a tissue to her nose and wiped it dry, and like a little child she thanked me in a pitiful, stuffed-up voice.

We spent a windy night playing cards together, the two of us, a gale wind howling outside. When the kotatsu and the stove were not enough to keep the cold at bay, we put on thick padded clothes and curled up face to face. I couldn't hear anything but the wind; it felt like we might be the only things in the world.

As she played the ace of spades she asked about Kazuya and me. She seemed to want to learn more about the Kazuya she didn't know. Whenever she asked, I evaded her questions, and she would suddenly laugh. I'd think to myself, *She just can't see what's coming, can she?*

As she dealt out the cards she said, "I just remembered the time when Kazuya started eating a card. He was still little. I was his older sister, so I thought I had to take care of him."

She cheerfully told the story of how Kazuya had started to chew on a playing card and she hadn't known what to do about it.

And as I laughed and nodded, I felt a love for Saori and Kazuya well up inside my chest—so much I thought I might cry.

When it was my turn to cut the deck I asked, "Saori, do you remember your parents' funeral? The way Kazuya told it, it was kind of odd. He was standing next to you on a hill a small distance from your house. From there you could see the many people dressed in black down below…"

It was a vision I'd seen in my left eye.

A young man wearing black funeral clothes came up to the brother and sister on the hill. He spoke to them and tears quickly came to Saori's eyes. The young man's eyes were sad too.

I wanted to know what the youth had said. My left eye couldn't pass on his voice to me.

Saori, still small at the time, hugged the young man and cried.

"Did it happen like that? I only remember it vaguely." She rested her chin in her hands and closed her eyes. "That boy was the one who caused our parents' accident—the one who didn't tie the ropes properly…"

Saori had felt so much pity for the young man. After all, he'd only just gotten out of high school. He apologized to Saori and Kazuya again and again, told them he had left his hometown to come work in Kaede, told them about his own parents.

"I wonder why he told you all that stuff."

"He must have wanted me to hear it."

Two weeks after the funeral, the young man hanged himself. In the suicide note he wrote that he felt responsible for their parents' deaths.

That was what Saori quietly told me.

✳

When I had time to spare from my investigation I put the binder full of my eye's memories into my backpack and walked around town. The binder was heavy—when I held it in my arms as I walked, I felt like an ascetic monk.

I needed to find proof of the kidnapping and captivity of that little girl, but to do so I needed to follow Kazuya's footsteps.

I walked through the town and stood in places he had seen. I went to his elementary school and fondly recalled his memories.

Alongside the highway that cut through town was a supermarket, and behind it there was a small gap between the outer wall and a chicken-wire fence. Kazuya had walked through it as a young boy. Now I walked through it too. My line of vision was far higher from the ground than his had been, so I wasn't seeing exactly the same view as was in my left eye's vision. Yet still my heart raced—in a way I felt I had become the young Kazuya.

I walked down a street lined with utility poles and I stopped to listen at an empty, lonely park.

Kaede was a logging town. I came across a brace of trees being felled as the sound of chain saws rang through the air. A man in work clothes was sliding the whirling blade into the trunk of a tree, spraying wood chips about. I moved in for a closer look, but was shooed away because of the danger. Soon the tree's trunk cracked and snapped and the tree fell.

I took the binder from my backpack and read it as I walked through the town, like a tourist with a guidebook.

One hand supported the book of memories, the other turned the pages—although the gloves I wore made that difficult. Worse yet, my arm grew sore from bearing the binder's weight.

Blown about by the cold wind, I walked. A small distance from the homes of the town I found an abandoned railway line. A gravel path ran along the top of a hill thick with dead grass and the two rails, turned crimson with rust, followed its length as far as I could see.

I put the binder back into my backpack and jumped onto one of the rails, careful not to fall off as I walked. The past me with all her memories had apparently enjoyed exceptional coordination, but the present me couldn't walk more than a few feet down the rail without losing her balance and slipping off it.

From atop the hill with the abandoned line I could see the whole town nestled between the mountains. The town had changed since Kazuya had seen it. Roads had disappeared and new buildings had been built. I even found the exact same view as one I had seen in my left eye, and I saw houses I hadn't recorded in the journal.

My left eye remembered scenery that no longer was. That eye, taken from Kazuya and transplanted into me, was like a nugget of the past itself. Like a piece of hard candy, it slowly melted away, the past flowing into my optic nerve.

The abandoned rail eventually terminated at the edge of the forest in the place I'd seen, some time before, from the train station platform. The season had changed, so the trees in the background were now bare, skeletal. But the abandoned train car was just as it had been. The cold wind was blowing and there were no voices of children playing. But within the quiet the hulking mass of rust had not moved—not even a little—from where it had been in my left eye's memory.

Exhaling white breath, I ran to the train car and stepped inside. The walls of the car kept out the wind, preserving at least a little warmth in the space. But the interior was emptier than I'd imagined. Everything had been removed—even the seats. I hadn't known it from my vision, but the train car had been discarded as nothing but a shell. I felt a little lonely.

That's right, I recalled, *Kazuya was shunned by the group of kids. They wouldn't let him play with them.*

Kazuya was often alone in the memories of my left eye. Some visions showed him playing with friends, but more frequently I saw him walking alone. Maybe anyone's memories would be as limned with loneliness.

I went to the lumber mill next. I was hesitant to go inside, so from in front of the building I looked at where Kazuya's father had worked and where his parents had lost their lives. The worksite was fenced off by chicken wire, but the scent of fresh-cut wood drifted through the air. I covered the bottom half of my face with a scarf I'd borrowed from Saori, and as I stamped my feet to keep the cold away I tried to picture the inside of the lumber mill. I wasn't sure how accurate my imagination was—the real building probably wasn't crammed full of wood shavings.

But when I happened to glance at what seemed to be the entrance to the lumber mill's office, I saw a woman whose face I knew. It was Saori. I waved my hands and called out to her, and she looked at me, startled.

"I don't come here much," she said, "but there was something I wanted to find out about my parents."

She told me that some of her father's old coworkers still worked there and she had been listening to them reminisce.

We walked side by side back to Melancholy Grove. Saori was silent. She seemed to be thinking of her dead parents and of the young man who, feeling responsible for the accident, had killed himself.

I opened the door to the café and went inside, noticing first Kimura and then a few customers I didn't recognize. The café didn't seem to be very popular, but I knew by now that other customers did come from time to time.

As I went to sit down at the counter I found myself paralyzed, unable to move. It felt like the warmth of the space heater and the soft yellow light had utterly vanished.

In a seat in the dark corner sat Shiozaki. He didn't notice
the existence or the comings and goings of any of the other
customers—at least that was the impression I got from how he
sat staring, elbows on the table, fingers interlocked.

I was nervous. I wished I could turn around and get out of
there as quickly as I could, but that would have looked abnormal
given that I had just come inside. Quietly, I sat at the counter.

"Nami?"

It was a moment before I noticed that Saori was calling my
name. As she tied the strings on her apron she asked, "Have you
had lunch? Do you want something?"

I said I wanted to eat.

I told myself not to look over at Shiozaki, but my eyes went
in his direction.

Just as I finished eating my lunch he stood. I noticed it out
of the corner of my eye. His footsteps sounded on the wooden
floorboards. As he approached my breath caught.

Just after he had passed me, the footsteps stopped.

"I haven't seen you in a while, Shiraki."

I made a desperate nod. Thoughts of the kidnapped Hitomi
and the dead Kazuya appeared in my mind. I felt rage, yes, but
inside the terror was beating it out. I felt like a tiny animal, unable to do anything but close my eyes and wait quietly until the
monster had passed.

When he left I exhaled, disheartened by my cowardice.

Kyoko passed Shiozaki on her way in. She was holding a hardcover book in one hand and when she saw me she waved.

She sat in her usual seat and said to Saori, "House blend,
please."

"Sure…"

Saori's response seemed halfhearted.

At the window next to the table Kyoko opened her book.

✳

When Saori was quiet she was contemplating the dead. She never came out and told me so, but that's what I thought anyway.

I can explain. Say she was gazing out the window of the living room. Her uncle's house was built on a slope and looked down upon the road that passed it. Even if there weren't anyone walking along the road, Saori would be seeing Kazuya on his way to school or her father heading to work.

I'd also seen her staring at the washing machine as it hummed. Her thoughts were on the other side of the washer—watching her mother, no doubt. Her uncle's house wasn't where she had grown up with her parents, but from the look in her eyes I knew she was seeing her mother.

Times like that, I could never get myself to speak to her. From behind she looked so tired and thin. I pitied her.

I saw the past inside my left eye. For Saori the picture films of the past were inside her head. Just as I longed for Kazuya's visions, Saori too turned her thoughts to those who were no longer with us.

After dinner back at her house, she said, "It's been two months now, but it still doesn't feel like Kazuya is really gone. Why is that? Maybe it's because it just wasn't that sad for me."

Saori's uncle was late getting home from work, so we ate together, just the two of us. The television was off and the evening quiet, and I could hear her every word, her every sniffle.

We were gazing at a cup on top of the kotatsu. Kazuya had used it often when he was alive.

"You've got it backwards. Couldn't it be that you haven't felt the sadness yet because it still doesn't feel like he's gone?"

"You're strange, Nami."

I tilted my head.

"With you it's like my brother is still here with me." She waved it off. "By the way, did you know? Kazuya's left eye was transplanted into someone else's body."

That was a subject I was very interested in hearing about.

"One of his eyes was removed after the accident and was taken away. It's what he wanted."

"He wanted it?"

"This all happened about a year ago. He had a sty on his eyelid and had to go to an eye doctor, and for a little while he had to have a bandage over his eye. Maybe about three days."

She told me that at the hospital Kazuya had read a pamphlet about eye transplants and had decided to become a donor.

"Kazuya had beautiful eyes. He had large pupils and a steady gaze." Saori's voice was soft, like she was remembering. "What had that boy seen during the course of his life?"

She was ever chasing after the shadows of the dead.

Whenever Sumida gave her a sunny greeting as she entered the café, Saori would return it with a smile. And that was all I saw at first. But as I watched her I started to sense that somewhere inside her heart, Saori was focused on the dead. Sometimes, in the middle of their conversations, she would glance over at the seat where Kazuya used to sit.

The past flows on. You die and fade away. Like streets and railroads vanish from a town, so too do people become no more. And the world becomes a little different. But Saori kept thinking of those who had left the world as if time had stopped.

Saori's world, frozen in time, reminded me of her keepsake of her brother—the broken gold watch.

Her uncle was the same way.

There was a Buddhist altar in the room on the other side of the sliding paper door of the room where I slept, and on the altar rested photos for Kazuya and their parents and their uncle's wife.

One cold morning I had been savoring the warmth inside my futon when I heard a noise in the next room. I got up. Disheveled, I moved on all fours to the sliding door and opened it to see Saori's uncle tidying the shrine. Then he pressed his hands together.

He looked at me and said, "Did I wake you?"

I shook my head, then slowly moved next to him. I sat in the formal seiza position, joining my hands together. He seemed to think I was sleepwalking.

"When my wife was alive," he said weakly, "I hit her once. I don't remember why. I don't know why I was always so short-tempered."

I looked at the photograph of his wife. She had died from pneumonia.

Every now and then I'd see him attending to the altar. It was hard to say anything to him, so I just watched his back.

He was deeply remorseful.

One day I helped at the café. Saori had gone somewhere and I had been recruited by Kimura to fill her place. Not that I did much helping—there were few customers that day. My only tasks were to listen to Kimura complain and to keep him from picking on Sumida.

After a time Kimura disappeared.

"Sumida, take over for me, will you?"

I handed him my apron and headed outside to look for Kimura.

Sumida's eyes widened. Flustered, he said, "What, wait. What am I supposed to do?"

Kimura was behind the café. It took me a moment to realize what he was doing. He was setting out a great many shoes in the sun. He'd made a line of shoes—there were maybe thirty of them, well worn. There were all kinds of shoes, some small enough for a young child, all the way to large ones.

"What are these?"

"They're shoes my friend left. He had this strange habit of saving all his shoes and never throwing them out. He died and these shoes are all that he left behind."

Apparently whenever Kimura had some spare time, he lined the shoes up on the ground and dried them in the sun. *Even if he is as large as a bear, he's still a sensitive guy.*

"I'm lining them up in the order he wore them. The ones on left end he wore as a child. The ones on the right he wore just

before he died. See these guys here, the leather ones?" He pointed
at a pair of small shoes near the left end of the row. "He was
wearing those when we first met."

He pointed at another pair on the right. "He was wearing these
when the café first opened, although I wasn't the owner yet. One
of my uncles opened it."

History lived in that row of shoes. They were like a timeline.

Kimura pointed at the pair of new-looking shoes on the far
right. "He took these shoes off before jumping to his death from
a railway bridge. They were still at the entryway of his house.
The night he killed himself he walked through the cold barefoot,
all the way from his house to the bridge."

When he'd finished talking, I went inside to my backpack and
pulled out the binder. Kimura's story had made me remember a
strange vision I'd seen in my left eye.

"What are you doing?" asked Sumida, the apron wrapped
around his skinny frame. He was looking at me with deep interest.
The getup suited him more than I'd have thought. He would have
made a good stay-at-home dad.

"This is my secret book and I can't show you."

Hiding the binder from him, I glanced over the pages.

I thought I might have been mistaken, but I wasn't: Kazuya's
eye had seen that night.

He had been walking the dark road home from middle school,
pushing his bicycle up the hill. I knew it had to have been middle
school, because that was when he rode his bike to school.

Beneath the streetlamps he passed a man walking the opposite
way. The man was looking up at the sky as he walked and hadn't
seemed to notice Kazuya or much of anything else.

The peculiar thing was, the man was barefoot.

※

I'm not sure whether I should call it the beginning or what led
to the beginning, but whatever it was that came to Kazuya—I
saw it.

It happened when I was having trouble deciding if I should go back to Shiozaki's house and try the search again. I was walking the serpentine slopes toward the house. Passing by the place Kazuya had lost his life, I noticed the side road leading to where Kyoko lived. It was lined with peaceful cedars, and the endless row of trees seemed to swallow all noise.

A car was coming up the road behind me. Worried that it might be Shiozaki, I stiffened, but thankfully it was a compact car I didn't recognize.

The car stopped in front of me and a man's face leaned out the driver's-side window.

"Excuse me, I seem to be lost. Could you help me out?"

When I started to walk toward the car my left eye suddenly grew warm. The sight of the car stopped beside the cedar trees matched a vision tucked away inside my eye.

I'd experienced so many visions of the left eye's memories since coming to that town that, paying no mind to the abrupt playback, I walked up to the driver.

To the man in my right eye I said, "Um...I'm not really familiar with the roads around here. I'm sorry."

In my left eye Kazuya was walking down a road fenced by cedar trees. It could very well have been the same road I was standing on at that moment. A car was parked in front of him, just like the scene before me. He approached the car and started to walk past.

Whenever I saw something in my right eye that didn't match what I saw in my left, I lost my equilibrium and my legs became unsteady. To prevent that from happening, I usually shut both my eyes during my visions. This time, because there was another person in front of me, I didn't.

"Oh...Well, if I keep going along this road, I'll get to the next prefecture, right?"

As I nodded in answer to his question a feeling came over me that could have stopped my heart.

Kazuya passed alongside the car and happened to glance in the rear window. In the back seat a girl had been left sleeping.

Her eyes were closed, but I had seen her picture so many times her face had been burned into my head. It was Hitomi.

Kazuya didn't seem to have thought anything of it; he looked away from the window and back at the road before him. He hadn't seen the driver's seat or the license plate of the car.

There the memory ended.

I had stopped hearing what the man who needed directions was saying. In my shock my mind had blanked and I could no longer understand the words he was speaking. Eventually he gave up and drove off.

By chance Kazuya had witnessed the car Hitomi had ridden in. He might not have known about her yet. In that vision, how were her arms and legs? I hadn't been able to tell for sure.

Kazuya must have seen Hitomi's picture later, on the news or in the paper. Whether it was soon after her kidnapping or just two months ago, I couldn't know. But whenever it was, he had remembered seeing her lying in the back seat of that car.

Had Kazuya known the car belonged to Shiozaki? The car in the vision didn't look like the one he drove now. Had he bought a new one or did he perhaps have two cars?

Or maybe Kazuya had seen the car on the road that led to Shiozaki's house? If so, that could be how he learned that the blue brick house was where the kidnapper lived.

I decided to investigate the road that led to Shiozaki's house. I thought I might find the location I'd just seen in the vision. But all of the roads in this area were lined with cedar trees like that one was, making it difficult to pinpoint the right place. In the end, without finding anything, I headed back toward Melancholy Grove.

On the way back, Saori appeared from the side road that connected to Kyoko's house. I called out to her, and she looked at me with a surprised expression.

"Today's delivery day," she said.

✳

One day Shiozaki forgot his coat inside the café. Kimura found it still draped over the back of his seat.

After a moment of hesitation I found the courage to declare, "I'll take it to his house."

"Don't worry about it," Kimura said. "He'll just come back tomorrow."

But I wasn't about to let the opportunity escape. Only rarely would I have a legitimate excuse to visit his house. If I brought him something he'd lost, I might be able to look around inside his home without drawing suspicion.

Finally Kimura decided I could go.

Sumida, who had heard most of the conversation, gave me a ride to the blue house. He drove the car through the gate and onto Shiozaki's property. There wasn't any reason to worry that our presence would be suspect, but as we approached the house I couldn't help feeling afraid.

At the front of the house was a wide graveled drive. Shiozaki's black car was there, alone. Sumida parked next to it.

I climbed out of the passenger seat and looked up at the front of the building. It wasn't tall like a castle or anything like that. The withered trees crowding around the house might have even been taller, their slender, leafless limbs outstretched like hair standing on end. The house was surrounded.

The angle of the sun cast shadows over the front of the house. Its blue bricks shrouded in black, the building had become the embodiment of shadow itself, a cavern that had opened up in space. If a rift were ever to open in our world, that house revealed how dark the hollow, bottomless blackness on the other side would be.

Hitomi Aizawa is there, in the cellar. As the thought came over me a tremor ran through my body.

"This won't take long, right?" said Sumida, who hadn't gotten out of the car. I got the very strong impression that he didn't want to spend a single moment outside the car's heated interior.

Thinking I'd feel more safe with him along, I said, "Come with me, Sumida."

He pretended not to hear me.

Left with no other option, I held the coat to my chest and walked to the house. Earlier, when no one was looking, I had searched the pockets but found nothing inside.

Fearfully I stood at the front door. It was made from black wood and had a gold-colored doorknob.

I rang the doorbell. From my place outside the front door I could hear the clear chime sounding inside.

After a short time Shiozaki appeared. His sharp eyes peered down at me from behind a pair of thin-framed glasses.

My heart raced and my words tumbled together. With my dry mouth I somehow managed to communicate that I had come to return his coat to him.

He said, "Thanks," and looked at the car behind me. "That's Sumida's car, isn't it? So he came too."

Never have I felt so relieved to have another person with me as I did at that moment. *There's nothing this man can do to me.*

"Since you came all the way out here, why don't you come in for some coffee?"

I nodded at the suggestion.

I went back to the car and reported Shiozaki's offer to Sumida. With sleepiness in his eyes, he got out of the car.

We went inside. It was a Western-style home; he didn't even have us take our shoes off.

The walls and floors were simple. There weren't any chandeliers or red carpet. The house had the cool reserve of a monastery or a historic school building.

The age of the building gave it a gloomy air. The rooms were illuminated not with pure white fluorescent light, but with old, dim lightbulbs. Everything about the house plucked at the thread of anxiety deep in my heart.

Sumida and I were led into the parlor. In the center of the room was a sofa and a coffee table. A short bookcase sat along one of the walls, its shelves jammed full with foreign editions.

A painting in a black frame hung on the wall, and when I asked

about it Shiozaki said he had painted it. It depicted an elderly
woman holding a sack of apples in her arms.

Shiozaki brought us coffee.

I looked around the room to see if anything might trigger heat
in my left eye. But the box of memories stayed shut. Had Kazuya
never stepped inside this room?

"This is all antique," said Sumida, patting at the sofa. It was
one of those you sink right into. "I don't think I could even fit
this couch into the room I live in."

"Almost all the furniture was left here by a previous tenant."

I asked, "Do you think that person inherited it from the one
before?"

Shiozaki tilted his head. "I wouldn't know. I never met him."

He had moved to the house almost half a year before. Hitomi
had disappeared a year ago—had he brought her here?

While Sumida and Shiozaki were talking, I stood and noncha-
lantly asked if I could use the bathroom. Shiozaki told me where
it was and I left the parlor.

It would be simple, I thought, to intentionally forget the directions to the bathroom. Then it wouldn't appear unnatural for me
to open the door to the wrong room.

I walked down the hallway, and making sure that nobody
was around, I opened the doors to the other rooms. I wanted
to make a detailed search, but fearful that Shiozaki would find
me, I couldn't make myself step into any of the rooms. As I went
by each room, I peeked inside, and when I saw nothing there,
I quickly shut the door again. Some rooms looked like studios,
others hadn't any furniture at all.

The hallways twisted like a digestive tract through the spacious house. They hadn't been designed to be complicated—at
least I thought they hadn't—and yet at each intersection I found
myself losing track of where I was. As I walked along the black
floorboards, I started to feel the illusion of the halls languidly
moving like the peristalsis of the intestines.

Hitomi may be somewhere inside this house. When the thought came to me, I found it hard to breathe. *Even though she's so close I still can't save her. Damn it!*

Near the center of the house was a stairway. The ceiling opened up into a stairwell, and I could see the handrails of the second floor hallway. *What's up there?* Of course, I hadn't the courage to go up and see. If I were caught upstairs he'd be suspicious of me for sure.

I opened the door to another room. *There's not much time. I have to get back to the two of them and I have to do it fast.*

Inside the room, there it was:

Women's clothing, hanging on the wall—a plain green blouse and a black skirt. But whose were they?

As I asked myself that question, I sensed someone standing behind me. I turned to look. Shiozaki.

"I left my wife's things in here."

He explained that even though she had died, he still couldn't bring himself to throw them away.

Through my panic, I managed to apologize. "I'm sorry, I got lost..." I was too frightened to look him in the eye.

"Nami," called Sumida, "let's go back."

Shiozaki saw us out and we drove away in Sumida's car. We left the blue house and started down the slope lined with cedar trees.

"Oh," I said in a half whisper, "he said he was going to repair a broken wall. He bought the supplies to do it, but..."

That was how he'd explained it to me at least.

"Repair? What?" Sumida asked, his hands at the wheel.

I asked him if there really had been an earthquake.

"I guess you could call it that, but it was actually just a small tremor."

We were in agreement—there was no reason for any broken walls in that house.

3—AN AUTHOR OF FAIRY TALES

Miki watched the car drive away. He closed the front door, turned the lock, and went upstairs to the study.

"I heard talking," said Hitomi from the couch. "Was it that visitor who's been snooping around the house lately?"

Miki shrugged.

"Tell me what happened."

Miki started to explain, but it was more trouble than it was worth so he stopped.

"I kept quiet and didn't cry out for help, but it wasn't to protect you, you know. So don't get the wrong idea. If I'd said something, you would have had to kill somebody, wouldn't you?"

She corrected herself. "Sorry, not kill. It's hard for you to kill anything."

He told the girl that he could certainly kill someone if he wanted. All he had to do was sever the head.

"But if somebody found a corpse in that shape, there'd be trouble, right?"

In that case, he'd make it look like an accident, he explained.

Say he needed to kill a man. Miki couldn't kill the guy by pushing him from a height or using a machine to cut him up. Miki's victims wouldn't die from anything done directly by Miki's own hands. Running down the man with a car wouldn't work either.

But Miki could, for example, get him drunk or make him take sleeping pills, and then push him in front of a car or make him walk along a cliffside and wait for him to fall on his own.

In the case of the former, Miki wouldn't have killed him, the driver would have. And with the latter, it would be suicide. As long as Miki didn't do it himself his mysterious power wouldn't interfere.

"Do you know that for sure? Have you tried it?"

When Miki didn't answer, Hitomi looked as if that was answer enough.

Miki thought back to the conversation he'd had downstairs. *Was the visitor in my house just now? We had a perfectly ordinary chat*...He couldn't tell if he had been suspected.

If things go the wrong way, I might have to abandon this place and move somewhere else.

But first I need to locate—and silence—the visitor. If I do it right, I won't need to find a new home.

4

I went back home once. My father had been telling me to go to my doctor's exam and I felt the longer I put it off, the harder it would be to go back.

To be honest, I wasn't looking forward to it. I had few memories from the time I awoke in the hospital and went to live in that house, and fewer still that I could call fun. My head was occupied with the things Kazuya had seen—the landscapes, Saori, and Kaede's past.

When I told Saori I was going home, she nodded, looking sad. "That's good. You should get back to your own parents."

"Can I come back?"

"When?"

"In four days."

She made a surprised face. "Do you dislike your family that much?"

I solemnly intended to return to Kaede right away. *I still have an important job to do. I have to save Hitomi.* I had lost sight of the solution and was still trying to devise a way to find proof that Shiozaki was the kidnapper.

"Nami..." said Saori, her tone serious. "You've never told me about your family. I know it's not my business, but I've been worrying about how you get along with them. About how maybe you ran away and came here. It isn't right."

After a moment, I fearfully asked, "Do you not want me to come back here?"

"Of course I want you to come back. I just want you to have a talk with your parents—a real talk—and then I want you to come back."

I had Sumida drive me to the train station. Just as when I'd first come to Kaede, I watched the town from the passenger-side window. The cedar trees, the utility poles, and the bridges that spanned the valleys all passed by my window, until finally we emerged into the open space before the station. Nearby was a college, the municipal hospital, and a row of businesses.

Sumida stopped the car in front of the station and asked, "Nami, you're coming back, right? Give me a call when you do and I'll come get you. Saori will be lonely with you gone. When you're at the café everything goes smoothly, just like when Kazuya was alive."

"Everything goes smoothly?"

"Well, what I mean is, it's like you fit perfectly into his place."

I asked him about Kazuya, and he told me that they had been friends for just about the last year of Kazuya's life.

"One night, exactly one year before the accident, I carried him back to the café. He was completely drunk."

"I heard about that. That was the day you met him and Saori."

"Yeah. But when he came to, he had forgotten who I was." He chuckled. "After that we'd come out here, around the train station, and we went to see movies together—stuff like that."

He told me how on one hot, humid summer day, they had gone to a hill covered in fresh green grass. Sumida had skipped his college classes, and Kazuya had already dropped out of school entirely and was spending his aimless days wandering around town. With nothing much else to do, they had tried knocking over some empty cans by throwing rocks at them.

"Now that I mention it," Sumida said softly, as if in shock, "we never really did anything. Just threw rocks. What a couple of losers we were."

"That's not true. I'm jealous of you."

What Sumida had described—the time they had spent idly together—sounded lovely to me. I thought it would be nice to just be in the summer sunlight, to let the days just pass by.

"Thank you for being his friend," I said.

I got out of the car, waved goodbye to Sumida, and went into the station.

The raven key chain hanging inside Sumida's car suddenly reminded me of the fairy tale book at the café. The drawing of the raven pecking his beak at the child's eye must have left a strong impression on me. I decided I would read the story when I returned.

＊

It was a few hours by bullet train.

When I arrived at the station nearest my house, it was already evening. I passed through the turnstile and emerged onto the road in front of the station. The western sky shone red. In the twilight, the rows of stores around the station looked as though they were lit by colored lights.

With a reluctant heart, I walked the distance to the front of my house. Saori had said what she had said, but I still didn't know what to tell my parents. Several times I stopped to decide if I should go home or if I should just turn around and return to Kaede.

But I had already told my father I'd be coming home that day. I didn't want to change the plan.

I arrived at the house with SHIRAKI written on the nameplate. It looked unfamiliar, just another white house like you'd see in any neighborhood.

I rang the doorbell and my mother opened the front door.

When she saw my face her smile disappeared, replaced by a mixed expression.

After a moment I said, "I'm home." She looked away and nodded, and I came inside.

I don't know what to do. I don't know what to say. Fighting back the urge to cry, I followed my mother down the hall.

I didn't hate my mother, but I knew she hated me. *I have to say something. We have to talk.* And yet I was too scared, and I couldn't find the words. It was so bad that I wondered, *Would she just ignore me and pretend she hadn't heard?*

My father in the living room said, "Welcome home."

"I'm sorry I left like that."

Complex emotions flickered across his face, but he said that what was done was done.

The three of us ate dinner. At first my mother and I were silent. To ease the tension my father talked, and every once in a while I threw in a *Yeah?* or an *Uh-huh.* I felt bad for him.

"Where have you been?" he asked. I hadn't told him my exact whereabouts over the phone.

"I was at a friend's house. In the mountains."

I told them about Saori and Melancholy Grove, about Kimura and Sumida.

I talked about how I played cards with Saori, about how Kimura was always whacking Sumida on the head with a tray. As I spoke I started to enjoy it and I couldn't keep the smile from my face. I couldn't explain why, but when I described these people and all that I'd felt, I thought I could go on talking forever.

After a while I noticed that my father had set his elbow on the table and, with his chin resting in his hand, was staring at me.

"That's good," he said. "It's a relief to see you so excited. You're not who you used to be, but I'm glad to see your old smile back again."

My mother's irritation was plain as she stood and began to clear the dishes.

That night I walked out of my room and heard my parents

arguing downstairs. I couldn't hear what they were saying, but I sensed the argument was about me. Now and then I was able to make out the words "Nami" and "that girl."

I sat on the steps and listened to their fight from the shadows. The argument ended before I could grasp what it had been about and the lights downstairs went out. Total darkness and quiet reigned over the house.

The stairway was cold, but I remained sitting there. I thought about a concept that should have been obvious—*I have parents.*

Until that very moment I had felt like the mother and father in this house were not my real parents. Maybe, having lost my memory, it was only natural to feel that way. When Saori told me to talk with my parents, I had wondered if a mom and a dad were really so important.

But they had been arguing about me. They each had their own thoughts about me. I didn't know if what they had said about me had been positive or negative. But they had argued—that was what mattered. Before, I'd imagined that they were worried about me, but I thought of their worry as if it weren't connected to me. Even though I had lost all my memories, in the end I was still their child.

✳

The doctor said that memory was a mysterious thing.

I had come to the hospital—the one where my grandfather had had me undergo the illegal operation—to have my eye examined. With a feeling of nostalgia, I sat before the mustached, just-past-middle-age doctor.

He pressed his thumb below my left eye to the point where I was making the *akanbe* face and told me to look up and down, then left and right. He put my eye under more strain than I tended to, but it held up fine.

He asked me some questions, like, "Do you ever feel any sudden pain in the eye?" and I shook my head no.

"How about your memory?"

"It still hasn't come back."

"I see. Well, it could come back at any time, or you may start to remember things bit by bit."

I was surprised. I had almost entirely stopped thinking about the possibility of my memory returning.

"The brain is a fickle thing," said the doctor. He went on to tell me about the patient of a brain surgeon acquaintance of his.

This patient had lost his memory in a motorcycle accident. He had forgotten everything that had happened to him over the previous ten years. He started a new life for himself and then, two years later, his forgotten memories had slowly come back.

"Sometimes it all comes back at once. Other times people regain their memories slowly, bit by bit. Of course, some never do get their memory back. And there are cases where they've forgotten their sweetheart and in the end they break up. But you're still young. You may yet remember your past."

I thought again about what it would be like for that to happen. I'd go back to being Nami. I couldn't imagine it.

I recalled the me I'd seen in the videotape who still had her memories. Me, confidently playing the piano. My fingers caressing the keys, the sound flooding out. I couldn't believe that my awkward self could ever be like that.

I became uneasy. *If that happened what would become of the current me?* I asked the doctor about it.

"I couldn't say."

He touched his mustache, looking a bit uncomfortable.

He told me that, as my memories came back, I would slowly return to my old self. But I would still remember everything that had happened during the time I had been without memory. I was a little relieved to hear it. As my memories came back, I wouldn't forget Saori and Kazuya.

"What would happen if I were in a situation where the me with my memories and the me without them would have completely different thoughts about something?"

"I've heard something about that."

The doctor told me about a man with a positive attitude who had lost his memory and then become a negative person. But eventually his memory came back and he was reborn a positive man. About the time he spent without his memories he said, "It was like I was dreaming."

The man completely remembered—and understood—his negativity. And yet he felt like it had all been a dream.

"The amount of time amnesiacs tend to go without their memories is trifling compared to the amount of time that has passed from their birth to the moment they lost their memory. It's like a scab atop a vast number of memories. And when the scab peels off, everything you are thinking now may seem like a long dream."

All the way home from the hospital, I thought only of that.

When my memory comes back, what will happen to me? When I return to the me everyone likes, the me that is good at school and can play the piano, what will happen to this insecure me?

Had the previous me been the kind of girl to feel the loneliness of say, walking alone, head lowered, through the cold wind? Had she ever hated herself and wanted to die because she wasn't able to do anything right? Had she ever been envious—or resentful—of the people who everyone seemed to love?

That Nami had seventeen years of history. I had only two months. *If my memory were to come back, would I think of the me who's having these thoughts right now as little and naive, just a leading role within a dream?*

At first, I hadn't dreamt when I was asleep. But lately I'd been having dreams about Saori and Sumida and the rest. And once I'd had a dream in which I was hit by a car. I opened my eyes in the darkness to find myself suddenly rolling down a slope and tumbling onto the road. The nightmare was terrifyingly real. The dream of being struck by that dark blue car burned into my eyelids and for days it was all I could think about.

But most dreams I forgot after waking up. *If my memories*

were to return, would I also forget who I am now? Would the awareness of my present distress fade away?

I felt like Nami was a stranger to me. But deep down I knew that wasn't true at all.

✳

I spent the next two days with an uneasy feeling.

During that time I thought back over all the things I'd experienced.

I remembered how sad I had been when I couldn't play the piano—that had been the most painful experience. I sighed just thinking of it.

Oh yeah, I wonder how that Yuri girl who sat in front of me is doing? She had talked of nothing but who I had been when I still had my memory, and every time she'd done so I'd felt a little sad.

I remembered when my left eye had suddenly heated up and what Kazuya had seen.

Of all the things I remembered, the majority had been given to me by Kazuya. I loved everything he had seen in his life. I loved his past and I loved Kazuya who had seen it all.

Into his eyes he had burned the moment of a bird flapping its wings. When a fish opened its mouth at the surface of the water to beg for food, he had observed it. He saw leaves falling and milk spilling. I felt closer to Kazuya than anyone else.

Whenever I recalled all I'd seen and everything I'd thought during these last two and a half months, I was sad. No matter how happy the memory my chest felt heavy with the thought of it.

One night my mother and I were alone in the house. Dad was working late and hadn't come home yet.

There was an uneasiness between us. Neither had tried to talk to the other. I didn't know what to say. I was sure my mother didn't know either. Even if she did hate me, I wanted to believe that she just didn't know how to start a conversation with me. Both of us were nervous and didn't know how to handle it.

As my mother made dinner I stared at her back—it was as if I were seeing it for the first time since I woke up in the hospital.

Her back was small. Threads of gray were mixed in her hair. She was wearing a sweater, and she was cutting up carrots with a *chop chop chop* of the knife.

That was all there was to the image; it made my heart feel like it would break.

"Mother..." I said to her. She stopped her movements, her shoulders shaking.

I stood in front of her and looked into her eyes. She turned her head away to avoid looking at me.

"Hey, Mother... You used to love me so much, and that's why you hate me now—now that I can't do anything and I don't have my memory, right?"

She didn't answer. *That's fine*, I thought.

"A doctor told me that there was a chance that my memory will come back. He's an eye doctor, but he knows a lot of people who have recovered from amnesia in a matter of years. He said I might return to my old self."

But I want you to listen to me now. Compared to who I used to be, the me now is just some underachiever who can't do anything. But seeing what I've seen I've learned to think in my own way.

When my memory comes back I may not even care about how worried and upset I've been over something as trivial as this. But who I am now is everything to me.

At first I hated myself for being worthless. But not anymore.

Even if my memory does return, I never want to forget who I am now. I want to always remember how I'm frightened and hurt by the littlest things.

I love who I am now. And I want you to accept me too.

"I'm sorry, but I think I'm going to leave again tomorrow. I really am sorry."

With that I left my mother and went upstairs to my room.
Early the next morning, without seeing anyone, I left home.

＊

I called Sumida from the station and he came to pick me up.
When I got in the car he said, "You're back soon."

"There are still a few things I need to do here. How's Saori
doing?"

"She seems kind of down lately," he confided.

Sumida told me another fun story about Kazuya that day. I lived
for every fresh bit of information about Kazuya I could find.

We stopped by Sumida's apartment—a fairly new two-story
building not far from the station—before going back to Kaede.
He had forgotten to set the recording timer on his DVR. I asked
him about the building, and he said it had been built not even a
year before. He was a junior at a college roughly a twenty-minute
drive from the station. His first two years he had lived a little
farther away, but he'd grown tired of the long daily commute and
moved to the new apartment just after it had been built.

I waited in the car while Sumida went to his apartment to set
the recording. When he came back, he sat in the driver's seat and
looked up at the windows of the building and said, "Kazuya came
over here to hang out all the time."

"Really? Did he stay over?"

"When Saori kicked him out, he did." He smiled, amused, and
then shrugged.

Careful not to say too much, I said, "I'd love to hear about it."

I must have said it in a more serious tone than I'd thought,
because he sighed. Then, in the car, with the engine still off, I
listened to him talk about times he had spent with Kazuya.

Kazuya had been a smart boy back when he was in middle
school. But in high school, classes had become more difficult and
his grades had started to fall. Of course, Sumida hadn't met him

until college—Sumida only knew about all this because Kazuya had told him.

Kazuya barely made it into college—not the same one as Sumida went to—but by then he'd lost interest in studying.

"He dropped out and stopped doing anything with himself."

For whatever reason, Kazuya hadn't been in a hurry to make anything of his life. After he stopped going to school he spent every day as if time had stopped, doing whatever he felt like. And by that I don't mean to imply that he did anything in particular. Rather, when he quit his classes he stopped seeing his friends. Until he met Sumida nobody ever called him; his peers had stopped coming to see him. Alone, he walked Kaede until struck by some thought, such as *I should see what the view is from the top of that hill,* or *I should go climb the jungle gym at my old grade school.*

"He was like a hermit," Sumida said, deep emotion in his voice.

When Saori got mad at Kazuya for being lazy and not doing anything with himself, he'd escape to Sumida's apartment.

I started to feel giddy.

In the car on the way to Kaede I could think of nothing but Kazuya. Sumida tried talking to me as he drove, but I only gave half-hearted responses and eventually he gave up, shrugged, and let me be.

I sat there picturing it—Kazuya walking through Kaede in the summer, when the earth was covered with life. As he walked through grass as tall as he was, Kazuya brushed the leaves with his hand. A bird sat chirping on the edge of the roof of a house and Kazuya drew near, then watched as the bird flew away in alarm. As he walked and watched and felt the wind, he might have almost been having a one-on-one conversation with the world.

Reflected in the side-view mirror, my left eye stared back at me.

I loved Kazuya. I had been trying not to think about what kind of feeling it was. *It's just the kind of affection you feel for someone close to you,* I told myself. *If it's anything more than that it'll hurt. He's dead.*

But not only did I have those feelings for him, I also, oddly enough, thought of him as myself. Sometimes I even wondered if his soul had possessed my empty body. Of course, I only felt that way because I'd taken in so much of what he'd seen. I didn't think it was a bad thing. But when I tried to think about who I was, I couldn't find a simple answer.

Who am I? Without my memories, I'm not Nami. I'm a lot like Kazuya, but I'm not him either.

Now that I'm back in Kaede, pushing myself to seek vengeance for Kazuya, how long will I be able to remain me?

Soon we had entered Kaede. It was already dusk—the journey from my house had taken all day.

Once more I looked at the outside of Melancholy Grove. Inside would be Kimura, the bearlike manager, and behind the counter, that stuffed-up part-timer would be blowing her nose.

She met me with a smile and said, "Welcome back!"

I thought I might cry. Even if my memory were to come back, I didn't want to forget how I felt at that moment.

"Nami, did you talk with your parents?" Saori asked.

I answered vaguely, "Yeah, well, a little."

"Isn't school starting up again for you? Is it okay for you to be here?"

"Hmmmmm…It might not be okay, but you don't have to worry about it."

Saori put her elbows on the counter, resting her chin in her hands, and looked at me sharply. "You're not planning on skipping school, are you?"

Anxiously I drew my hands to my chest, covering my heart.

She laughed and said, "You can't hide anything from me!"

As we talked the thought that I might disappear became more and more painful.

No, I'm not going to disappear. I don't know if my memory is ever coming back, but even if it does, I won't forget about Saori and the rest of them.

It's just…when I become Nami again, the deep feelings I now have for them may change. That was my fear.

After we ate dinner at her uncle's house, I told Saori about how I skipped school a lot and about how I wasn't getting along with my mother. The only part I left out was why.

"In time things will get better," she said softly, consolingly. "Time is the best doctor they say."

"Maybe the doctor is out."

I really wanted to tell her that I had amnesia. But I couldn't confess it to her without revealing that I had lied about being Kazuya's friend.

Someday, if this is all over, I'll tell her. I'll tell her why I'm here.

✳

That night, as I was brushing my teeth before bed, I heard the sound of the front door opening. I rinsed out my mouth and went to the door, where I noticed that Mr. Ishino's worn-out shoes were gone. The sliding front door had a lattice pattern of frosted glass. I could see the old man on the other side.

Without thinking anything else of it I opened the door to say good night.

He was sitting on the steps that led down to the front gate. His back was small and hunched over. He didn't seem like the same person Kazuya's left eye had seen. It was as if he had lost his strength and withered away.

When he noticed I was the one who had opened the door he gave me a weak smile, lowered his head a little, and said, "Hey."

"I'm going to bed. Good night." Before I went back inside, I asked from the doorway, "What are you doing?"

He seemed to have trouble answering. I started to worry that I had asked a rude question.

"I was thinking of my wife."

He looked over at the washing line at the side of the house. He was sitting just where he could see it. That was where she had collapsed and passed on.

"I'm sorry, I shouldn't have asked..."

I wanted to cry.

"It's okay. I just have a lot on my mind."

Outside it was cold and still. The darkness of night had stripped away all warmth.

It seemed like he was going to keep sitting there, like he was punishing himself for something.

He was apologizing to his wife. He had been violent toward her, and his regret had made him how he was now.

He was meditating in the freezing cold, but I felt I shouldn't interfere with his sacred ritual.

And yet my feet stayed in place. From the front door I said to his back, "Kazuya told me about your wife."

I had seen it in my left eye.

One night the old man had passed out drunk in the living room. His wife—standing above him with an expression that said, "Well, what else can I do?"—had covered him with a blanket. That was the whole inconsequential vision.

But somehow her expression had overflowed with kindness for her husband, though I didn't know why.

I told him about the love she had shown for him as if I had heard it from Kazuya.

"I'm sure she didn't feel any resentment or unhappiness...At least that's what Kazuya said."

He went quiet.

I turned to go back inside.

"Thank you," he said without looking at me.

I got into my futon and thought, *She had to have known. She had to have thought he would feel like this after she died. Maybe that's how she could have had that expression. Maybe she could see him for who he was, and that's how she could be kind to him.*

She saw into the future.

Would just anyone have noticed her? Kazuya hadn't passed the moment by. Was it a coincidence that of all the many sights he had seen, that moment had burned vividly into his eyes? I don't think it was. Kazuya had realized the beauty of that moment and turned his eyes upon it.

❋

I knew Hitomi was inside that blue brick house. But without any solid proof of Shiozaki's guilt I couldn't accuse him of anything.

In the café Shiozaki spoke to me. "I noticed I hadn't seen you in a while, but then I heard you went back to your own home."

"Yeah," I answered. On the inside I was screaming.

He's the one who caused Kazuya's accident. I was nervous. Nervous and infuriated. Trying to hold back my fear, I took care not to say anything unusual.

But with that he walked past me to his table at the rear of the café. Not until he sat did I feel relief.

Sometimes I stayed at Melancholy Grove until the sun set and the café closed. When I did, I would walk the nighttime streets home with Saori. To get to her uncle's house we had to walk along a dark road that cut through the forest. Saori said it was nothing to worry about, but I couldn't help it.

That particular day I planned to stay at the café until it closed, so I had some time to kill there talking and reading.

On the shelf with the magazines and comic books, I saw the fairy tale book I'd noticed before—*The Eye's Memory.* I remembered its creepy illustrations. Maybe that was why, as if on command, I took the book into my hands.

I sat at the counter and started to read. As I turned the pages, stirred-up air danced under my nose. I was struck by a strange premonition that I was about to see something bad.

I read a little bit. The main character was a talking raven.

As I continued, I noticed that some parts of the story were similar to my own experiences. The blind girl put the eyes the raven gave her into her eye sockets, and then in her dreams saw what the eyes had seen.

I thought the illustration of the raven taking out people's eyeballs for the girl was horrifying—nothing I'd want a child to see.

But when I finished the story, the picture of the raven gliding through the air, eyeball in his beak, stuck with me, very clear in my mind. The image was so strong I could almost hear his wings flapping.

The raven didn't want the girl to learn of the evil he'd done. He didn't want her to know that he wasn't a human. He'd struggled with it. And then, that ending.

"Even if it wasn't going to have a happy ending," I said to Saori, "I feel so sorry for the girl's parents the way it concluded."

She had been waiting behind the counter to hear what I thought of the tale. She made her fingers into the shape of a pistol, pointed it at me, and said, "Same here."

"Is this book here because Kimura likes it?"

"I don't think it's his. One day it was just there on the shelf."

As I flipped through the pages once more, a realization came to me. Near the beginning the raven takes the eye of the baker's son, and when the boy sees the raven's beak clutching his own eye, he's surprised at first and then becomes angry. And that was odd. Wouldn't he have felt pain? It seemed like pain had been left out altogether.

I looked for the name of the author and found it: Shun Miki. A man's name.

Saori and I walked home, shivering in the cold. Saori had always been talkative with me, but this night she was silent, something on her mind. I wondered if something was troubling her and then I remembered what Sumida had said.

"What are you thinking about?"

"Well..." Saori muttered, "Kyoko."

That was an answer I hadn't expected. Why would she be worried about Kyoko?

"You know," I said, "that one time, you were coming from the road that goes to her house..."

"I had gone to visit her. I wanted to talk to her." When I asked why, she wouldn't tell me, giving me only an ambiguous smile.

After we had walked in silence for a while, we came upon her uncle's house.

"When Kazuya said that he wanted to donate his eyes, did you oppose it?"

"Just a little. But it didn't really bother me much."

"Why not?"

"Well, because it's what he wanted. And isn't it a little exciting to think that his eyes are still alive somewhere out there?"

She laughed. Then she told me about when he had filled out the consent form.

"A year ago he went to see his eye doctor. He came home with a pamphlet about organ transplants."

He had filled out the form in front of her, saying his eye would be given to someone else after his death.

Family consent was required for organ donors, and Saori gave hers. Hearing her talk about it, I was filled with emotion.

If the two of them hadn't done that, what would have happened to me? At the very least I would never have come here. I would never have been able to make these cherished memories. Then, someday my memory would have returned and my feelings would have changed, and I would never have known the sadness of not wanting to forget who I was.

Unfortunately, I hadn't seen that fateful event in the memories of my left eye. Might I yet see it? I certainly hoped so.

Then suddenly I realized why I hadn't seen it.

"When you signed those papers, did Kazuya have a bandage over his eye?"

"Why do you ask?" She looked at me with curiosity, then told me that he had. "He had the bandages on for about three days and yeah, I think he had them on then."

"Was it his right eye or his left?"

"His left eye."

The eye transplanted into my face had been covered by bandages. No matter how much time might pass by, I would never see him settling those papers, because the eye had never seen it.

At that moment I became aware of a certain possibility. His left eye had been prevented from recording these events because it had been covered with bandages...Maybe there was a similar explanation for the discrepancy in the path from the accident site to Shiozaki's house.

What if when he was escaping from the house after seeing Hitomi through the cellar window something had covered his eye? Or he had closed his eyes. What if while the eye was blinded he had crossed the road, jumped over the guardrail, and fallen down the concrete wall. Then his eyesight had returned, and he'd run through the cedar trees, rolled down the slope, and gotten hit by the car.

Would the vision have gone black while his left eye was covered? When I had seen it in the library I'd been in shock, and I might not have noticed the vision going dark. All he had done was cross a road and fall. It would have taken only five seconds.

One mystery solved.

Hitomi is in Shiozaki's house. She must be. And I was right—that house must be the same one Kazuya saw.

After some hesitation I borrowed Mr. Ishino's phone to call the police. As it was cordless I was able to make the call away from Saori and her uncle. Had they heard me talking, explaining myself would have been difficult—they thought I was calling my parents.

Telling myself, *I'm right about this*, I summoned the courage to push those three crucial numbers: 1–1–0. Until that moment I had thought it pointless to call the police, but I had to at least try.

Over the line came a voice that sounded like it belonged to a middle-aged man; it informed me I was talking to the police.

I started by asking about a missing girl named Hitomi Aizawa. "Um...Do you—do you know who she is?"

He didn't.

"She went missing over a year ago."

Then I told him that there was a chance she was being held captive in someone's house.

From the phone came a half-hearted, "Oh..." Then he said, "Well, we'll investigate it on our end. We'll need to call you back. What's your phone number?"

For a moment I didn't say anything. The phone number would have to be Mr. Ishino's number. *If the police call it and he or Saori answers, what will they think about me? I might have to confess to them, under awkward circumstances, that I've been lying about my friendship with Kazuya.* I didn't want that to happen.

"Um...Do I absolutely have to tell you?"

Immediately his tone turned distrustful.

I realized that by not telling him the number, I'd made him suspicious of me. But there was nothing to do about it; the damage was done.

He accused me of pulling a prank. I insisted I wasn't, but the call ended without my having gotten anywhere.

The next day I went to Melancholy Grove with new resolve. Shiozaki always came at one in the afternoon. I talked with Kyoko until then.

She seemed interested in Saori.

In the middle of our conversation she said casually, "I wonder how Saori feels about her brother."

She may not have fully accepted that he's dead. That was what I thought, but I couldn't find the right words to say it.

"I get the feeling she still thinks about him a lot," said Kyoko.

I told her about the gold watch that he had with him at the time of the crash, and how Saori kept it as a keepsake.

"A watch?"

"It broke in the accident. Its hands stopped at the moment of impact."

I thought back to what Saori had said on the way home the day before. What had Saori and Kyoko talked about? I wanted to know but hesitated to ask.

The clock inside the café pointed to one o'clock. The door opened and the clear chime rang, announcing the arrival of a customer.

Shiozaki entered in his usual black coat, walking with un-wavering, evenly paced steps. He crossed in front of the counter, headed for the dark area in back.

I lowered my head and brought forth my courage. I was scared. But now that the police thought I was pranking them, I couldn't think of any other way.

"What's wrong?" Kyoko tilted her head.

"It's nothing." I gave her a slight smile, stood, and walked over to the table where Shiozaki sat.

From inside my pocket I took out an old newspaper clipping. Printed on it was Hitomi Aizawa's photograph.

I stopped in front of him and said, "Shiozaki."

His eyes met mine. "Hello."

I noticed that my body was shaking. *If I'm going to turn back, now's my chance*. But I didn't know what else there was for me to do.

"There's something I'd like to ask you." I held out Hitomi's photograph. "I'm looking for this girl. Do you know her?"

I struggled to hide the wavering in my voice. He took the newspaper clipping from my hand. As he did our fingers touched. The dreadful coldness of his hand made me feel as if my whole body had been covered in ice.

For a short time, he looked at the picture. Then he looked at me.

"Can't say I do." He handed the clipping back to me.

That was all we said to each other that day in the café.

I had expected that kind of response. But if he was the kidnap-per, he wouldn't be able to maintain his composure after seeing that picture.

He must be wondering why I'm looking for Hitomi, and why I asked him about it. To find out—or to keep me from talking and to keep her hidden—he might resort to violence.

Good. Let him, I thought. Because the moment he did, I'd have my chance to expose him for what he was.

PART 4

1—AN AUTHOR OF FAIRY TALES

"You're waiting for your chance, aren't you?" said Hitomi from the sofa. "Or is it that you think another killing—or the addition of a new resident to the cellar—would be too risky?"

Miki was packing all of his belongings. When he had moved to the house he hadn't brought much with him, so he had very little to pack—mostly clothes and books. But his other preparations were taking him days to finish.

"When I wanted to see the outside, you took the car, remember? I was seen then," Hitomi said. "And just because you bought a new one, that doesn't mean anything. That visitor knows your face. And your name too. You can't escape. You'll have to deal with it."

She narrowed her eyes and smiled calmly. Sitting on the sofa like that, the limbless girl looked like a doll.

Leaving her there, Miki went down to the cellar. Almost all of the rooms in the house were in order except for that one.

As he came into the cellar he heard Yukie singing. It was the same sad English song she always sang. Her voice came from the darkness beyond the reach of the room's dim light, echoing off the bare brick walls, filling the cellar.

He transferred the large pile of bricks from the corner of the room to the foot of the steps. It took him a number of trips to move them all.

Yukie's singing stopped.

"What are you doing?" she asked from the darkness. Then suddenly she gave a painful groan and said, "My ankle's on a jagged rock and it's hurting!"

"Sorry," Shinichi apologized. Miki could hear the sound of their massive body moving about.

He told them that he was leaving the house.

"Oh, I see," said Shinichi. Miki sensed his nod. "So this is goodbye, then."

"What do you mean?" asked Yukie.

"I'll explain it to you later," Shinichi answered.

Miki left the cellar and went back to the second-floor study where Hitomi was. When the girl in the sack saw him, her face went sad.

"If you're not thinking of taking me with you, then you either have to kill me or you have to hide me somewhere nobody will ever find me. You're trying the latter. Listen, just one last time, I want to see the sun."

Miki picked her up in his arms. The girl was just a head and a torso and he lifted her easily. Her long hair, brightly shimmering as if it were damp, flowed through the air as he moved.

"When you get caught, I'll testify that you were good to me."

Miki laid her down next to the window.

2

After showing Hitomi's picture to Shiozaki, I spent my time battling fear. *He could strike at any moment*, I thought.

The café kitchen was equipped with an assortment of potential weapons. At least five chef's knives, ranging from small to large, were easily available. But I didn't feel like taking any of them. Having to spend my days with a knife hidden inside my coat seemed like too much trouble. Besides, I didn't have any confidence that if he came from behind and pinned my arms I'd be able to stab him anyway.

In the end I decided to take a paring knife I'd found in the back of one of the cupboards. It was small, the kind that folds shut. I didn't know if it would actually be of any help, but I needed a blade to steady my heart.

I wrote a letter to Saori and her uncle. *If anything happens to me they'll search my things. They'll find the letter, learn why I came to Kaede, and why I suddenly vanished.*

If I disappear the police will have to act. I wrote about Shiozaki in the letter. If he attacks me, I win.

Every morning I realized anew that I was still alive. When I walked outside and when I was alone at home, I looked in all directions and listened for every sound. My heart was always beating fast. Even the slightest noise would make me nearly scream.

But Shiozaki didn't come to me. In fact, he had even stopped coming to Melancholy Grove.

Everything has an ending. But I didn't know if this would be a happy ending.

It was three days since I had shown the photo to Shiozaki.

It was to be the last day of my inquiry.

✳

The morning was terribly cold, and when I awoke my hands and feet were freezing. My toes tingled with a faint numbness. I curled up in the futon, wrapping my hands around my feet to warm them. As I did I felt strangely at peace. I cherished the moment.

Soon my heart began to beat faster. I opened my eyes, a premonition piercing through me. It was indistinct but had to do with my investigation. *This has to come to an end someday, I'm sure of it. And when it does, it will be on a day with a cold morning, like this one.* I couldn't explain why, but I was convinced of it.

I turned my thoughts to Kazuya and then Hitomi, and finally I crept out from the futon.

"And to think it's April," Saori's uncle grumbled. He put his arms through the sleeves of his jacket and left for work. After we saw him off, Saori and I headed for the café.

I was worried about what I should do if Shiozaki appeared while Saori and I were walking together. Saori, through no fault of her own, would be drawn into my plan. To be honest, I'd spent as much time as possible away from Saori the past two days.

But after three days without contact from Shiozaki I had stopped taking as many precautions. Although that morning's premonition was still on my mind, I figured we could at least walk together.

"Spring break is ending soon," Saori said to me. Her breath was white. Her nose was red, and it caused her to sniffle constantly as she talked.

"Yeah," I said. "I think the new school year starts the day after tomorrow."

"So you'll be studying for the college exams now."

Will I be at the opening ceremony? I didn't want to go home with things left unfinished.

"I want to stay here longer."

Saori looked at me uneasily.

The café had a large space heater. I shamelessly sat down in the seat closest to it and read through *The Eye's Memory* again. By the time the hands of the clock pointed to twelve not a single customer had come.

A little before noon Saori left. I was sitting by the heater thinking about Shiozaki when she took off her apron and said, "I'm going to Kyoko's house for a bit. Say bye to the boss for me."

I nodded. Kimura was back in the kitchen. After she had left, I went to tell him.

"But this isn't delivery day," he said, touching his mustache.

Shiozaki had always come to Melancholy Grove at one in the afternoon. But when there was no sign of him at one, my emotions became a complicated mixture of relief and worry.

It was unsettling. I didn't know what he was thinking or where he was. *Maybe he's already escaped.*

When I came to that thought it felt right.

"That's one less regular," Kimura grumbled. "What the hell happened to him?" He looked disappointed that Shiozaki had stopped coming—and maybe even a little worried about him.

Sumida, who had been talking with Kimura, said, his straw still in his mouth, "And he didn't say anything about going on a vacation." His glass of orange juice was empty save for the ice.

Sumida had popped in an hour after Saori had left. Of course, he'd come to see her. When I had told him she was out, he had looked dejected, his head lowering.

I considered further my surmise that Shiozaki had fled.

If he did, then what's at his home? Did he dispose of all the evidence before he left the house? What evidence would there be? Something he'd needed to keep Hitomi captive?

First, her clothes. Clothes Hitomi would wear...I had seen women's clothing inside the house. But the Hitomi Kazuya had seen hadn't had any arms or legs and was wrapped in a sack. In that case she wouldn't be able to wear regular clothing.

But maybe the clothing I had seen was what she'd been wearing at the time of her kidnapping.

After following my thoughts that far, I realized something else that would be necessary for a captive. A place to keep her. *If Shiozaki had gotten rid of all the evidence, would he also have disguised the existence of the cellar?* It seemed like the windows had been covered by the brick planters within the last two months. All he had to do was seal up the entrance and no one would ever discover the cellar was there.

What other evidence would there be? What could be used to identify him as the kidnapper?

I stood. I was angered by my foolishness. And I was terrified. Wasn't there something important, something I had to find?

Hitomi Aizawa herself. If anyone were to find her alive, it would be fatal for him. So, what would he do?

He might take her with him, or he might make sure she stays silent forever.

I had to go straight to Shiozaki's house.

✳

"I need you to drive me somewhere!"

Sumida looked at me in surprise. "What? Where?"

"It doesn't matter! Get up!" I tugged at the sleeve of his sweater and pulled him to his feet. "I'll tell you in the car!"

Behind the counter Kimura watched us, looking amused. "Just drive her," he ordered Sumida, his voice calm. I didn't know if he said it because my distress irritated him, but whatever his reason, I was thankful he did.

I pushed Sumida out the front of the café. I left without paying— not wanting to take the time, I decided I'd pay later.

The outside must have been cold, but I was too excited to feel it. I found Sumida's car in the café parking lot and opened the passenger-side door. We got in.

"First," he said in a calming voice, "you need to settle down. You stretched out my sleeve pulling it like that."

"I'm sorry." I took a deep breath. "But I'm in a hurry. So hurry to Shiozaki's house."

Sumida opened his mouth in surprise. "Why?"

"I'll explain on the way. First, please, just start the car."

He quietly turned the ignition and started the car. We left the Melancholy Grove parking lot and headed for Shiozaki's house.

"So tell me why. Why am I driving to Shiozaki's house?"

I wasn't sure whether or not I should tell him about Hitomi. When I considered it a little more rationally, I thought that I really shouldn't get him involved. But in the end, I decided to tell him of the possibility that Shiozaki had kidnapped a little girl.

"I don't want you to be shocked when I say this."

"I can't be any more shocked than when I first saw that fierce look on your face."

"I need you to listen to me seriously."

After a beat Sumida said, "Okay," and nodded. His eyes were fixed on the road ahead. Suddenly I felt reassured. *It's better to go with him than by myself*, I thought.

I told him about Hitomi, and then about my surmise that she was being kept in the cellar of Shiozaki's blue brick house.

Everything else, like how Shiozaki had caused Kazuya's death, I refrained from discussing. Telling him about my left eye would have made things complicated.

"Three days ago, I showed a newspaper clipping to Shiozaki. It had Hitomi's photograph on it."

I explained that I had been waiting for Shiozaki to come after me, but I had just arrived at the conclusion that he had silenced the girl and fled.

Sumida listened earnestly to me. When I had finished, he said, his face pale and his voice weak, "But...Shiozaki? I can't believe it."

"Please believe me."

"But..."

The car advanced along the snaking road that led to the house. The road began to slope uphill; both sides were flanked with cedar trees. We passed the site where Kazuya had died.

I said, "That's fine. You don't need to believe me. I'll go to the house alone and you can wait in the car. There's a strong chance that Shiozaki may still be there. It's going to be dangerous. If I don't come back, I want you to go the police." I was scared, but I didn't want to be unreasonable with him.

"It's going to be dangerous?"

"Probably. But I have a weapon of sorts. A paring knife."

I thought I saw Sumida's face grow even paler.

"But...even so, I can't let you go alone."

I was so grateful for his words I thought I might cry.

We went around a corner and passed the side road to Kyoko's house.

Soon I could see the short leafless trees that mingled with the frozen-looking cedars farther up the slope.

Nothing moved, as if the merciless cold had imprisoned all life. The trees might have been carved from stone.

Low clouds shut away the sun, shading everything in gloomy darkness.

Finally the blue brick house came into view above the slope. A chill ran down my spine.

"Don't take the car onto the property," I said. "We'll park close by and walk the rest of the way."

"Why's that?"

"Otherwise, if Shiozaki is still there he might notice us."

I wanted one more look around the house before we opened the door. Sumida drove the compact car up the inclined road. I closed my eyes and cast off the surging terror. My body was trembling, and not from the temperature. I hugged my body and endured.

I made a silent prayer to Kazuya's left eye.

When he came to the house to save Hitomi, how much terror did he endure?

Give me courage.

The car stopped. We were on the side of the road not far from the gate of the house.

"Are you ready?" asked Sumida, his face ashen.

I nodded and stepped out of the car.

3

Two stone gateposts as tall as myself stood on either side of the road leading to the grounds of Shiozaki's house. The rusted iron doors of the gate had been left open. Ducking our heads a bit, Sumida and I passed through it.

We emerged from the narrow bush-lined path to see the blue brick house before us. Although you could easily find taller buildings, its two stories were large enough to envelop the sky. The tip of its gabled roof pointed straight up at the low gray clouds.

The house seemed like a giant demon pregnant with darkness. As I looked at it, some helpless little thing within the deepest reaches of my soul began to tremble. No matter how positive and true my feelings were, the moment I saw that house I couldn't help but realize I was just one solitary person.

Blue is the color of darkness and loneliness. As you descend deeper into the sea, you enter depths where light cannot reach. The blue of the water's surface and the darkness of the sea below are not two separate things. The color of the house before me was cold testament to that fact.

Though it was still afternoon, clouds covered the sun, making it dark outside—maybe dark enough that you'd need to have the lights on inside.

But the windows on this side of the house revealed only a still darkness. It didn't seem like anyone was there.

In front was a large gravel drive for cars to park. Shiozaki's black car was there. Alone.

"I wonder if Shiozaki is still home," I said to Sumida. I was nervous and my voice sounded stilted to my ears.

"He might have left his car when he fled."

We were half hidden in the woods that surrounded the house. The forest was so quiet I could hear ringing in my ears. Occasionally a bird would flap its wings somewhere; that was the only sound.

As I stood, enthralled by the quiet, I saw a lone raven on the roof. It was just a black dot, like someone had taken the tip of a needle and poked a hole in space. The bird was keeping watch, swiveling its black neck in search of intruders.

We decided to start our search by circling around the outside of the house from opposite sides.

"Sumida, you go to the right. I'll search the left."

"If anything happens," Sumida said with a worried look, "scream."

He moved, hiding himself between the trees. Doing the same, I advanced through the forest toward the left-hand side of the house.

Separated from Sumida, I suddenly felt very alone. Sumida wasn't strong—rather, his thin frame and arms made him look frail. But having someone around was a comfort.

The blue brick wall shot straight up from the ground, and with each step closer, I felt it loom ever higher. When I finally reached the house I looked up. The wall occupied over half the sky above.

As I stared silently at the wall, my eyes went out of focus and I started to feel dizzy. The orderly rows of bricks buried themselves deep into my mind, and from their other side I sensed screams of agony and terror.

Waves of nausea and anxiety swept over me. I steadied my hand on the trunk of the tree next to me and closed my eyes to calm myself down. Struggling to breathe, I gulped for air.

With my entire body I sensed the forest and the house. Cold fingertips of air brushed my cheeks. I could feel the tension all across the surface of my skin as it took in the isolation and the cold.

Had Kazuya felt like this too? When he came to rescue Hitomi and he searched around the outside of the house, had he been afraid?

After he first saw Hitomi, had he come like this to investigate before the day he tried to break the window? He might have. After all he had come with that screwdriver hidden in his pocket, prepared to break in.

Now I'm doing the same things he did. I have inherited his purpose and am reenacting Hitomi's rescue.

My breath steady, I opened my eyes.

I had stood there with my eyes shut for around ten seconds. That was all the time I had needed to find the handful of courage it took to step forward.

I moved out from between the trees and pressed my body against the wall. Careful not to make any sound, I moved along the side of the house.

Had I been noticed? From atop the house I heard the flapping of the raven's wings as it flew away.

4—AN AUTHOR OF FAIRY TALES

Miki was in the study. He had finished most of his packing, and all that was left for him to do was seal off the cellar and leave. With the help of an acquaintance, the house would easily pass to a new tenant.

He would leave behind the desk and the chair, the clock and the curtains and such. The house would be almost as it had been when he came to it. Only his personal belongings would come with him.

Suddenly remembering something, Miki opened the desk drawer. He took out the object inside and looked at it for a time. It was the object the visitor had dropped outside the house.

Just then, Miki thought he heard the flapping of a bird's wings outside.

If it were any other time, he wouldn't have thought anything of it. But right then, as he was about to make his disappearance, the sound was disconcerting.

He slipped the object into his pocket.

He looked out the study window—nothing out of the ordinary.

Miki left the room and walked down the second-floor hallway. The open stairwell at the top of the stairs looked down on the first floor. The hallway around the stairwell made an L-shape, terminating at a window.

Miki approached the window and put his face to the glass, looking out the southern side of the house. Not wanting to make any noise he didn't open the window, but with the window closed he couldn't see directly below.

And yet, for an instant, just beyond the very edge of the windowsill, he saw the shoulder of someone moving around to the back of the house. Whoever it was was pressed against the brick wall, moving around the side of the house, searching.

Miki moved. Quietly, he descended the staircase.

A sack of bricks and plaster had been left at the bottom of the steps. He had brought them from the cellar a little bit at a time.

Chance put the hammer in Miki's hand. He had left his toolbox at the bottom of the stairs just in case he needed it to seal off the basement; the hammer was inside. The head of the hammer was covered in rust, but heavy enough and perfectly suited for smashing.

Miki headed for the visitor.

5

I walked along the walls of the house. I figured that if I hugged the walls, I wouldn't be easily seen from the second floor. I kept my shoulders and palms against the bricks as I moved. The walls were cold and dry. My white breath brushed the rows of rectangular bricks and faded into the air.

The house wasn't shaped like a simple four-sided box. Sections where rooms jutted out made sharp corners of the exterior walls. At each turn I held my breath, frightened that Shiozaki would suddenly appear before me.

I carefully peeked into the windows one by one. Nearly all of them had their curtains closed. *Shiozaki isn't here after all.* There was a feeling of emptiness only found in a vacant home.

Here and there along the sides of the house were a few brick-work planters. Not much grew within them—just some dead brown grass. Sometimes thin dry branches poked out of the dirt, signs that shrubs had once grown there. Now, their leaves had gone and only withered stems remained.

The southwest corner of the house most closely matched the memory I'd seen in my left eye. The last time I'd come, I'd been convinced that Kazuya had been here.

Again I stood in that spot. But sure enough, the cellar window Kazuya had seen was gone. At the intersection of the wall and the earth wasn't a window but a planter.

I dug into the dirt inside the planter, but the earth was frozen, hard to dig into with my bare hands. The bricks of the planter were set with mortar and wouldn't come apart.

This must have been built hastily sometime in the past two months. There might be a weakness in it somewhere. If there was I never found it.

I stopped thinking about it. I wanted to avoid staying in the same place for long.

Continuing around to the back, I saw the shed I had noticed

before. It might have been built along with the house. The wooden
boards from which it was made were old and starting to rot. Apparently they had once been white, but the paint had peeled off,
revealing stains from the rainwater.

Some boards were starting to come off in places, allowing the
darkness inside to peek out. I gripped the shed's door handle and
tried to open it, but the door wouldn't budge. I put my strength
into it and it gave. Nothing was inside. Empty.

That was when I noticed the window.

The window was in the wall shared by the shed, a little bit
above me. It didn't seem to have closed curtains. I don't mean
to say there weren't curtains—there were, but they were cinched
open on either side, allowing an unobstructed view of the home's
interior.

I looked around to make sure I was alone.

The window was high up. Because the house was built on a
slope, even windows on the same floor ended up being at differ-
ing heights outside.

I peered through the shed window to get a look inside the
house. I slipped my toes between the boards on the side of the
shed, gripped the windowsill, and lifted myself up.

My nose came up to the windowpane.

I looked inside.

6—AN AUTHOR OF FAIRY TALES

Miki came out through the front door and walked along the
walls of the house. The figure he'd caught a glimpse of from the
second floor seemed to have been moving around the west side
of the house; he was right behind.

Miki thought about the visitor. This wasn't the first time someone had sniffed out his secret.

He'd never really taken any care to hide his crimes.

Not even his first murder, when he'd suddenly shoved the

woman who'd asked him for directions off a cliff. Looking back at it he still didn't know why he'd done it. He never thought about the consequences of getting caught. He felt like he wouldn't even mind being captured.

But if Miki could get away with it, he intended to. If he could silence the visitor who had come to his house, he would.

Hammer firmly in hand, he crept forward. Finally, after passing a number of places where the walls jutted out, he stopped.

From around the next corner had come a glimpse of clothing. His latest visitor was there.

The visitor seemed unaware that the master of the house was watching. Still hidden, Miki hushed his breath.

It's what always happens. How many have come to this house now?

It had been the same at the last place he'd lived. He recalled what had happened then. A housewife had been the visitor that time. *She'd seen me walking outside and had looked at me suspiciously. Maybe I'd seemed strange for avoiding all contact with my neighbors. I buried two people in the mountains when I lived there. Had she suspected me? I could have killed her, but I chose another option since her family might have made a fuss over her sudden disappearance. In the end I thought it would be simpler to just move someplace else before she could find conclusive proof.*

And so Miki had come to Kaede.

He pressed his face and shoulders against the brick wall and looked again at the visitor.

White clouds of breath hung in the air as the visitor peered through a window.

Miki searched his memory for what might be on the other side of that window. He remembered what he had left there at once.

And he knew it was time for him to act.

Hitomi had said she wanted to see the sun.

If she hadn't made that request, Miki might not have needed to silence the visitor. All he'd had left to do was seal off the cellar and leave.

But Hitomi was on the other side of the window. He had laid her down there with his own arms.

The visitor seemed to have seen her.

Although it was small and restrained, the visitor let out a cry of surprise.

7

There wasn't much of anything on the other side of the window, just a bookshelf lined with the spines of oversized books—art books, perhaps. Several paintings leaned, unhung, against the side of the bookcase. Shiozaki must have been using the room for storage.

Not sure whether I should feel relieved or bewildered, I lowered myself from the shed. Is Shiozaki really not here after all?

Suddenly, a shadow fell in my path. I was about to scream when I realized it was Sumida. I felt my strength drain from my body.

"Was there anything?" he asked.

I shook my head.

We decided to go inside.

We tried the front but it was locked and wouldn't open. But Sumida had found a back door on the northern side of the house. When I turned the handle it opened quietly, unlocked.

The inside was dark. Not only was it cloudy outside, but we were on the northern side of the house. I couldn't rely on my eyes to see anything and I debated whether or not to turn on the lights, thinking it might be dangerous if Shiozaki was around. But Sumida, unconcerned with such thoughts, quickly flipped the switch.

"It's fine, there's nobody here."

"We need to be more careful," I said, but inside I was feeling the confidence of having the two of us together again.

The back door had led into the kitchen.

The small, dim light revealed an old refrigerator and cabinets. Within the quiet, I could hear the low hum of the fridge.

The sink was free of dirty dishes and refuse, and there were no signs that anyone had cooked there recently. But rather than having been well cleaned, the kitchen might just have been in disuse.

We checked from room to room, but found nobody anywhere.

In one room that might have been in use as a studio, a half-finished work had been left—a painting of the house's yard. On a table smeared with paint sat a cup holding paintbrushes.

The clothes Shiozaki had said had belonged to his wife were still there, and more women's clothing had been neatly folded and packed into a semi-transparent storage box.

None looked the right size for Hitomi to wear; more than that, they all looked like clothes an adult would choose.

After we had looked inside an empty bathroom, Sumida said, "Nobody's here."

If he was still nervous it didn't show. He even seemed doubtful that Hitomi was being held here, that Shiozaki was her kidnapper. He didn't come out and say so, but I could tell from his tone.

We walked the dim hallways in search of a door we hadn't yet opened. There had to be an entrance to the cellar, but we found no doors that looked like one.

In the hallway Sumida said, "Nami, let's go. Something must be wrong with your theory."

I was downcast. I didn't see how that could be. But I was unsure of what to do and had no reply.

"There's still the second floor," I said.

"I won't go."

He put his hands on his hips and stood fast.

I went up the stairs alone. At the top, a hallway wrapped around the stairwell, with several doors along the walkway.

One led to a room that looked like Shiozaki's bedroom. Another had an old wooden desk.

In the room with the desk I started feeling more and more unsure. No matter where I looked—nothing.

Just moments before, when Sumida had started doubting me,

I'd felt angry. But now I could see that his questioning me wasn't so strange.

As I searched each room, my fear of the house began to fade. From the outside it had seemed like a demon's lair, something grotesque within. But the more I saw things like Shiozaki's painting of a dog running through a meadow, the television in the living room, the labeled video cassettes, the more my dread faded away.

Why isn't there an entrance to the cellar? Why haven't I found anything I could use as evidence? Bewildered, I walked through the rooms.

My eyes landed on a window. If the curtains had been shut, I might never have seen it.

From here I could see the forest. And on the side of a mountain a little ways out stood another building that looked like the house we were in.

That house also appeared to be built from brick. But its walls were a different color. Shiozaki's house was made from blue bricks; the one out the window was red.

That could be Kyoko's house. Hadn't Kimura said that Kyoko also lived in a brick house?

The location seemed right. But since I'd never been near her house this was the first time I'd seen it.

A theory formed inside me, one I hadn't thought of before.

What if Kazuya had been wearing blue sunglasses the day he tried to save Hitomi?

Even if it were a different color, the image of the house could have burned into his left eye as blue.

No, that shouldn't be true. In what I saw there had been no hint he'd been wearing sunglasses. I rejected the idea.

But somewhere a part of me wasn't certain enough to laugh it off entirely. Rather, my anxieties were growing.

That's right. In Kazuya's memory, the cellar had a window. But Shiozaki's house doesn't have one—only those planters.

I had been assuming that the planters had been hastily built in the past two months. *But in that short a time, could the dead grass have grown in the dirt within? It's winter. Could the grass have grown from nothing and then died? Besides, wouldn't it be more logical to assume the planters had been here from before?*

I stood frozen in the room on the second floor. If the window Kazuya had seen was in the cellar in Kyoko's house, I'd made a terrible error.

I left the room. I didn't have the patience to go down the stairs. Leaning over the railing above the stairwell, I looked down at the first-floor hall.

"Sumida!"

He walked to the foot of the stairs, looked up at me, and tilted his head. "Have you had enough?"

"Get your car! We need to go to Kyoko's house!"

His eyes widened in surprise.

"I'll explain later!"

He didn't seem convinced, but he ran toward the front door.

As I flew down the steps, I thought, *This isn't the house Kazuya saw. There's another brick house. And if I'm right, Saori is in danger. Just this afternoon she said she was going to Kyoko's.*

I have to hurry. I leapt over the last few steps in one bound.

8—AN AUTHOR OF FAIRY TALES

Miki wondered, *What had Hitomi's expression been on the other side of the window?*

Had the visitor noticed her missing limbs? She's a bizarre sight, wriggling inside her sack.

Likely apprehensive of what—or who—was near, the visitor had quickly stifled any reaction.

Miki took a step toward the visitor. Just then, from his pocket came the faint noise of metal objects jostling each other.

Inside his pocket were his car keys and a gold watch—the one the visitor had dropped behind his house.

Just a tiny sound, but enough to reveal his presence.

He heard the visitor take off running.

Miki came out from the corner where he had been hiding.

He needed to chase. He needed to silence that visitor.

9

I cleared the stairs and aimed for the front door. Sumida would be about to start the car, and I needed to get to him as quickly as possible.

Then came something I hadn't expected in the least.

If my ears hadn't picked it up, I might never have stopped there.

I thought I'd heard someone singing.

I halted at the bottom of the stairs. The voice was incredibly faint, just barely audible—a woman's voice, trembling and unsteady. The lyrics seemed to be in English.

Maybe there's a television or a radio on in one of the rooms. I should just ignore it and hurry to Kyoko's house. But despite those thoughts, part of me wanted to find the source of the singing.

That's it. I just need to calm down and think it through.

Even if Kazuya had been wearing blue sunglasses, that doesn't mean the red brick would appear blue. It's a simple concept...

When I walked away from the staircase, the singing grew softer until I could no longer hear it. The voice was loudest when I stood in front of a cabinet at the rear of the staircase.

The old wooden cabinet had been placed in the recessed wall behind the staircase. I pressed my ear against the sliding door of the cabinet and closed my eyes.

The song sounded like it came from behind the cabinet.

I was almost positive. *Something is back there and this cabinet has been put here to hide it.*

A tremor shot through my body. Any thought of going to Kyoko's house was long gone.

There was nothing inside the cabinet. Had it had been left empty to make it easier to move?

It was light—light enough for me to move when I put my muscle into it. I slid it aside, revealing a hole in the wall.

The wall seemed to have originally been covered in the same milky-white wallpaper as the rest of the house, and all but one section of it had peeled off. The hole was about as big as a person, its edges damaged brick.

I saw hinges behind the edge of the brickwork, and I got the impression the bricks had been meant to conceal what was in fact a doorway.

Through the opening, I saw a narrow stairway leading down. A dim light hung from the ceiling, illuminating the stairway—long and narrow like the throat of some creature.

The singing was coming from below. I was certain that the sound wasn't coming from a radio or a TV but from a person.

It's a cellar. There's a cellar after all.

Cautiously I went down the stairway one step at a time. I was so nervous I could barely breathe, and I could feel my heart beating furiously.

The walls on either side of the staircase were exposed brick, and I kept my hands on them to keep from falling down the steps.

As I neared the bottom the air grew dank. Humidity coiled around me and pressed in at me from all directions, sticky and thick enough to choke me, the darkness a liquid flooding the room.

I emerged from the stairway into a dark room. The ceiling was crossed with support beams for the floor above. A single light-bulb hung from the ceiling, already emitting a weak light when I came in. Occasionally it flickered, like it was almost dead. The light wasn't strong enough to reach the edges of the space. The darkness seemed so thick the room might extend into infinity. Several support posts were visible in the light—or I should say, were standing there like ghosts half vanishing into the darkness. The dirt floor was hardened and felt like stone under my feet.

In the wide space before me was a large wooden desk. Toward

the back of the cellar stood a cluster of shelving units lined up like library stacks.

The wooden desk seemed to have been used as a workbench. Saws and hammers and other tools were strewn across its surface. One of the hammers appeared curiously new.

On top of the workbench I found what looked like a scalpel of the sort that had been used in my surgery; its dull silver reflected the flickering light. The entire surface of the desk was covered with black stains.

I shook away a thought—that the stains were traces of human blood that had seeped into the table and changed color over time. *No, it's just oil*, I told myself.

An assortment of boxes had been placed in front of the storage shelves, perhaps a collection of all the things in the house that had, in their age, fallen into disuse. Maybe these were all things that had been in the house since the time it was built. There was a pendulum clock without a face and a baby carriage draped with a drab-colored blanket.

The woman's voice kept singing. The song floated out from somewhere in the darkness that the lone lightbulb couldn't sweep away. I couldn't understand the English lyrics, but her ephemeral voice carried with it sorrow—it was as if the teeming darkness itself were crying and the song were its tears.

I tried to call out to the singer, but my voice didn't come. The words kept sticking in the back of my dry throat. When I finally spoke, my voice was trembling, weak.

"Is there...anyone here?"

As the words were swallowed up by the darkness, the singing stopped. For a moment silence fell across the room.

Then a woman's voice—the same one that had been singing—came from the shadows behind the shelves. "Who are you?" The voice carried a hint of fear.

"You must be Hitomi Aizawa," I said, approaching the source of the voice. I passed the side of the workbench and walked toward the shelves. I felt like I was in an unfamiliar world—a dark world with no sun, no morning, and no night, just a single dim lightbulb.

"She's not Hitomi."

I stopped next to one of the posts. That was a young man's voice and it had come from behind the same shelves.

"I'm Shinichi Hisamoto. Yukie Mochinaga's the one who first replied to you."

My mind whirled. It was the first I'd heard either of those names. I had thought Hitomi was the only one in the cellar.

"What about Hitomi?"

In a lowered voice, the man who had identified himself as Shinichi said, "She must be sleeping now. Let's keep our voices down so we don't wake her."

I could hear them whispering to each other over by the shelves. From out of the darkness, their voices tickled my ears like the rustling of paper scraps. I couldn't see them in the dark, but I felt their stares piercing me.

It was eerie. My legs wouldn't move any closer to them. I didn't want to take even a single step away from the pool of weak light. The two of them, two people with their own will, had been hiding in the cellar. I didn't know what to think anymore.

"You wouldn't happen to be one of Shiozaki's friends, would you?" It was Yukie's voice. Not knowing why his name should come up, I was confused. "When he heard you talk, he made the slightest reaction."

"Is he...here?"

"He's next to us." Shinichi's voice. "He isn't able to speak, but when he heard you he made a faint moan."

Shiozaki is here. And he isn't able to speak. I felt like it must all be a joke.

The low ceiling weighed down on me, a giant slab of darkness that seemed about to crush me. Enduring the feeling of claustrophobia and with my hand on one of the support pillars, I peered into the darkness where they hid.

I could sense them back there. I could feel the gathered darkness stir. But I still couldn't see them.

Some things were hanging from the ceiling next to me. Several dozen slender threads with fishhooks on their ends. Looking closely, I saw some bits of dried matter stuck to the hooks.

"Why can't Shiozaki talk?" I asked.

After a pause, Shinichi answered. "He's sitting, his arms hugging his knees, with stakes driven into his entire body. He can't move and he can't speak. I think his lungs must have been punctured. Of course he's still alive, though."

"Like that, how could he be?" My voice raised a little, and I felt the vast darkness lurking in the cellar shake.

"But he is—although I can't explain it well." His voice was unsure. He said soothingly, "Please, speak a little more quietly."

Just then, one of the storage shelves rocked, like someone had bumped into it. It didn't tip over, but when it tilted, a box on one of the shelves toppled to the floor and landed with a thud.

I put my hand over my mouth and stepped back.

When the shelves had rocked, the dim light of the lightbulb had reached to the edge of where the two were hiding. Like a phantom they had appeared for an instant before vanishing.

I thought I must have seen it wrong. That or I had gone crazy.

"Don't make that face." Yukie's voice. It carried sadness in it. "We can see you, you know."

"Why..." I started to say, but it took everything just to recover my breath. Seeing them had dashed away the last shreds of my composure. The only reason I hadn't run away screaming was because I was cowering, unable to move.

"We've had surgery," said Shinichi.

"Surgery?"

"Everyone who comes here undergoes some kind of surgery. Good surgery. And then we get shut away. Strangely enough, it doesn't hurt. It's like time stands still and we feel completely free." After a pause he continued, "Speaking of which, are you the new resident of the cellar?"

What does he mean, resident of the cellar? Does he mean like how he and the rest of them were brought here?

"I've come to rescue you," I said to the darkness. "Where is Hitomi?"

First, I have to get her out of here—now. If I stay here any longer I'll go crazy. This thick darkness clutching at my hands and feet will stretch its tendrils deep into my mind and devour it. I need to get above ground and feel the light. Then I'll get help and return. I need to get Shinichi's and Yukie's bodies back to normal.

"Hitomi is in the carriage. It's her bed." Shinichi's voice.

Keeping my attention on the darkness where they hid, I approached the carriage. It was small and old. The cloth was torn and cobwebs hung from the handle. Its once silver-colored wheels were covered with rust and losing their shape. A blanket was draped over the top of it, and I couldn't see inside.

I wanted to cry. When Hitomi had been kidnapped, she'd been fourteen. Now she was fifteen. No matter how much she could bend her knees, there was no way she could fit in this tiny carriage.

I removed the blanket and tears came to my eyes.

Underneath the blanket was a girl's face, so small you could fit your hands around it. Her delicate cheeks were sickly white. I could see the pale veins running beneath her skin. Her long, messy hair looked as if it hadn't been washed in some time.

The light fell across her face. She winced and groaned, and then her eyes opened a crack. She noticed me beside her. With an expression like she thought she might still be dreaming, she smiled.

"Hey," she said.

I choked up. She was in a sack only big enough for her torso, yet she was packed inside. The sack was closed shut around her neck with a red necktie.

"Who..." Hitomi spoke in a soft, sweet voice. "Who are you? Were you brought here?"

No. I shook my head. I wanted to explain that I had come to rescue her, but the words wouldn't come. She kept asking me questions. "You were brought here in a car too, weren't you? Hey, did you see the raven? Even now, when I sleep, I see it in my dreams."

As she spoke her words had a pleasant enunciation, like the hopping of a rabbit. There in the darkness that voice felt like my only savior.

"Yeah, I saw the raven. It was up on the roof when I came in."

"No, not like that. The one that was, you know, swaying."

Swaying?

"I guess he did say he was buying a new car. But he liked that key chain so much, I figured he would have put it in the new car too."

I thought I'd leave Hitomi in the carriage and just get out of the cellar. As I started to run for the steps, someone was already coming down them. It was Sumida.

"There you are, Nami," he said. I came up to him and slapped him across the face. The sound rang through the cellar.

"It was you," I said.

Without flinching, he stared at me. The swaying little raven. Hitomi had seen the key chain. When he had brought her here in his car, that image had burned into her eyes.

10—AN AUTHOR OF FAIRY TALES

Through the forest, Miki chased the visitor. As he went farther from his house, the leafless trees of the forest started to give way to conifers.

Suddenly he lost sight of the visitor. The visitor had slipped and fallen down the slope. A road was ahead.

He heard the screeching of tires—and then the visitor was struck by a car. Miki watched from behind a tree.

The driver got out of the car. It was a middle-aged man. The man looked about, saw there were no other cars around, and got back into his own. And then the white car drove off, leaving the visitor lying in the road.

11

Keeping his eyes fixed upon me, Sumida approached the carriage. His movements were slow and confident, like those of a cat.

Overwhelmed, I stepped aside.

He placed his hand on the lip of the carriage and looked down at Hitomi inside.

"How do you feel?" he asked.

With her eyes closed, she replied, "So-so."

"So Shiozaki wasn't the kidnapper," I said.

More than anger at his betrayal, I felt unnerved. I still didn't understand everything that had happened, but one thing I remembered from when we'd first sneaked into the house:

"You knew where the light switch was."

Despite being at the dark rear entrance of someone else's home, Sumida had found the switch immediately, without having to look for it. I couldn't think of it as a coincidence any longer. He was familiar with the inside of the house.

His hand still upon the carriage, Sumida turned to me. "The other day, for the first time in a while, I came down to this cellar." His expression and voice were virtually unchanged from how they'd been in the café. "We came to bring Shiozaki his coat, right? Do you remember what you said on the way back?"

In the car I had told him that Shiozaki had described one of his walls as damaged, but that I hadn't seen any walls like that.

"I thought it wasn't possible, but it turned out you were right. There had been damage to one of the walls—the one I put up to hide the cellar. By the time we came over, he had noticed the cracks, but the cabinet was covering the wall."

"The cabinet?"

He nodded. "I covered up the door with bricks a long time ago and hid it with the cabinet. When Shiozaki moved in he didn't know there was a cellar. But an earthquake put cracks in the wall and he was able to hear Yukie singing. Shiozaki told me all this himself. Did you talk with Yukie?"

He pointed to the back of the room.

I could feel them staring at Sumida and me.

"So Shiozaki discovered the cellar?"

"When I came to see him, he still didn't really know. I guess he thought it was a radio or something."

Sumida explained that Shiozaki had intended to break down the wall. He had bought the hammer for this purpose, passing it off to me as a tool to repair the wall.

"Then when it looked like he'd discover the cellar, you..." I glanced at the back of the cellar. I couldn't see him, but Shiozaki was back there in the darkness with Shinichi and Yukie.

"Who's Shiozaki?" Hitomi's innocent voice came from the carriage.

"He's the one who moved in here after I left," said Sumida. "The one I brought down here before."

Remembering, she said, "Oh, that's right. The shish kebab."

The cellar seemed to be operating under different rules than the surface. I struggled to keep from fainting with dizziness. The low ceiling and the thick darkness pressed into my fragile mind from all directions.

"Three days ago, with my own hands, I tore down the wall I'd built a year before."

With the finality of an oracle reciting his prophecy, he said that I'd come and found that hole.

He turned from the carriage and stepped toward me.

"Stay back!"

My tearful voice echoed in the room.

He stopped.

"You used to live here?"

He nodded and told me that he had lived here until a year

before, that he had amputated Hitomi's arms and legs in the room where we stood.

"When I left, I bricked over the entrance and the windows of the cellar."

The windows.

"You built those brick planters outside, right? To hide the windows..."

"Most of them were already there. I just added one more."

The dead plants hadn't been in the planter because he'd replanted them there from somewhere else—they had grown, and withered, over the course of a year.

But I don't understand. In the memory of my left eye, the window wasn't covered over. Two months ago, when Kazuya died, Shiozaki was living in this house.

Suddenly I realized I had come to the wrong conclusion. But such a convergence of coincidences would have had to occur, I never even considered the possibility.

"You told me that you met Kazuya a year ago. Was that true?"

"He was a visitor."

"A visitor?"

"That's what I call people who find out what I do and come snooping around—searching around my house, asking people about me. Mr. Hisamoto over in the back of the room, he was a visitor too. I found him outside the house."

"And you found Kazuya looking into the cellar window?"

He nodded. "Exactly one year ago."

I held my hand to my mouth and started to sob.

My suspicion was correct. That vision in my left eye wasn't of his death two months before, it was from an event a year before.

The vision I saw in the library had ended when Kazuya was struck by the car. Maybe the driver had noticed and tried to brake—I wouldn't have heard it. Of course I had assumed that Kazuya died. But could I have known for sure?

He hadn't died then. Examined from this perspective, the inconsistency between the place I had seen in my left eye and the site of the fatal accident was only natural—they were two different places.

Sumida took one step closer to me. Unable even to scream, I took one step back, shaking my head.

"One year ago, Kazuya peeked inside the cellar window. The week before, I started having the feeling someone was watching me. You came here looking for Hitomi because Kazuya told you about her, didn't you?"

I covered my ears with my hands. But I could still hear him speak.

"When Kazuya was at the window, he noticed me and ran. But while he was trying to escape, he was struck by a car and fell unconscious. The car drove away, a hit and run."

He took another step toward me.

"The problem was after that. You might not believe what I'm about to tell you, but by some chance it happened. When he came to, he didn't remember anything. Not me, not the house. He had clean forgotten everything that had happened the previous week."

Amnesia. I see. My head was too filled with fear to be able to think about much, but that, strangely enough, I could understand.

"I didn't kill him. I didn't bring him down here either."

"Why didn't you?"

At first, he wasn't sure how to answer. He considered it, then replied, "I just didn't." He added, "I added chance upon chance."

"And then," said Hitomi, "He took him—he took the visitor—to the café."

Saori had first met Sumida a year ago, when he came into the café with her brother passed-out drunk in his arms. Saori had once told me, "Kazuya had moaned, 'Take me to Melancholy Grove.'"

But Kazuya hadn't been passed-out drunk. He'd been half conscious, hit by a car. Sumida had been lying when he said he'd met Kazuya in town.

And then they had started spending time together as friends.

Sumida was standing only steps away from me. His body

was slim and didn't seem to have much strength. But it still had enough strength to catch and silence me.

The stale air of the cellar was thick with tension, so that even as I inhaled, I felt like I was suffocating.

Sumida was frightening. His eyes weren't fierce or vicious, nor were they empty. He gazed at me analytically. He had the visage of an experimenter, a doctor, a researcher.

"Right after it happened, I left this house and moved to an apartment by the station. After I'd closed up the cellar, of course."

Will my fate be decided when he's done talking? I shifted my arms and legs to see if I still had the strength to run.

"But there's something strange," I said. "Given what you've said, Hitomi and the rest must have been left in this cellar for nearly a year. How are they still alive?"

"That's the way they are now. Their wounds aren't closed. So they live. Time has stopped for them, and they can sing and talk away in this sunless room. I bought a new lightbulb and left the switch on when I closed up the room."

He looked up at the lightbulb on the ceiling, flickering, nearly dead.

"I've been bored," Hitomi said in her small voice.

It was nearly time for me to steel my determination. I took one step back and to the side. Inside I was praying.

"What about Saori? Did you keep going to Melancholy Grove after you moved because of your feelings for her?"

He fixed his placid eyes on me. In the end he never answered me, but in that moment, I learned something about him.

Sumida took another step toward me. *It's now or never*, I thought. I was afraid, but it was my fear that impelled me to flee.

With all of my strength I sprang at him, striking with my shoulder.

I thought I heard a number of voices gasp in the back of the room.

The impact rocked through my body. My breath caught. I rebounded from the collision.

Sumida toppled into the tangle of fishhooks hanging from the ceiling. He struggled to pull free. The hooks caught in his clothing, their countless arms pulling at him.

I ran. I knew he would soon come after me.

I flew up the stairs to the surface. It wasn't a particularly long staircase, but no matter how hard I pushed my legs to move, the light of the hallway above seemed to grow no nearer. I had no sense of advancing up the steps—it was as though I were treading water.

Although it felt like it took a long time, it was probably quick. I finally made it up the last of the steps and into the hallway. The freshness of the air was dizzying.

I turned for the front door and ran. My footsteps rang on the floorboards as I dashed down the hall.

The large black doorway to the outside was in front of me. I grabbed the gold-colored doorknob and turned it.

But what happened wasn't what I expected. The door only opened a crack—barely wide enough to slip my hand through. Again and again I tried with all my strength to pull it open, but it wouldn't move. Then I noticed an extension cord wrapped around the doorknob. It would take time to untie it.

I realized immediately that Sumida had put it there. Through waves of panic I remembered the back door.

I turned and ran down the hall.

Just as I passed the side of the stairs, I felt my foot strike something. I had fallen before realizing Sumida's foot had thrust out from the entrance to the cellar.

It didn't hurt. I'd been running as fast as I could when I stumbled and slammed straight into the side of an open door leading to one of the rooms, but, as if I had fallen onto a cushion, I didn't feel any pain.

I thought, *I can still run*, and as I started to pull myself up, I saw it.

My right foot was bent at an unnatural angle. Although I didn't know why, it didn't hurt. Rather, it felt warm and pleasant.

I couldn't understand what was happening to my body. I assumed that my fear and my panic were keeping me from feeling any pain.

Sumida stood before me, a cut on his cheek—probably from where it had caught on one of the fishhooks. His clothes were torn in places, several hooks still caught in them. He must have ripped himself free with all his strength.

I pulled the paring knife from my pocket, holding it in my left hand. My hand was shaking. Somewhere inside me I doubted the tiny blade would be enough for me to intimidate him enough for me to flee. But it was all I had.

The moment I unfolded the blade, he kicked my hand, pinning it between his shoe and the wall. It didn't hurt. It felt like nothing more than a strong gust of wind.

The knife fell to the floor. He picked it up. Alarm rang through my head. But I couldn't move.

At first I didn't know what was happening. He pushed into my stomach with the hand that held the knife. I only barely felt the pressure.

"This won't do," he said, looking at the knife, which was now only a handle. The blade seemed to have folded back in.

He gripped my neck, holding me in place, then touched my stomach through my shirt.

I wriggled to get away from his hand, and I heard the blade of the knife strike the floor. It must have been caught in my shirt.

I don't hurt anywhere. I'm fine. But then I realized my left hand wasn't moving. Even when I tried to move it, it only made a hiccuping twitch.

I looked at Sumida's face. His eyes were directed at my stomach.

I followed them. My shirt was torn. I had been stabbed. The wound was surrounded by red, but it wasn't bleeding much.

Something strange was hanging from the wound, dangling through the hole torn in my shirt.

At first I thought it looked like an umbilical cord.

I looked at Sumida's hand. His fingers were red. He had

put them into my stomach—I suppose to pull the cord out.

I think the only reason I didn't lose my sanity on the spot was because the thing coming out from my stomach didn't look like it could possibly be my own. When I scooped it up with my hand, it felt warm.

A brain-numbing intoxication flowed from the wound. A peculiar feeling of happiness enveloped me.

I got the feeling I had discovered the reason the residents of the basement didn't have any fear of Sumida.

My mind felt like it was drifting through warm water, and through it I heard Sumida's far-off voice.

You can't run.

An unrelenting vitality flowed from the wound and filled me from the tips of my fingers to the core of my mind.

I loathed it. Some deep-down part of me that no one could violate resisted.

Sumida reached his hand out to me. But to his surprise, I shook free.

I made it to the nearest room and shut the door. I went to lock it, but the door had no lock. I moved to the window. My one foot was completely immobile and I had to drag it behind me as I went.

Behind me the door opened. Sumida was coming after me. He knew I had no escape. He watched my movements with the calm eyes of a spectator.

The window was easy to open. If it had been locked, I would have tried to burst through, but luckily even my meager strength was enough to open it. I shoved my body through the rectangular opening.

I fell backward onto the ground, the impact knocking the wind out of me. But the warmth overflowing from my wound stopped any pain.

Lying on the ground I realized I had fallen next to one of the planters. Right before my eyes were the blue bricks of the planter

hiding the window Kazuya had been looking in a year before—
God's idea of a joke. I wanted to laugh.

Sumida came out the window, deftly passing his slender frame
through it and then landing on the ground.

I hadn't the strength to get up. Still collapsed on the ground,
I looked up at him. "Why do you do this?"

"Well, I don't know why." He seemed to have never spent
much time thinking about it. He responded as if the question
were unimportant and didn't deserve an answer. "It's not that I
want to kill people. I just do it to keep them from talking."

I started to crawl away. The fingers on my left hand were paralyzed, but I could still move the arm. Propping my upper body
on my left elbow and my other hand, I swept my left leg across
the ground. My right leg, immobile, dragged behind me.

The ground should have felt cold, but it didn't—I just felt the
unpleasant sensation of dirt rubbing against me. I tried not to
think about the viscera hanging from my wound.

Sumida walked beside me; I could feel him staring down at me.

Without looking up, I spoke. "Was Kazuya's death two months
ago really just an accident?"

I had the faint hope that nothing more would happen to me as
long as I kept asking him questions. *As long as he's still talking,
he won't kill me.*

My arm, tired from supporting my body, began to tremble.
Its strength gave way, and my face fell to the ground, knocking
gravel into my mouth.

"I made it look like an accident."

Sumida put his foot on the long, thin thing that trailed from my
stomach. I kept going. I could feel it slipping out from inside me.
The barely audible sound of it passing out of the wound reached
into my mind. I felt my stomach start to cave in.

"I blindfolded him and broke his limbs, then dragged him to
the slope and pushed him in front of an oncoming car."

Sumida explained that he hadn't removed the blindfold until

just before it happened. Kazuya had never known why his arms
and legs wouldn't move.

I made it to the corner of the house and hooked the fingers of
my right hand around its edge.

How long are my intestines? I'd been relying on my arm to
drag myself forward, my body scraping across the earth, my
guts—pinned down by Sumida's foot—sliding out.

Having made it that far, I gave up crawling any farther. I raised
my upper body and sat, leaning against the corner of the house.
I aimed my face, dirty with mud and tears, at him. "Why would
you do something like that?"

"Kazuya's memory started coming back—slowly, and not all
at once. About the house, about when he had come to the house
with that bandage over his eye. He was confused by the memories
and he was starting to talk about them."

And so Sumida, worried Kazuya would soon remember everything, had had to silence him...

Sumida stood before me. He seemed terribly tall as he looked
down at me, probably because I was sitting with my butt on the
ground.

The gray sky at his back, he said, as if trying to reason with
a small child, "All right, that's enough now, isn't it? It was just
bad luck that you ended up a visitor too."

He bent down, circled his hands around my neck. His slender
face was right in front of my eyes now.

"It won't hurt. I've gotten quite good at breaking necks."

My right hand moved to where he couldn't see it. I ran my hand
through the gutter at the base of the house and there, among the
dirt and rotted leaves, my fingers found it.

"You're wrong," I said through my tears. "It wasn't bad luck.
I meant to find you."

Summoning the last shreds of my strength, I shoved it into
Sumida. For one year, Kazuya's flathead screwdriver had awaited
just this moment.

12—AN AUTHOR OF FAIRY TALES

Miki walked over to the man lying on the pavement. The man wasn't dead. He seemed only unconscious, with no visible injuries.

Miki had to decide whether to kill the man or bring him back to the house to make sure he'd never talk.

Then the man in Miki's arms groaned. His eye must have healed. When he had stopped by Miki's house the other day white bandages had covered one eye. Now the bandages were gone.

The man opened his eyes a crack. They were unfocused and didn't look straight at Miki.

But the man seemed to have noticed someone was by his side.

Miki knew he had to silence the man before anybody else passed by. But just as Miki had prepared himself for it, the man spoke: "Who...Where am I?"

Miki dragged the man to the side of the road and asked him some questions. The last thing the man remembered was ordering coffee at a café.

"Who are you?" asked the man.

"It doesn't matter."

The man nodded weakly, as if floating through a dream.

Miki still held the hammer in his hand. He raised it. If he smashed the man's brain, death would come.

The man, barely holding onto consciousness, closed his eyes. Just as Miki's hammer was about to bring death, he said, "Please, could you take me to Melancholy Grove?"

Miki decided to take a chance and spare the man's life. If he had lost his memory, there was no need to kill him. Besides, getting rid of the evidence would be tricky. Miki would have to either leave the body by the road or haul it back up to the house, and either option meant bothersome work.

He discarded the hammer in some nearby bushes. Lending his shoulder to the man, he walked him back to the café. Miki had never been inside, but he knew where it was. He'd frequently passed by it in his car.

By the time the two arrived at Melancholy Grove, night had fallen. There were few streetlights and the light of the café seemed to float alone in the darkness.

The man had passed out during the walk, so Miki was carrying him over his shoulder when he opened the door.

The woman behind the counter, upon seeing the man slumped over Miki's back, cried out, "Kazuya!"

Miki lowered him into one of the booths.

As the woman tended to the man, she bowed her head and said, "I'm so sorry my little brother put you through this."

Miki told her that the man had been passed out drunk. Her brother didn't smell of alcohol, but she didn't question the lie.

"This is bad," she said, reaching for him. "He's got a bump on the head."

Miki explained that the man had tripped and fallen on the walk to the café.

Miki looked around and saw there were no customers. He wondered if the woman at the counter was the owner, but she seemed too young. Maybe she was just a part-timer.

Miki left to go home. The woman called out to stop him, but he pretended not to have heard.

He put the café behind him and headed for his house. As he walked through the darkness he thought about the inside of the café, about the unconscious man.

The face of the woman caring for her brother rose in his mind. She looked like his childhood friend from the hospital, the little girl whose arms had ended at her elbows. If the little girl had grown up, she might have had a face like that woman's.

He became aware that his fingers were playing with the object inside his pocket—the gold watch the man had presumably dropped while searching outside Miki's home.

He stopped and thought a while. *There's no need to give it back.*

But a few minutes later he was opening the door to the café.

The woman clasped her hands around the watch more emotionally than he had expected. "Thank you for coming all the way back. This watch is very important to him." Warmly she asked, "What's your name?"

She looks just like her.

Miki gave his real name.

"Nice to meet you, Sumida." She set the watch on the counter. The metal clunked against the surface.

As Miki turned to leave again, the woman grabbed his arm.

"Please, have some coffee before you go."

She flashed her white teeth at him and seated him at the counter, halfway by force.

The secondhand of the watch was moving at a steady pace.

PART 5

1

Three days after I was taken to the hospital, I was allowed visitors.

That day, I lay in bed thinking absently about the past. Well, I say the past, but even my oldest memories were only two and a half months old.

After I had lost both my left eye and my memories, I'd awoken in a white hospital room just like this one. At the time, I hadn't known anything. I still didn't know what I spent my time thinking about then. I suspected I didn't think anything at all—I wasn't sure I'd had the means to, that I even knew how.

I only remembered one thing—how terribly anxious I had felt.

The door to my hospital room opened. So far the only people who had come were doctors, nurses, and policemen. This time it was different. The ban on seeing me had been lifted and someone had come.

At the door to the room was a face I knew.

Still lying on the bed, I asked, "You came all the way here?"

My mother nodded. Her eyes were puffy and red.

※

The day before my mother visited, some policemen had come to talk to me—three of them, all in black suits.

I invited them to sit, but none of them even considered it. They looked down at me lying in bed, not even allowed to sit up because the movement might reopen my stomach wound. When they spoke it was all business. They informed me that they did not want me to speak publicly about my encounter with Sumida. Because it was such a bizarre incident, the newspapers and TV would make a big fuss, which wouldn't be good.

Don't talk to anyone about the incident. I promised them I wouldn't.

In the end, I never did tell them about my left eye.

What I had experienced in that house was highly unusual. At least, that's what all the many examinations of my body indicated. The doctors were still mystified as to how I had been able to move given my injuries. I'd explained to them that there hadn't been any pain, but all the doctors could do was tilt their heads and test me further.

Hitomi and the others had probably had to undergo even more tests than I. But I hadn't seen any of them since the police had taken us from the house.

After the three policemen had finished their duties, they prepared to leave. I stopped them. "Where's Hitomi?"

One answered me.

He explained that she was being examined in another hospital and that after she recovered, she would return to her parents.

"And Shiozaki?"

After a silence, he told me Shiozaki had died. In the middle of his examination he had stopped breathing—peacefully, as if he were drifting off to sleep. One of the stakes had scratched his heart.

I have no way of knowing if the officer was telling the truth or not.

"Thank you for the information," I said.

He started to walk away but stopped. He asked me the question I had already been asked many times before.

In the cellar they'd found signs that someone other than the victims they had rescued had been injured. He asked me if there had been anyone else down there.

Each time I was asked that question my answer was the same: I shook my head and said, "I don't know. The only ones I found down there were Hitomi Aizawa and Mr. Shiozaki."

*

Back then...

After I'd made sure Sumida was dead, I gathered up the long thing that hung from my stomach. I didn't even scream. I was singularly focused on stuffing the dirt-covered thing back into my wound. Thinking back on it now, I wasn't acting normally, but at the time I earnestly believed that was the best solution.

There was no pain. My stomach, my left hand, and my contorted right leg were enveloped in a blissful warmth, and the sensation left my head in a haze.

My body felt heavy, sluggish. I was terribly exhausted, but leaning against the wall for support, I was able to stand. Somehow I used my left leg to drag myself back to the window I had jumped from; here I returned inside. The front door wouldn't have opened due to the extension cord, and there was a strong chance the same had been done to the back door. I was only able to lift myself up and through the window through sheer force of will—I knew I had to call for help.

After I contacted the police and an ambulance I returned to the cellar. Forgetting that my right leg didn't work, I tried to walk on both legs.

Even with Sumida gone the darkness in the cellar was thick. I announced to Hitomi and the wriggling bodies in the back that Sumida was dead.

"I thought so." Hitomi's whisper came from the carriage. "Please take me to him."

I wasn't sure if that was a good idea, but I decided to carry her back to Sumida's body. The fingers on my left hand wouldn't move, but that didn't prevent me from being able to hold her. Hitomi was light and small and warm. She felt like little more than a ball of body heat.

With the girl in my arms, I slowly climbed the stairs—a difficult task with only one working leg. I unwrapped the extension cord from the front door and went around the house toward the southwest corner. The effort used up nearly the last of my strength.

Sumida lay still on the ground, the screwdriver stuck in his eyeball. Although I didn't have any medical knowledge, I was pretty sure it had passed into his brain.

Hitomi gazed at him from my arms and quietly cried. Even thinking back on it now, her tears didn't seem like those for a person who had done her harm. I still don't know exactly how she felt toward him.

Knowing I hadn't the strength to make it back to the cellar, I waited at the front door for the police to arrive.

I sat, leaning my back against a beam at the side of the doorway and hugging Hitomi's small body against my chest.

"Thank you for coming to save me," she said. "I'll be able to go home now, won't I?"

I nodded. My consciousness was starting to fade, although not due to any pain—my exhaustion was a warm blanket wrapping around my mind.

"Is it okay for me to sleep?" I asked. Before she could answer my eyes had closed.

The patrol car's siren woke me from my dream. A policeman came running up, saw Hitomi, and recoiled.

"There are three more in the cellar," I said.

The cop's face paled, but he entered the house. After a while he returned and with his hand over his mouth told me there was only one person inside.

"That's okay," Hitomi said. "I'm sure she must be remembering it wrong."

The policeman's eyes, filled with dread, moved back and forth from Hitomi to me. Then he ran back to his car to call for backup.

"It's fine this way." Hitomi looked at me and winked.

I realized that what I had seen after I dozed off had not been a dream.

There had been the sound of the front door opening, and then I had sensed something large pass right by me. I felt the pressure of the air against my cheek.

I lifted my eyelids a crack to see. The thing was a bizarre mass of body parts. Its two heads were exchanging goodbyes with Hitomi. They extended one of their many arms to lovingly pat the girl. The arm was slender, like that of a child.

Then, wriggling their limbs like the legs of a spider, they disappeared into the forest.

"Let's keep those two a secret," said Hitomi.

I winked at her, closing my left eye as if to say, *I'll forget all about them.*

2

The incident was handled as a case of abduction and false imprisonment. The kidnapper was Michio Sumida. From a newspaper article I learned he had been a college student who wrote fairy tales on the side.

Saori came to visit me often. The hospital was in a prosperous part of the city. She, unable to drive, had Kimura or Kyoko drive her there.

She brought me all kinds of manga and books to keep me from getting too bored.

She never asked me about what had happened inside the house. She must have sensed it had been a nightmare and was considerate enough not to bring it up.

The newspapers Saori brought me reported the incident pretty much as it had happened, with only a few small distortions. They said that Sumida, the previous tenant of the house, had been hiding Hitomi Aizawa in the cellar. When Shiozaki found out, Sumida took action against him too. I'd gotten involved and been injured.

No magazine or newspaper article I read mentioned anything about Hitomi's limbs or how Sumida had kept her alive for a whole year. But one of the magazines did have a feature about Sumida as a person and the stories he'd written under the name Shun Miki.

He was born an only child and grew up in a hospital. In high school he made his debut as an author of fairy tales and moved into his own apartment near his school.

After he graduated from high school he went to college. While he attended classes he supported himself by writing fairy tales. The house he had rented was the blue house in Kaede, where he lived for two years. After that—a year ago—he had moved to a newly built apartment building near his school.

When he moved out of the house, Shiozaki had moved in.

No one had learned of Shinichi and Yukie. The police might have had their suspicions, but nothing about the two had been published in the magazines. *When had they become residents of the cellar?*

Hitomi was kidnapped a year before, and Kazuya must have gone to the house soon after. Shinichi and Yukie were probably already in the cellar by then.

Sumida had told me that Kazuya had come to the house. Why then didn't my left eye show me any memories of it when I set foot inside? Why had it not seen any keys to open the box of those particular memories? What bad luck. If only some vision had played from when Kazuya visited the house, I might have realized Sumida was the kidnapper.

Then I remembered something. *That's right. A year ago, Kazuya had a bandage over his eye. His left eye. If that was when he went to the house, the eye wouldn't have seen a thing.*

In the weekly magazines and on the news shows, many theorized about why Sumida had injured and killed people.

There were a lot of theories—he had a sadistic personality, he held a deep hatred for his fellow man, he was copying criminals from other countries. But I felt like all of them were wrong.

The Sumida I saw was calmer than that—like a scientist. I remembered how he had quietly looked down at me as I lay flat on the ground, my guts trailing from my body. Somehow, in that dreadful memory I envisioned him dressed in a doctor's white lab coat. That wasn't how it had really been, but something made me picture him that way. He hadn't wanted to kill people. Maybe he had just wanted to take them apart to see what life was.

Whether it was a blessing from God or the devil's curse I couldn't say, but his scalpel had held a mysterious power. I think I could wonder about the nature of his power forever and still never find a satisfactory explanation. That blissful feeling as my innards had dragged along through the dirt, that feeling of gentle light enveloping the world, of my body turning into feathers—that hadn't been some kind of telepathic mind trick or drug-induced hallucination. If this existence were just a motion picture projected onto a thin, fragile screen, I believe his power was a darkness that crawled through a tiny hole in the screen to slowly blot out the picture.

I read in the weekly magazines that, according to evidence found near his high school apartment, Sumida had likely committed many other crimes over a period of time. I don't know if that was true or not.

Once, Saori saw me reading one of those articles and her face grew sad. She didn't say anything, but I wondered if she was thinking about Sumida. After that I made sure I never read about the incident in front of her.

In the end I never told anyone that Sumida had taken Kazuya's life. I felt it would hurt Saori more than if she thought it had just been an accident.

Once when Saori was sitting with me, peeling an apple, I asked her, "Hey, what were you doing at Kyoko's house?"

"Nothing in particular," she said. Then she told me about a time she went there on a delivery.

"I just happened to see it there—a photograph of Kyoko and this kid..."

She had seen the kid somewhere before. The boy's young face hadn't yet matured, but she was certain.

I didn't expect what came next.

"He was the boy who came to apologize to Kazuya and me at our parents' funeral."

"The one who worked at the lumber mill?"

She nodded.

That young man had caused the accident that took away their parents. Overcome with guilt, he had killed himself in Kaede.

After that, Saori had asked her parents' coworkers for the boy's name.

"Kyoko's husband had died too."

The name the coworkers gave her had been the same as Kyoko's before her husband's death.

Kyoko had probably moved to Kaede because of the boy.

"I wasn't able to bring it up with her right away. But after a few days I went back to her house to ask."

At first Kyoko had denied it. But Saori kept coming by her house to talk, and eventually she admitted that what Saori believed was true.

When Saori finished talking, she gazed into my eyes. The wound in my stomach had started to close, but I still couldn't sit up. Lying there, I took in her stare.

She put a piece of apple in my mouth even though I hadn't asked her to, and I had to work my jaw up and down. As the sun shone in through the window, I chewed the apple—its crunching sound broke the silence in the room.

"Sis, there's something I haven't told you..." When the words came out of my mouth, nothing about them felt unnatural. Saori seemed to feel the same way. "I never knew Kazuya."

"Yeah?"

I didn't know if she would believe me, but I began to tell her the strange story of my left eye. The parts about Kazuya's accident and the things related to the incident—those I would keep secret.

3

Until the wound in my stomach healed and the bones in my arms and my legs stitched themselves back together, my body felt strange and distant. Any feelings of pain were dulled and I could barely sense changes of temperature. I had no appetite—I felt like I didn't even need to eat to stay alive.

Hitomi, her arms and legs removed by Sumida, had lived in that cellar for one year. Everyone said she had survived on canned food.

I couldn't quite explain why, but I thought they were wrong. I think a power, like the one I felt in my body, had disconnected her from the natural cycle of life and death.

When my injuries had completely healed my body returned to normal.

After I was released from the hospital, I returned to my life at home. To be honest, I hadn't wanted to go back to school, but Saori and my mother wanted me to, so I did. I still did poorly in academics and in sports.

But in my own way—I don't know how—I managed to make friends who would talk to me. After that school gradually grew more fun.

Whenever school was on break I returned to Kaede. I was worried I might become a nuisance, but Saori's uncle gladly allowed me to stay. Because Saori hadn't told anyone about my eye, he still misunderstood my relationship with Kazuya.

I could remember how lonely it had felt the very first time the three of us ate dinner together, with each of us feeling as if the other two didn't exist. But that had changed. It wasn't exactly a dramatic change, but there was a warmth and a happiness around the dinner table. I supposed it was because Saori and her uncle were being gradually released from the spell in which the dead had held them. It was what I had hoped for them.

I visited Kazuya's grave. Because I went alone, without telling Saori, I had a lot of trouble finding the place where he rested. Finally, after I had worn out my tired and stumbling feet so much I thought I might die, I found the Fuyutsuki family grave.

I told Kazuya everything, though I was sure he already knew. After all, his eye had been there through the final moments.

A layer of thin clouds covered the sky, and the sun shone behind them. Standing between the rows of gravestones, I closed my eyes, and inside myself, I thanked him.

Thank you. Thank you for showing me your memories. Because you were always with me, I never gave up. Because of you, I could fight till the end.

I was choked up by the love inside me, and my salty tears spilled to the ground.

✳

I visited Kimura and Kyoko at Melancholy Grove. They had become accustomed to my presence at the café, and whenever I didn't show up for a while, they couldn't help but worry about me.

I sat in Kazuya's seat at the counter, and when Kimura brought me a café au lait, I thought back—as was my habit—to the first time I had come to the café. I looked around the interior, and everything I saw had a memory.

My eyes turned to Shiozaki's painting.

"I guess they discovered it among his belongings, but..." According to Kimura Shiozaki's wife had been born in Kaede.

"You mean the woman in the painting?" I asked.

He nodded.

I walked over to the painting and focused my eyes on it— otherwise I wouldn't have been able to see the tiny figure dressed in red standing on the shore of the lake.

"When I asked what her name was, it turned out I knew her. She used to be a regular here."

She had died in another place, and Shiozaki had moved to the town where she'd been born. He hadn't offered the painting to the café out of simple generosity.

I finally understood. Everyone in this town was seeing visions of the dead.

Once when I had gone a while without visiting them, Kyoko and Saori both said, "Nami, there's something a little different about you."

"What's different about me?" I asked, but they couldn't give me a clear answer. Looking back on it now, maybe change had come to me without my noticing, and they had subconsciously picked up on it.

Kyoko and Saori were like mother and daughter. Whenever Saori had the time, she went to Kyoko's house and the two would talk—not just of those who had died, but lighter talk and gossip.

Sometimes Saori would play with her brother's watch, turning her sad face toward its unmoving secondhand. But I knew that, slowly, one click at a time, that watch, stopped at the time of Kazuya's death, was moving again.

In the café I read Sumida's book *The Eye's Memory* again—the story of the girl who put eyes into her head and saw dreams.

Kazuya's eye had gradually ceased to show me visions. More and more I found myself at the end of a day thinking, *Oh, I didn't see any of Kazuya's memories today.*

Maybe I'd already seen everything that had been burned into the eye. Or maybe I'd stopped seeing them because the eye had become completely integrated with my body. I had a feeling it was the latter. The eye only showed the past of another person. If it replayed all the things I'd already seen for myself, I'd be overwhelmed.

At first when I stopped seeing Kazuya's memories, I was sad. But soon it just felt normal.

Sumida was in my final vision. He sat beside Kazuya in the

bright sunlight and they threw rocks at empty cans. It was the first memory I'd seen that was about Sumida.

The vision in the library hadn't been of Kazuya's death. After Sumida had blindfolded him and taken him to the side of the road, Sumida had pushed him in front of a car and killed him. I hadn't actually seen the moment Kazuya died.

Well, that was what I thought, until one day I realized I was wrong. I had seen that moment.

Some time ago, I'd experienced a vivid nightmare in which I was hit by a car.

The darkness of my closed eyes must have overlapped with the darkness in the blindfold Sumida had used to cover Kazuya's eyes, and the memory was drawn out. When I was asleep—or maybe I'd just dozed off—I saw myself jumping in front of a car. I had incorrectly assumed it was just a dream. Of course, there was no way I could know for sure. Maybe I was wrong. But I believed I saw the moment of Kazuya's death.

In the brief flash of the nightmare, the car was blue. Later I learned that the car that had killed Kazuya was blue. In the vision from the library, the car was white. And when I had that vivid nightmare, I hadn't yet known the color of the car that killed him. I think the car being blue shows that I wasn't just having a dream.

I closed the book and waved Saori over to order some coffee. Just then I noticed the vase of flowers sitting on the counter, and I recalled the vision I'd seen of Saori knocking it over. Strangely, the flowers in the vase seemed exactly the same as the ones in the vision.

Are they fake? I touched them; they were real. *Maybe Kimura has Saori keep only the same kind of flowers here.*

"A long time ago," Kimura said, "Sumida picked those flowers as a present for Saori. And they're still alive. Isn't that something?"

Beyond the white flowers, Saori blew her nose.

4

That summer, as I sat in the breeze of my air conditioner, I suddenly remembered it.

I can't quite explain what "it" was. It wasn't a distinct memory, and it had no real form.

But it felt strange and out of place in my head, like an object caught in my throat refusing to go down. It brought a rift between the world as I knew it and the world of reality. If I had to compare it to something, I'd liken it to that uncomfortable feeling you can get right before you wake up, when you start to realize you may be in a dream.

I thought it might be a sign that my memory was coming back.

I was right.

✳

Gradually my memories returned. And although I had been fearing it, it happened so naturally and so gently that I didn't try to resist.

Before I knew it, I could recall the name of a teacher I'd had in grade school and I remembered when my family had gone on a vacation. It became strange to think that I hadn't been able to play the piano. At school my grades skyrocketed, something which pleased me greatly.

"Are you really Nami?" Saori tilted her head and pulled at my ear. I dodged free from her hand, crying out through fits of laughter, *Hey, stop it! This isn't a disguise! I'm me!*

She put an elbow on the counter and said, a little sadly, "You seem at peace." Later, thinking back on that moment, I wondered if it had been her farewell to her brother.

I should have always been aware I was myself, but that demon of total forgetfulness, with skill so fine I didn't even notice it happening, separated me from myself. Then all that remained was the me who had existed prior to the loss of my eye. I don't want you to misunderstand me—"me" and "my memories" are two separate things.

I have my memories of my time in Kaede. I remember what I did. But when I think back upon who I was then, I'm like another person. The way I interacted with people, the way I thought—everything about me was different.

My mother says I was a completely different person, all the way down to my mannerisms. "I've never seen you so fearful," she'd say.

Before then I had always enjoyed listening to people and telling them my thoughts in return. When I suddenly changed into a person who almost never talked to anyone, my mother hadn't known how to cope.

I looked at my left eye in the mirror. It had been a long time since one of Kazuya's memories had come to life. No matter what I looked at, nothing became a key to unlock the box of memories.

Sometimes I'd start to wonder, *Did any of it really happen?*

Then the letter came from the police.

✳

Summer passed and I continued attending cram school in preparation for the looming college entrance exams. One night when I came home my father handed me an envelope.

The envelope was a charming pale blue. The second I saw it the image of Hitomi Aizawa flashed into my head. The sack around her body back in the cellar had been the same pale blue, soft to the touch.

Her name was above the return address.

I went upstairs to my room, sat at my desk, and opened the envelope. Inside was a letter from Hitomi, written for her by her mother. Not knowing my address, she had asked the police to forward it to me.

In the letter she wrote words of thanks and said she wanted
to meet me to talk, if only once.

I read and reread the letter I don't know how many times.
Already I had come to think of that day as something that hadn't
really happened, just some nightmare. But now I gathered my
memories, one after another. They seemed almost as if they belonged to somebody else.

Hitomi Aizawa's small body nestled in the carriage.

And Shinichi Hisamoto and Yukie Mochinaga.

I hadn't heard any talk of those two being discovered. Did they
still live up in the mountains? Or had they never really existed?

I pictured them. Their giant form concealed among the quiet
trees. Crawling into an opening in the rock face when it rained,
the two of them watching the falling raindrops. Wriggling their
carelessly placed limbs to carry them into the darkness away
from the sight of others...

I took out my binder and set it atop my desk. For the first
time in a long while I opened the records of the visions of my
left eye.

Not that long ago I carried this heavy thing as I walked that
town. The pages, worn ragged from all the times I'd flipped through
them, contained handwriting that didn't seem my own.

They stored every last detail—the scenery young Kazuya had
seen, Saori's expressions—everything in the visions his left eye
had shown me.

I turned the pages one by one.

That's when that feeling, the one I'd nearly forgotten, came to
me again. My left eye—Kazuya's eye—suddenly grew warm.

I was flustered, taken by surprise. Ever since my own memories
had returned the eye had remained dormant.

Quickly I saw that the pages of the binder were doubled over
each other, with differences between the pages in my right eye and
the ones in my left. I gently closed my eyes. The sight of my right
eye went dark and the vision in my left eye pulled into focus.

My viewpoint lifted from the rows of words written upon

the notebook paper. What I saw wasn't my room. It was Kaede.

In front of me were abandoned train tracks stretching off into the distance. Off to one side mountains blanketed with conifers soared up into the sky. They looked pitch black in the weak sunlight. On the other side the sleepy town spread out among the lines of tall transmission towers. In my left eye, I was walking across hills of withered grass, looking at the binder I held in my hands.

I knew immediately that it wasn't one of Kazuya's memories.

My left eye remembers. It remembers how I searched for Hitomi, how I pursued her kidnapper. How I looked for the blue brick house, how I walked the streets. How I endured loneliness as I wandered over the windy landscape. How hopeless and adrift I felt, not knowing what to do. It all burned into the eye.

And I'm seeing it. The rusted rail lines continuing into the distant forest. My feet on top of one of the rails. Myself tottering along it, trying not to fall.

That memory was still inside my head. I even knew what I had been thinking at the time. But it wasn't the way I thought anymore. My interests were different and so were my immediate reactions.

Therefore, she wasn't me. Just as she herself had thought, that girl, fearful and without her memories, was an entirely different person.

Intellectuals, or those who can be entirely dispassionate, might claim that she never existed. Or that she was just me without my memories.

Sitting at the desk with the binder spread open before me, I closed my eyes and silently prayed. When she had ceased to be, it was equivalent to a person's death. I never wanted to hear anyone tell me that she'd never existed, or that she was some scab atop my lost memories. That girl, with all her ineptness, was different from me—and she was real.

Besides, if the eye only ever showed me the memories of other people…

That girl, who only existed in this world for a brief time, faced great difficulties and suffered because of them. I knew exactly how hard it had been for her.

Everyone at school had talked about me. She was constantly compared with me, and she pitied herself for who she was. She couldn't seem to do anything right and she thought herself inferior.

But she wasn't defeated. No matter what terrors she found before her, she never backed down.

My eyes still shut, I put my head on top of the desk. I left my room as she had rearranged it. The still night came in through the window, the cool air of a summer just passed. It'd been half a year since she had gone to Kaede.

And as I watched the memory of her walking atop the rails beneath the cloudy sky, that heavy weight in her hands, I promised myself:

I will never forget. I will remember you, you who lived stronger than anyone I know. Forever.

AFTERWORD

Originally published in the Japanese paperback edition of *Black Fairy Tale*.

Hello, I'm Otsuichi. How are you all doing? I've been spending my days finding sustenance from the self-serve drink stations in family restaurants. The wind was strong today and almost knocked me over as I was going home from the restaurant. I barely avoided falling onto the side of the road and getting run over by a truck. It would have been better if I had.

By the way, *Black Fairy Tale* is now in paperback, although I didn't perform any major revisions on it. Owners of the hardcover edition need not purchase this in search of any changes.

Black Fairy Tale was the first work I'd written longer than two hundred pages of *genko yoshi* manuscript. Having just graduated from college, I decided not to look for a job, instead seeking to make my living as an author.

"I don't care if it ends up as garbage, I just need to complete a long-form work. If I want to survive as a professional writer, the novel is a barrier I must overcome."

That was my impetus for writing *Black Fairy Tale*. And this bizarre thing was the result. Everyone, I'm really sorry.

Anyway, today at the family restaurant, I read through the galley for *Black Fairy Tale*. Galleys—the manuscripts that are made just before a book is printed—serve as the final check for things like typos and omitted words, or phrases I want to change. With a red pen firmly in hand, I had to read through it carefully with open eyes. I confronted the galley, occasionally quenching my thirst at the drink station.

But I had written *Black Fairy Tale* while I was still honing my craft. Each time I saw my infantile self in the spaces between the words, my temperature rose and my pulse quickened.

I was ashamed. The words I'd written utterly shamed me. I couldn't even read them. If I had to describe it, I'd say it would be like if you were forced to read a diary from your teenage years. I never kept one myself, but that's exactly how it would feel.

I read one line, and I could feel my cheeks turn bright red. I read a second line, and my hand holding the red pen started to shake, and I began to stamp my feet under the table. I read a third line and thought, "Damn it, no more!" and I rolled up the galley and whacked it against the wall.

When I'd read up to the second chapter, I reached the limit of my shame, and my nerves broke.

Soon those embarrassing words would be printed and sent out into the world. Faced with the nearly unbearable humiliation, something in the back of my skull snapped. I realized I was about to make a strange monkeylike cry and frantically held it in.

Witnessing this suspicious behavior was a family—a boy in grade school, perhaps, and his parents—in the next booth.

Stop it. Don't look at me. Don't stare at me like you should feel sorry for me.

In each hand I gripped one half of a pair of disposable chopsticks, and I held them in a menacing pose. I glared at the family, and they looked away, like they had seen something offensive. I'm sure they were laughing at me on the inside. By the looks in their eyes, I could follow their silent conversation:

Mother: "Dear, did you see that young man at the next table in that dreadful tracksuit? He's that Otsuichi, the guy whose infantile and clumsy novel is being turned into a paperback."

Son: "I don't want to grow up to be like him."

Father: "That's right, Takashi, be smart. Don't get some crazy idea about writing an embarrassing novel."

Son: "Yeah, I'm going to study hard and become a decent member of society. While I'm in college, I'll look for a job. I won't think about making a living as a writer."

Takashi...Oh, Takashi...You are smart. Well put, Takashi. I stared at him, the wooden chopsticks still gripped in my hands. His mother hugged him in an effort to keep him from my sight.

Takashi was right. Why hadn't I tried to line up a job before I graduated from college? Why did I get the idea I'd write for a living? Without that notion, I'd never have written a full-length novel. I wouldn't have written *Black Fairy Tale*. And I wouldn't be distraught over this galley.

When the rest of my classmates were lining up their future employment, I was helping my friends make independent movies and getting short stories published in magazines. Those activities provided me a respite when I would feel a nervous breakdown coming on in a seminar. The thought of finding employment hurt my head too much to think about. I was running from having to put on a suit and go to interviews and take tests. Now my former classmates wear business suits, and I put on my unwashed tracksuit.

My classmates' suit-and-tie appearances put me to shame. They jostle about in society and grow as people. Then there's me, sitting in the corner of a family restaurant, slurping away at the sweet juice from the drink station like some stag beetle finding sustenance. I don't grow. My days are days of sloth. Where did I go wrong? It makes me want to cry. It makes me want to die.

Takashi, don't be like me. Live a proper life. Keep playing baseball. Don't make your parents cry.

I bestowed my biggest smile upon the boy in the next booth, and I gave him a cheer. Takashi's mother stood and took her boy by the hand to the register. They moved quickly, trying to escape my view. When they had left, I returned to my revisions, mindful not to let my heart break. But as I worked, my mind was still on Takashi. Good luck, Takashi. Whatever you do, just don't become a writer. Find a good company to work for and give your parents something out of your first paycheck. Please, I beg of you.

When I finished with the galley, I left the restaurant and ped-
aled my bike back to my apartment. Pushed about by the wind,
I nearly fell over. Moments later, a truck passed right beside me.
I was mad at the driver. Why didn't you hit me? Why hadn't you
driven another thirty centimeters to the left, you damn no-good
driver?

So I lived on. And without incident, this paperback was published.

—Otsuichi, March 18, 2004

ABOUT THE AUTHOR

Born 1978 in Fukuoka, Otsuichi won the Sixth Jump Short Fiction/Nonfiction Prize when he was seventeen with his debut novella *Summer, Fireworks, and My Corpse*. Now recognized as one of the most talented young fantasy/horror writers in Japan, his other English-language works include the short story collection *Calling You* and the Honkaku Mystery Prize-winning novel *Goth*. Otsuichi's *ZOO*, published in English by Haikasoru, was nominated for the Shirley Jackson Award for best single-author collection of 2009.